the FOUR WINDS

The FOUR WINDS

KRISTIN HANNAH

MACMILLAN

First published 2021 by St Martin's Press,
an imprint of St Martin's Publishing Group, New York

First published in the UK 2021 by Macmillan
an imprint of Pan Macmillan
The Smithson, 6 Briset Street, London EC1M 5NR
EU representative: Macmillan Publishers Ireland Limited,
Mallard Lodge, Lansdowne Village, Dublin 4
Associated companies throughout the world
www.panmacmillan.com

ISBN 978-1-5290-5456-9

Photograph credits: page 3 by Mark Taylor Cunningham / Shutterstock.com;
page 59, FSA photo (Dust Bowl farm, Coldwater District, Texas), Library of Congress,
Prints & Photographs Division, FSA/OWI Collection; page 193,
Dust Bowl, AP Photo; page 285, FSA photo (work camp), Library of
Congress, Prints & Photographs Division, FSA/OWI Collection

Illustration by sergio34 / Shutterstock.com

3 5 7 9 8 6 4 2

A CIP catalogue record for this book is available from the British Library.

Printed and bound by CPI Group (UK) Ltd, Croydon, CR0 4YY

Visit **www.panmacmillan.com** to read more about all our books
and to buy them. You will also find features, author interviews and
news of any author events, and you can sign up for e-newsletters
so that you're always first to hear about our new releases.

Dad, this one's for you.

PROLOGUE

Hope is a coin I carry: an American penny, given to me by a man I came to love. There were times in my journey when it felt as if that penny and the hope it represented were the only things that kept me going.

I came west in search of a better life, but my American dream was turned into a nightmare by poverty and hardship and greed. These past few years have been a time of things lost: Jobs. Homes. Food.

The land we loved turned on us, broke us all, even the stubborn old men who used to talk about the weather and congratulate each other on the season's bumper wheat crop. *A man's got to fight out here to make a living,* they'd say to each other.

A man.

It was always about the men. They seemed to think it meant nothing to cook and clean and bear children and tend gardens. But we women of the Great Plains worked from sunup to sundown, too, toiled on wheat farms until we were as dry and baked as the land we loved.

Sometimes, when I close my eyes, I swear I can still taste the dust . . .

1921

To damage the earth is to damage your children.

—WENDELL BERRY,
FARMER AND POET

ONE

Elsa Wolcott had spent years in enforced solitude, reading fictional adventures and imagining other lives. In her lonely bedroom, surrounded by the novels that had become her friends, she sometimes dared to dream of an adventure of her own, but not often. Her family repeatedly told her that it was the illness she'd survived in childhood that had transformed her life and left it fragile and solitary, and on good days, she believed it.

On bad days, like today, she knew that she had always been an outsider in her own family. They had sensed the lack in her early on, seen that she didn't fit in.

There was a pain that came with constant disapproval; a sense of having lost something unnamed, unknown. Elsa had survived it by being quiet, by not demanding or seeking attention, by accepting that she was loved, but unliked. The hurt had become so commonplace, she rarely noticed it. She knew it had nothing to do with the illness to which her rejection was usually ascribed.

But now, as she sat in the parlor, in her favorite chair, she closed the book in her lap and thought about it. *The Age of Innocence* had awakened something in her, reminded her keenly of the passage of time.

Tomorrow was her birthday.

Twenty-five.

Young by most accounts. An age when men drank bathtub gin and drove recklessly and listened to ragtime music and danced with women who wore headbands and fringed dresses.

For women, it was different.

Hope began to dim for a woman when she turned twenty. By twenty-two, the whispers in town and at church would have begun, the long, sad looks. By twenty-five, the die was cast. An unmarried woman was a spinster. "On the shelf," they called her, shaking heads and *tsk*-ing at her lost opportunities. Usually people wondered *why*, what had turned a perfectly ordinary woman from a good family into a spinster. But in Elsa's case, everyone knew. They must think she was deaf, the way they talked about her. *Poor thing. Skinny as a rake handle. Not nearly as pretty as her sisters.*

Prettiness. Elsa knew that was the crux of it. She was not an attractive woman. On her best day, in her best dress, a stranger might say she was handsome, but never more. She was "too" everything—too tall, too thin, too pale, too unsure of herself.

Elsa had attended both of her sisters' weddings. Neither had asked her to stand with them at the altar, and Elsa understood. At nearly six feet, she was taller than the grooms; she would ruin the photographs, and image was everything to the Wolcotts. Her parents prized it above all else.

It didn't take a genius to look down the road of Elsa's life and see her future. She would stay here, in her parents' house on Rock Road, being cared for by Maria, the maid who'd managed the household forever. Someday, when Maria retired, Elsa would be left to care for her parents, and then, when they were gone, she would be alone.

And what would she have to show for her life? How would her time on this earth be marked? Who would remember her, and for what?

She closed her eyes and let a familiar, long-held dream tiptoe in: She imagined herself living somewhere else. In her own home. She could hear children's laughter. *Her* children.

A life, not merely an existence. That was her dream: a world in which her life and her choices were not defined by the rheumatic fever she'd contracted at fourteen, a life where she uncovered strengths heretofore unknown, where she was judged on more than her appearance.

The front door banged open and her family came stomping into the house. They moved as they always did, in a chattering, laughing knot, her portly father in the lead, red-faced from drink, her two beautiful younger sisters, Charlotte and Suzanna, fanned out like swan wings on either side of him, her elegant mother bringing up the rear, talking to her handsome sons-in-law.

Her father stopped. "Elsa," he said. "Why are you still up?"

"I wanted to talk to you."

"At this hour?" her mother said. "You look flushed. Do you have a fever?"

"I haven't had a fever in years, Mama. You know that." Elsa got to her feet, twisted her hands together, and stared at the family.

Now, she thought. She had to do it. She couldn't lose her nerve again.

"Papa." At first she said it too softly to be heard, so she tried again, actually raising her voice. "Papa."

He looked at her.

"I will be twenty-five tomorrow," Elsa said.

Her mother appeared to be irritated by the reminder. "We know that, Elsa."

"Yes, of course. I merely want to say that I've come to a decision."

That quieted the family.

"I . . . There's a college in Chicago that teaches literature and accepts women. I want to take classes—"

"Elsinore," her father said. "What need is there for you to be educated? You were too ill to finish school as it was. It's a ridiculous idea."

It was difficult to stand there, seeing her failings reflected in so many eyes. *Fight for yourself. Be brave.*

"But, Papa, I am a grown woman. I haven't been sick since I was fourteen. I believe the doctor was . . . hasty in his diagnosis. I'm fine now. Truly. I could become a teacher. Or a writer . . ."

"A writer?" Papa said. "Have you some hidden talent of which we are all unaware?"

His stare cut her down.

"It's possible," she said weakly.

Papa turned to Elsa's mother. "Mrs. Wolcott, give her something to calm her down."

"I'm hardly hysterical, Papa."

Elsa knew it was over. This was not a battle she could win. She was to stay quiet and out of sight, not to go out into the world. "I'm fine. I'll go upstairs."

She turned away from her family, none of whom was looking at her now that the moment had passed. She had vanished from the room somehow, in that way she had of dissolving in place.

She wished she'd never read *The Age of Innocence*. What good came from all this unexpressed longing? She would never fall in love, never have a child of her own.

As she climbed the stairs, she heard music coming from below. They were listening to the new Victrola.

She paused.

Go down, pull up a chair.

She closed her bedroom door sharply, shutting out the sounds from below. She wouldn't be welcomed down there.

In the mirror above her washstand, she saw her own reflection. Her pale face looked as if it had been stretched by unkind hands into a sharp chin point. Her long, corn-silk blond hair was flyaway thin and straight in a time when waves were all the rage. Her mother hadn't allowed her to cut it in the fashion of the day, saying it would look even worse short. Everything about Elsa was colorless, washed out, except for her blue eyes.

She lit her bedside lamp and withdrew one of her most treasured novels from her nightstand.

Memoirs of a Woman of Pleasure.

Elsa climbed into bed and lost herself in the scandalous story, felt a frightening, sinful need to touch herself, and almost gave in. The ache that came with the words was almost unbearable; a physical pain of yearning.

She closed the book, feeling more outcast now than when she'd begun. Restless. Unsatisfied.

If she didn't do something soon, something drastic, her future would look no different from her present. She would stay in this house for all her life, defined day and night by an illness she'd had a decade ago and an unattractiveness that couldn't be changed. She would never know the thrill of a man's touch or the comfort of sharing a bed. She would never hold her own child. Never have a home of her own.

⌇

THAT NIGHT, ELSA WAS plagued by longing. By the next morning, she knew she had to do something to change her life.

But what?

Not every woman was beautiful, or even pretty. Others had suffered childhood fevers and gone on to live full lives. The damage done to her heart was all medical conjecture as far as she could tell. Not once had it failed to beat or given her cause for real alarm. She had to believe there was grit in her, even if it had never been tested or revealed. How could anyone know for sure? She had never been allowed to run or play or dance. She'd been forced to quit school at fourteen, so she'd never had a beau. She'd spent the bulk of her life in her own room, reading fictional adventures, making up stories, finishing her education on her own.

There had to be opportunities out there, but where would she find them?

The library. Books held the answer to every question.

She made her bed and went to the washstand and combed her waist-length blond hair into a deep side part and braided it, then dressed in a plain navy-blue crepe dress, silk stockings, and black heels. A cloche, kid gloves, and a handbag completed her outfit.

She went down the stairs, grateful that her mother was still asleep at this early morning hour. Mama didn't like Elsa exerting herself except for Sunday church services, at which Mama always asked the congregation to pray for Elsa's health. Elsa drank a cup of coffee and headed out into the sunshine of a mid-May morning.

The Texas Panhandle town of Dalhart stretched out in front of her, wakening beneath a bright sun. Up and down the wooden boardwalks, doors opened, CLOSED signs were turned around. Beyond town, beneath an immense blue sky, the flat Great Plains stretched forever, a sea of prosperous farmland.

Dalhart was the county seat, and these were booming economic times. Ever since the train had been routed through here on its way from Kansas to New Mexico, Dalhart had expanded. A new water tower dominated the skyline. The Great War had turned these acres into a gold mine of wheat and corn. *Wheat will win the war!* was a phrase that still filled the farmers with pride. They had done their part.

The tractor had come along in time to make life easier, and good crop years—rain and high prices—had allowed farmers to plow more land and grow more wheat. The drought of 1908, long talked about by old-timers, had been all but forgotten. Rain had fallen steadily for years, making everyone in town rich, none more so than her father, who took both cash and notes for the farm equipment he sold.

Farmers gathered this morning outside the diner to talk about crop prices, and women herded their children to school. Only a few years ago, there had been horse-and-buggies in the streets; now automobiles chugged their way into the golden, glowing future, horns honking, smoke billowing. Dalhart was a town—fast becoming a city—of box suppers and square dances and Sunday morning services. Hard work and like-minded people creating good lives from the soil.

Elsa stepped up onto the boardwalk that ran alongside Main Street. The boards beneath her feet gave a little with each step, made her feel as if she were bouncing. A few flower boxes hung from stores' eaves, adding splashes of much-needed color. The town's Beautification League tended them with care. She passed the savings and loan and the new Ford dealership. It still amazed her that a person could go to a store, pick out an automobile, and drive it home the same day.

Beside her, the mercantile opened its doors and the proprietor, Mr. Hurst, stepped out, holding a broom. He was wearing shirtsleeves rolled up to expose his beefy forearms. A nose like a fire hydrant, squat and round, dominated his ruddy face. He was one of the richest men in town. He owned the mercantile, the diner, the ice-cream counter, and the apothecary. Only the Wolcotts had been in town longer. They, too, were third-generation Texans, and proud of it. Elsa's beloved grandfather, Walter, had called himself a Texas Ranger until the day he died.

"Hey, Miss Wolcott," the storekeeper said, pushing the few strands of hair he still had away from his florid face. "What a beautiful day it's looking to be. You headed to the library?"

"I am," she answered. "Where else?"

"I have some new red silk in. Tell your sisters. It would make a fine dress."

Elsa stopped.

Red silk.

She had never worn red silk. "Show me. Please."

"Ah! Of course. You could surprise them with it."

Mr. Hurst bustled her into the store. Everywhere Elsa looked, she saw color: boxes full of peas and strawberries, stacks of lavender soap, each bar wrapped in tissue paper, bags of flour and sugar, jars of pickles.

He led her past sets of china and silverware and folded multicolored tablecloths and aprons, to a stack of fabrics. He rifled through, pulled out a folded length of ruby-red silk.

Elsa took off her kid gloves, laid them aside, and reached for the silk. She had never touched anything so soft. And today *was* her birthday. . . .

"With Charlotte's coloring—"

"I'll take it," Elsa said. Had she put a slightly rude emphasis on *I'll*? Yes. She must have. Mr. Hurst was eyeing her strangely.

Mr. Hurst wrapped the fabric in brown paper and secured it with twine and handed it to her.

Elsa was just about to leave when she saw a beaded, glittery silver headband. It was exactly the sort of thing the Countess Olenska might wear in *The Age of Innocence*.

$$\gamma$$

ELSA WALKED HOME FROM the library with the brown-paper-wrapped red silk held tightly to her chest.

She opened the ornate black scrolled gate and stepped into her mother's world—a garden that was clipped and contained and smelled of jasmine and roses. At the end of a hedged path stood the large Wolcott home, built just after the Civil War by her grandfather for the woman he loved.

Elsa still missed her grandfather every day. He had been a blustery man, given to drink and arguing, but what he'd loved, he'd loved with abandon. He'd grieved the loss of his wife for years. He'd been the only Wolcott besides Elsa who loved reading, and he'd frequently taken her side in family disagreements. *Don't worry about dying, Elsa. Worry about not living. Be brave.*

No one had said anything like that to her since his death, and she missed him all the time. His stories about the lawless early years in

Texas, in Laredo and Dallas and Austin and out on the Great Plains, were the best of her memories.

He would have told her to buy the red silk for sure.

Mama looked up from her roses, tipped her new sunbonnet back, and said, "Elsa. Where have you been?"

"Library."

"You should have let Papa drive you. The walk is too much for you."

"I'm fine, Mama."

Honestly. It sometimes seemed they wanted her to be ill.

Elsa tightened her hold on the package of silk.

"Go lie down. It's going to get hot. Ask Maria to make you some lemonade." Mama went back to cutting her flowers, dropping them into her woven basket.

Elsa walked to the front door, stepping into the home's shadowy interior. On days that promised to be hot, all the shades were drawn. In this part of the state, that meant a lot of dark-interiored days. Closing the door behind her, she heard Maria in the kitchen, singing to herself in Spanish.

Elsa slipped through the house and went up the stairs to her bedroom. There, she unwrapped the brown paper and stared down at the vibrant ruby-red silk. She couldn't help but touch it. The softness soothed her, somehow, reminded her of the ribbon she'd held as a child when she sucked her thumb.

Could she do it, do this wild thing that was suddenly in her mind? It started with her appearance. . . .

Be brave.

Elsa grabbed a handful of her waist-length hair and cut it off at the chin. She felt a little crazed but kept cutting until she stood with long strands of pale-blond hair scattered at her feet.

A knock at the door startled Elsa so badly that she dropped the scissors. They clattered onto the dresser.

The door opened. Her mother walked into the room, saw Elsa's butchered hair, and stopped. "What have you done?"

"I wanted—"

"You can't leave the house until it grows out. What would people say?"

"Young women are wearing bobs, Mother."

"Not nice young women, Elsinore. I will bring you a hat."

"I just wanted to be pretty," Elsa said.

The pity in her mother's eyes was more than Elsa could bear.

TWO

For days, Elsa stayed hidden in her room, saying that she felt unwell. In truth, she couldn't face her father with her jaggedly cut hair and the need it exposed. At first she tried to read. Books had always been her solace; novels gave her the space to be bold, brave, beautiful, if only in her own imagination.

But the red silk whispered to her, called out, until she finally put her books away and began to make a dress pattern out of newsprint. Once she'd done that, it seemed silly not to go further, so she cut out the fabric and began to sew, just to entertain herself.

As she sewed, she began to feel a remarkable sensation: *hope*.

Finally, on a Saturday evening, she held up the finished dress. It was the epitome of big-city fashion—a V-neck bodice and dropped waist, a handkerchief hemline; thoroughly, daringly modern. A dress for the kind of woman who danced all night and didn't have a care in the world. *Flappers,* they were being called. Young women who flaunted their independence, who drank hooch and smoked cigarettes, and danced in dresses that showed off their legs.

She had to at least try it on, even if she never wore it outside of these four walls.

She took a bath and shaved her legs and smoothed silk stockings up her bare skin. She coiled her damp hair into pin curls and prayed they would create *some* wave. While her hair dried, she snuck into her mother's room and borrowed some cosmetics from the vanity. From downstairs she heard the Victrola playing music.

At last, she brushed out her slightly wavy hair and fit the glamorous silver headband on her brow. She stepped into the dress; it floated into place, airy as a cloud. The handkerchief hemline accentuated her long legs.

Leaning close to the mirror, she lined her blue eyes with black kohl and brushed a streak of pale rose powder across her sharp cheekbones. Red lipstick made her lips look fuller, just as the ladies' magazines always promised.

She looked at herself in the mirror and thought: *Oh, my Lord. I'm almost pretty.*

"You can do this," she said out loud. *Be brave.*

As she walked out of the room and went down the stairs, she felt a surprising confidence. All her life, she'd been told she was unattractive. But not now . . .

Her mother was the first to notice. She smacked Papa hard enough to make him look up from his paperback *Farm Journal*.

His face creased into frown lines. "What are you wearing?"

"I—I made it," Elsa said, clasping her hands together nervously.

Papa snapped his *Farm Journal* shut. "Your hair. Good God. And that harlot dress. Return to your room and do not shame yourself further."

Elsa turned to her mother for help. "This is the newest fashion—"

"Not for godly women, Elsinore. Your *knees* are showing. This isn't New York City."

"Go," Papa said. "*Now.*"

Elsa started to comply. Then she thought about what it meant to obey and she stopped. Grandpa Walt would tell her not to give in.

She forced her chin up. "I am going to the speakeasy tonight to listen to music."

"You will not." Papa rose. "I forbid it."

Elsa ran to the door, afraid that if she slowed, she'd stop. She lurched outside and kept running, ignoring the voices that called for her. She didn't stop until her ragged breathing forced it.

In town, the speakeasy was tucked in between an old livery station, now boarded up in this era of automobiles, and a bakery. Since the Eighteenth Amendment had been ratified and Prohibition had begun, she'd watched both women and men disappear behind the speakeasy's wooden door. And, contrary to her mother's opinion, many of the young women were dressed just as Elsa was.

She walked down the wooden steps to the closed door and knocked. A slit she hadn't noticed slid open; a pair of squinty eyes appeared. A jazzy piano tune and cigar smoke wafted through the opening. "Password," said a familiar voice.

"Password?"

"Miss Wolcott. You lost?"

"No, Frank. I've a hankering to hear some music," she said, proud of herself for sounding so calm.

"Your old man'd whoop my hide if I let you in here. Go on home. No need for a girl like you to walk the streets dressed like that. Only trouble comes of it."

The panel slid shut. She could still hear music behind the locked door. "Ain't We Got Fun." A whiff of cigar smoke lingered in the air.

Elsa stood there a moment, confused. She couldn't even go in? Why not? Sure, Prohibition made drinking illegal, but everyone in town wet their whistles in places like this and the cops looked the other way.

She walked aimlessly up the street, toward the county courthouse.

That was when she saw a man headed her way.

Tall and lanky, he was, with thick black hair partially tamed by glistening pomade. He wore dusty black pants that clung to his narrow hips and a white shirt buttoned to his neck under a beige sweater, with only the knot showing of his plaid tie. A leather newsboy cap sat at a jaunty angle on his head.

As he walked toward her, she saw how young he was—not more than eighteen, probably, with sun-darkened skin and brown eyes. (Bedroom eyes, according to her romantic novels.)

"Hello, ma'am." He stopped and smiled, took off his cap.

"Are you talking to m-me?"

"I don't see anyone else around here. I'm Raffaello Martinelli. You live in Dalhart?"

Italian. Good Lord. Her father wouldn't want her to look at this kid, let alone speak to him.

"I do."

"Not me. I'm from the bustling metropolis of Lonesome Tree, up toward the Oklahoma border. Don't blink or you'll miss it. What's your name?"

"Elsa Wolcott," she said.

"Like the tractor supply? Hey, I know your dad." He smiled. "What are you doing out here all by your lonesome in that pretty dress, Elsa Wolcott?"

Be Fanny Hill. Be bold. This might be her only chance. When she got home, Papa was probably going to lock her up. "I'm . . . lonely, I guess."

Raffaello's dark eyes widened. His Adam's apple slid up and down in a quick swallow.

Eternity passed while she waited for him to speak.

"I'm lonely, too."

He reached for her hand.

Elsa almost pulled away; that was how stunned she was.

When had she last been touched?

It's just a touch, Elsa. Don't be a ninny.

He was so handsome she felt a little sick. Would he be like the boys who'd teased and bullied her in school, called her Anyone Else behind her back? Moonlight and shadow sculpted his face—high cheekbones, a broad, flat forehead, a sharp, straight nose, and lips so full she couldn't help thinking about the sinful novels she read.

"Come with me, Els."

He renamed her, just like that, turned her into a different woman. She felt a shiver move through her at the intimacy of it.

He led her through a shadowy, empty alley and across the dark street. "Toot, toot, Tootsie! Goodbye" floated from the speakeasy's open windows.

He led her past the new train depot and out of town and toward a smart new Model T Ford farm truck with a large wooden-slat-sided bed.

"Nice truck," she said.

"Good year for wheat. You like driving at night?"

"Sure." She climbed into the passenger seat and he started up the engine. The cab shuddered as they drove north.

In less than a mile, with Dalhart in their rearview mirror, there was nothing to see. No hills, no valleys, no trees, no rivers, just a starry sky so big it seemed to have swallowed the world.

He drove down the bumpy, divoted road and turned onto the old Steward homestead. Once famous throughout the county for the size of its barn, the place had been abandoned in the last drought, and the small house behind the barn had been boarded up for years.

He pulled up in front of the empty barn and turned off the engine, then sat there a moment, staring ahead. The silence between them was broken only by their breathing and the tick of the dying engine.

He turned off the headlights and opened his door, then came around to open hers.

She looked at him, watched him reach out and take her hand and help her out of the truck.

He could have taken a step back, but he didn't, and so she could smell the whiskey on his breath and the lavender his mother must have used in ironing or washing his shirt.

He smiled at her, and she smiled back, feeling hopeful.

He spread a pair of quilts out in the wooden bed of the truck and they climbed in.

They lay side by side, staring up at the immense, star-splattered night sky.

"How old are you?" Elsa asked.

"Eighteen, but my mother treats me as if I'm a kid. I had to sneak out to be here tonight. She worries too much about what people think. You're lucky."

"Lucky?"

"You can walk around by yourself at night, in that dress, without a chaperone."

"My father is none too happy about it, I can tell you."

"But you did it. You broke away. D'ya ever think life must be bigger than what we see here, Els?"

"I do," she said.

"I mean . . . somewhere people our age are drinking bathtub gin and dancing to jazz music. Women are smoking in public." He sighed. "And here we are."

"I cut my hair off," she said. "You would have thought I killed someone, the way my father reacted."

"The old are just old. My folks came here from Sicily with only a few bucks. They tell me the story all the time and show me their lucky penny. As if it's *lucky* to end up here."

"You're a man, Raffaello. You can do anything, go anywhere."

"Call me Rafe. My mom says it sounds more American, but if they cared so much about being American, they should have named me George. Or Lincoln." He sighed. "It sure is nice to say these things out loud, for once. You're a good listener, Els."

"Thank you . . . Rafe."

He rolled onto his side. She felt his gaze on her face and tried to keep breathing evenly.

"Can I kiss you, Elsa?"

She could barely nod.

He leaned over and kissed her cheek. His lips softened against her skin; at the touch, she felt herself come alive.

He trailed kisses along her throat, and it made her want to touch him, but she didn't dare. Good women almost certainly didn't do such things.

"Can I . . . do more, Elsa?"

"You mean . . ."

"Love you?"

Elsa had dreamed of a moment like this, prayed for it, sculpted it out of scraps from the books she'd read, but now it was here. Real. A man was asking to love her.

"Yes," she whispered.

"Are you sure?"

She nodded.

He drew back, fumbled with his belt, undid it, pulled it free, and threw it. The buckle clacked against the side of the truck as he pulled off his pants.

He pushed up her red silk dress; it slid up her body, tickling, arousing her. She saw her bare legs in the moonlight as he pulled down her bloomers. Warm night air touched her, made her shiver. She held her legs together until he eased them apart and climbed on top of her.

Sweet God.

She closed her eyes and he thrust himself inside of her. It hurt so badly she cried out.

Elsa clamped her mouth shut to stay silent.

He groaned and shuddered and went limp on top of her. She felt his heavy breath in the crook of her neck.

He rolled off her but remained close. "Wowza," he said.

It sounded as if there were a smile in his voice, but how could that be? She must have done something wrong. That couldn't be . . . it.

"You're something special, Elsa," he said.

"It was . . . good?" she dared to ask.

"It was *great*," he said.

She wanted to roll onto her side and study his face. Kiss him. These stars she'd seen a million times. He was something new, and he'd wanted her. The effect of that was a staggering upheaval to her world. An opportunity she'd never really imagined. *Can I love you?* he'd asked. Maybe they would fall asleep together and—

"Well, I reckon I'd best get you home, Els. My dad will tan my hide if I'm not on the tractor at dawn. We're plowing up another hundred and twenty acres tomorrow to plant more wheat."

"Oh," she said. "Right. Of course."

꙳

ELSA CLOSED THE TRUCK door and stared through the open window at Rafe, who smiled, slowly raised his hand, and then drove away.

What kind of goodbye was it? Would he want to see her again?

Look at him. Of course not.

Besides, he lived in Lonesome Tree. That was thirty miles away. And if she did happen to see him in Dalhart, it wouldn't matter.

He was Italian. Catholic. Young. Nothing about him was acceptable to her family.

She opened the gate and entered her mother's fragrant world. From now on, blooming night jasmine would always make Elsa think of him . . .

At the house, she opened the front door and stepped into the shadowy parlor.

As she closed the door, she heard a creaking sound and she stopped. Moonlight bled through the window. She saw her father standing by the Victrola.

"Who are you?" he said, coming toward her.

Elsa's beaded silver headband slipped down; she pushed it back up. "Y-your daughter."

"Damn right. My father fought to make Texas a part of the United States. He joined the Rangers and fought in Laredo and was shot and nearly died. Our blood is in this ground."

"Y-yes. I know, but—"

Elsa didn't see his hand come up until it was too close to duck. He cracked her across the jaw so hard she lost her balance and fell to the floor.

She scrambled back into the corner to get away. "Papa—"

"You shame us. Get out of my sight."

Elsa lurched to her feet, ran up the stairs, and slammed her bedroom door shut.

With shaking hands, she lit the lamp by her bed and undressed.

There was a red mark above her breast. (Had Rafe done that?) A bruise was already discoloring her jaw, and her hair was a mess from lovemaking, if that was what it could be called.

Even so, she would do it again if she could. She would let her father hit her, yell at her, slander her, or disinherit her.

She knew now what she hadn't known before, hadn't even suspected: she would do anything, suffer anything, to be loved, even if it was just for a night.

⁂

THE NEXT MORNING, ELSA woke to sunlight streaming through the open window. The red dress hung over the closet door. The ache in her jaw reminded her of last night, as did the pain that lingered after Rafe's loving. One she wanted to forget; one she wanted to remember.

Her iron bed was piled with quilts she had made, often sewing by candlelight during the cold winter months. At the foot of her bed stood her hope chest, lovingly filled with embroidered linens and a fine white lawn nightdress and the wedding quilt Elsa had begun when she was twelve years old, before her unattractiveness had been revealed to be not a phase but a permanence. By the time Elsa started her monthlies, Mama had quietly stopped talking about Elsa's wedding and stopped beading scraps of Alençon lace. Enough for half a dress lay folded between pieces of tissue.

There was a knock at the door.

Elsa sat up. "Come in."

Mama entered the room, her fashionable day shoes making no sound on the rag rug that covered most of the wooden floor. She was a tall woman, with broad shoulders and a no-nonsense demeanor; she lived a life above reproach, chaired church committees, ran the Beautification League, and kept her voice low even when she was angry. Nothing and no one could ruffle Minerva Wolcott. She claimed it was a family trait, inherited from ancestors who had come to Texas when no other white face could be seen for a six-day horse ride.

Mama sat down on the edge of the bed. Her hair, dyed black, was drawn back into a chignon that heightened the severity of her sharp features. She reached out and touched the tender bruise on Elsa's jaw. "My father would have done much worse to me."

"But—"

"No *buts*, Elsinore." She leaned forward, tucked a ragged lock of Elsa's shorn blond hair behind her ear. "I suspect I will hear gossip today in town. *Gossip.* About one of my daughters." She heaved a heavy sigh. "Did you get into trouble?"

"No, Mama."

"So, you're still a good girl?"

Elsa nodded, unable to say the lie aloud.

Mama's forefinger moved down, touched Elsa's chin, tilted her face up. She studied Elsa, slowly frowning, assessing. "A pretty dress doesn't make one pretty, dear."

"I just wanted—"

"We won't speak of it, and nothing like it will ever happen again."

Mama stood, smoothing her lavender crepe skirt, although no wrinkles had formed or would dare to. Distance spread between them, as solid as any fence. "You are unmarriageable, Elsinore, even with all our money and standing. No man of note wants an unattractive wife who looms over him. And if a man did come along who could overlook your weaknesses, certainly he would not dismiss a tarnished reputation. Learn to be happy with real life. Throw away your silly romantic novels."

Mama took the red silk dress on her way out.

THREE

In the years since the Great War, patriotism ran high in Dalhart. That, combined with rain and rising wheat prices, gave everyone a reason to celebrate the Fourth of July. In town, store windows advertised Independence Day sales and bells clanged merrily as folks went in and out of the merchants' stores, stocking up on food and drink for the festivities.

Usually Elsa looked forward to the celebration, but the past few weeks had been difficult. Since her night with Rafe, Elsa had felt caged. Restless. Unhappy.

Not that anyone in her family looked closely enough at her to see the difference. Instead of voicing her discontent, she buried it and went on. It was all she knew to do.

She kept her head down and pretended nothing had changed. She stayed in her bedroom as much as she could, even in the ragged heat of summer. She had books delivered from the library—suitable books—and read them from cover to cover. She embroidered dish towels and pillowcases. At supper, she listened to her parents' conversation and nodded when she needed to. At church, she wore a cloche over her scandalously short hair and made the excuse that she didn't feel well and was left alone.

On the few instances when she dared to look up from a beloved book and stare out the window, she saw the emptiness of a spinster's future stretching out to the flat horizon and beyond.

Accept.

The bruise on her jaw had faded. No one—not even her sisters—had remarked upon it. Life returned to normal at the Wolcott house.

Elsa imagined herself as the fictional Lady of Shalott, a woman trapped in a tower, cursed, unable to leave her room, forever doomed to watch the bustling of life outside. If anyone noticed her sudden quiet, they didn't remark upon it or ask the cause. In truth, it was not so different. She'd learned how to disappear in place long ago. She was like one of those animals whose defense mechanism is to blend into the landscape and become invisible. It was her way of dealing with rejection: Say nothing and disappear. Never fight back. If she remained quiet enough, people eventually forgot she was there and left her alone.

"Elsa!" her father yelled up the stairs. "It's time to go. Don't make us late."

Elsa pulled on her kid gloves—required even in this terrible heat—and pinned a straw hat in place. Then she went downstairs.

Elsa stopped halfway down the stairs, unable to keep going. What if Rafe was at the party?

The Fourth of July was one of those rare events where the whole county gathered. Usually the different towns celebrated in their own halls, but for this party, people came from miles around.

"Let's go," Papa said. "Your mother hates to be late."

Elsa followed her parents out to her father's brand-new bottle-green Model T Runabout roadster. They climbed in, squished together on the heavy leather seat. Although they lived in town and the grange hall was close, they had a lot of food to carry, and Mama wouldn't be caught dead walking to a party.

The Dalhart Grange Hall had been decorated in layers of red, white, and blue bunting. A dozen or so cars were parked out front. Most belonged to the farmers who'd done well in the past few years and the bankers who had financed all that growth. Great care had been taken by the women of the Beautification League, so the lawn out front was a lush green. Flowers grew in bright profusion alongside the steps that led up to the front door. The grounds were full of children playing, laughing, running. Elsa couldn't see any teenagers, but they were here somewhere, probably sneaking stolen kisses in shadowy corners.

Papa parked in the street and turned off the engine.

Elsa heard music. Party noise drifted through open doors: chattering, coughing, laughing. A pair of fiddles played along with a banjo and a guitar: "Second Hand Rose."

Papa opened the trunk, revealing the food Maria had spent days preparing. Food Mama would take credit for making. Family recipes, handed down from her Texas pioneer ancestors—molasses stack cakes, Aunt Bertha's spicy gingerbread, upside-down peach cake, and Grandpa Walt's favorite ham with red-eye gravy and grits—every item designed to remind people of the Wolcotts' deep place in Texas history.

Elsa fell into step behind her parents, carrying a still-warm Dutch oven toward the wooden grange hall.

Inside, colorful quilts had been used for everything from decorations to tablecloths. Along the back wall were several long tables filled with food: pork roasts and rich, dark stews, trays full of green beans cooked in bacon fat. There would undoubtably be chicken salads, potato salads, sausage and biscuits, breads, cornbread, cakes, and pies of all kinds. Everyone in the county loved a party and the women worked hard to impress each other. There would be smoked hams, rabbit sausage, loaves of bread with freshly churned butter, hard-boiled eggs, fruit pies, and platters full of hot dogs. Mama led the way to the corner table, where the women of the Beautification League were busy rearranging the offerings.

Elsa saw her sisters standing with the women of the Beautification League. Suzanna was wearing a blouse made from Elsa's red silk. Charlotte wore a red silk scarf at her throat.

Elsa stopped; the sight of her sisters in that red silk made her heartsick.

Papa joined the men clustered in loud conversation beside the stage.

Even though Prohibition made liquor illegal, there was plenty to be had for the men, who were a tough, sturdy group of immigrants from Russia, Germany, Italy, and Ireland. They'd come here with nothing and made something out of that nothing and they didn't cotton to being told how to live, not by each other or by a government that hardly seemed to know the Great Plains existed. Although they tended to look a little worn, many of the men had plenty of money in the bank. When wheat sold for a dollar thirty a bushel and cost forty cents to grow, everyone in town was happy. With enough land, a man could become rich.

"Dalhart is on its way," Papa said loudly enough to be heard above the music. "I'm gonna build us a damn opera house next year. Why should we have to go to Amarillo for a little culture?"

"We need electricity in town. That's the ticket," Mr. Hurst added.

Mama continued to rearrange the food, which had never yet been done to her standards in her absence. Charlotte and Suzanna laughed with their pretty, well-dressed friends, most of whom were young mothers.

Elsa spotted Rafe, standing with the other Italian families in the corner by a food table. His black hair, floppy on top and shorter along his ears, needed cutting. The pomade he'd used made it shiny but couldn't quite control it. He wore a plain shirt, worn at the elbows, brown pants, saddle-leather brown suspenders, and a plaid bow tie. A pretty, dark-haired girl clung to his arm.

In the six weeks since she'd seen Rafe, his face had been further tanned by hours in the fields.

Look this way, she thought, and then: *No, don't.*

He would pretend not to know her. Or, worse, not even to see her.

Elsa forced herself to move forward, hearing her heels click on the hardwood dance floor.

She put the Dutch oven down on the white-clothed table.

"Heavens, Elsa. Ham in the middle of the dessert table. Whatever are you thinking?" Mama said.

Elsa took the pot up and carried it to the next table. Each step took her closer to Rafe.

She set the pot down as quietly as possible.

Rafe looked over, saw her. He didn't smile; worse, his gaze cut worriedly to the girl standing next to him.

Elsa immediately looked away. She couldn't stand here, longing like this. It was suffocating. And the last thing in the world she wanted was to be ignored by him all night.

"Mama?" she said, moving in beside her mother. "Mama?"

"You see I am speaking to Mrs. Tolliver?"

"Yes. I'm sorry. It's just . . ." *Don't look at him.* "I'm not feeling well."

"Too much excitement, I imagine," Mama said, glancing at her friend.

"I think I should go home," Elsa said.

Mama nodded. "Of course."

Elsa was careful not to look at Rafe as she walked toward the open door. Couples spun past her on the dance floor.

She opened the door and stepped out into the warm, golden early evening. The door banged shut behind her, softening the strains of the fiddle music and the stomp of dancing feet.

She made her way through the collection of parked cars, past the horse-drawn wagons that brought the less successful farmers to town for events like this.

Main Street was quiet now, bathed in a butterscotch glow that would soon melt into night. She stepped up onto the boardwalk.

"Els?"

She stopped, turned slowly.

"I'm sorry, Els," Rafe said, looking uncomfortable.

"Sorry?"

"I should have spoken up back there. Waved or something."

"Oh."

He came closer, so close she could feel the warmth emanating from him and smell the trace scent of wheat.

"I understand, Rafe. She's lovely."

"Gia Composto. Our parents decided we would marry before we could walk." He leaned closer. She felt his warm breath on her cheek.

"I dreamed about you," he said in a rush.

"Y-you did?"

He nodded, looking a little embarrassed.

She felt as if she'd just edged toward a cliff; below was a fall that could break her bones. His look, his voice. She stared into his eyes, which were dark as night and soulful and just a little sad, although what he could possibly have to be sad about, she couldn't imagine.

"Meet me tonight," he said. "Midnight. At the old Steward barn."

꒰

ELSA LAY IN BED, fully dressed.

She shouldn't go. That much was obvious. The bruise on her jaw had healed, but the mark of it remained beneath the surface. Good women did not do the thing Rafe had asked of her.

She heard her parents come home, climb the stairs, open and close their bedroom door down the hall.

The bedside clock read 9:40.

Elsa lay there, breathing shallowly, as the house quieted.

Waiting.

She shouldn't go.

It didn't matter how frequently she said it in her head, because not once, not for one moment, had she considered following her own advice.

At eleven-thirty, she got out of bed. The room was still stiflingly hot, but her window looked out on the Great Plains night sky. Her childhood portal to adventure. How often had she stood at this window and sent her dreams into those unknown universes?

She opened the window and climbed out onto the metal flower trellis. It seemed as if she were crawling into the starlit sky itself.

When she dropped onto the thick grass, she paused, waited nervously to be detected, but no lights came on inside. She crept over to the side of the house and retrieved one of her sisters' old bicycles. Climbing aboard, she pedaled out to the road and down Main Street and out of town.

The world at night was big and lonesome in a way that locals had become used to, illuminated only by starlight, pinpricks of white in a dark world. There were no homes out here, nothing but darkness for miles.

She pulled up to the old barn and dismounted, setting her bicycle in the blanket of buffalo grass beside the road.

He wouldn't show up.

Of course he wouldn't.

She could remember every word he'd said to her, few as they were, and every nuance of expression on his face as he spoke. The way his smile started on one side and kind of slid slowly into place. The pale comma of a scar along his jaw, the way one incisor poked out just a little.

I dreamed of you.

Meet me tonight.

Had she answered him? Or had she just stood there, mute? She couldn't remember.

But here she was, standing all alone in front of an abandoned barn.

Fool that she was.

There would be hell to pay if she got caught.

She stepped forward, her brown oxford heels crunching on tiny stones on the road. The barn loomed up before her, the peak of the roof seeming to get caught on the fishhook moon. Slats were missing; fallen boards lay scattered.

Elsa hugged herself as if she were cold, but in truth she was uncomfortably warm.

How long did she stand there? Long enough to begin to feel sick to her stomach. She was about to give up when she heard a car engine. She turned, saw a pair of headlights coming down the road.

Elsa was so shocked she couldn't move.

He was driving too fast, being reckless. Gravel spit out from the tires. His horn blared: *ah ooh gah.*

He must have jumped on the brake, because the truck fishtailed to a stop. Dust rose up around him.

Rafe jumped out of the car in a hurry. "Els," he said, grinning, producing a bouquet of purple and pink flowers.

"Y-you brought me flowers?"

He reached into the cab and produced a bottle. "And some gin!"

Elsa had no idea how to respond to either.

He handed her the flowers. She looked into his eyes, and she thought, *This.* She would pay any price for it.

"I want you, Els," he whispered.

She followed him into the back of the truck.

The quilts were already spread out. Elsa smoothed them a little and lay down. Only a thin thread of light came from the scythed moon.

Rafe lay down beside her.

She felt his body along hers, heard his breathing.

"Did you think about me?" he asked.

"Yes."

"Me, too. About you, I mean. About this." He began unbuttoning her bodice.

Fire where he touched her. An unraveling. She couldn't still herself, couldn't hide it.

He pushed her dress up and pulled her bloomers down and she felt the night air on her skin. All of it aroused her, the air on her skin, her own nakedness, the way he was breathing.

She longed to touch him, taste him, tell him where she wanted—needed—to be touched, but fear of humiliation kept her silent. Anything she said was bound to be wrong, unladylike, and she wanted so much to make him happy.

Before she was ready, he was inside of her, thrusting hard, groaning. Seconds later, he collapsed on top of her, shuddering, breathing quickly.

He whispered something unintelligible into her ear. She hoped it was romantic.

Elsa touched the stubble of beard along his jaw. Her touch was so soft and tenuous that she didn't think he felt it.

"I will miss you, Els," he said.

Elsa brought her hand back quickly. "Where are you going?"

He opened the bottle of gin and took a long drink, then handed it to her. "My folks are making me go to college." He rolled onto his side and rested his head on one hand and stared at her as she took a stinging, fiery drink and clamped a hand over her mouth.

He took another drink. "My mom wants me to graduate from college so I'll be a real American. Or something like that."

"College," she said wistfully.

"Yeah. Stupid, huh? I don't need book learning. I want to see Times Square and the Brooklyn Bridge and Hollywood. Learn by *doing*. See the world." He took another drink. "What do you dream of, Els?"

She was so surprised to be asked, it took her a moment to answer. "Having a child, I guess. Maybe a home of my own."

He grinned. "Heck, that don't count. A woman wanting a baby is like a seed wanting to grow. What else?"

"You'll laugh."

"I won't. I promise."

"I want to be brave," she said, almost too softly to be heard.

"What scares you?"

"Everything," she said. "My grandfather was a Texas Ranger. He used to tell me to stand up and fight. But for what? I don't know. It sounds silly when I say it out loud . . ."

She felt his gaze on her and hoped the night was kind to her face.

"You ain't like any other girl I know," he said, tucking a lock of hair behind her ear.

"When do you leave?"

"August. That gives us some time. If you'll meet me again."

Elsa smiled. "Yes."

She would take whatever she could get from Rafe and pay whatever price there was for it. Even going to hell. He'd made her feel more beautiful in one minute than the rest of the world had in twenty-five years.

FOUR

By mid-August, the flowers in the few hanging planters and window boxes in downtown Dalhart were scorched and leggy. Fewer merchants could find the energy to prune and water in this heat, and the flowers wouldn't last much longer either way. Mr. Hurst waved listlessly as Elsa passed him on her way home from the library.

As Elsa opened the gate, the cloying, sickeningly sweet scent of the garden overpowered her. She clamped a hand over her mouth but there was no way to hold back her sickness. She vomited on her mother's favorite American Beauty roses.

Elsa kept dry-heaving long after there was nothing left in her stomach. Finally, she wiped her mouth and straightened, feeling shaky.

She heard a rustling beside her.

Mama was kneeling in the garden, wearing a woven sun hat and an apron over her cotton day dress. She set down her clippers and got to her feet. The pockets of her gardening apron bulged with cuttings. How was it that the thorns didn't bother her?

"Elsa," Mama said, her voice surprisingly sharp. "Didn't you get sick a few days ago?"

"I'm fine."

Mama pulled off her gloves, one finger at a time, as she walked toward Elsa.

She laid the back of her hand against Elsa's forehead. "You're not fevered."

"I'm fine. It's just an upset stomach."

Elsa waited for Mama to speak. It was obvious she was thinking something; her face was drawn into a frown, which was something she tried never to do. *A lady doesn't reveal emotions,* was one of her favorite adages. Elsa had heard it every time she'd cried from loneliness or begged to be allowed to go to a dance.

Mama studied Elsa. "It couldn't be."

"What?"

"Have you dishonored us?"

"What?"

"Have you been with a man?"

Of *course* Mama could see Elsa's secret. Every book Elsa had ever read romanticized the mother-daughter bond. Even if Mama didn't always show her love (affection being another thing a lady should conceal), Elsa knew how bound they were.

She reached out for her mother's hands, took them in her own, felt her mother's instinctive flinch. "I've wanted to tell you. I have. I've been so alone with these feelings that confuse me. And he—"

Mama wrenched her hands back.

Elsa heard the gate creak open and snap shut in the quiet that had settled in between Elsa and her mother.

"Good Lord, women, why are you standing out in this vexing heat? Surely a glass of cold tea would be the ticket."

"Your daughter is expecting," Mama said.

"Charlotte? It's about durn time. I thought—"

"No," Mama snapped. "Elsinore."

"Me?" Elsa said. *Expecting?*

It couldn't be true. She and Rafe had only been together a few times. And each coupling had been so fast. Over almost before it began. Surely no child could come from that.

But what did she know of such things? A mother didn't explain sex to her daughter until the wedding day, and Elsa had never had a wedding, so her mother had never spoken to her of passion or having children, it having been assumed Elsa would never experience any of it. All Elsa knew of sex and procreation came from novels. And, frankly, details were scarce.

"*Elsa?*" Papa said.

"Yes," was her mother's barely there answer.

Papa grabbed Elsa by the arm and yanked her close. "Who ruined you?"

"No, Papa—"

"Tell me his name right now, or as God is my witness, I will go door to door and ask every man in this town if he ruined my daughter."

Elsa imagined that: Papa dragging her from door to door, a modern-day Hester Prynne; him banging on doors, asking men like Mr. Hurst or Mr. McLaney, *Have you ruined this woman?*

Sooner or later, she and her father would leave town and head out to the farms . . .

He would do it. She knew he would. There was no stopping her father once he'd made up his mind. "I'll leave," she said. "I'll leave right now. Go out on my own."

"It must have been . . . you know . . . a crime," Mama said. "No man would—"

"Want me?" Elsa said, spinning to face her mother. "No man could ever want me. You've told me that all my life. You've all made sure I understood that I was ugly and unlovable, but it isn't true. Rafe wanted me. He—"

"Martinelli," Papa said, his voice thick with disgust. "An Eye-talian. His father bought a thresher from me this year. Sweet God. When people hear . . ." He shoved Elsa away from him. "Go to your room. I need to think."

Elsa stumbled away. She wanted to say something, but what words could fix this? She walked up the porch steps and into the house.

Maria stood in the archway to the kitchen, holding a silver candlestick and a rag. "Miss Wolcott, are you all right?"

"No, Maria, I'm not."

Elsa ran upstairs to her room. She felt the start of tears and denied herself the relief they promised.

She touched her flat, nearly concave stomach. She couldn't imagine a baby in her, growing secretly. Surely a woman would know such a thing.

An hour passed, then another. What were they talking about, her parents? What would they do to her? Beat her, lock her away, call the police and report a fictitious crime?

She paced. She sat. She paced again. Outside her window, she saw evening start to fall.

They would throw her out and she would wander the Great Plains, destitute and ruined, until it was time for her to give birth, which she would do alone, in squalor, and her body would give out on her at last. She would die in childbirth.

So would the baby.

Stop it. Her parents wouldn't do that to her. They couldn't. They loved her.

At last, the bedroom door opened. Mama stood there, looking unusually harried and discomfited. "Pack a bag, Elsa."

"Where am I going? Will it be like Gertrude Renke? She was gone for months after that scandal with Theodore. Then she came home, and no one ever said a thing about it."

"Pack your bag."

Elsa knelt beside her bed and pulled out her suitcase. The last time it had been used was when she went to the hospital in Amarillo. Eleven years ago.

She pulled clothes from her closet without thought or design and folded them into her open suitcase.

Elsa stared at her overstuffed bookcase. Books lay on top, were stacked on the floor beside it. More books covered her nightstand. Asking her to choose among them was like having to choose between air and water.

"I haven't all day to wait," Mama said.

Elsa picked out *The Wonderful Wizard of Oz*, *Sense and Sensibility*, *Jane Eyre*, and *Wuthering Heights*. She left *The Age of Innocence*, which in a way had started all of this.

She put the four novels in her suitcase and clasped it shut.

"No Bible, I see. Come," Mama said. "Let's go."

Elsa followed her mother out of the house. They crossed through the garden and approached Papa, who stood by the roadster.

"It can't come back on us, Eugene," Mama said. "She'll have to marry him."

Elsa stopped. "Marry him?" In all the hours she'd had to imagine her terrible fate, this had not even occurred to her. "You can't be serious. He's only eighteen."

Mama made a sound of disgust.

Papa opened the passenger door and waited impatiently for Elsa to get into the car. As soon as she was seated, he slammed her door, took his place in the driver's seat, and started the engine.

"Just take me to the train station."

Papa turned on his headlights. "You afraid your Eye-talian won't want you? Too late, missy. You won't simply disappear. Oh, no. You will face the consequences of your sin."

A few miles out of Dalhart, there was nothing to see but the yellow beams of the twin headlights. Every minute, every mile tightened Elsa's fear until she felt she might simply break apart.

Lonesome Tree was a nothing little town tucked up toward the Oklahoma border. They blew through it at twenty miles per hour.

Two miles later, the headlights shone on a mailbox that read: MARTINELLI. Papa turned onto a long dirt driveway, which was lined on both sides by cottonwood trees and fenced with barbed wire attached to whatever wood the Martinellis had been able to find in this mostly treeless land.

The car pulled into a well-tended yard and stopped in front of a whitewashed farmhouse with a covered front porch and dormer windows that looked out to the road.

Papa honked his horn. Loudly. One. Two. Three times.

A man came out of the barn, holding an ax casually over one shoulder. As he stepped into the glow of the headlights, Elsa saw that he wore the farmer's uniform in these parts: patched dungarees and a shirt with the sleeves rolled up.

A woman walked out of the house and joined the man. She was petite, with black hair woven into a coronet. She wore a green plaid dress and a crisp white apron. She was as beautiful as Rafe was handsome; they shared the same sculpted face, high cheekbones, and full lips, the same olive complexion.

Papa got out of the car, then walked around to the passenger door, opened it, and yanked Elsa to her feet.

"Eugene," the farmer said. "I'm up-to-date on my thresher payments, aren't I?"

Papa ignored him, yelled: "Rafe Martinelli!"

Elsa wished the earth would open up and swallow her. She knew what the farmer and his wife saw when they looked at her: a spinster, skinny as a length of twine, tall as most men, hair cut unevenly, her narrow, sharp-chinned face as plain as a dirt field. Her thin lips were chapped, torn, and bloody. She'd been chewing on them nervously. The suitcase in her right hand was small, a testament to the fact that she was a woman who owned almost nothing.

Rafe appeared on the porch.

"What can we do for yah, Eugene?" Mr. Martinelli said.

"Your boy has ruined my daughter, Tony. She's expecting."

Elsa saw the way Mrs. Martinelli's face changed at that, how the look in her eyes went from kind to suspicious. An appraising, judging look in which Elsa was condemned as either a liar or a loose woman or both.

This was how people in town would see Elsa now: the old maid who'd seduced a boy and been ruined. Elsa held herself together with sheer willpower, refusing to give voice to the scream that filled her head.

Shame.

She thought she'd known shame before, would have said it was even the ordinary course of things, but now she saw the difference. In her family she'd felt ashamed for being unattractive, unmarriageable. She'd let that shame become a part of her, let it weave through her body and mind, become the connective tissue that held her together. But in that shame, there had been hope that one day they would see past all of that to the real her, the sister/daughter she was in her mind. A flower closed up tightly, waiting for the sunlight to fall on furled petals, desperate to bloom.

This shame was different. She'd brought it on herself and, worse, she had destroyed this poor young man's life.

Rafe came down the steps and moved in beside his parents.

Standing in the glare of the headlights, the Martinelli family stared at her in what could only be described as horror.

"Your son took advantage of my daughter," Papa said.

Mr. Martinelli frowned. "How do you know—"

"Papa," Elsa whispered. "Please don't . . ."

Rafe stepped forward. "Els," he said. "Are you okay?"

Elsa wanted to cry at that small kindness.

"It can't be true," Mrs. Martinelli said. "He's engaged to Gia Composto."

"Engaged?" Elsa said to Rafe.

His face turned red. "Last week."

Elsa swallowed hard and nodded matter-of-factly. "I never thought you . . . you know. I mean, I understand. I'll go. This is for me to deal with."

She took a step back.

"Oh, no, you don't, missy." Papa looked at Mr. Martinelli. "The Wolcotts are a good family. Respected in Dalhart. I expect your boy to make this right." He gave Elsa one last look of disgust. "Either way, I don't ever want to see you again, Elsinore. You're no daughter of mine."

On that, he strode back to his still-running roadster and drove away.

Elsa was left standing there, holding her suitcase.

"Raffaello," Mr. Martinelli said, turning his gaze to his son. "Is it true?"

Rafe flinched, unable to quite meet his father's gaze. "Yeah."

"*Madonna mia,*" Mrs. Martinelli said, then rattled off something further in Italian. Angry, that was all Elsa got from it. She slapped Rafe on the back of the head, a loud crack of sound, and then began yelling: "Send her away, Antonio. *Puttana.*"

Mr. Martinelli pulled his wife away from them.

"I'm sorry, Rafe," Elsa said when they were alone. Shame was drowning her. She heard Mrs. Martinelli yell, "No," and then, again: "*Puttana.*"

A moment later, Mr. Martinelli returned to Elsa, looking older than when he'd left. He was craggy-looking—his brow thrust out, tufted by sagebrush eyebrows; the bumpy arch of a nose that looked to have been broken more than once; a blunt plate of a chin. An old-fashioned cowcatcher mustache covered most of his upper lip. Every bit of bad Panhandle Texas weather showed on his deeply tanned face, created wrinkles along his forehead like year rings in a tree trunk. "I'm Tony," he said, and then cocked his head toward his wife, who stood about fifteen feet away. "My wife . . . Rose."

Elsa nodded. She knew he was one of the many farmers who bought supplies from her father each season on credit and paid it back after harvest. They had met at a few county gatherings, but not many. The Wolcotts didn't socialize with people like the Martinellis.

"Rafe," he went on, looking at his son. "Introduce your girl properly."

Your girl.

Not your hussy, your Jezebel.

Elsa had never been anyone's *girl.* And she was too long in the tooth to be a girl anyway.

"Papa, this is Elsa Wolcott," Rafe said in a voice that cracked on the last word.

"No. No. No," Mrs. Martinelli shouted. Her hands slammed onto her hips. "He's going to college in three days, Tony. We've paid the deposit. How do we even know this woman is in the family way? It could be a lie. A baby—"

"Changes everything," said Mr. Martinelli. He added something in Italian, and his words silenced his wife.

"You'll marry her," Mr. Martinelli said to Rafe.

Mrs. Martinelli cursed loudly in Italian; at least it sounded like a curse.

Rafe nodded at his father. He looked as frightened as Elsa felt.

"What about his future, Tony?" Mrs. Martinelli said. "All of our dreams for him?"

Mr. Martinelli didn't look at his wife. "It's the end of all that, Rose."

ELSA STOOD SILENTLY BY. Time seemed to slow down and stretch out as Rafe stared at her. The silence around them would have been complete but for the chickens squawking from the pen and a hog rooting lazily through the dirt.

"I'll get her settled," Mrs. Martinelli said tightly, her face a mask of displeasure. "You boys go finish up for the night."

Mr. Martinelli and Rafe walked away without a word.

Elsa thought, *Leave. Just walk away.* That was what they wanted her to do. If she walked away now, this family could go on with their lives.

But where would she go?

How would she live?

She pressed a hand to her flat belly and thought about the life growing in there.

A baby.

How was it that in all the maelstrom of shame and regret, she'd missed the only thing that mattered?

She would be a mother. A *mother*. There would be a baby who would love her, whom she would love.

A miracle.

She turned away from Mrs. Martinelli and began the long walk down the driveway. She heard each of her footsteps, and the cotton-woods chattering in the breeze.

"Wait!"

Elsa stopped. Turned back.

Mrs. Martinelli stood directly behind her, hands fisted, mouth set in a hard line of disapproval. She was so small a good breeze might topple her, and yet the force emanating from her was unmistakable. "Where are you going?"

"What do you care? Away."

"Your parents will accept you back, ruined?"

"Hardly."

"So . . ."

"I'm sorry," Elsa said. "I didn't mean to ruin your son's life. Or dash your hopes for him. I just . . . it doesn't matter now."

Elsa felt like a giraffe looming over this petite, exotic-looking woman.

"So that's it? You just leave?"

"Isn't that what you want me to do?"

Mrs. Martinelli stepped closer, looked up, studying Elsa intently. Long, uncomfortable moments passed. "How old are you?"

"Twenty-five."

Mrs. Martinelli did not look pleased by that. "Will you convert to Catholicism?"

It took Elsa a moment to understand what was happening. They were negotiating.

Catholic.

Her parents would be mortified. Her family would disown her.

They already had. *You're no daughter of mine.*

"Yes," Elsa said. Her child would need the comfort of a faith and the Martinellis would be her only family.

Mrs. Martinelli nodded crisply. "Good. Then—"

"Will you love this child?" Elsa asked. "As you would have loved one borne by Gia?"

Mrs. Martinelli looked surprised.

"Or will you just put up with this *puttana*'s child?" Elsa didn't know what the word meant, but she knew it wasn't kind. "Because I know about growing up in a household where love is withheld. I won't do that to my child."

"When you are a mother, you will know how I feel right now," Mrs. Martinelli said at last. "The dreams for your children are so . . . so . . ." She stopped, looked away as tears filled her eyes, then went on. "You cannot imagine the sacrifices we made so that Raffaello could have a better life than we've had."

Elsa realized the pain she'd caused this woman, and her shame intensified. It was all she could do not to apologize again.

"The baby, I will love," Mrs. Martinelli said into the silence. "My first grandchild."

Elsa heard the unvoiced remainder loud and clear: *You, I will not,* but just that word, *love,* was enough to steady Elsa's heart and shore up her fragile resolve.

She could live among these strangers unwanted; invisibility was a skill she'd learned. What mattered now was the baby.

She pressed a hand to her stomach, thinking, *You, you, little one, you will be loved by me and love me in return.*

Nothing else mattered.

I will be a mother.

For this child, Elsa would marry a man who didn't love her and join a family who didn't want her. From now on, all her choices would be thusly made.

For her child.

"Where should I put my things?"

FIVE

ᕬ

Mrs. Martinelli walked so fast it was hard to keep up with her. "Are you hungry?" the diminutive woman asked as she bounded up the steps and strode past the collection of mismatched chairs on the porch.

"No, ma'am."

Mrs. Martinelli opened the front door and stepped inside. Elsa followed her into the house. In the parlor, she saw a collection of wooden furniture and a scarred oval cocktail table. Crocheted white doilies hung on the backs of chairs. There were large crucifixes hanging on two of the walls

Catholic.

What did that mean, really? What had Elsa promised to become?

Mrs. Martinelli moved through the sitting room and went down a narrow hallway, past an open door that revealed a copper bathing tub and a washstand. No toilet.

No indoor plumbing?

At the end of the hall, Mrs. Martinelli pushed a door open.

A boy's bedroom, complete with sports trophies on the dresser. An unmade bed faced a large window, framed by blue chambray curtains. Elsa saw a photo of Gia Composto on the bedside table. A suitcase—no doubt packed for college—lay on the bed.

Mrs. Martinelli scooped up the photograph and tossed the suitcase under the bed. "You will stay here, alone, until the wedding. Rafe can sleep in the barn. He loves that on a hot night anyway." Mrs. Martinelli lit a lamp. "I will speak to Father Michael promptly. No need to draw this out." She frowned. "I will need to talk to the Compostos."

"Perhaps Rafe should do that," Elsa said.

Mrs. Martinelli looked up. The small woman was a study in contradictions: she moved with the fast, furtive motions of a bird and looked fragile, but Elsa's overwhelming impression was of strength. Toughness. She remembered Rafe's family story, how Tony and Rose had come to America from Sicily with only a few dollars between them. Together they had found this land and survived on it, lived for years in a sod dugout they'd built themselves. Only tough women lasted on Texas farmland.

"I think he owes her that," Elsa added.

"Wash up. Put your things away," Mrs. Martinelli said. "We will see you in the morning. Things often look better in sunlight."

"I don't," Elsa said.

Mrs. Martinelli studied Elsa for an agonizing moment, obviously found her lacking, and then walked away, closing the door behind her.

Elsa sat down on the edge of the bed, unable suddenly to catch her breath.

There was a quiet knock on the door.

"Come in," she said.

Rafe opened the door and stood in the opening, his face dusty. He took off his cap, twisted it in his hands.

Then, slowly, he closed the door behind him. He came toward her, sat down on the bed. The springs protested at the additional weight.

She glanced sideways at him, seeing his perfect profile. *So handsome.*

"I'm sorry," she said.

"Aw, heck, Els, I didn't want to go to college anyhow." He gave her a strained smile; black hair flopped across one eye. "I didn't want to stay here, either, but . . ."

They looked at each other.

At last he took her hand, held it. "I'll try to be a good husband," he said.

Elsa wanted to tighten her hold on his hand, give a squeeze to show how much those words meant to her, but she didn't dare. She was afraid that if she really held on to him, she'd never let go. She had to be cautious from now on, treat him as she would a skittish cat; be careful to never move too fast or need too much.

She said nothing, and in time, he let go of her hand and left her in his bedroom, sitting on his bed, alone.

THE NEXT MORNING, ELSA woke late. She pushed the hair from her face. Fine strands were stuck to her cheek; she'd cried in her sleep.

Good. Better to cry at night when no one could see. She didn't want to reveal her weakness to this new family.

She went to the washstand and splashed lukewarm water on her face, then she brushed her teeth and combed her hair.

Last night, as she'd unpacked, she'd realized how wrong her clothes were for farm life. She was a town girl; what did she know about life on the land? All she'd brought were crepe dresses and silk stockings and heels. Church clothes.

She slipped into her plainest day dress, a charcoal-gray with pearl buttons and lace at the collar, then pulled up her stockings and stepped into the black heels she'd worn yesterday.

The house smelled of bacon and coffee. Her stomach grumbled, reminding her she hadn't eaten since yesterday's lunch.

The kitchen—a bright yellow-wallpapered room with gingham

curtains and white linoleum flooring—was empty. Dishes drying on the counter attested to the fact that Elsa had slept through breakfast. What time did these people waken? It was only nine.

Elsa went outside and saw the Martinelli farm in full sunlight. Hundreds of acres of shorn wheat fanned out in all directions, a sea of dry, cut, golden stalks, with the homestead part taking up a few acres in the middle of it all.

A driveway cut through the fields, a brown ribbon of dirt bordered by cottonwoods and fencing. The farm itself consisted of the house, a big wooden barn, a horse corral, a cow paddock, a hog pen, a chicken coop, several outbuildings, and a windmill. Behind the house was an orchard, a small vineyard, and a fenced vegetable garden. Mrs. Martinelli was in the garden, bent over.

Mr. Martinelli came out of the barn and approached her. "Good morning," he said. "Walk with me."

He led her along the edge of the harvested wheat field; the shorn crop struck her as broken, somehow, devastated. Much like herself. A gentle breeze rustled what remained, made a shushing sound.

"You are a town girl," Mr. Martinelli said in a thick Italian accent.

"Not anymore, I guess."

"This is a good answer." He bent down, scooped up a handful of dirt. "My land tells its story if you listen. The story of our family. We plant, we tend, we harvest. I make wine from grape cuttings that I brought here from Sicily, and the wine I make reminds me of my father. It binds us, this land, one to another, as it has for generations. Now it will bind you to us."

"I've never tended to anything."

He looked at her. "Do you want to change that?"

Elsa saw compassion in his dark eyes, as if he knew how afraid she'd been in her life, but she had to be imagining it. All he knew about her was that she was here now and she'd brought his son down with her.

"Beginnings are only that, Elsa. When Rosalba and I came here

from Sicily, we had seventeen dollars and a dream. That was our beginning. But it wasn't what gave us this good life. We have this land because we worked for it, because no matter how hard life was, we stayed
here. This land provided for us. It will provide for you, too, if you let it."

Elsa had never thought of land that way, as something that an-
chored a person, gave one a life. The idea of it, of staying here and
finding a good life and a place to belong, seduced her as nothing
ever had.

She would do her best to become a Martinelli through and through,
so she could join their story, perhaps even take it as her own and pass it
on to the child she carried. She would do anything, become anyone, to
ensure that this family loved the baby unconditionally as one of their
own. "I want that, Mr. Martinelli," she said at last. "I want to belong
here."

He smiled. "I saw that in you, Elsa."

Elsa started to thank him, but was interrupted by Mrs. Martinelli,
who called out to her husband as she walked toward them carrying a
basket full of ripe tomatoes and greenery. "Elsa," she said, coming to a
stop. "How nice to see you up."

"I . . . overslept."

Mrs. Martinelli nodded. "Follow me."

In the kitchen, Mrs. Martinelli took the vegetables from her basket
and laid them on the table: plump red tomatoes, yellow onions, green
herbs, clumps of garlic. Elsa had never seen so much garlic at one time.

"What can you cook?" she asked Elsa, tying an apron on.

"C-coffee."

Mrs. Martinelli stopped. "You can't cook? At your age?"

"I'm sorry, Mrs. Martinelli. No, but—"

"Can you clean?"

"Well . . . I'm sure I can learn to."

Mrs. Martinelli crossed her arms. "What can you do?"

"Sew. Embroider. Darn. Read."

"A lady. *Madonna mia.*" She looked around the spotless kitchen. "Fine. Then I will teach you to cook. We will start with *arancini.* And call me Rose."

༯

THE WEDDING WAS A hushed, hurried affair with no celebration before or after. Rafe slipped a plain band on Elsa's finger and said, "I do," and that was pretty much that. He looked to be in physical pain throughout the brief ceremony.

On their wedding night, they came together in the darkness and sealed their vows with their bodies, just as they had done with their words, their passion as silent as the night around them.

In the days and weeks and months that followed, he tried to be a good husband and she tried to be a good wife.

At first, in Rose's eyes at least, Elsa seemed unable to do anything right. She cut her finger when chopping tomatoes and burned her wrist taking freshly baked bread out of the oven. She couldn't tell a ripe squash from an unripe one. Stuffing zucchini flowers was nearly impossible for someone as clumsy as Elsa. She converted to Catholicism and listened to Mass in Latin, not understanding a word but finding a strange comfort in the beautiful sound of it all; she memorized prayers and learned the rosaries and kept one always in her apron pocket. She took confession and sat in a small, dark closet and told Father Michael her sins and he prayed for her and absolved her. At first none of this made much sense to her, but in time it became both familiar and routine, a part of her new life, like no meat on Fridays or the myriad saints' days that they celebrated.

Elsa learned—to her surprise and to her mother-in-law's—that she wasn't a quitter. She woke up each morning well before her husband and got into the kitchen in time to make coffee. She learned to make and eat and love food she had never heard of, made from ingredients she'd never seen—olive oil, fettuccine, *arancini,* pancetta. She learned how to disappear on a farm: work harder than anyone else and don't complain.

In time, a new and unexpected feeling of belonging began to creep in. She spent hours in the garden kneeling in the dirt, watching seeds she planted sprout and push up from the earth and turn green, and each one felt like a new beginning. A promise for the future. She learned to pick the rich purple Nero d'Avola grapes and turn them into a wine that Tony swore was as good as his father could make. She learned the peace that came with looking out at a newly tilled field and the hope those fields inspired.

Here, she sometimes thought, standing on land she cared for, *here* her child would flourish, would run and play and learn the stories told by the ground and the grapes and the wheat.

꘎

THROUGHOUT THE WINTER, SNOW fell, and they hunkered down in the farmhouse, settling into a new routine; the women spent long hours cleaning, sewing, darning, and knitting, while the men took care of the animals and readied the farm equipment for the coming spring. On snowy evenings they huddled around the fire and Elsa read stories aloud and Tony played his fiddle. Elsa learned little things about her husband—that he snored loudly and was restless in his sleep, that he often woke with a cry in the middle of the night, shaken by nightmares.

It's quiet enough on this land to make you mad, he said sometimes, and Elsa tried to understand what he meant. Mostly she just let him talk and waited for him to reach out for her, which he did, but rarely and always in the dark. She knew the sight of her growing belly frightened him. When he did talk to her, he usually smelled of wine or whiskey; he would smile then, spin stories of their imagined, someday life in Hollywood or New York. In truth, Elsa never knew quite what to say to the handsome, quicksilver man she'd married, but spoken words had never been her forte and she didn't have the courage to tell him how she felt anyway, that she'd found an unexpected strength in herself on this farm, and in her love for both her husband and his parents she'd become almost fierce. Instead, she did what she'd always done in the face of a painful rejection: she disappeared and held her tongue and waited—sometimes desperately—for her husband to see the woman she'd become.

In February, rain came to the Great Plains, nourishing the seeds planted in the soil. By March, the land was vibrant with new growth—green for miles. Tony stood by his fields in the evening, staring out at the growing wheat.

On this particularly blue, sunlit day, Elsa had opened every window in the house. A cool breeze moved through, carrying the scent of new life with it.

She stood at the stove, browning bread crumbs in the delicious, nutty-flavored, imported olive oil they purchased at the general store. The pungent aroma of garlic browning in hot oil filled the kitchen. They used these bread crumbs, mixed with cheese and fresh parsley, on everything from vegetables to pasta.

On the table behind her, a crockery bowl full of flour, ground from last year's abundant crop, waited to be turned into bread dough. The Victrola in the sitting room played a "Santa Lucia" record loudly enough that Elsa felt compelled to sing along, even though she didn't understand the words.

A pain came without warning, stabbed her deep in the abdomen, doubling her over. She tried to be still, held her stomach, waited it out.

But another pain came, minutes later, worse than the first. "Rose!"

Rose rushed into the house, her arms full of laundry to be washed.

"It's . . ." Elsa's water broke, splashed down her stockinged legs, and puddled on the floor. The sight plunged Elsa into panic. For the past months, she'd felt herself getting stronger, but now, as pain upended her, she couldn't think of anything except the doctor telling her so long ago not to get overexcited, not to put strain on her heart.

What if he'd been right? She looked up in terror. "I'm not ready, Rose."

Rose put down the laundry. "No one is ever ready."

Elsa couldn't catch her breath. Another pain hit, wrenched through her stomach.

"Look at me," Rose said. She took Elsa's face in her hands, although she had to get on her tiptoes to do so. "This is normal." She took Elsa by the hand and led her to the bedroom, where she stripped the bed and threw the quilts and sheets on the floor.

She undressed Elsa, who should have been ashamed to be seen that way, with her swollen belly and shapeless limbs, but the pain was so great she didn't care.

Such *teeth* in this pain. Gnawing at her, then spitting her out to breathe for a moment and then biting again.

"Go ahead and scream," Rose said, helping Elsa to the bed.

Elsa lost her hold on time, on everything but the pain. She screamed out when she needed to and panted like a dog in between.

Rose positioned Elsa as if she were a doll, spread her bare legs wide open. "I see the head, Elsa. You can push now."

Elsa pushed and strained and screamed. "My . . . heart's going to stop," she said, panting. She should have told them she was sick, that she wasn't supposed to have children, that she could die. "If it does—"

"It's bad luck to speak of such things, Elsa. Push."

Elsa gave one last desperate push, felt a great whooshing relief, and sagged back into the pillows, exhausted.

A baby's cry filled the room.

"A beautiful little girl with a good set of lungs." Rose cut and tied off the umbilical cord, then wrapped the baby up in one of the many blankets they'd knitted over the long winter and handed the bundle to Elsa.

Elsa took her daughter in her arms and stared down at her in awe. Love filled her to the brim and spilled over in tears. She'd never felt anything like it before, a heady, exhilarating combination of joy and fear. "Hello, baby girl."

The baby quieted, blinked up at her.

Rose reached into the velvet pouch she wore as a necklace around her throat. Inside the pouch was an American penny. Rose kissed the penny and held it out for Elsa to see. The coin had two wheat shafts imprinted on the back. "Tony found this on the street outside my parents' home on the day we were to leave on the boat for America. Can you imagine such good fortune? The wheat revealed our destiny. A *sign,* we said to each other, and it has been true. This coin will watch over another generation now," Rose said, looking at Elsa. "My beautiful granddaughter."

"I want to call her Loreda," Elsa said. "For my grandfather, who was born in Laredo."

Rose sounded out the unfamiliar name. "Lor-ay-da. Beautiful. Most American, I think," she said, placing the penny in Elsa's hand. "Believe me, Elsa, this little girl will love you as no one ever has . . . and make you crazy and try your soul. Often all at the same time."

In Rose's dark, tear-brightened eyes, Elsa saw a perfect reflection of her own emotions and a soul-deep understanding of this bond— motherhood—shared by women for millennia.

She also saw more affection than she'd ever seen in her own mother's eyes. "Welcome to the family," Rose said in an uneven voice, and Elsa knew she was talking to her as well as to Loreda.

1934

I see one-third of a nation ill-housed, ill-clad, ill-nourished. . . . The test of our progress is not whether we add more to the abundance of those who have much; it is whether we provide enough for those who have too little.

—FRANKLIN D. ROOSEVELT

SIX

It was so hot that every now and then a bird fell from the sky, landing with a little thump on the hard-packed dirt. The chickens sat in dusty heaps on the ground, their heads lolled forward, and the last two cows stood together, too hot and tired to move. A listless breeze moved through the farm, plucking at the empty clothesline.

The driveway that led to the farmhouse was still hemmed in on either side by makeshift posts and barbed wire, but in several places the posts had fallen down. The trees on either side were skeletal, barely alive. This farm had been reconfigured by wind and drought, sculpted into a land of tumbleweeds and starving mesquite.

Years of drought, combined with the economic ravages of the Great Depression, had brought the Great Plains to its knees.

They'd suffered through these dry years in the Texas Panhandle, but with the whole country devastated by the Crash of '29 and twelve million people out of work, the big-city newspapers didn't bother covering the drought. The government offered no assistance, not that the farmers wanted it anyway. They were too proud to live on the dole. All they wanted was for rain to soften the soil and sprout the seeds so the wheat and corn would once again lift their golden arms toward the sky.

The rains had begun to slow in '31, and in the last three years there had been almost none at all. This year, so far, they had had less than five inches. Not enough to fill a pitcher for tea, let alone water thousands of acres of wheat.

Now, on another record-breaking hot day in late August, Elsa sat in the driver's seat of the old wagon, her hands sweating and itching inside her suede gloves as she handled the reins. There was no money for gas anymore, so the truck had become a relic stored in the barn, like the tractor and the plow.

A straw hat, once white and now brown with dust, was pulled low on her sunburned forehead, and she'd tied a blue bandanna around her throat. Grit in her eyes made her squint as she made a clicking sound with her teeth and tongue and maneuvered the wagon off the farm and onto the main road. Milo's plodding, even clip-clop steps rang out on the hard-packed dirt. Birds sat on telephone wires strung between the poles.

It was not quite three o'clock in the afternoon when she pulled into Lonesome Tree. The town was quiet, hunkered down in the heat. There were no townspeople out shopping, no women gathered outside the storefronts. Those days were as gone as green lawns.

The hat shop was boarded up, as was the apothecary, the soda foun-tain, and the diner. The Rialto Movie Theater was hanging on by a thread; it showed one matinee a week, but few could afford to attend. Raggedly dressed people stood in line for food at the Presbyterian church, metal spoons and cups in hand. The children, freckled and sun-burned and as whittled down as their parents, were quiet.

The lone tree on Main Street, a plains cottonwood that was the town's namesake, was dying. Each time Elsa came to town it looked a little worse.

The wagon rolled forward, wheels clacking, passing the boarded-up county welfare building (there was lots of need, but no funds), and the blank-eyed jail that was busier than ever with drifters and hobos and no-account train tramps. The doctor's office was still open, but the bakery was out of business. Most of the buildings were single story and made of wood. In the wet years, they'd been repainted yearly. Now they were untended and turning gray.

Elsa said, "Whoa, Milo," and pulled up on the reins. The horse and wagon clanked to a stop. The gelding shook his head, snorted tiredly. He hated being out in this heat, too.

Elsa stared at the Silo Saloon. The squat, square building, half as wide and twice as long as any other Main Street building, had two windows that faced the street. One had been broken last year in a fight between two drunks and had never been fixed. Rows of dirty tape closed the square. The saloon had been built in the 1880s for the cowboys of the three-million-acre XIT Ranch that ran along the Texas–New Mexico border. The ranch was long gone and most of the cowboys had moved on, but the Silo remained.

In the months since Prohibition had been repealed, places like the Silo had reopened for business, but the Depression had left fewer and fewer men with spare pennies for beer.

Elsa tied the gelding to a hitching post and smoothed the front of her damp cotton dress. She'd made the dress herself, from old flour sacks. Everyone made clothes from grain and flour sacks these days. The manufacturers of the sacks had even begun printing pretty designs on the material. It was a small thing, those floral patterns, but anything that made a woman feel pretty in these hard times was worth its weight in gold. Elsa made sure that the dress, once fitted to her figure and now bagging at her narrowing hips and bust, was buttoned up to her throat. It was a sad fact that she was thirty-eight years old, a grown woman with two children, and she still hated to enter a place like this. Although she hadn't seen her parents for years, it turned out that a parent's disapproval was a powerful, lingering voice that shaped and defined one's self-image.

Elsa steeled herself and opened the door. Inside, the long, narrow saloon was as drab and untended as the town itself. The smoky air smelled of spilled hooch and men's sweat. A mahogany bar had been worn to a satin finish by fifty years of men drinking at it. Faded, shredded barstools were positioned along it; most were empty now in the middle of a hot summer day.

Rafe sat slumped on one of them, elbows on the bar, an empty shot glass in front of him, his head hung forward. Black hair curtained his face from view. He wore faded, patched dungarees and a shirt made of plain beige flour-sack fabric. A brown, hand-rolled cigarette burned between two dirty fingers.

In the back of the saloon, an old man chuckled. "Watch out, Rafe. The sheriff's in town." His voice was slurred, his mouth almost lost in the tufts of his gray beard.

The barkeep looked up, a dirty rag slung over his shoulder. "Howdy, Elsa," he said. "You come to pay his tab?"

Perfect. There was no money to buy the children new shoes or to replace her last pair of stockings, and now her husband was drinking on credit.

She felt awkward and unattractive in her baggy flour-sack dress and thick cotton hose, with the fraying leather of her shoes making her big feet look even bigger.

"Rafe?" she said quietly, coming up behind him, laying a bare hand on his shoulder, hoping to gentle him with touch, as she would a skittish colt.

"I meant to have one drink." He let out a ragged sigh.

Elsa couldn't count the number of times her husband's sentences began with *I meant*. In the first years of their marriage, he'd tried. She'd *seen* him trying to love her, to be happy, but the drought had drained her husband, just as it had dried out the land. In the past four years, he'd stopped spinning dreams for the future. Three years ago, they'd buried a son, but even that loss hadn't broken him the way poverty and the drought had. "Your father was counting on you to help him plant fall potatoes this afternoon."

"Yeah."

"The kids need potatoes," Elsa said.

He cocked his head, just enough so he could see her through the dust black of his hair. "You think I don't know that?"

I think you've been sitting here drinking up what little money we have, so how can I know what you know? Loreda needs new shoes, she thought but didn't dare say out loud.

"I'm a bad father, Elsa, and a worse husband. Why do you stay with me?"

Because I love you.

The look in his dark eyes broke her heart yet again. She *did* love her husband as deeply as she loved her children, Loreda and Anthony, and as deeply as she'd come to love the Martinellis and the land. Elsa had discovered within herself a nearly bottomless capacity for love. And, God help her, it was her doomed, unshakable love for Rafe, as much as anything, that repeatedly rendered her mute, made her withdraw so that she wouldn't seem pathetic. Sometimes, especially on the nights he didn't come to their bed at all, she felt she deserved better and that maybe if she stood up and demanded more, she would receive it. Then she would remember the things her parents had said about her, the unattractiveness that had never changed, and she would remain silent.

"Come on, Elsa, take me home. I can't wait to spend the rest of the day rooting through the dirt to plant potatoes that will die without rain."

She steadied him as he stumbled out of the saloon, and helped him up into the wagon. She took the reins and slapped them across the bay gelding's butt. Milo snorted tiredly and began the long, plodding journey through town, past the abandoned grange hall where the Rotary and Kiwanis Clubs used to meet.

Rafe leaned against Elsa, placing a gentle, long-fingered hand on her thigh. "I'm sorry, Els," he said in his soft-spoken, what-have-I-done voice.

"It's okay," she said, meaning it from the bottom of her heart. As long as he was beside her, it was okay. She would always forgive him.

As little as he gave her, as frayed as his affection for her sometimes was, she lived in fear of losing it. Losing him. Just as she feared losing her moody, adolescent daughter's love.

Lately, that fear had grown almost too big to handle.

Loreda had turned twelve and immediately become angry. Gone overnight were the days of mother-daughter gardening and reading hour at night, when they'd discussed Heathcliff's nature and Jane Eyre's strength. Loreda had always been a daddy's girl, but as a child she'd had room in her heart for both of her parents. For everyone, really. Loreda had been the happiest of children, always laughing and clapping and demanding attention. For years, she had only been able to sleep if Elsa was in bed with her, stroking her hair.

Gone, all of it.

Elsa grieved daily for the loss of that closeness with her firstborn. At first she'd tried to scale the walls of her daughter's adolescent, irrational anger; she'd volleyed back with words of love, but Loreda's continuing, thriving impatience with Elsa had done worse than grind her down. It had resurrected all the insecurities of childhood. Somewhere along the way, Elsa had begun to withdraw from Loreda, first hoping that her daughter would grow out of her mood swings, and then—worse—believing that Loreda had finally seen the lack in Elsa that her own family had seen.

Elsa felt a deeply rooted shame in her daughter's rejection. In her hurt, she did what she'd always done: she disappeared. But all the while, she waited, prayed, that both her husband and her daughter would someday see how much she loved them and they would love her in return. Until then, she dared not push too hard or demand too much. The price could be too high.

There was something she hadn't known when she went into marriage and became a mother that she knew now: it was only possible to live without love when you'd never known it.

֍

ON THIS FIRST DAY of school, the town's only remaining teacher, Nicole Buslik, stood at the chalkboard, chalk in hand. Her auburn hair had worked free from its constraints and become a fuzzy nimbus around her heat-flushed face. Sweat turned the lace at her throat a shade darker and Loreda was pretty sure Mrs. Buslik was afraid to lift her arms and show sweat stains.

Twelve-year-old Loreda sat at her desk, slumped forward, not paying attention to today's lesson. It was just more blather about what had gone wrong. The Great Depression, the drought, blah, blah, blah.

It had been "hard times" for as long as Loreda could remember. Oh, in the early years, the time before memory, she knew rains had fallen, season after season, nourishing the land. Pretty much all Loreda remembered of the green years was the sight of her grandfather's wheat, golden stalks dancing beneath an enormous blue sky. The sound of rustling. The image of tractors rolling over the ground twenty-four hours a day, plowing the earth, churning up more and more fields. A horde of mechanical insects chewing up the ground.

When had the bad years begun, exactly? It was hard to pinpoint. There were so many choices. The stock market crash of 1929, some would say, but not the folks around here. Loreda had been seven years old then, and she remembered some of that time. Folks lined up outside the savings and loan. Grandpa complaining about bad wheat prices. Grandma lighting candles and keeping them lit, whispering prayers with her rosary.

That had been bad, the crash, but most of the hardship landed in cities Loreda had never been to. Nineteen twenty-nine had been a good rain year, which meant a good crop year, which meant times had been good enough for the Martinellis.

Grandpa kept riding his tractor, kept planting wheat, even as the prices plummeted because of the Depression. He'd even bought a brand-new Ford Model AA stake-bed farm truck. Daddy had smiled often then and told her stories of faraway lands while Mom did chores.

The last good crop had been 1930, the year Loreda turned eight. She remembered her birthday. A beautiful spring day. Presents. Grandma's tiramisu with candles poking up from the cocoa-powder topping. Her best friend, Stella, had been allowed to spend the night for the first time. Daddy had taught them how to dance the Charleston while Grandpa accompanied them on the fiddle.

And then the rains slowed and never started up again. *Drought.*

These days, green fields were a distant memory, a mirage of her youth. The adults looked as parched as the ground. Grandpa spent hours standing in his dead wheat fields, scooping the dry earth into his callused hands, watching it fall away through his fingers. He grieved for his dying grapes and told anyone who would listen that he'd brought the first vines from Italy, stuffed in his pockets. Grandma had built altars everywhere, doubled the number of crucifixes on the walls, and made them all pray for rain each Sunday. Sometimes the whole town came together in the schoolhouse to pray for rain. All different religions begging God for moisture: the Presbyterians, the Baptists, the Irish and the Italian Catholics, each in their own rows. The Mexicans had their own church built hundreds of years ago.

Everyone talked about the drought constantly and missed the good old days. Except her mother.

Loreda sighed heavily.

Had there ever been any fun in her mother? If so, it was another of Loreda's lost memories. Sometimes, when she lay in bed, drifting toward sleep, she thought she remembered the sound of her mother's laughter, the feel of her touch, even a whispered, *Be brave,* just before a good-night kiss.

More and more, though, those memories felt manufactured, false. She couldn't remember the last time her mother laughed about anything.

All Mom did was work.

Work, work, work. As if that would save them.

Loreda couldn't remember when exactly she'd begun to be angered by her mother's . . . disappearance. There was no other word for it. Her mother rose well before the sun and worked. Day after day. Hour after hour. She harped constantly about saving food and not dirtying clothes and not wasting water.

Loreda couldn't imagine how her handsome, charming, funny father had ever fallen in love with Mom. Loreda had once told her father that Mom seemed afraid of laughter. He had said, "Now, Lolo," in that way of his, with his head cocked and a smile that meant he wouldn't talk of it. He never complained about his wife, but Loreda knew how he felt, so she complained for him. It brought them closer, proved how alike they were, she and Daddy.

As alike as peas in a pod. Everyone said so.

Like Daddy, Loreda saw how limited life was on a wheat farm in the Texas Panhandle, and she had no intention of becoming like her mother. She was not going to sit on this dying wheat farm for her whole life, withering and wrinkling beneath a sun so hot it melted rubber. She was not going to waste her every prayer on rain. Not a chance.

She was going to travel the world and write about her adventures. Someday she would be as famous as Nellie Bly.

Someday.

She watched a brown field mouse creep along the baseboard under the window. It stopped at the teacher's desk, sipped at a blot of fallen ink. When it looked up, blue painted its tiny nose.

Loreda elbowed Stella Devereaux, who sat at the desk next to Loreda.

Stella looked up, bleary-eyed from the heat.

Loreda indicated the mouse.

Stella almost smiled.

A bell rang and the mouse ran into the corner and disappeared into its hole.

Loreda got to her feet. Her flour-sack dress felt sticky with sweat. She grabbed her book bag and fell into step with Stella. Usually they'd be talking nonstop on the way out, about boys or books or places they wanted to see or movies coming to the Rialto Theater, but today it was too hot to make the effort.

Loreda's little brother, Anthony, was the first one to the door, as usual. At seven, Ant ran like an unbroken colt, all bent elbows and loose joints. More spirited than any of the other children, Ant always had a spring in his step. He was dressed in faded, patched dungarees that were inches too short, the ragged hems revealing ankles as skinny as broom handles and shoes with holes in the toes. His freckled, angular face was tanned to the color of saddle leather, with big red patches of sunburn on his cheeks. A cap hid the fact that his black hair was dirty. Outside, he saw his parents in the wagon and waved broadly and started to run. He had never known anything but drought, not really, and so he played and laughed like an ordinary boy. Stella's younger sister, Sophia, tried gamely to keep up with him.

"How does your mom always sit up so tall in this heat?" Stella said. She was the only kid in class wearing new shoes and a dress made from real gingham. Times weren't so bad for the Devereaux family, but Loreda's grandpa said all the banks were in trouble.

"It doesn't matter how hot it is, she never complains."

"My mom doesn't say much, either, but you should hear my sister. Ever since she got married, she cries like a stuck pig about all the work it takes to be a wife."

"I ain't getting married," Loreda said. "My dad and me are going to go to Hollywood together someday."

"Your mom won't mind?"

Loreda shrugged. Who knew what bothered her mom? And who cared?

Stella and Sophia turned left and headed toward their home on the other side of town.

Ant ran up to the wagon.

"Hey, Mommy," Ant said, his grin showing off a new lost tooth. "Daddy."

"Howdy, son," Daddy said. "Climb into the back."

"D'ya wanna see what I drew in class today? Missus Buslik says—"

"Get in the wagon, Anthony," Daddy said. "I'll see your artwork at home, when the sun goes down and we are out of this damnable heat."

Ant's face fell in disappointment.

Loreda hated how sad and beaten her dad looked. The drought was sucking him dry. He and Loreda were bright stars who needed to shine. He said so all the time. "You wanna go to the movies tomorrow, Daddy?" she said, staring up at him adoringly. "*Little Miss Marker* is playing again."

"There's no money for that, Loreda," Mom said. "Climb in the back with your brother."

"How about—"

"Get in the wagon, Loreda," Mom said.

Loreda tossed her book bag into the back of the wagon and climbed in. She and Ant sat close together on the dusty old quilt that they kept in the back.

Mom snapped the reins and they were off.

Swaying with the motion of the wagon, Loreda stared out at the dry land. The air smelled of dust and heat. They passed the rotting carcass of a steer, its ribs sticking up, its horns reaching out from the sand. Flies buzzed around it. A crow landed on the carcass, cawed proprietarily, and began plucking at the bones. There was an abandoned Model T beside it, doors open, tires buried up to the axle in dry soil.

To their left stood a small farmhouse, unshaded by trees, surrounded by brown earth. A pair of signs—AUCTION and FORECLOSURE—were hammered to the front door.

In the yard, a jalopy was stuffed to the gills with people and junk. Tied to the back end were a stack of buckets, a cast-iron frying pan, and a wooden crate full of mason jars and sacks of wheat. The running engine puffed black smoke into the air and rattled the metal frame. Pots and pans had been tied wherever there was something to tie them to. Two children stood on the rusty running boards and a woman with a sad face and lanky hair sat in the passenger seat holding a baby.

The farmer—Will Bunting—stood by the driver's-side door, dressed in coveralls and a shirt with only one sleeve. A banged-up cowboy hat was pulled low over his dusty face.

"Whoa," Mom said, drawing the gelding to a halt, tilting back her sun hat.

"Heyya, Rafe," Will said, spitting tobacco into the dirt at his feet. "Elsa." He pulled away from the overburdened car, walked slowly toward the wagon. When he got there, he stopped, said nothing, shoved his hands in his pockets.

"Where yah goin'?" Daddy asked.

"We're licked," Will said. "You know my boy, Kallson, died this summer?" He glanced back at his wife. "And now there's the new one. Can't take it no more. We're leaving."

Loreda straightened. They were *leaving*?

Mom frowned. "But your land—"

"Bank's land now. Couldn't make the payments."

"Where will you go?" Daddy asked.

Will pulled a creased flyer out of his back pocket. "California. Land of milk and honey, they say. Don't need honey. Just work."

"How do you know it's true?" Daddy said, taking the flyer from him. *Jobs for everyone! Land of opportunity! Go West to California!*

"I don't."

"You can't just leave," Mom said.

"Too late for us. A family can only bury so much. Tell your folks I said goodbye."

Will turned and walked back to his dusty car and climbed into the driver's seat. The metal door clanged shut.

Mom clicked her tongue and snapped the reins and Milo began plodding forward again. Loreda watched the jalopy drive past them in a cloud of dust, unable suddenly to think about anything else. *Leaving.* They could go to one of the places she and Daddy talked about: San Francisco or Hollywood or New York.

"Glenn and Mary Lynn Mounger left last week," Daddy said. "They headed for California, just up and left in that old Packard of theirs."

It was a long moment before Mom said, "You remember the news-reel we saw? Breadlines in Chicago. People living in shacks and card-board boxes in Central Park. At least here we've got eggs and milk."

Daddy sighed. Loreda felt the pain of that sound, the hurt that came with it. Mom *would* say no. "Yeah, I reckon." He dropped the flyer to the floor of the wagon. "My folks would never leave anyhow."

"Never," Mom agreed.

❧

THAT NIGHT, LOREDA SAT out on the porch swing after supper.

Leave.

The sun set slowly on the farm around her, night swallowing the flat, brown, dry land. One of their cows lowed plaintively for water. Soon, in the darkness, her grandfather would start watering the livestock, car-rying buckets of water from the well one by one, while Grandma and Mom watered the garden.

The creaking whine of the porch swing chain seemed loud amid the quiet. She heard the jangling of the party-line telephone come from inside the house. These days, a phone call meant nothing fun; all anyone talked about was the drought.

Except her father. He wasn't anything like the farmers or shopkeep-ers. Every other man seemed to live or die by land and weather and crops. Like her grandfather.

When Loreda had been young and the rain reliable, when the wheat grew tall and golden, Grandpa Tony smiled all the time and drank rye on the weekends and played his fiddle at town parties. He used to take her by the hand and walk with her through the whispering wheat and tell her that if she listened, there were stories coming from the stalks themselves. He would get a clump of dirt in his big, callused hand and hold it out to her as if it were a diamond and say, "This will all be yours one day, and it will pass to your children, and then to your children's children." *The land:* he said it the way Father Michael said *God*.

And Grandma and Mom? They were like all the farm wives in Lonesome Tree. They worked their fingers to the bone, rarely laughing and hardly talking. When they did talk, it was never about anything interesting.

Daddy was the only one who talked about ideas or choices or dreams. He talked about travel and adventures and all the lives a person could live. He'd repeatedly told Loreda that there was a big beautiful world beyond this farm.

She heard the door open behind her. The aroma of stewed tomatoes and fried pancetta and cooked garlic wafted her way.

Daddy came out onto the porch, closed the door quietly behind him. Lighting up a cigarette, he sat down on the swing beside her. She smelled the sweetness of wine on his breath. They were supposed to be conserving everything, but Daddy refused to give up on his wine or his hooch. He said drinking was the only thing keeping him sane. He loved to drop a slippery, sweet slice of preserved peach into his after-supper wine.

Loreda leaned into him. He put an arm around her and pulled her close as they glided forward and back. "You're quiet, Loreda. That ain't like my girl."

The farm transitioned around them into a dark world full of sounds: the windmill thumping, bringing up their precious water, chickens scratching, hogs rooting in the dirt.

"This drought," Loreda said, pronouncing the dreaded word like everyone did around here. *Drouth.* She fell silent, choosing her words with care. "It's killing the land."

"Yep." He finished the cigarette, stubbed it out into the pot full of dead flowers beside him.

Loreda pulled the flyer out of her pocket, unfolded it with care.

California. Land of milk and honey.

"Mrs. Buslik says there's jobs in California. Money lying in the streets. Stella said her uncle sent a postcard saying there's jobs in Oregon."

"I doubt there's money lying in the streets, Loreda. This Depression is worse in the cities. Last I read, over thirteen million folks were out of jobs. You've seen the tramps that ride the trains. There's a Hooverville in Oklahoma City that'd make you cry. Families living in apple carts. Come winter, they'll be dying of cold on park benches."

"They aren't dying of cold in California. You could get a job. Maybe work on the railroad."

Daddy sighed, and in that exhalation of his breath, she knew what he was thinking. That was how in tune she was with him. "My parents— and your mom—will never leave this land."

"But—"

"It'll rain," Daddy said, but there was something sorrowful about the way he said it, almost as if he didn't want rain to save them.

"Do you have to be a farmer?"

He turned. She saw the frown that bunched his thick black brows. "I was born one."

"You always tell me this is America. A person can be anything."

"Yeah, well. I made a bad choice a few years back, and . . . well . . . sometimes your life is chosen for you." After that, he was quiet for a long time.

"What bad choice?"

He didn't look at her. His body was sitting beside her, but his mind was somewhere else.

"I don't want to dry up here and die," Loreda said.

At last he said, "It'll rain."

SEVEN

A nother scorcher of a day, and not even ten in the morning. So far, September had offered no respite from the heat.

Elsa knelt on the linoleum kitchen floor, scrubbing hard. She had already been up for hours. It was best to do chores in the relative cool of dawn and dusk.

A scuffling sound caught her attention. She saw a tarantula, body as big as an apple, scurrying out from its hiding place in the corner. She got to her feet and used the mop to chase it outside. It was crueler to send the spider back out into the heat than to crush it with her shoe. Besides, she barely had the energy to stomp on the spider, let alone the will strong enough to care. She had trouble lately doing anything that didn't result in food or water.

The key to life in this dry heat was conservation of everything: water, food, emotion. That last one was the biggest challenge.

She knew how unhappy Rafe and Loreda were. The two of them, as alike as grains of sand, had more trouble these days than the rest of them. Not that anyone on the farm was happy. How could they be? But Tony and Rose and Elsa were the kind of people who expected life to be hard and had become tougher to survive. Her in-laws had worked for years—him on the railroad, her in a shirtwaist factory—to earn the money to buy their land. Their first dwelling here had been a dugout made of sod bricks that they'd built themselves. They might have come off the boat as Anthony and Rosalba, but hard work and the land had turned them into Tony and Rose. Americans. They would die of thirst and hunger before they'd give that up. And although Elsa hadn't been born a farmer, she'd become one.

In the past thirteen years, she'd learned to love this land and this farm more than she would have imagined possible. In the good years, spring had been a time of joy for her, watching her garden grow, and autumn had been a time of pride; she'd loved seeing her labor on the shelves of the root cellar: jars filled with vegetables and fruits—red tomatoes, glistening peaches, and cinnamon-scented apples. Rolls of spiced pancetta made from pork belly and cured hams hanging from hooks overhead. Boxes overflowing with potatoes and onions and garlic from the garden.

The Martinellis had welcomed Elsa in and she repaid that unexpected kindness with a deep devotion, a fierce love for them and their ways, but even as Elsa had merged deeper into the family, Rafe had veered away. He was unhappy, had been for years, and now Loreda was following her father's path. Of course she was. It was impossible not to be captivated by Rafe's charm and caught up in his impossible dreams. His smile could light up the room. He'd fed his impressionable, mercurial daughter a steady diet of dreams when she was young; now he passed along his dis-satisfaction. Elsa knew he said things to Loreda, complained of things that he wouldn't say to his parents or his wife. Loreda had the greatest part of Rafe's heart, and had from her first breath.

Elsa went back to scrubbing the kitchen floor, and then went on to scrub the floors in all eight rooms, washing dust off the woodwork and window-sills. When she finished that chore, she gathered up the rugs and took them outside and hung them, beating the dirt out of them with a stick.

The wind picked up, ruffled her dress. She paused in beating the rug, sweat running down her face, between her breasts, and tented a hand over her eyes. Past the outhouse, a murky, urine-yellow haze burnished the sky.

Elsa tilted her sun hat back, stared out at the sickly yellow horizon.

Dust storm. The newest scourge of the Great Plains.

The sky changed color, turned red-brown.

Wind picked up, barreled across the farm from the south.

A Russian thistle hit her in the face, tore the skin from her cheek. A tumbleweed spiraled past. A board flew off the chicken coop and cracked into the side of the house.

Rafe and Tony came running out of the barn.

Elsa pulled her bandanna up over her mouth and nose.

The cows mooed angrily and pushed into each other, pointing their bony butts into the dust storm. Static electricity made their tails stand out. A flotilla of birds flew past them, flapping hard, cawing and squawking, outrunning the dust.

Rafe's Stetson flew off his head and tumbled toward the barbed-wire fence and was caught on a spike. "Get inside," he yelled. "I'll take care of the animals."

"The kids!"

"Mrs. Buslik knows what to do. Go inside."

Her kids. *Out in this.*

The wind was howling now, slamming into them, shoving them sideways. Elsa bent into it and fought her way to the house against the wind-driven dust.

She inched up the uneven stairs and across the gritty porch and grabbed the metal doorknob. A current of static electricity knocked her off her feet. She lay there a second, dazed, coughing, trying to breathe.

The door opened.

Rose yanked her to her feet, pulled her into the rattling, howling house.

Elsa and Rose ran from window to window, securing the newspaper and rag coverings over the glass and sills. Dust rained down from the ceilings, wafted from infinitesimal cracks in the window frames and walls. The candles on the makeshift altar blew out. Centipedes crawled out from the walls, hundreds of them, and slithered across the floor, looking for somewhere to hide.

A blast of wind hit the house, so hard it seemed the roof would be torn off.

And the *noise*.

It was like a locomotive bearing down on them, engines grinding. The house shuddered as if breathing too hard; a banshee wind howled, mad as hell.

The door opened and her husband and Tony staggered in. Tony slammed the door shut behind them and threw the bolt. A crucifix fell to the floor.

Elsa leaned back against the shuddering wall.

Elsa could hear her mother-in-law's breathy, scratchy voice as she prayed.

Elsa reached sideways, took her hand.

Rafe moved in beside Elsa. She could tell that they were both thinking the same thing: What if the children had been out on the playground? This storm had come up *fast*. With everything dying these days, there were no strong roots to anchor the soil to the earth. A wind like this could blow whole farms away. At least that was how it felt.

"They'll be okay," he said, hacking through the dust.

"How do you know?" she yelled above the sound of the storm.

The despair in her husband's eyes was all the answer he had.

❧

LOREDA SAT ON THE floor of the quaking schoolhouse, her brother tucked in close beside her, both wearing bandannas drawn over their mouths and noses bandit-style. Ant was trying to be brave, but he flinched every time a particularly fierce gust of wind hit the building and rattled the glass.

Dust rained down from the ceiling. Loreda felt it collecting in her hair, on her shoulders. Wind battered the wooden walls, wailed in a high, almost human scream. Panicked birds kept hitting the glass.

When the storm first struck, Mrs. Buslik had called them all in and made them sit together in the corner farthest from the windows. She'd tried reading a story, but no one could concentrate, and in time no one could hear her voice, so she gave up and closed the book.

There had been at least ten of these dust storms in the past year. One day this spring, the wind and dirt had blown for twelve straight hours, so long that they'd had to cook and eat and do chores in the raging dust.

Grandma and Mom said they should pray.

Pray.

As if lighting candles and kneeling could stop all of this. Clearly, if God was watching the people of the Great Plains, He wanted them to either leave or die.

When the storm finally ended and silence swept into the schoolhouse, the children sat there, traumatized and big-eyed and covered in dirt.

Mrs. Buslik slowly unfolded from her seat on the floor. As she stood, dirt rained down from her lap. The sand outline of her body on the floor remained behind, a dirt design. She went to the door, opened it to reveal a beautiful blue sky.

Loreda saw Mrs. Buslik sigh with relief. The exhalation made her cough. "Okay, kids," she said in a scratchy voice. "It's over."

Ant looked at Loreda. His freckled face was brown with dirt above the bandanna that covered his mouth and nose. By rubbing his eyes, he'd given himself a raccoon look. Tears hung stubbornly onto his lashes, looking like beads of mud.

She pulled down her bandanna. "Come on, Ant," she said. Her voice was thin and scratchy.

Loreda and Stella and Ant retrieved their book bags and empty lunch pails and left the schoolhouse. Sophia shuffled along behind them, her head hung.

Loreda held Ant's hand firmly in hers as she stepped from the building.

Town was catastrophe-quiet. The carbide arc streetlamps—such a source of community pride four years ago when they had been installed—were lit because people and cars and animals needed light to find safety in the storm.

They walked up Main Street. Tumbleweeds were caught in the boardwalk. Windows were boarded up, from both the Depression and the dust storms.

When they neared the train depot, Stella said, "It's gettin' bad, Lolo," quietly, as if she were afraid her voice would carry all the way to her parents' house.

Loreda had no answer to that. In the Martinelli house it had been bad for years. She watched Stella walk away, shoulders hunched as if to protect her from whatever hardship was waiting; she climbed over a new dune of sand that had been swept into the street and turned the corner on her way home. Sophia followed her sister.

Loreda and Ant kept walking. It felt as if they were the only two people left in the world.

They passed several FOR SALE signs on fence posts, and then there was nothing. No houses, no fences, no animals, no windmills. Just endless brown-gold dirt molded into hills and dunes. Sand piled up at the base of the telephone poles. One pole was down.

Loreda was the first to hear the slow, dull clip-clop of hooves.

"Mommy!" Ant yelled.

Loreda looked up.

Mom drove the wagon toward them; she sat strained forward, as if she wanted Milo to move faster, faster, but the poor old gelding was as exhausted and thirsty as the rest of them.

Ant pulled free and started to run.

Mom brought the horse to a halt and jumped down from the wagon. She ran toward them, her face brown with dirt, her dress shredded into fraying strips from the waist down, apron flapping, her pale blond hair brown with dust.

Mom swept Ant into a hug, pulled him off his feet, twirled him around, as if she'd thought she'd never see him again, and covered his dirty face with kisses.

Loreda remembered those kisses; Mom had smelled of lavender soap and talcum powder in the good years.

Not anymore. Loreda couldn't remember the last time she'd let Mom kiss her. Loreda didn't want the kind of love that trapped. She wanted to be told she could fly high, be anything and go anywhere—she wanted the things her father wanted. Someday she would smoke cigarettes and go to jazz clubs and get a job. Be *modern*.

Her mother's idea of a woman's place was too sad for Loreda to bear.

Mom helped Ant up into the wagon's front seat, then came to stand in front of Loreda. "You okay?" Mom asked, tucking the hair behind Loreda's ear, her touch lingering there.

"Yeah. Great," Loreda said, hearing the sharpness in her voice. She knew it was wrong to be angry with her mother now—the weather wasn't her fault—but Loreda couldn't help herself. She was mad at the world, and somehow that meant she was mad at her mom most of all.

"Ant looks like he's been crying."

"He was scared."

"I'm glad his big sister was with him."

How could Mom smile at a time like this? It was irritating.

"You know your teeth are brown with dirt?" Loreda said.

Her mother flinched and instantly stopped smiling.

Loreda had hurt Mom's feelings. Again.

Loreda suddenly felt like crying. Before her mom could see the emotion, Loreda headed for the back of the wagon.

"You can sit up here with us," Mom said.

"Seeing where we're going ain't any better than seeing where we've been. The view never changes."

"Isn't," Mom corrected automatically.

"Oh, right," Loreda said. "Education is everything."

As they headed home, Loreda stared out at the flat, flat land.

All the trees that lined their driveway were dying. The hot, dry years had turned them a sick gray-brown; their leaves had turned into crunchy, blackened confetti and been swept away by the wind. Only three of them were even still standing. The dusty soil lay in heaps and dunes at the base of every fence post. Nothing grew or thrived in the fields. There was not a blade of green grass anywhere. Russian thistles—tumbleweed—and yucca were the only living plants to be seen. The rotting body of something—a jackrabbit, maybe—lay in a heap of sand; crows picked at it.

Mom pulled the wagon to a stop in the yard. Milo pawed at the hard earth beneath his hooves. "Loreda, you put Milo away. I'll get the preserved lemons and make lemonade," Mom said.

"Fine," Loreda said glumly. She climbed out of the wagon and took hold of the reins and led the horse and wagon toward the barn.

Poor Milo moved so slowly Loreda couldn't help feeling sorry for this bay gelding that had once been her best friend in the whole world. "It's okay, boy. We all feel like that."

She petted his velvet-soft muzzle, remembering the day her daddy had taught her to ride. It had been a bluebird day, with wheat a sea of gold all around. She'd been scared. So scared, to climb all the way up onto that grown-up-sized saddle.

Daddy helped her up, whispered, "Don't worry," and moved back beside Mom, who looked as nervous as Loreda felt.

Loreda hadn't fallen off once. Daddy told her she was a natural and told the family at supper that Loreda was the best little horsewoman he'd ever seen.

Loreda had soaked up his praise, grown to fit it. And after that, for years, she and Milo had been inseparable. She did her homework in his stall whenever she could, both of them munching on carrots she pulled from the garden.

"I miss you, boy," Loreda said, stroking the side of his head.

The gelding snorted, blew wet, sandy mucus on Loreda's bare arm. "Ick."

Loreda opened the double doors of the barn that was her grandfather's pride and joy. The large barn had a wide center aisle where the tractor and truck were parked, and two stalls on either side, both of which opened onto corrals. Two for the horses and two for the cows. A loft that had once been stacked with fragrant green bales of hay was emptying fast. Everyone knew it was her daddy's favorite hiding spot, that loft; he loved to sit up there and smoke cigarettes and drink hooch and dream big dreams. He stayed up there more and more these days.

As Loreda unharnessed the gelding, she smelled the rubber on the tires and the metallic taint of the engine along with the comforting aromas of sweet hay and manure. In the side-by-side stalls at the end, their other gelding, Bruno, snorted softly in greeting, banged his nose into the stall door.

"I'll get you boys some water," Loreda said, easing the slimy bit out of Milo's mouth. She turned him into his stall, the back of which opened out to the corral.

As she closed the stall door, clicked it shut, she heard something. What?

She left the barn, stepped outside, and looked around.

There it was again. A deep rumbling. Not thunder. There wasn't a cloud in the sky.

The ground trembled beneath her feet, made a loud, crunching, splintering sound.

A crack opened up in the earth, a giant snaking zigzag.

Boom.

Dust geysered into the air, dirt crashed into the new crevasse, the sides crumbled away. A part of the barbed-wire fence fell into the opening. New cracks crawled off from the main one, like branches on a tree limb.

A fifty-foot zigzagging crevasse opened in the yard. Dead roots stuck out from the crumbling dirt sides like skeletal hands.

Loreda stared at it in horror. She had heard stories of this, the land breaking open from dryness, but she'd thought it was a myth . . .

Now, it wasn't just the animals and the people who were drying up. The land itself was dying.

LOREDA AND HER DADDY were in their favorite place, sitting side by side on the platform beneath the giant blades of the windmill. As the sky turned red in the last few moments before darkfall, she could see to the very end of the world she knew and imagine what lay beyond.

"I want to see the ocean," Loreda said. It was a game they played, imagining other lives they would someday live. She couldn't remember now when they'd begun; she just knew that it felt more important these days because of the new sadness in her father. At least it felt new. She sometimes wondered if his sadness had always been there and she'd just finally grown up enough to see it.

"You will, Lolo."

Usually he said, *We will.*

He slumped forward, rested his forearms on his thighs. Thick black hair fell in unruly waves over his broad forehead; it was cut close to the sides of his head but Mom didn't have time to tend it closely and the edges were ragged.

"You want to see the Brooklyn Bridge, remember?" Loreda said. It scared her to think of her father's unhappiness. She hardly got to spend any time with him lately and she loved him more than anything in the world, he who made her feel like a special girl with a big future.

He'd taught her to dream. He was the opposite of her dour, workhorse mom, who just plodded forward, doing chores, never having any fun. They even looked alike, she and her daddy. Everyone said so. The same thick black hair and fine-boned faces, the same full lips. The only thing Loreda had inherited from her mother was her blue eyes, but even with her mother's eyes, Loreda saw things the way her daddy did.

"Sure, Lolo. How could I forget? You and I will see the world someday. We will stand at the top of the Empire State Building or attend a movie premiere on Hollywood Boulevard. Hell, we might even—"

"Rafe!"

Mom stood at the base of the windmill, looking up. In her brown kerchief and flour-sack dress and sagging stockings, she looked practically as old as Grandma. As always, she stood ramrod stiff. She had perfected an unyielding, unforgiving stance: shoulders back, spine straight, chin up. Wisps of corn-silk-fine pale blond hair crept out from beneath her kerchief.

"Hey, Elsa. You found us." Daddy flashed Loreda a conspiratorial smile.

"Your father wants help watering while it's cool," Mom said. "And I know a girl who has chores to finish."

Daddy bumped his shoulder against Loreda's and then climbed down the windmill. The boards creaked and swayed at his steps. He jumped down the last few feet, faced Mom.

Loreda crawled down behind him, but she wasn't fast enough. When she got down, her father was already headed toward the barn.

"How come you can't let anyone have any fun?" she said to her mother.

"I want you and your father to have fun, Loreda, but I've had a long day and I need your help putting the laundry away."

"You're so *mean*," Loreda said.

"I am not mean, Loreda," Mom said.

Loreda heard the hurt in her mother's voice but didn't care. That anger of hers, always so close to the surface, surged up, uncontrollable. "Don't you care that Daddy is unhappy?"

"Life is tough, Loreda. You need to be tougher or it will turn you inside out, as it has your father."

"Life isn't what makes my daddy sad."

"Oh, really? Tell me, then, with all your worldly experience, what is it that makes your father unhappy?"

"You," Loreda said.

EIGHT

One hundred and four degrees in the shade, and the well was drying up. The water in the tank had to be carefully conserved, carried by the bucketful to the house. At night, they gave the animals what water they could.

The vegetables that Elsa and Rose had tended with such loving care were dead. Between yesterday's wind and dust and the relentless sun, every plant had either been torn out by the roots or lay wilted and dead.

She heard Rose come up beside her.

"There's no point watering," Elsa said.

"No."

She heard the heartbreak in her mother-in-law's voice and wished she could say something to help.

"You've been awfully quiet today," Rose said.

"Unlike my usual chatty self," Elsa said to deflect a conversation she didn't want to have.

Rose bumped her shoulder against Elsa's arm. "Tell me what is wrong. Besides the obvious, of course."

"Loreda is angry at me. All of the time. I swear, before I even speak, she gets mad at whatever it is I'm about to say."

"She is at that age."

"It's more than that, I think."

Rose stared out at the devastated fields. "My son," she said. "*Stupido.* He is filling her head with dreams."

"He's unhappy."

"*Pssht,*" Rose said impatiently. "Who isn't? Look at what is happening."

"My parents, my family," Elsa said quietly. This was something she rarely talked about, a pain too deep for words, especially when words wouldn't change anything; Loreda's opinion of Elsa lately had brought all that heartache of youth back. Elsa remembered the day she'd taken Loreda, swaddled in pink, to her parents' house, hoping her marriage would allow them to accept her again. Elsa had worked for weeks on a lovely pink dress for the baby, trimmed it in lace. She knit a matching cap. Finally, she borrowed the truck and drove to Dalhart alone, pulling up at the back gate. She remembered every moment in detail: *Walking up the path; the smell of roses. Everything in bloom. A clear blue sky. Bees buzzing around the roses.*

She had felt both nervous and proud. She was a wife now, with a baby girl so beautiful even strangers remarked upon it.

Knocking on the door. The sound of footsteps, heels on hardwood. Mama answering the door, dressed for church, wearing pearls. Papa in a brown suit.

"*Look,*" *Elsa had said, her smile unsteady, her eyes filling with unwanted tears. "My daughter, Loreda."*

Mama, craning her neck, peering down at Loreda's small, perfect face.

"*Look, Eugene, how dark her skin is. Take your disgrace away, Elsinore.*"

The door, slamming shut.

Elsa had made a point of never seeing them or speaking to them again, but even so, their absence caused an ache that wouldn't go away.

Apparently you couldn't stop loving some people, or needing their love, even when you knew better.

"Yes?" Rose said, looking up at her.

"They didn't love me. I never knew why. But now Loreda has turned so angry, I wonder if she sees me the same way they did. I could never do anything right in their eyes, either."

"Do you remember what I told you on the day Loreda was born?"

Elsa almost smiled. "That she would love me as no one else ever would and make me crazy and try my soul?"

"*Sì*. And you see how right I was?"

"About part of it, I guess. She certainly breaks my heart."

"Yes. I was a trial to my poor *mamma*, too. The love, it comes in the beginning of her life and at the end of yours. God is cruel that way. Your heart, is it too broken to love?"

"Of course not."

"So, you go on." She shrugged, as if to say, *Motherhood*. "What choice is there for us?"

"It just . . . hurts."

Rose was silent for a while; finally, she said, "Yes."

In the distant field, Tony and Rafe were hard at work, planting winter wheat in ground that was as powdery as flour at the surface and hard beneath. For three years, they'd planted wheat and prayed for rain and gotten too little and grown no crop at all.

"This season it will be better," Rose said.

"We still have milk and eggs to sell. And soap." Small blessings mattered. Elsa and Rose combined their individual optimism into a communal hope, stronger and more durable in the combination.

Rose put an arm around Elsa's waist, and Elsa leaned into the smaller woman. From the moment of Loreda's birth, and in all the years since, Rose had become Elsa's mother in every way that mattered. Even if they didn't speak of their love, or share their feelings in long, heartfelt conversations, the bond was there. Sturdy. They'd sewn their lives together in the silent way of women unused to conversation. Day after day, they worked together, prayed together, held their growing family together through the hardships of farm life. When Elsa had lost her third child—a son who never drew breath—it was Rose who held Elsa and let her cry, and said, *Some lives are not ours to hold on to; God makes His choices without us.* Rose, who spoke for the first time about her own lost children, had showed Elsa that grief could be borne one day, one chore, at a time.

"I'll go water the animals," Elsa said.

Rose nodded. "I'll dig up what I can."

Elsa grabbed a metal bucket from the porch and wiped the grit from its inside. At the pump, she put on gloves to protect her hands from the blazing-hot metal and pumped a bucketful of water.

Carrying the sloshing pail carefully back to the house, not wanting to spill a precious drop, she was nearing the barn when she heard a sound, like a saw blade grinding over metal.

She slowed, listened, heard it again.

She set down the bucket and moved around the corner of the barn and saw Rafe standing by the new crack in the ground, his arms propped on the head of a rake, his hat pulled low on his downcast face. *Crying.*

Elsa walked over to him, stood silently by. Words were something she could never pull up easily, not for him. She was always afraid of saying the wrong thing, of pushing him away when she wanted to draw him near. He was like Loreda, full of mercurial moods and given to bouts of passion. It frightened her, those moods she could neither tame nor understand. So she held her tongue.

"I don't know how long I can stand all of this," he said.

"It will rain soon. You'll see."

"How can you not break?" he said, wiping his eyes with the back of his hand.

Elsa didn't know how to answer that. They were parents. They had to stay strong for the children. Or did he mean something else? "Because the kids need us not to."

He sighed, and she knew she'd said the wrong thing.

⌇

THAT SEPTEMBER, HEAT ROARED across the Great Plains, day after day, week after week, burning away whatever had survived the summer.

Elsa stopped sleeping well, or at all, really. She was plagued by nightmares of emaciated children and dying crops. The livestock—two horses and two cows, all bones and hollows—were being kept alive by eating the prickly Russian thistles that grew wild. The small amount of hay they'd harvested was nearly gone. The animals stood still for hours at a time, as if afraid that every step could kill them. In the hottest part of the day, when the temperature rose above 115 degrees, their eyes became glassy and unfocused. When they could, the family carried pails of water to the corral, but it was always too little. Every drop of water that came up from the well had to be carefully conserved. The chickens rarely moved, they were so lethargic; they lay like feathered heaps in the dirt, not even bothering to squawk when they were disturbed. Eggs were still being laid, and each one was like a nugget of gold, although Elsa feared that each one would be their last.

Today, like most mornings, she was awake before the rooster crowed.

She lay in bed, trying not to think about the dead garden or the dried-up ground or the coming winter. When sunlight began to stream through the windows, she sat up and read a chapter of *Jane Eyre,* letting the familiar words soothe and comfort her. Then she put the novel aside and got out of bed, careful not to waken Rafe. After dressing, she took a moment to stare down at her sleeping husband. He'd been out in the barn until late last night and finally stumbled to bed smelling of whiskey.

She had been restless, too, but neither had turned to the other for solace. They didn't know how, she supposed; they'd never learned to comfort each other. Or maybe there was no comfort to be found when life was so bad.

What she knew was that the slim hold she'd had on him was loosening. In the past few weeks, she'd noticed how frequently he turned away from her. Was it since the dust storms had ruined their fields and tripled the work? Or since he'd planted the winter wheat with his father?

He stayed up late, reading newspapers as if they were adventure novels, staring out windows, studying maps. When he finally stumbled to bed, he rolled away from her and thumped into a sleep so deep that sometimes she feared he had died during the night.

Last night, as so often, when he finally came to their bed, she lay in the dark, aching for him to turn to her, touch her, but even if he had, they both would have remained unsatisfied. He never spoke while they were intimate, not even whispers about his need, and he rushed through the act as if he regretted it before he began. Sometimes Elsa felt lonelier when their lovemaking ended than she had been before it began. He said he stayed away from her because she conceived so easily, but she knew the truth was darker than that. As always, it came down to her unattractiveness. Of course he had difficulty wanting her. And clearly, she was not good in bed; he rushed through it so.

In earlier years, she had dreamed of boldly reaching for him, changing how they touched each other, exploring his body with her hands and her mouth; then, upon waking, she'd felt frustrated and swollen with a desire she could neither express nor share. She'd waited years for him to see it, see *her*, and reach out.

Lately, though, that dream felt far away. Or maybe she was just too tired and worn out these days to believe in it.

She left their bedroom and walked down the hallway. She paused at each of the kid's bedroom doors and peered in. The peacefulness in their sleeping faces squeezed her heart. At times like this, she remembered Loreda when she'd been young and happy, always laughing, her arms thrown open for a hug. When Elsa had been Loreda's favorite person in the world.

She went into the kitchen, which smelled of coffee and baking bread. Her in-laws didn't sleep anymore, either. Like her, they held on to the unproven hope/belief that more work might save them.

Pouring herself a cup of black coffee, she drank it quickly and washed out the cup, then stepped into her brown shoes—the heels almost worn away—and grabbed her sun hat.

Outside, she squinted into the bright sun, tented a gloved hand over her eyes.

Tony was already at work, taking advantage of the relative cool of the morning. He was putting up hay—what little there was—and doing it early because he was afraid the afternoon heat would kill their horses. Both geldings moved more slowly every day. Sometimes the lowing moans of their hunger was enough to make Elsa weep.

Elsa waved at her father-in-law and he waved back. Tying on her hat, she made a quick stop at the outhouse and then hauled water by the pailful to the kitchen for laundry. There was no reason to water the orchard or the garden anymore. By the time she finished carrying water, her arms ached and she was sweating. At last, she went to her own little garden. She'd hollowed out a square of ground directly below the kitchen window, in a narrow patch of morning shade. It was too small to grow anything of value, so she'd planted some flower seeds. All she wanted was a little green, maybe even a splash of color.

She knelt in the powdery dirt, rearranging the stones she'd set in a semicircle to delineate the garden. The latest wind had pushed a few out of place. In the center, still standing, was her precious calico aster, with its leggy brown stems and defiant green leaves.

"If you can just make it through this heat wave, it will cool down soon," Elsa said, pouring a few precious drops of water onto the soil, watching it darken instantly. "I know you want to bloom."

"Talking to your little friend again?"

Elsa sat back on her heels and looked up, blinded for a moment by the bright sun.

Rafe stood in a halo of yellow light. He rarely bothered to shave these days, so the lower half of his face was covered in thick, dark stubble.

He knelt on one knee beside her and laid a hand on her shoulder. She could feel the slight dampness in his palm, the way his hand trembled from last night's drinking.

Elsa couldn't help leaning into his touch just enough to make his hold feel possessive.

"I'm sorry if I woke you up when I got in," he said.

She turned. The brim of her straw hat touched the brim of his, made a scratching sound. "It was nothing."

"I don't know how you can stand all this."

"All this?"

"Our life. Digging for scraps. Being hungry. How skinny our kids are."

"We have more than lots of folks have these days."

"You want too little, Elsa."

"You make that sound like a bad thing."

"You're a good woman."

He made that sound like a bad thing, too. Elsa didn't know how to respond, and in the silence of her confusion, he rose slowly, tiredly to his feet.

She stood in front of him, tilted her face up. She knew what he saw: a tall, unattractive woman with sunburned, peeling skin and a mouth that was too big, and eyes that seemed to have drunk all the color God allotted her.

"I need to get to work," he said. "It's already so goddamn hot I can't breathe."

Elsa stared after him, thinking, *Look back, smile,* but he didn't, and finally she stopped waiting and headed in to start the laundry.

THE FIRST PIONEER DAYS celebration had taken place in 1905, back in the days when Lonesome Tree was a vast plain of blue-green buffalo grass and the XIT Ranch employed a thousand cowboys. Homesteaders had been drawn to this land by brochures that promised they could grow cabbages the size of baby carriages, and wheat. All without irrigation. Dry farming, it was called, and it was promised to them here.

Indeed.

Loreda was pretty sure the party was really about men celebrating themselves.

"You look beautiful," Mom said, coming into Loreda's bedroom without even knocking. Loreda felt a rush of irritation at the intrusion. She bit back an angry remark about privacy.

Mom came up behind her; for a moment their faces were reflected together in the mirror above Loreda's washstand. Beside Loreda's tanned skin and blunt-cut black hair, Mom's pallor was remarkable. How was it that Mom's skin never tanned, just burned and peeled? She hadn't even bothered to do anything with her hair beyond braiding it in a coronet. Stella's mom always wore cosmetics and had her hair pinned and curled, even in these hard times.

Mom didn't even *try* to look good. The dress she wore—a floral flour-sack housedress with a button-up bodice—was at least a size too big and just exaggerated how tall and thin she was.

"I'm sorry I couldn't make you a new dress or at least buy you some socks. Next year. When it rains."

Loreda couldn't imagine how her mother could even say those words anymore. Loreda pulled away, smoothing the waves she'd coaxed into her chin-length hair and ruffling her bangs. "Where's Daddy?"

"He's hitching up the wagon."

Loreda turned. "Can Stella spend the night after?"

"Sure," Mom said. "But you'll have to do your chores in the morning."

Loreda was so happy, she actually hugged her mother, but Mom ruined it by hanging on too long and squeezing too hard.

Loreda yanked free.

Mom looked sad. "Go downstairs," she said. "Help Grandma pack up the food."

Loreda bolted out of the bedroom and hurried down to the kitchen, where Grandma was already busy packing up the pot of minestrone soup. A plateful of her cannoli with sweetened ricotta filling waited on the table. Both of which only the other Italian families would eat.

Loreda covered the tray of desserts with a dish towel and carried it out to the wagon. She climbed up into the back and sat close to her father, who put his arm around her and held her close. Grandma and Grandpa took their places up front. Mom was the last one to climb up into the back of the wagon.

Ant tucked in close to Mom and talked constantly, his high-pitched voice rising in excitement as they neared the town. Daddy, she noticed, was uncharacteristically quiet.

Lonesome Tree appeared on the horizon, a meager town squatted on a table-flat plain, surrounded by nothing.

Only the water tower stood tall against the cloudless blue sky.

Once, patriotism had run high in town. Loreda remembered how the old men used to talk about the Great War at every community gathering. Who fought, who died, and who grew the wheat to feed the troops. Back then, Pioneer Days had been an expression of the farmers' pride in themselves and a celebration of their hard work. *Americans! Prosperous!* They'd draped the stores of Main Street in red, white, and blue bunting and planted American flags in the flowerpots and painted patriotic slogans on the windows. The men had gathered to drink and smoke and congratulate each other on winning the war and turning grazing land into farmland. They drank homemade hooch and played music on their fiddles and guitars while the women did all the work.

Or that was how Loreda saw it. In the week leading up to the celebration, Mom and Grandma Rose cooked more, made more home-made macaroni, did more laundry, and had to darn or repair every scrap of clothing that was to be worn. No matter how dire times were, how tight money was, Mom wanted her children to look presentable.

Today there was no bunting (too hot to put up, she figured, or else some woman finally said, *Why bother?*), no flowers or flags in the flowerpots, no patriotic slogans. Instead, Loreda saw hobos gathered around the train de-pot, wearing rags, their back pockets turned inside out in what were being called Hoover flags. A shoe with holes was a Hoover shoe. Everyone knew who to blame for the Depression but not how to fix it.

Clop-clop-clop down Main Street. Only two automobiles were parked out here. Both belonged to bankers. Banksters, they were called these days, for the way they cheated hardworking folk out of their land and then went bust and closed their doors, keeping the money people had thought was safe.

Grandpa maneuvered the horse and wagon up to the schoolhouse and parked.

Loreda heard music wafting through the open doors and the sound of stomping feet. She launched herself out of the wagon and hurried to the schoolhouse.

Inside, the party was *on*. A makeshift band played in the corner and a few couples were dancing.

Off to the right were the food tables. There wasn't a lot of food out, but after the years of drought, Loreda knew it was a feast the women had worried and slaved over.

"Loreda!"

Loreda saw Stella moving toward her. As usual, Stella and her younger sister, Sophia, were the only girls in the room in pretty new party dresses.

Loreda felt a pinch of jealousy and put it aside. Stella was her best friend. Who cared about dresses?

Loreda and Stella came together as they always did, grasping hands, heads tilted together.

"Say, what's the story, morning glory?" Loreda said, trying to sound in the know.

"I'm behind the grind, don'tcha know?" Stella answered.

Stella's parents came up behind the girls, stopped to talk to the Martinellis.

Loreda heard Mr. Devereaux say, "I got another postcard from my brother-in-law. There's railroad work in Oregon. You should think about it, Tony. Rafe."

Like women had no opinions.

And her grandfather's reply: "I don't blame nobody for leaving, Ralph, but it ain't for us. This land . . ."

Not that again. The land.

Loreda pulled Stella away from the grown-ups.

Ant ran past them, wearing a gas mask that made him look like an insect. He bumped into Loreda and giggled and ran away again, arms outstretched as if he were flying.

"The Red Cross donated a big box of gas masks to the bank—for the kids to wear during dust storms. My mom is handing 'em out tonight."

"Gas masks," Loreda said, shaking her head. "Jeepers."

"It's getting worse, my dad says."

"We are *not* talking about gas masks. This is a party, for gosh sakes," Loreda said. She reached out, took hold of Stella's hands. "My mom said you can spend the night tonight. I got some magazines from the library. There's a picture of Clark Gable that will make you swoon."

Stella pulled back, looked away.

"What's wrong?"

"The bank is closing," Stella said.

"Oh."

"My uncle Jimmy—the one in Portland, Oregon? He sent my dad a postcard. He reckons the railroad is hiring, and there's no dust storms out there."

Loreda took a step back. She didn't want to hear what was coming.

"We're leaving."

NINE

Loreda leaned out her bedroom window and screamed in frustration. Below her, the chickens squawked in response. "Fly away, you idiot birds. Can't you tell we're dying here?"

Stella was leaving.

Loreda's best—and only—friend in Lonesome Tree was leaving.

The room seemed to close in on her, becoming so small she couldn't breathe. She went downstairs. The house was still, no wind poking at the cracks, no wood settling onto its foundations.

She moved easily in the dark. In the past month they'd turned off the party-line phone—no money to pay for it—and now they were really out here all alone. She found the front door and went outside. A bright moon shone out, glazing the barn's roof with silvered light.

She smelled the sunbaked dirt and a hint of chicken manure and . . . cigarette smoke? Following the smell of it, she walked around the side of the farmhouse.

Beneath the windmill, she saw the red glow of a cigarette tip rise and fall and rise again. *Daddy.* So he couldn't sleep, either.

As she approached him, she saw his red eyes and the tear streaks on his cheeks. He'd been out here in the dark, all alone, smoking and crying. "Daddy?"

"Hey, doll. You caught me."

He tried to sound casual, but the obvious pretense made her feel even worse. If there was one person she trusted to tell her the truth, it was her father. But now it was so bad he was *crying*.

"You heard the Devereauxs are leaving?"

"I'm sorry, Lolo."

"I'm tired of *I'm sorry*s," Loreda said. "We could leave, too. Like the Devereauxs and the Moungers and the Mulls. Just go."

"They were all talking about leaving at the shindig tonight. Most folks are like your grandparents. They'd rather die here than leave."

"Do they know we might *actually* die here?"

"Oh. They know, believe me. Tonight, your grandfather said—and I quote: *Bury me here, boys. I ain't leaving.*" He exhaled smoke. "They say they're doing it for our future. As if this patch of dirt is all we could ever want."

"Maybe we could convince them to leave."

Her father laughed. "And maybe Milo will sprout wings and fly away."

"Could we leave without them? Lots of folks are leaving. You always say this is America, where anything is possible. We could go to California. Or you could get a railroad job in Oregon."

Loreda heard footsteps. Moments later, Mom appeared, dressed in her ratty old robe and work boots, her fine hair all whichaway.

"Rafe," Mom said, sounding relieved, as if she thought he might have run off. It was pathetic how close an eye Mom kept on Daddy. On all of them. She was more of a cop than a parent, and she took the fun out of everything. "I missed you when I woke. I thought . . ."

"I'm here," he said.

Mom's smile was as thin as everything else about her. "Come inside. Both of you. It's late."

"Sure, Els," Daddy said.

Loreda hated how beaten her father sounded, how his fire went out around her mother. She sucked the life out of everyone with her sad, long-suffering looks. "This is all your fault."

Mom said, "What am I to blame for now, Loreda? The weather? The Depression?"

Daddy touched Loreda, shook his head. *Don't.*

Mom waited a moment for Loreda to speak, then turned away and headed for the house.

Daddy followed.

"We could leave," Loreda said to her father, who kept walking as if he hadn't heard. "Anything is possible."

❧

THE NEXT MORNING, ELSA woke well before dawn and found Rafe's side of the bed empty. He'd slept in the barn again. Lately he preferred it to being with her. With a sigh, she got dressed and left her room.

In the dark kitchen, Rose stood at the dry sink, her hands deep in water that she'd hauled from the well and poured into the sink. A large cracked mixing bowl lay drying on towels on the counter beside her. Towels Elsa had embroidered by hand, at night, by candlelight, in Rafe's favorite colors. She had thought that making a perfect home was the answer to making a marriage happy. Clean sheets scented with lavender, embroidered pillowcases, hand-knit scarves. She'd filled hours with such tasks, poured her heart and soul into them, using thread to say the words she could not utter.

A pot of coffee sat on the woodstove, pumping a comforting aroma into the room. A tray of rectangular chickpea *panelle* was on the table and a tablespoon of olive oil popped in a cast-iron pan on the stove. Beside it, oatmeal bubbled in a pot.

"Morning," Elsa said. She removed a spatula from the drawer and lowered two of the *panelle* into the hot oil. These would be the midday meal, eaten like a sandwich, squeezed with precious drops of preserved lemon.

"You look tired," Rose said, not unkindly.

"Rafe isn't sleeping well."

"If he'd stop drinking in the barn at night it might help."

Elsa poured herself a cup of coffee and leaned against the cabbage-rose-papered wall. She noticed the corner of the flooring where the linoleum was coming up. Then she went to turn the *panelle* over, seeing a nice brown crust on them.

Rose moved in beside her, took over the cooking.

Elsa began to take apart the butter churn. The parts needed to be washed and scalded and put back together in a precise, numbered order and then stacked for the next use. It was the perfect chore to keep one's mind occupied.

A centipede crawled out of its hiding place and plopped onto the counter. Elsa took out a pair of knives and chopped it into pieces. Sharing the house with centipedes and spiders and other insects had become commonplace. Every living thing on the Great Plains sought safety from the dust storms.

The two women worked in companionable silence until the sun came up and the children stumbled out of their bedrooms.

"I'll feed them," Rose said. "Why don't you take Rafe some coffee?"

Elsa was grateful for her mother-in-law's insight. Smiling, Elsa said, "Thank you," poured her husband a cup of coffee, and went outside.

The sun was a bright yellow glow in a cloudless cornflower-blue sky. Instead of noticing the latest destruction to the land—broken fence posts, damage to the windmill, dirt piles growing in size—she focused instead on the good news. If she hurried, she would be able to do laundry today, bleach everything into whiteness. There was something about fresh sheets hanging on the line that lifted her spirits. Perhaps it was simply a vision of having accomplished a thing that improved her family's life, even if no one noticed.

Tony was up on the windmill repairing a blade. The *bang-bang-bang* of his hammer echoed across the endless brown plain.

Rafe was in the last place in the world she expected him to be: the family cemetery. A small brown plot of land delineated by a sagging picket fence. Once, it had included a beautiful garden, with pink morning glories crawling up and over the white picket fence and a carpet of blue-green buffalo grass on the ground. Elsa used to spend an hour here every Sunday, rain, heat, or snow, but she hadn't been out here as often lately. As always, the headstones reminded her of her lost son, of the dreams she'd spun for him while he was in her womb and the pain that had softened over time but never gone away.

She unclicked the gate, which hung askew on a broken hinge. Dozens of white pickets lay on the ground; some had broken, others had been yanked out of the ground by the savage wind.

Four gray headstones stood from the dirt. Three of Rose and Tony's children—all daughters—and Lorenzo . . .

Rafe was kneeling in front of their son's headstone. *Lorenzo Walter Martinelli, b. 1931, d. 1931.*

Elsa knelt beside him, laid a hand on his shoulder.

He turned to her. She had never seen such pain in his eyes, not even when they'd buried their newborn son. Rafe had been only twenty-eight when he'd held his tiny, unbreathing child in his arms and cried for their loss. He had, to the best of her knowledge, never come out here, never knelt at this grave.

"I miss him, too," Elsa said, stumbling a little over the words.

"Old Man Orloff butchered his last steer this week. The poor thing was full of dirt."

"Yes." Elsa frowned at the odd change in topic.

"Ant asked me why his stomach hurt all the time. How could I tell him that the land is killing him?" He stood, took her by the hand, and pulled her up to stand with him. "Let's go."

"Go?"

"West. To California. People are leaving every day. I hear there are railroad jobs to be had. And maybe I'll qualify for that program of FDR's. The Conservation Corps."

"We don't have money for gas."

"We could walk. Jump on trains. Folks will give us rides. We will get there. The kids are tough."

"*Tough?*" She pulled free of his hold, took a step back. "They don't have shoes that fit. We have no money. No food. You've seen the Hooverville photos, what it's like out there. Anthony is seven. How far do you think he can walk? You want him to jump on a moving train?"

"California is different," he said stubbornly. "There are jobs there."

"Your parents won't leave. You know that."

"We could go without them?" He made it a question, not a statement, and she could see how ashamed he was to even ask it.

"Go without them?"

Rafe ran a hand through his hair and looked out over the dead wheat fields and the graves already on this land. "This damnable wind and drought will kill them. And us. I can't stand it anymore. I can't."

"Rafe . . . you can't mean this."

This land was his heritage, their future, their children's future. The kids would grow up on this land, always knowing their history, knowing who they were and who they'd come from. They'd learn the pride that came with a good day's work. They would *belong* somewhere. Rafe didn't know how it felt not to belong, the pain of it, but Elsa did, and she would never inflict that heartache on her children. This was *home*. He had to know that hard times ended. Land endured. Family endured. How could he think they could just leave Tony and Rose here alone? It was unconscionable, unthinkable. "When it rains—"

"Christ, I hate that sentence," he said, sounding more bitter than she'd ever heard him.

She saw the agony in his eyes, the disappointment, the anger.

Elsa wanted to reach out and touch him but didn't dare. *I love you* burned in her dry throat. "I just think—"

"I know what you think."

He walked away and didn't look back.

>⟨

LEAVE. JUST GIVE UP on this land and walk away with nothing.

Actually *walk* away. She was still thinking about it hours later, well after night had fallen.

She couldn't imagine joining the horde of jobless, homeless hobos and migrants who were headed west. She'd heard it was dangerous to jump onto those trains, that legs and feet could be cut off, bodies severed in half by the giant metal wheels. And there was crime out there, bad men who'd left their consciences along with their families. Elsa was not a brave woman.

Still.

She loved her husband. She'd vowed to love, honor, and obey him. Surely "follow him" was understood.

Should she have told him they'd go to California? At least talked about it? Maybe in the spring, if they'd had rain and a crop, there would be money for gas.

And God knew he was unhappy here. So was Loreda.

Perhaps they could leave—all of them—and come back when the drought ended.

Why not?

This land would wait for them.

She could at least discuss it with him properly, make him see that she was his wife and they were a team and if he wanted this enough, she would do it. She would leave this land she had come to love, the only home she'd ever had.

For him.

She threw a shawl over her worn lawn nightgown, then stepped into the rubber boots by the front door and went outside.

Where was he? Out on the windmill, alone, chewing on his disappointment? Or had he hitched up the wagon and gone to the Silo so he could sit at the bar and drink whiskey?

It was nearly nine o'clock and the farm was quiet.

The only light on in the house shone in Loreda's upstairs window. Her daughter was in bed reading, just as Elsa had done at her age. She walked out into the yard. The chickens roused themselves lethargically as she passed by and quieted quickly. She heard music coming from her in-laws' bedroom. Tony was playing music on his fiddle. Elsa knew that music was how he spoke to Rose in these hard times, how he reminded them of their past and their future, how he said, *I love you.*

She saw Rafe in the darkness by the corral, an upright slash of black against the black slats of the corral, all of it sheened silver by the light of a waxing moon. The bright orange tip of his cigarette.

He heard her footsteps, she could tell.

Rafe pulled away from the corral, stubbed out his cigarette, and dropped the unsmoked portion into his shirt pocket. Tony's love song wafted toward them.

Elsa stopped in front of Rafe. All it would take was the smallest movement and she could rest her hand on his shoulder. She knew the faded blue chambray of his work shirt would feel warm after this long, hot day. She'd hemmed and washed and stitched and folded every garment he owned and knew each one by touch.

How was it possible that Elsa was close enough to her husband that she could feel the heat coming off him and smell the whiskey and cigarettes on his breath and still feel as if an ocean sloshed between them?

He surprised her by taking her hand and pulling her into his arms.

"You remember that first night of ours, out in the truck in front of Steward's barn?"

Elsa nodded uncertainly. These were things they didn't speak of.

"You said you wanted to be brave. I just wanted . . . to be somewhere else."

Elsa stared up at him, saw his pain, and it hurt her, too. "Oh, Rafe—"

He kissed her on the lips, long and slow and deep, letting his tongue taste hers. "You were my first kiss," he whispered, drawing back just enough to look at her. "Remember me then?"

It was the most romantic thing he'd ever said to her, and it filled her with hope. "Always," she whispered.

Tony's music stopped, leaving a heavy silence behind. Insects sang their staccato songs. The geldings moved listlessly in the corral, bumping the fencing with their noses, reminding them that they were hungry.

The night around them was black, the huge sky bright with stars. Maybe those were other universes she saw up there.

It felt beautiful and romantic, and just now, the two of them could be alone on the planet, attended to only by the sounds of the night.

"You're thinking about California," she began, trying to find the right words to begin a new conversation.

"Yeah. Ant walking one thousand miles on bad shoes. Us in a bread-line somewhere. You were right. We can't go."

"Maybe in the spring—"

Rafe silenced her with a kiss. "Go to bed," he murmured. "I'll be there soon."

Elsa felt him pulling away, releasing her. "Rafe, I think we should talk about—"

"Don't fret, Els," he said. "I'll come to bed shortly. We can talk then. I just need to water the animals."

Elsa wanted to stop him and make him listen, but such boldness was beyond her. Deep down, she was always afraid of how flimsy her hold on him was. She couldn't test it.

But she *would* reach for him tonight, touch him with the kind of intimacy she dreamed of. She would overcome whatever was wrong with her and finally please him.

She would. And when they were finished making love, she would talk to him about leaving, talk seriously. More important, she would listen.

She returned to their room and paced. Finally, she went to the window and peeled away the dirt-crusted rags and newspaper that covered the sill and pane.

She could see the windmill, a slash of black lines, a flower almost, silhouetted against the bejeweled night sky.

Rafe was there, leaning against the frame, almost indistinguishable from the windmill. He was smoking.

She climbed into bed and pulled the quilt up around her and waited for her husband.

⅀

THE NEXT THING ELSA knew, it was daylight and she smelled coffee. The rich, bitter aroma drew her out of the comfort of her bed. She finger-combed her hair and slipped into a housedress, trying not to be hurt that Rafe hadn't come to their bed again last night.

She rebraided her hair and wrapped it in a coil at the back of her head, pinning it in place and then covering it with the kerchief.

She checked on her children—letting them sleep in on this Saturday morning—and headed to the kitchen, where a pot full of last night's potato water had been saved to make bread.

All they had for breakfast was wheat cereal, so she got it started. Thank God they had one cow that was still producing milk.

Loreda was the first to stumble out of her small second-floor bedroom. Her black bob was a rat's nest of tangles and curls. A sunburn peeled in patches across her cheeks. "Wheat cereal. Yum," she said, heading to the icebox. Opening it, she took out the yellow crockery pitcher that held a bit of precious cream and carried it over to the oilcloth-draped table, where the speckled bowls and plates were already in place, upside down to protect from dust. She turned over three bowls.

Ant came out next, climbed up into the chair beside his sister. "I want pancakes," he grumbled.

"I'll put some corn syrup in your cereal," Elsa said.

Elsa served up the cereal, doctored it with cream and added a little corn syrup to each bowl, and then set down two glasses of cold buttermilk.

As the children ate—silently—Elsa headed for the barn. Wind and shifting sand had changed the landscape overnight again, filled in much of the giant crack that had cut through their property.

As she passed the hog pen, she saw their only remaining hog kneeling lethargically on the hard-packed earth, and the John Deere one-horse seed drill, unused now, half buried in sand. Beyond that, she saw Rose in the orchard, looking for apples on the cracked ground.

In the pen, their two cows stood side by side, heads down, mooing pathetically. Their ribs stood out, their bellies shrunken, their hides blistered with sores. Elsa couldn't help but remember a few years ago, when the younger of the two cows, Bella, had been born. Elsa had fed her by bottle because the cow's mother hadn't survived the birth. Rose had taught Elsa how to make the bottle and get the unsteady calf to take it. Sometimes Bella still followed Elsa around the yard like a pet.

"Hey, Bella," Elsa said, stroking the cow's sunken side.

Bella looked up, her big brown eyes blinded by dirt, and mooed plaintively.

"I know," Elsa said, taking a bucket from the fence post.

Elsa led Bella into the relative coolness of the barn, tied her to the center post, and pulled out the milking stool. She couldn't help glancing up into the hayloft—nearly empty now of hay. She was pretty sure Rafe had slept there last night. Again.

Elsa had always loved this chore. It had taken her a long time to catch on in the beginning; she had heard a hundred *tsk*s from Rose as Elsa tried to master the technique, but master it she had, and now it was one of her favorite chores. She loved being with Bella, loved the sweet smell of fresh milk, the hollow clanking as the first stream hit the metal bucket. She even loved what came next: carrying the bucket of fresh, warm milk to the house, pouring it into the separator, cranking the machine by hand, skimming off the rich yellow cream, saving the whole milk to feed her family and using skim milk for the animals.

Elsa reached out for the cow's barely swollen udder, touched the wind-chapped teats gently.

The cow bellowed in pain.

"I'm sorry, Bella," Elsa said. She tried again, squeezing as gently as she could, pulling down slowly.

A stream of dirt-brown milk squirted out, smelling fecund. Each day, it seemed, milking took longer to reach white, usable milk. The first streams were always dirty like this. Elsa dumped out the brown milk, cleaned the bucket, and tried again. She never gave up, no matter how sad Bella's moans made her or how long it took to get clean milk.

When she finished, getting less than they needed, she turned the poor cow out into the paddock.

As she passed the horse stalls, Milo and Bruno both snorted heavily and bit at the door, trying to eat the wood.

As she locked the barn door behind her, she heard a gunshot.

What now?

She turned, saw her father-in-law at the hog pen. He lowered his rifle as their last hog staggered sideways and collapsed.

"Thank God," Elsa murmured to herself. Meat for the children.

She waved at him as he hefted the dead hog into a wheelbarrow and headed to the barn to hang it for slaughter.

A tumbleweed rolled lazily past her, pushed along by a gentle breeze. Her gaze followed it to the fence line, where the Russian thistles survived against all odds, growing stubbornly even in the drought, against the wind. The cows ate them when there was nothing else. So did the horses.

She took the milk into the house and then went outside again, crossing the expanse of dirt that lay between the barn and the fence. The wind plucked at her kerchief, as if trying to stop her.

The Russian thistles were a tangle of prickles and stems, barely green. Wiry. Tough. Spikes as sharp as pins.

She pulled her gloves from her apron pocket and put them on. Making a bowl of her apron, she eased her hand past the sharp prickly ends and plucked off a green shoot.

She tasted it.

Not bad. Maybe they could be cooked gently in olive oil, wine, garlic, and herbs. Would they taste like artichokes? Tony loved his artichokes. Or maybe pickling them was the answer . . .

Tomorrow she'd get everyone picking them and find a way to preserve them.

At noon, when she'd picked as many as her apron could hold, she went back to the house.

Inside, Elsa found the children and Tony already seated at the table for the midday meal.

"I found some grapes," Ant said, bouncing in his seat, beaming at his contribution.

Elsa tousled his hair, felt its texture. "Bath tonight for a little boy I know."

"Do I hafta?"

Elsa smiled. "I can smell you from here. Yep."

Tony pulled off his hat, revealing a strip of white skin across his brow, and sat down. He downed an entire glass of tea in two gulps, then wiped his mouth with the back of his hand.

Rose came into the kitchen and poured her husband a glass of red wine.

Tony dug into his plate of *arancini*. It was a family favorite: rice balls filled with creamy cheese, swimming in a pancetta-and-garlic-flavored tomato sauce.

Elsa put her pile of thistles into a bowl and set it by the dry sink.

"What's that?" Rose asked, wiping her hands on her apron.

"Thistles. I think I can figure out a way to make them palatable. They almost taste like artichokes."

Rose sighed. "It's come to that. Italians eating horse food. *Madonna mia.*"

"Where's Rafe?" Elsa asked, looking around. "I need to talk to him."

"Ain't seen him all day," Ant said. "I looked, too."

Elsa walked out to the porch, rang the bell for the midday meal, and waited, looking out over the farm.

The horses and wagon were here, so he hadn't gone to town.

Maybe he was in their room.

She headed back into the house and went into their bedroom. Sunlight made the pale white walls look golden. A large framed portrait of Jesus stared at her.

The room was empty—just the bed and the chest of drawers she shared with her husband and the washstand with its oval mirror that captured her image. Everything was as it should be, except . . .

There were marks on the floor, coming out from beneath her bed, as if something had been put under the bed or taken out from underneath it.

She lifted the quilt and looked underneath the bed. She saw her suitcase, the one she'd brought into her marriage, and the box of baby clothes she'd saved just in case.

Something was missing. What?

She dropped to her knees for a better look. What was missing?

Rafe's suitcase. The one he'd packed all those years ago to go off to college. The one he'd unpacked when her father left Elsa here.

She glanced sideways. His clothes were gone from the hooks by the door, as was his hat.

She got up slowly and went to the dresser, opened the top drawer. His drawer.

One blue chambray shirt was all that was left.

TEN

She couldn't believe he'd left in the middle of the night without a word.

She'd spent thirteen years living with him, sharing his bed at night, bearing his children. She'd known he'd never been in love with her, but *this*?

She walked out of her room, saw the family—her family, their family—seated at the table, talking. Ant was retelling his grape-finding story.

Rose looked up, saw Elsa, and frowned. "Elsa?"

Elsa wanted to tell Rose this terrible thing and be held, but she couldn't say anything until she was sure. Maybe he had walked to town for . . . something.

With all of his belongings.

"I have . . . errands," Elsa said, seeing Rose's disbelief.

Elsa hurried out of the house and grabbed Loreda's bicycle. Climbing aboard, she pedaled through the thick dirt that layered the driveway, her legs working hard. More than once she had to zigzag around the dead branches of the fallen trees, which had been exposed in the last dust storm. She stopped at the mailbox, looked in. Nothing.

On the way to town, she didn't see a single automobile or wagon out on the road in this heat. Birds congregated on the telephone wires overhead, chattered down at her. Several cows and horses roamed free, plaintively moaning for food and water. Unable to butcher or care for their animals, farmers had let them go to fend for themselves.

By the time she reached Lonesome Tree, her hair had worked itself free from the pins she'd used to hold it back from her face, and her kerchief was damp.

On Main Street, she stopped. A tumbleweed rolled past her, scraped her bare calf. Lonesome Tree lay anesthetized before her, shops boarded up, nothing green, the town's namesake cottonwood half dead; up and down the street boards had been ripped away by the wind.

She pedaled toward the train depot and got off the bike.

Maybe he was still here.

Inside was a room full of empty benches. A dirty floor. A whites-only water fountain.

She walked to the ticket window. Behind a small, arched opening sat a man in a dusty white shirt with black elbow guards.

"Hello, Mr. McElvaine."

"Heya, Miz Martinelli," the man said.

"Was my husband here recently? Did he buy a ticket?"

He looked down at the papers on his desk.

"Please, sir. Do not make me interrogate you. This is humiliating enough for me, wouldn't you agree?"

"He didn't have any money."

"Did he say where he wanted to go?"

"You don't want me to say."

"I do."

He sighed and looked up at her. "He said, 'Anywhere but here.'"

"He said that?"

"If it helps, he pret' near looked ready to cry."

The man pulled out a crumpled, stained envelope and pushed it through the iron bars of the ticket window. "He said to give you this."

"He knew I'd come?"

"Wives always do."

She drew in a steadying breath. "So, if he had no money, maybe—"

"He done what they all do."

"All?"

"Men all over the county been leavin' their families. Families been abandonin' their kids and kin. I never seen nothing like it. A man over in Cimarron County kilt his whole family 'fore he left."

"Where do they go with no money?"

"West, ma'am. Most of 'em. They jump on the first train that comes through town."

"Maybe he'll come back."

The man sighed. "I ain't seen one of 'em come back yet."

>-

ELSA STOOD IN FRONT of the depot. Slowly, as if it were combustible, she opened Rafe's letter. The paper was wrinkled and dusty and appeared blotched by moisture. His tears?

Elsa,

I'm sorry. I know the words don't matter, may be worse than nothing.

I'm dying here, that's all I know. One more day on this farm and I might put a gun to my head. I'm weak. You are strong. You love this land and this life in a way I never could.

Tell my parents and my children I love them. You are all better off without me. Please, don't look for me. I don't want to be found. I don't know where I'm going anyway.

R

Elsa couldn't even cry.

Heartache had been a part of her life so long it had become as familiar as the color of her hair or the slight curve in her spine. Sometimes it
was the lens through which she viewed her world and sometimes it was
the blindfold she wore so she didn't see. But it was always there. She
knew it was her own fault, somehow, her doing, even though in all her
desperate musings for the foundation of it, she'd never been able to see
the flaw in herself that had proven to be so defining. Her parents had
seen it. Her father, certainly. And her younger, more beautiful sisters,
too. They had all sensed the lack in Elsa. Loreda certainly saw it.

Everyone—including Elsa—had assumed she would live an apol-
ogetic life, hidden among the needs of other, more vibrant people. The
caretaker, the tender, the woman left behind to keep the home fires
burning.

And then she had met Rafe.

Her handsome, charming, moody husband.

"Hold your head up," she said out loud.

She had children to think about. Two small people who needed to
be comforted in the wake of their father's betrayal.

Children who would grow up knowing that their father had abandoned them at this tender time.

Children who, like Elsa, would be shaped by heartache.

꒰

BY THE TIME ELSA got back to the farm, she felt as if she were a
machine slowly breaking down. Her family was in the house, bustling
about. Rose and Loreda were in the kitchen, making pasta, and Ant and
Tony were in the sitting room, rubbing oil into the straps of a leather
harness.

The children's lives would never be the same after today. Their opinions of everything would change, but especially their opinions of themselves, of the durability of love and the truth of their family. They would

know forever that their father hadn't loved their mother—or them—enough to stay with them through hard times.

What did a good mother do in this circumstance? Did she tell the harsh, ugly truth?

Or was a lie better?

If Elsa lied to protect her children from Rafe's selfishness and to protect Rafe from their resentment, it might be a long while before the truth came out, if it ever did.

Elsa walked past Tony and Ant in the sitting room and went into the kitchen, where her daughter was working the pasta dough on the flour-dusted table. Elsa squeezed her daughter's thin shoulder. It was all she could do not to pull her into her arms for a fierce hug, but frankly, Elsa couldn't handle another rejection right now.

Loreda pulled away. "Where's Daddy?"

"Yeah," Ant said from the sitting room, "where is he? I wanna show him the arrowhead Grandpa and I found."

Rose was at the stove, adding salt to a pot filled with water. She looked at Elsa and turned off the burner.

"Have you been crying?" Loreda asked.

"It's just watery eyes from all the dust," Elsa said, forcing a tight smile. "Can you kids go look for potatoes? I need to talk to Grandma and Grandpa."

"Now?" Loreda whined. "I hate doing that."

"Now," Elsa said. "Take your brother."

"Come on, Ant," Loreda said, pushing the dough away from her, "let's go root through the dirt like pigs."

Ant giggled. "I like bein' a pig."

"You would."

The kids shuffled out of the house and banged the door shut behind them.

Rose stared at Elsa. "You're scaring me."

Elsa headed into the sitting room, went straight to Tony's bottle of rye, and poured herself a drink.

It tasted awful enough that she poured a second one and drank that, too.

"*Madonna mia,*" Rose said quietly. "I have never seen you take one drink in all these years, and now you take two."

Rose came up behind Elsa, put a hand on her shoulder.

"Elsa," Tony said, putting the harness aside and standing up. "What is it?"

"It's Rafe."

"Rafe?" Rose frowned.

"He left," Elsa said.

"Rafe left?" Tony said. "To go where?"

"He left," Elsa said tiredly.

"Back to that damn tavern?" Tony said. "I told him—"

"No," Elsa said. "He left Lonesome Tree. On a train. Or so I'm told."

Rose stared at Elsa. "He *left*? No. He wouldn't do that. I know he's unhappy, but . . ."

"For God's sake, Rose," Tony said. "We are all unhappy. Dirt is raining from the sky. The trees are falling over dead. Animals are dying. We're all unhappy."

"He wanted to go to California," Elsa said. "I said no. It was a mistake. I was going to talk to him about it, but . . ." She pulled the letter out of her pocket and handed it to them.

Rose took it in trembling hands and read it, her lips moving silently over the words. Tears filled her eyes when she looked up.

"Son of a bitch," Tony said, crumpling the letter. "That's what comes of coddling the boy."

Rose looked stricken. "He'll be back," she said.

The three of them stared at each other. Absence could fill a room to overflowing, apparently.

The front door banged opened. Loreda and Ant came back with dirty hands and dirty faces and three small potatoes between them.

"It's barely any use." Loreda stopped. "What's wrong? Who died?"

Elsa set down her glass. "I need to talk to you two."

Rose put a hand over her mouth; Elsa understood. Saying these words aloud would change the children's lives.

Rose pulled Elsa into a tight hug, then let her go.

Elsa turned to face the children.

Their faces unraveled her. Both of them were such spitting images of their father. She went to them, pulled them into her arms, both at once. Ant happily hugged her back. Loreda struggled to break free.

"You're smothering me," Loreda complained.

Elsa let Loreda go.

"Where's Daddy?" Ant asked.

Elsa smoothed her son's hair back from his freckled face. "Come with me." She led them out onto the porch, where they all sat on the porch swing. Elsa pulled Ant onto her lap to make room.

"What's wrong now?" Loreda said, sounding put-upon.

Elsa drew a breath, pushed off, let the swing rock backward and forward. Lord, she wished her grandpa were here to say, *Be brave,* and give her a little push. "Your father has left—"

Loreda looked impatient. "Oh, yeah? Where'd he go?"

And there it was. The moment to lie or tell the truth.

He's taken a job out of town to save us. It would be easy to say, harder to prove when no money or letters came, when month after month, he didn't come home. But they wouldn't cry themselves to sleep, either.

Only Elsa would.

"Mom?" Loreda said sharply. "Where did Dad go?"

"I don't know," Elsa said. "He left us."

"Wait. *What?*" Loreda jumped off the swing. "You mean—"

"He's gone, Lolo," Elsa said. "Apparently he jumped on a train."

"DON'T YOU CALL ME THAT. Only he can call me that," Loreda screamed.

Elsa felt fragile enough that she feared there were tears in her eyes. "I'm sorry."

"He left *you*," Loreda said.

"Yes."

"I HATE YOU!" Loreda ran down the porch steps and disappeared around the corner of the house.

Ant twisted around to look up at Elsa. His confusion was heartbreaking. "When's he comin' back?"

"I don't think he will come back, Ant."

"But . . . we need him."

"I know, baby; it hurts." She stroked his hair back from his face.

Tears filled his eyes and seeing that made her own eyes sting, but she refused to cry in front of Ant.

"I want my daddy. I want my daddy . . ."

Elsa held her son close and let him cry. "I know, baby. I know . . ."

She couldn't think of anything else to say.

⨎

LOREDA CLIMBED UP THE windmill and sat on the platform beneath the giant blades, her knees drawn up. The wood was warm beneath her, heated by the sun.

How could Daddy do this? How could he leave his family on the farm without crops or water? How could he leave—

Me.

It hurt so much she couldn't breathe when she thought of it.

"Come back," she screamed.

The blue, sunlit Great Plains sky swallowed her feeble cry and left her there, alone, feeling small and lonely.

How could he abandon her when he knew how much she wanted to leave this farm? She was like him, not like Mom and Grandma and

Grandpa. Loreda didn't want to be a farmer; she wanted to go out into the great big world and become a writer and write something important. She wanted to leave Texas.

She felt the windmill rattle and thought, Great, now Mom was going to come up, looking all pathetic, and try to comfort Loreda. Mom was the very last person Loreda wanted to see now.

"Go away," Loreda said, wiping her eyes. "This is all your fault."

Mom sighed. She looked pale, almost fragile, but that was ridiculous. Mom was about as fragile as a yucca root.

Mom continued climbing up to the platform and sat down beside Loreda, in the place her daddy always sat, and it made Loreda suddenly furious. "You don't belong there," she said. "It's where . . ." Her voice broke.

Mom laid a hand on Loreda's thigh. "Honey—"

"No. *No.*" Loreda wrenched free. "I don't want to hear some lie about how it will be okay. Nothing will ever be okay again. You drove him away."

"I love your father, Loreda." Mom said it so quietly Loreda could barely hear it. She saw tears brighten her mother's eyes and thought, *I will not watch you cry.*

"He wouldn't leave me." The words felt ripped out of Loreda. She climbed down the windmill and ran, blinded by tears, back into the house, where Grandpa and Grandma sat on the settee, holding hands, looking like tornado survivors, stricken.

"Loreda," Grandma said. "Come back . . ."

Loreda barged up to her bedroom, and found Ant curled into a little ball on her bed, sucking his thumb.

The sight of him crying finally broke Loreda. She felt her own tears burn, fall.

"He left us?" Ant said. "Really?"

"Not us. Her. He's probably waiting for us somewhere."

Ant sat up. "Like an adventure?"

"Yes." Loreda wiped her eyes, thinking, *Of course.* "Like an adventure."

Elsa remained on the platform, staring out, seeing nothing. The thought of climbing down, walking back into the house, into her bedroom—her bed—was more than she could bear. So she stayed there, thinking of all the things she'd done wrong that had led to this moment and wondering what her life would be like now.

She felt a brush of wind lift her hair. She was so lost in her thicket of pain, she barely noticed.

I should go after Loreda.

But she couldn't face her daughter's fury and heartache. Not yet.

She should have told Rafe she'd go west. Everything would be different now if she'd simply said, *Sure, Rafe, we'll go.* He would have stayed. They could have convinced Tony and Rose to come with them.

No.

That was a lie she couldn't tell herself even now. And how could Elsa and Rafe have left them behind? How could they have gone west with no car and no money?

Wind yanked the kerchief off her head.

Elsa saw her kerchief sail out into the air. The platform shook; the blades overhead creaked and spun.

Storm coming.

Elsa climbed down from the shaking platform. As she stepped onto the ground, a gust swept up topsoil and lifted it upward in a great, howling scoop and blew it sideways. Sand hit Elsa's face like tiny bits of glass.

Rose ran out of the house, yelled to Elsa, "Storm! Coming fast!"

Elsa ran to her mother-in-law. "The kids?"

"Inside."

Holding hands, they ran back to the house, bolting the door shut behind them. Inside, the walls quaked. Dust rained down from the ceiling. A blast of wind struck hard, rattled everything.

Rose jammed more wads of cloth and old newspapers in the windowsills.

"Kids!" Elsa screamed.

Ant came running into the sitting room, looking scared. "Mommy!" He threw himself at her.

Elsa clung to him. "Put on your gas mask," she said.

"I don't wanna. I can't breathe with it," Ant whined.

"Put it on, Anthony. And go sit under the kitchen table. Where's your sister?"

"Huh?"

"Go get Loreda. Tell her to put on her gas mask."

"Uh. I can't."

"Can't? Why not?"

He looked miserable. "I promised not to tell."

She lowered herself to her knees to look at him. Dirt rained down on them. "Anthony, where is your sister?"

"She ran away."

"What?"

Ant nodded glumly. "I tol' her it was a dumb idea."

Elsa rushed to Loreda's bedroom, shoved the door open.

No Loreda.

She saw something white through the falling dust.

A note on the dresser.

I'm going to find him.

Elsa rushed downstairs, yelled, "Loreda ran away," to Rose and Tony. "I'm taking the truck. Is there gas left in the tank?"

"A little," Tony yelled. "But you can't go out in this."

"I have to."

Elsa fished the long-unused keys from the junk bucket in the kitchen and went back out into the blasting, gritty dust storm. She pulled her bandanna up around her mouth and nose and squinted to protect her eyes.

Wind swirled in front of her. Static electricity made her hair stand up. Out where the fence used to be, she saw blue fires flare up from the barbed wire.

Feeling her way in the dust storm, she found the line they'd strung between the house and the barn.

She pulled herself along the rough rope toward the barn, flung the doors open. Wind swept through, breaking slats away, terrifying the horses.

Bruno bolted out of his stall, through a broken slat, and stood in the aisle, nostrils quivering in fear, panicked. He snorted at Elsa and ran out into the storm.

Elsa pulled the cover off the truck; the wind yanked the canvas from her grasp and sent it flying like an open sail into the hayloft. Milo whinnied in terror from his stall.

Elsa climbed into the driver's seat and stabbed the key into the ignition, turned hard. The engine coughed reluctantly to life. *Please let there be enough gas to find her.*

She drove out of the barn and into the storm, her hands tight on the wheel as the wind tried to push her into the ditch. A chain tied to the axle rattled along behind her, grounding the truck so the vehicle wouldn't short out.

In front of her, brown dirt blew sideways, her two headlights spearing into the gloom. At the end of the driveway, she thought: *Which way?*

Town.

Loreda would never turn the other way. There was nothing for miles between here and the Oklahoma border.

Elsa muscled the truck into a turn. The wind was behind her now, pushing her forward. She leaned forward, trying to see. She couldn't drive more than ten miles an hour.

In town, they'd turned the streetlamps on in the storm. Windows had been boarded up and doors battened down. Dust and sand and dirt and tumbleweeds blew down the street.

Elsa saw Loreda at the train depot, huddled against the closed door, hanging on to a suitcase the storm was trying to yank out of her hand.

Elsa parked the truck and got out. Thin halos of golden light glowed at the streetlamps, pinpricks in the brown murk.

"Loreda!" she screamed, her voice thin and scratchy in the maw.

"Mom!"

Elsa leaned into the storm; it ripped her dress and scraped her cheeks and blinded her. She staggered up the depot steps and pulled Loreda into her arms, holding her so tightly that for a second there was no storm, no wind clawing or sand biting, just them.

Thank you, God.

"We need to get into the depot," she said.

"The door's locked."

A window exploded beside them. Elsa let go of Loreda and clawed her way to the broken window, climbed over the glass teeth in the sill, felt sharp points jab her skin.

Once inside, she unlocked the front door and pulled Loreda inside and slammed the door shut.

The depot rattled around them; another window cracked. Elsa went to the water fountain and scooped up some lukewarm water and carried it back to Loreda, who drank greedily.

Elsa slumped down beside her daughter. Her eyes stung so badly she could hardly see.

"I'm sorry, Loreda."

"He wanted to go west, didn't he?" Loreda said.

The walls of the depot clattered and shook; the world felt as if it were falling apart.

"Yes."

"Why didn't you just say yes?"

Elsa sighed. "Your brother has no shoes. There's no money for gas. There's no money for anything. Your grandparents won't leave. All I saw were reasons not to go."

"I got here, and I didn't know where to go. He didn't want me to know."

"I know."

Elsa touched her daughter's back.

Loreda yanked sideways and scuttled away from the touch.

Elsa brought her hand back and sat there, knowing there was nothing she could say to fix this breach with her daughter. Rafe had abandoned them both, walked out on his children and his responsibilities, and it was *still* Elsa whom Loreda blamed.

THAT NIGHT, AFTER THE storm quieted, Elsa drove back to the farmhouse with Loreda. Somehow, Elsa found the strength to get herself and the children fed, and finally she tucked them into bed. All without crying in front of anyone. It felt like a major triumph. In the hours after Rafe's abandonment, Rose's pain had turned to seething anger that showed itself in outbursts in Italian. Loreda's despair had left her mute during their evening meal, and Ant's confusion was painful to see. Tony made eye contact with no one.

It occurred to Elsa as she walked into her bedroom—finally—that she hadn't spoken in a long time, hadn't bothered to even respond when spoken to. The pain of him leaving kept expanding inside of her, taking up more and more space.

There was no wind outside now, no forces of nature trying to break down the walls. Only silence. An occasional coyote howl, an every-now-and-then scurrying of some insect across their floor, but nothing else.

Elsa walked to the chest of drawers beneath the window. She opened Rafe's drawer to look at the only shirt he'd left behind. All she had of him now.

She picked it up, a pale blue chambray with brass snaps. She'd made it for him one Christmas. There was still a small brownish-red mark of her blood on one cuff, where she'd poked herself in the sewing.

She wrapped the shirt around her neck as if it were a scarf and walked aimlessly out into the starlit night, going nowhere. Maybe she would start walking and never stop . . . or never take this scarf off until one day, when she was old and gray, some child would ask about the crazy woman who wore a shirt for a scarf and she would say she couldn't recall how it had begun or whose shirt it was.

As she neared the mailbox, she saw Bruno, their gelding, dead, caught in the dried branches of the fallen trees, dirt caked in his open mouth. Tomorrow, they would have to dig into the hard, dry earth to bury him. Another terrible chore, another goodbye.

With a sigh, she walked back to the house, got into bed. The mattress felt too large for her alone, even if she spread her arms and legs wide. She folded her arms over her chest as if she were a corpse being washed and readied for burial, and stared up at the dusty ceiling.

All those years, all those prayers, all her hope that at last, someday, she would be loved, that her husband would turn to her and see her and love what he saw . . . gone.

Her parents had been right about her all along.

ELEVEN

Loreda knew she couldn't blame her mother for Daddy abandoning them, or not entirely. That was the sad, sorry truth she'd come to after a long and sleepless night.

Daddy had left them all. Once she'd seen that fact, she couldn't unsee it. Daddy had filled Loreda's head with dreams and told her he loved her, but in the end, he'd left her and walked away.

It made her feel hopeless for the first time in her life.

When she got up the next morning and saw the blue sky outside her window, she dressed in the same dirty clothes she'd run away in and didn't bother to brush her hair or teeth. What was the point? She was never going to get off this farm and if she didn't, who cared what she looked like?

She found Grandma Rose in the kitchen, with a breakfast of creamed wheat cereal bubbling on the stove. Grandma looked . . . clenched. There was no other word for it. She kept talking to herself in Italian, a language she refused to teach her grandchildren because she wanted them to be Americans.

Ant shuffled into the kitchen, kicking through the inch of dirt that covered the floor, and Loreda pulled out a chair for him at the oilcloth-draped table, where the bowls sat upside down at their places, covered in more dirt.

Loreda turned the bowls over and wiped them out, then sat down beside her brother, whose hunched shoulders made him look even younger as he ate cereal so tasteless that even cream and butter couldn't make it palatable.

Grandpa walked into the kitchen, buckling his tattered, patched overalls. "Coffee smells good, Rose." He tousled Ant's dirty hair.

Ant started to cry. It ended in a hacking cough. Loreda reached out to hold his hand. She felt like crying, too.

"How could he leave them?" Grandpa said to Grandma, who looked stricken.

"*Silenzio,*" she hissed. "What good are words?"

Grandpa released a heavy breath; the exhalation ended in a cough. He pressed a hand to his chest, as if the dirt from yesterday's storm had collected there.

Grandma Rose reached for the broom and dustpan. Loreda groaned out loud. They'd spend a whole day digging out from yesterday's storm—beating rugs, scooping dirt from windowsills, washing everything in the cupboards and putting it away again, upside down. And still more sweeping.

There was a knock at the front door.

"Daddy!" Loreda yelled, leaping to her feet.

She ran for the door, jerked it open.

The man standing there was dressed in rags, his face filthy.

He yanked off his tattered newsboy cap, curled it in his dirty hands. *Hungry.* Like all the hobos who stopped by here on their way "there."

This was what her daddy wanted? To be starving and alone, knocking on some stranger's door for food? *That* was better than staying?

Grandma moved in beside Loreda.

"I'm hungry, ma'am. If you've got any vittles to share, I'd be much obliged." The hobo's shirt was so discolored by dirt and sweat that it was impossible to determine its original color. Blue, maybe. Or gray. He wore dungarees with a belt he'd cinched tight at his waist. "I'd be happy to do some chores."

"We have cereal," Grandpa said. "And the porch could use sweeping."

They were used to hobos stopping by at mealtime, begging for food or offering work for a slice of bread. In times this hard, folks did what they could for those less fortunate. Most hobos did a chore or two and then headed off again. One of the tramps had drawn a symbol on their barn. A message to other wanderers. Supposedly it meant, *Stop here. Good folks.*

Grandpa studied the vagrant. "Where are you from, son?"

"Arkansas, sir."

"And how old are you?"

"Twenty-two, sir."

"How long you been on the road?"

"Long enough to get where I was a-goin', if'n I knew where that was."

"What makes a man just up and leave? Can you tell me that?" Grandpa asked.

They all looked at the hobo, who seemed to wrestle with the question. "Well, sir. I reckon you leave when you just can't stand your life where it is."

"And what about the family you left behind?" Grandma asked sharply. "Doesn't a man care what happens to his wife and kids?"

"If he did, he'd stay, I reckon," the hobo said.

"That ain't true," Loreda said.

"Let's get you that cereal, shall we?" Grandma said. "No use talking the day away."

⅔

"Loreda." Ant tugged on Loreda's sleeve. "Sumpin's wrong with Mommy."

Loreda pushed the tangled hair out of her eyes and leaned on the broom. She'd been sweeping long enough and hard enough to work up a sweat. "What do you mean?"

"She won't wake up."

"That's silly. Grandma said to let her sleep."

Ant's shoulders slumped. "I knew you wouldn't believe me."

"Fine."

Loreda followed Ant into their parents' bedroom. The small room was usually as neat as a pin, but now there was dirt everywhere, even on the bed. It was a sharp reminder that Dad had abandoned them; Mom hadn't even bothered to sweep before going to bed. And Mom was crazy about clean. "Mom?"

Mom lay in the double bed, her body positioned as far to the right as she could go, so that there was a big blank space to her left. She wore a dirty kerchief and a nightdress so old the cotton showed her skin in places. A blue chambray work shirt—Daddy's—lay coiled around her neck. Her face was almost as pale as the sheet, with her sharp cheekbones standing out above sunken cheeks.

Mom was always pale. Even out in the summer sun, she burned and peeled. She never tanned. But this . . .

She pushed Mom's shoulder gently. "Wake up, Mom."

Nothing.

"Go get Grandma. She's milking Bella," Loreda said to Ant.

Loreda poked her mom's arm, this time not gently. "Wake up, Mom. This isn't funny."

Loreda stared down at the woman who had always seemed indomitable, unyielding, humorless. Now she saw how delicate her mother was, how thin and pale. Lying in bed, wearing Daddy's shirt as a scarf, she looked fragile.

It was scary.

"Wake up, Mom. Come on."

Grandma walked into the room, carrying an empty metal bucket. "What's wrong?" Ant was right behind her, staying close.

"Mom won't wake up."

Grandma put down the metal bucket and lifted the cement-sack towel that covered the cracked porcelain pitcher on the nightstand. Silt-fine dust sifted to the floor. She dipped a washrag into water and wrung the excess into the basin, then placed the washrag on Mom's forehead. "She isn't feverish," Grandma said. Then: "Elsa?"

Mom didn't respond.

Grandma dragged a chair into the room and sat down by the bed. For a long time, she said nothing, just sat there. Then, finally, she sighed. "He left us, too, Elsa. It is not only you. He left all the people he said he loved. I'll never forgive him for that."

"Don't say that!" Loreda said.

"*Silenzio*," Grandma said. "A woman can die of a broken heart. Do not make it worse."

"It's her fault he left. She wouldn't go to California."

"In your vast experience with men and love, you decide this. Thank you for your genius, Loreda. I'm sure it's a comfort to your mama."

Grandma dabbed the cool wet washcloth on Mom's forehead. "I know how much it hurts right now, Elsa. You can't unlove someone even if you want to, even if he breaks your heart. I understand not wanting to wake up. Lord, with this life of ours, who could blame you. But your daughter needs you, especially now. She is as foolish as her father. Ant worries me, too." Grandma leaned closer, whispered, "Remember the first time you held Loreda and we both cried? Remember your son's laugh and how he squeezes so hard when he hugs you. Your children, Elsa. Remember Loreda . . . Anthony . . ."

Mom drew in a sharp, ragged breath, and sat up sharply, as if she'd been thrown ashore, and Grandma steadied her, took her in her arms and held her.

Loreda had never heard sobbing like this. She thought Mom might simply break in half at the force of her crying. When she was finally able to breathe without sobbing, Mom drew back, looking ravaged. There was no other word for it.

"Loreda, Ant, please leave us," Grandma said.

"What's wrong with her?" Loreda asked.

"Passion has a dark edge. If your father had ever grown up, he would have told you this instead of filling your head with fluff."

"Passion? What does that have to do with anything?"

"She's too young to understand, Rose," Elsa said.

Loreda hated to be told she was too young for anything. "I am not. Passion is good. Great. I *long* for it."

Grandma waved a hand impatiently. "Passion is a thunderstorm, there and gone. It nourishes, *sì*, but it drowns, too. Our land will save and protect you. This is something your father never learned. Be smarter than your selfish, foolish father, *cara*. Marry a man of the land, one who is reliable and true. One who will keep you steady."

Marriage again. Her grandmother's answer to every question. As if marrying well meant a good life. "How about if I just get a dog? It sounds about as exciting as the life you want for me."

"My son has spoiled you, Loreda, let you read too many romantic books. It will be the ruin of you."

"Reading? I doubt it."

"Out," Grandma said, pointing to the door. "Now."

"I don't want to be here anyway," Loreda said. "Come on, Ant."

"Good," Grandma said. "It's laundry day. Go get us water."

Loreda should have left five minutes ago.

❧

"HE NEVER LOVED ME," Elsa said. "Why would he?"

"Ah, *cara* . . ." Rose scooted closer, reached out to place her rough, work-reddened hand on Elsa's. "You know I lost three daughters.

Three. Two who never breathed in this world and one who did. But never did we really speak of it." Rose drew in a deep breath, exhaled it. "Each one I allowed myself to mourn briefly. I made myself believe in God's plan for me. I went to church and lit candles and prayed. I was never in my life as afraid as when I carried Raffaello in my womb. He was so *busy* in there. I found I couldn't think of him as anything but healthy and I grew afraid of my hope. If I saw a black cat, I would burst into tears. Spilled olive oil could send me rushing to church to combat bad luck. I didn't knit a single pair of booties or make a blanket or sew a christening gown. What I did do, it seems, was imagine him. He became real to me in a way the girls had not. When he finally was born—so hearty and hale and too beautiful to bear—I knew that God had forgiven me for whatever sin I'd committed that cost me my daughters. I loved him so much, I . . . couldn't discipline him, couldn't deny him. Tony told me I was spoiling him, but I thought, how could it hurt? He was a shooting star and he blinded me with his light. I . . . wanted so much for him. I wanted him to know love and prosperity and to be an American."

"And I came along."

Rose was still for a moment. "I remember every bit of that day. He was packed to go to college. *College.* A Martinelli. I was so proud, I'd told everyone."

"And then, me."

"Skinny as a willow switch, you were. Hair that needed tending. You looked like a young woman who didn't know how to smile. And you were too old for him, I thought."

"I was all those things."

"It took me months to see that you were a woman more capable of love and commitment than anyone I've ever known. You were the best thing that ever happened to my son. He's a fool to have missed that."

"It is a kind thing for you to say."

"But you can't believe it." Rose sighed. "What damage I did to

Raffaello by loving him too much, I fear your parents did to you by loving you too little."

"They tried to love me. Just as Rafe did."

"Did they?" Rose said.

"I was a sickly child. I had a fever as a teenager and it left me weakened. They told my parents that I would die young and that I have a damaged heart."

"And you believed them."

"Of course."

"Elsa, I don't know about your youth or your illness or what your parents said or did. But I know this. You have the heart of a lion. Don't believe anyone who tells you different. I've seen it. My son is a fool."

"The last thing he said to me before he left was, 'Remember me then.' I thought he was being romantic."

"I imagine it will hurt us all for a long time, but Loreda and Ant need you. Loreda needs to learn that it is this land that will save her, not her silly father."

"I want her to go to college, Rose. To be brave and have adventures."

"A girl?" Rose laughed. "Ant will be the one. Loreda will settle down. You'll see."

"I don't know if I want her to settle down, Rose. I'm in awe of her fire. Even if I'm the one who gets burned. I just . . . want her to be happy. It breaks my heart to see her as unhappy as her father was."

"You blame yourself when they are the ones to blame." Rose gave her a steady, reassuring look. "Remember, *cara,* hard times don't last. Land and family do."

TWELVE

In November, the first winter storm battered them from the north, leaving behind a fine layer of snow. Clean, glistening, and white, it dusted the windmill's rough blades, the chicken coop, the cows' hides, and the land itself.

Snow was a good sign. It meant water. Water meant crops. Crops meant food on the table.

On this particularly frigid day, Elsa stood at the kitchen table, rolling meatballs in hands that were pink and swollen and pocked with blisters. Chilblains were common this season and everyone in the house—in the county—had raw, burning throats and gritty, bloodshot eyes that itched from too many dust storms.

She placed the garlic-seasoned pork meatballs on a baking sheet and covered them with a towel, then went into the sitting room, where Rose sat by the stove darning socks.

Tony came into the house, stomped the snow from his boots, and slammed the door behind him. He made a chapel of his gloved hands and blew into them. His cheeks were red and roughened by cold, scoured by wind. His hair stuck out in frozen shards. "The windmill isn't pumping," he said. "Must be the cold." He walked over to the woodstove. Beside it, a barrel held their dwindling supply of cow chips. In these dust and drought years, the animals on the Great Plains were dying, and so this treeless land was losing the fuel source that the farmers had assumed would last forever. He fed a few into the fire. "There are still a few broken slats in the hog pen. I'd best go chop 'em up. We're going to need a roaring fire tonight."

"I'll go," Elsa said.

She retrieved her winter coat and gloves from the hook by the door and stepped out into the frosted world. Glittery, frozen tumbleweeds cartwheeled across the yard, breaking pieces off at every rotation.

She grabbed an ax from the wooden box.

Carrying it out to the empty hog pen, she surveyed the remaining slats and picked her spot, then lifted the ax, brought it down, and felt the *thunk* of metal on wood reverberate up through her shoulder, heard the *craaack* of the wood breaking.

It took her less than half an hour to destroy what was left of the hog pen and turn it into firewood.

⤳

THE SKY WAS SO gray it could smother a soul.

Elsa sat with Ant in the back of the wagon, bundled up in quilts. Loreda sat by herself, wrapped in blankets, her cheeks pink and chapped from the unseasonable cold. She had become increasingly silent and distant since Rafe had left. Elsa was surprised to realize that she preferred her daughter's loud anger to this quiet depression. Rose and Tony sat up front, with Tony handling the reins. All of them were dressed in what tattered clothes could be called their Sunday best.

Lonesome Tree was quiet on this late-November day. Quiet in the way of a dying town. Snow covered everything.

The Catholic church looked lonely. Half of the roof had been torn away last month, and the spire had been broken. One more good wind and it would be gone.

Tony parked the wagon out front, tied the horse to the hitching post. He hauled a bucket over to the pump, filled it, and left it for Milo.

Elsa tugged a felt cloche down over her braided hair and gathered her children close. Together, they climbed the creaking steps and walked into the church. Several broken windows had been repaired with plywood, making the altar dark.

In good years there hadn't been many Catholics in town, and these were far from good years. Every Sunday fewer came. The Irish Catholics had their own church, over in Dalhart, and the Mexicans worshipped in churches that had been built hundreds of years ago. But they were all losing members. Every church in the county was. More and more postcards and letters had begun to land in mailboxes in the Great Plains, containing notes from people in California and Oregon and Washington who had found jobs and were encouraging their kin to follow.

Elsa heard people coming in behind them. Unlike the old days, there was no gathering of women to gossip about recipes and no clot of men arguing about the weather. Even the children were quiet. The sound of hacking coughs rose above the squeaking of wooden pews.

In time, Father Michael stood before the altar and looked out at his much-diminished flock.

"We are being tested." He looked as tired as Elsa felt. As tired as they all felt. "Let us pray this snow means rain to come. Crops to come."

"God's no help," Loreda grumbled.

Rose elbowed Loreda hard.

"Tested does not mean forgotten," Father Michael said, peering through his small round glasses at Loreda. "Let us pray."

Elsa bowed her head. *God help us,* she thought but wasn't certain it was exactly a prayer. More of a desperate plea.

They prayed and sang and prayed some more and then filed up for Communion.

When it was over, they looked at their remaining friends and neighbors. No one made eye contact for long. Each was remembering the food and fellowship that used to grace their Sundays.

Outside, the Carrio family stood by the frosted water pump.

Mr. Carrio broke free of his family and strode toward them, his face shuttered tightly. No one wanted to show too much emotion these days, afraid a little could become too much in an instant.

"Tony," he said, pushing the hair back from his cold-reddened face. He was a shriveled, sinewy man, with a bulwark of a jaw and a thin nose.

Papa removed his hat, shook his friend's hand. "Where are the Cirillos?"

"Ray got a letter from his sister in Los Angeles," he said in a thick Italian accent. "Seems she's heeled. Got herself a good job. Him and Andrea and the kids are fixin' to head out that way, too. Says there ain't no reason to stay."

A silence followed.

"Wish we'd left already," Mr. Carrio said. "No money for gas now. You heard from your boy? He found work?"

"Not yet," Tony said tightly. None of them had told anyone the truth of Rafe's desertion. The idea of his betrayal and weakness becoming public was more than they could bear.

"Too bad," Mr. Carrio said. "Seems you're stuck."

"I'd never leave my land," Tony said.

Mr. Carrio's face darkened. "Ain't you figured it out, Tony? This land don't want us here. And it's gonna get worse."

❧

EVERY DAY OF THAT long, unseasonably cold winter, Elsa woke with a single purpose: keep her children fed. Each day their survival felt less certain. She woke in the dark, alone, and dressed without the benefit of light. Lord knew nothing good came of looking in a mirror anyway.

Her lips were always chapped with cold and swollen from her habit of biting down when she worried. And she was always worried. About the cold, about the crops, about her children's health. That was the worst of it. School had closed last week for good—it had fallen to twenty degrees in the schoolhouse. With the supply of cow chips disappearing, heating the school had become a luxury none of them could afford. So now Elsa had added schooling to her list of chores. For a woman who hadn't graduated from high school, being responsible for her children's education was a daunting ordeal, but she did it with zeal. If there was one thing she wanted above all else, it was for her children to have the opportunities that came with education.

It wasn't until nighttime, after prayers with her children, when she collapsed into her lonely bed, that she let herself think of Rafe, miss him, ache for him. She thought of how kind he'd always been and she wondered now if he would miss her, even some small bit. They had history together, after all, and she couldn't help loving him still. In spite of everything, all the pain and heartbreak and anger he'd left in his wake, when she closed her eyes at night, she missed him beside her, missed the sound of his breathing and the hope she'd felt that one day he would really love her. She'd think, *I wish I'd said, "I'll go to California,"* over and over until a fitful sleep came to save her.

Thank God for this farm and her children, because some days she still wanted to crawl in a hole and cry. Or maybe become one of those crazy women who wore pajamas and slippers all day and stood at a window awaiting the man who'd left. For the first time in her life, she understood the physical pain of betrayal. She would do almost anything to hide from it. Run. Drink. Take laudanum . . .

But she wasn't an *I*. She was a *we*. Her two beautiful children were counting on her, even if Loreda didn't know it yet.

On this cold late-December day, she woke late and dressed in every piece of clothing she owned, covering her stringy hair with both a red bandanna and the woolen hat Rose had knit her for Christmas.

She coiled Rafe's shirt around her throat like a scarf and went into the kitchen and put wheat cereal on to boil.

Today, *finally*, they were going to get help from the government. It was big news in town. Last Sunday at church, no one had been able to talk about anything else.

She slipped into her winter boots and walked outside, shivering instantly. She tossed handfuls of grain at the chickens and checked their water. The well had been troublesome during this freezing winter, only working sporadically. Thank God when it froze they could gather snow to keep the animals and themselves in water. She saw Tony chopping wood by the side of the house—barn boards being ripped down and cut into kindling.

She waved as she headed to the barn. At the corral, she snapped a lead rope onto Milo's halter.

The poor starving animal gave her such a sorrowful look that it gave her pause. "I know, boy. We all feel that way."

She led the bony gelding out into the bright blue day. She had just finished hitching him to the wagon when Tony appeared beside her.

She saw how red his cheeks were from the cold, saw the plumes of his breath and the weight loss that had sunken his face and eyes. For a man who had two religions—God and the land—he was dying a little each day, disappointed by them both. He spent long minutes throughout the day staring at his snow-covered winter-wheat fields, begging his God to let the wheat grow. "This meeting will be the answer," she said.

"I hope so," he said.

The season of cold had been hard on Loreda, too. She'd lost her father and her best friend and now school had closed. The dwindling of her world left her sullen and depressed.

Elsa heard the farmhouse door bang open. Footsteps clattered on the porch steps. Loreda and Ant shuffled toward the wagon, bundled up in anything that still fit. Rose came out behind them, carrying a box full of the goods they'd be selling in town.

Elsa and the children climbed into the back of the wagon with the box of goods to be sold.

Elsa wrapped Ant up in a quilt and held him close. Loreda would rather freeze than join them, so she sat across from them, shivering.

Tony snapped the reins and Milo plodded forward. In the wagon bed, soap clattered in the slatted box. Elsa kept one gloved hand on the stack of eggs to keep them from falling. "You know, Loreda, if you joined us just to get warm, I promise I would still know that you are angry."

"Very funny." Loreda crossed her arms; her teeth chattered.

"You're turning blue," Elsa said.

"No, I'm not."

"Sorta red, though," Ant said, grinning.

"Don't look at me," Loreda said.

"You're directly across from us," Elsa said.

Loreda pointedly looked away.

Ant giggled.

Loreda rolled her eyes.

Elsa turned her attention to the land.

Snow-covered, this landscape looked beautiful. There weren't many dwellings between town and the Martinelli farm, but several of the places along the way were abandoned. Cabins and shacks and dugouts and homes with boarded-up windows and FOR SALE signs plastered over foreclosure notices.

They passed the abandoned Mull place. Last she heard, Tom and Lorri had followed their kin to California on foot. *On foot.* How could anyone be that desperate? And Tom had been a lawyer by trade. It wasn't just farmers going broke these days.

So many were leaving.

Let's go to California.

Elsa pushed the thought away with force, although she knew it would come back to haunt her in the dark.

In town, Tony parked the wagon and tied Milo to a hitching post. Elsa retrieved the wooden box full of eggs and butter and soap and hefted it into her arms. On the few still-open storefronts, placards announced the arrival today of Hugh Bennett, a scientist from President Roosevelt's new Civilian Conservation Corps. In an attempt to put Americans back to work, FDR had created dozens of agencies, put folks to work documenting the Depression in words and photographs and in sweat labor, building bridges and fixing roads. Bennett had come all the way from Washington, D.C., to finally help the farmers.

Inside the mercantile, Elsa was struck by the empty shelves. Even so, there was a tantalizing collection of colors and aromas. Coffee, perfumes that hadn't been purchased in years, a box of apples. Here and there on the barren shelves were utensils and dress patterns and shade hats and bags of rice and sugar and tinned meat and canned milk. Stacks of gingham and polka-dot and striped fabric lay gathering dust, as did the stacks of eyelets and lace. Grain sacks had become the only fabric used for clothing.

She went up to the main counter, where Mr. Pavlov stood, wearing a weary smile and a white shirt that had seen better days. Once one of the richest men in town, he was now hanging on to his store by his fingernails, and everyone knew it. His family had moved in above the store when the bank foreclosed on his house.

"Martinellis," he said. "You in town for the meeting?"

Elsa set the box of goods on the counter.

"We are," Tony said. "You?"

"I'll walk over. I sure hope the government can help folks around here. I hate to see people give up and leave."

Tony nodded. "Most are staying, though."

"Farmers are tough."

"We've worked too hard and made too many sacrifices to walk away. Droughts end."

Mr. Pavlov nodded and glanced at the box Elsa had laid on the counter. "Chickens still laying. Good for you."

"That's Elsa's soap, too," Rose said. "Scented with lavender. Your missus loves it."

The children came up to stand beside Elsa. She couldn't help remembering how they'd once run around in here, oohing and aahing over candies, begging for treats.

Mr. Pavlov pushed the rimless glasses higher up on his nose. "What do you need?"

"Coffee. Sugar. Rice. Beans. Maybe some yeast? A tin of that nice olive oil, if you have it."

Mr. Pavlov did calculations in his head. When he was satisfied, he yanked on the basket that hung from a length of rope beside him. He grabbed a piece of paper, wrote on it: *Sugar. Coffee. Beans. Rice.* Then said, "No olive oil in stock and no charge for yeast," and put the list in the basket and pulled a lever that lifted to the second floor of the store, where his wife and daughter did the receipts.

Moments later, a heavyset girl came out from the back room hauling a sack of sugar, some coffee, a bag of rice, and another of beans.

Ant stared at the jar of licorice whips on the counter.

Elsa touched her son's head.

"Licorice is on special today," Mr. Pavlov said. "Two whips for the price of one. I could put it on a tab."

"You know I don't believe in handouts," Tony said. "And I don't know when we could pay."

"I know," Mr. Pavlov said. "My treat. Take two."

His kindness was the sort of thing that made life bearable out here. "Thank you, Mr. Pavlov," Elsa said.

Tony stowed the new goods in the back of the wagon and covered them with a tarp. Leaving Milo tied to the hitching post, they walked along the icy boardwalk toward the boarded-up schoolhouse, where several other horse-and-wagon teams waited outside.

"Ain't many folks here," Tony said.

Rose reached for his hand. "I heard Emmett got a postcard from his kin in Washington State. Railroad jobs there."

"They'll be sorry," Tony said. "Those jobs are a pipe dream. Gotta be. Millions are out of work. Let's say you do run off to Portland or Seattle and there ain't work. Then where will you be—in a strange place with no land and no job."

Elsa held Ant's hand. Together they climbed the steps up to the schoolhouse. Inside, the children's desks had been pushed out of the way, positioned along the walls. Plywood covered several of the broken windows. Someone had set up a row of chairs facing a portable movie screen.

"Oh, *boy*," Ant called out. "A movie!"

Tony led the family to a row in the back, where they sat with the other Italians who were left in town.

A few more folks filed in, no one saying much. A couple of the older folks coughed constantly, a reminder of the dust storms that had ravaged the land this fall.

The door banged shut and the lights went out.

There was a whir and clatter of sound; a black-and-white image appeared on the white screen: it was a howling windstorm blowing through a farm. Tumbleweeds cartwheeled past a boarded-up house.

The caption read: *30% of all the farmers on the Great Plains face foreclosure.*

The next image was of a Red Cross hospital, beds full, gray-uniformed nurses tending to coughing babies and old people. *Dust pneumonia takes a terrible toll.*

In the next image, farmers poured milk into the streets, where it disappeared instantly in the arid dirt.

Milk sells for below production costs . . .

Haggard, ragged men, women, and children drifted across a gray screen, looking ghostlike. A Hooverville encampment. Thousands living in cardboard boxes or broken-down cars or shacks cobbled together from cans and sheet metal. Folks standing in soup lines . . .

The movie snapped off. The lights came back on.

Elsa heard footsteps, boot heels clacking confidently on the hardwood floor. Like everyone else, Elsa turned.

Here was a man with presence, dressed better than anyone in town. He moved the makeshift movie screen out of the way, stepped over to the blackboard, picked up a piece of chalk, wrote *Farming methods,* and underlined the words.

He turned to face the crowd. "I'm Hugh Bennett. The President of the United States has appointed me to his new Conservation Corps. I've spent months touring the farmland of the Great Plains. Oklahoma, Kansas, Texas. I got to say, folks, this summer it was as dire in Lonesome Tree as anywhere I've seen. And who knows how long the drought will go on? I hear only a few of you even bothered to plant a crop this year."

"Don't you reckon we know it?" someone yelled, coughing.

"You know there's been no rain, friend. I'm here to tell you it's more than that. What's happening to your land is a dire ecological disaster, maybe the worst in our country's history, and you have to change your farming methods to stop it from getting worse."

"You sayin' it's our fault?" Tony said.

"I'm saying you contributed," Bennett said. "Oklahoma has lost almost four hundred and fifty million tons of topsoil. Truth is that you farmers have to see your part in it or this great land will die."

The Carrington family got up and walked out, slamming the door behind them. The Renke family followed.

"So, what do we do?" Tony asked.

"The way y'all farm the land is destroying it. You dug up the grasses which held the topsoil in place. The plow broke the prairie. When the rain died and the wind came up, there was nothing to stop your land from blowing away. This here is a man-made disaster, so we got to fix it. We need the grasses back. We need soil-conservation methods in place."

"It's the weather and the damn greedy banksters on Wall Street, closing their banks, taking our money, that's what's ruining us," Mr. Carrio said.

"FDR wants to pay y'all *not* to plant next year. We've got a conservation plan. You've got to rest some of this land, plant grass. But it isn't enough for one or two of you to do it. Y'all have to do it. You have to protect the Great Plains, not just your own acreage."

"That's it?" Mr. Pavlov said, standing up in a huff. "You're telling 'em not to plant next year? Grow grass? Why don't you just light a match on what's left? The farmers need *help*."

"FDR cares about the farmers. He knows you've been forgotten. He has a plan. To start with, the government will buy your livestock for sixteen bucks a head. If possible, we'll use your cattle to feed the poor. If not, if they're full of dirt, which I've seen out here, we'll pay you and bury them."

"That's it?" Tony said. "You brung us all the way down here to tell us the disaster is our fault, we need to plant grass, which ain't a crop that makes money, in land too dry to grow anything, in a drought—seeds we can't afford—and oh, yeah, kill your last living farm animal for sixteen lousy bucks."

"There's a plan for relief. We want to pay you not to grow crops. Might even get the banks to forgive mortgage payments."

"We don't want charity," someone called out. "We want *help*. We want water. What good is keeping our houses if the land is useless?"

"We're *farmers*. We want to plant our crops. We want to take care of ourselves."

"Enough," Tony said. He shoved his seat back and stood up. "Come on. We're leaving."

When Elsa glanced back, she saw the disappointment on Bennett's face as more families followed the Martinellis out of the schoolhouse.

THIRTEEN

Elsa stood in the falling snow. The sounds of the world were muffled by the airy flakes. Such a pretty, sparkling layer of white; she marveled that she could still find beauty in nature. As she headed down into the root cellar, she heard Bella's low, mournful moan. The poor cow was as hungry and thirsty as the rest of them. Shivering with cold, Elsa stared at the empty shelves. There should be boxes of onions and potatoes, mason jars full of fruits and vegetables; instead there were bare shelves.

And now . . . this news from the government expert.

Elsa had thought of the plains pioneers, people like Tony and Rose, as indomitable, invincible. People who had come to this vast, unknown country with nothing but a dream and who had tamed the land with grit and determination and hard work.

But apparently they'd misjudged the land. Or, worse, misused it.

She thought about their daily chores, done this week in a bitter, skin-biting cold, and tonight there would only be a slice of bread, a few of last season's soft potatoes, and a bit of smoked ham for supper. Not enough to fill any of their bellies. And then it would be time for bed and they would each go their own way, into their own black, frigid rooms, unwilling to waste precious fuel or money for anything as fanciful as light, and they would crawl into beds that always felt gritty no matter how often they changed the sheets, and try to fall asleep.

Now she took three shriveled potatoes from the box, trying not to notice how few were left, and walked back out into the falling snow.

"Mom?"

Elsa turned.

Loreda wore layers of ill-fitting clothes, and two pair of knee socks, which no doubt increased the discomfort of wearing outgrown shoes. In the past few months, Loreda had let her bob grow out and so her hair was almost to her shoulders. An uneven fringe of bangs hung past her nose and continually covered her eyes. She said it didn't matter what she looked like anymore because she had no friends.

Even so, her beauty was remarkable. No bad haircut or cheap frock could dim it. She had inherited her father's olive complexion and elegant bone structure and luxurious black hair. And those eyes, like Elsa's and yet more intensely blue. Almost violet. Someday men would see her across a crowded street and stop in their tracks.

Loreda's cheeks were bright pink; melted snowflakes glistened on her dark lashes and full lips. "I want to talk to you."

"Okay."

Loreda led the way up to the porch and sat down on the swing.

Elsa sat down beside her.

"I've been thinking," Loreda said.

"Oh, no," Elsa said quietly.

"I've been a crumb to you since Daddy . . . you know, made tracks."

Elsa was shocked by the acknowledgment. All she could think of to say was, "I know how much he hurt you."

"He isn't coming back, is he?

Elsa longed to touch her daughter's hair, brush it back from her forehead in the kind of intimate touch that had been possible years ago, back when Loreda's body had felt like an extension of her own and Elsa had thought that her daughter's bold heart must surely strengthen Elsa's weaker one. "I don't think so. No."

"I gave him the idea."

"Oh, honey. Don't take responsibility for his actions. He's a grown man. He did what he wanted to do."

Loreda was silent for a long time before she said, "That man from the government, he says this land is ruined."

"That's his opinion, I guess."

"It isn't a hard thing to believe."

"No."

"I should get a job," Loreda said. "Make some money . . . to help out."

"I'm proud of you for that, Loreda, but half of the country is out of work. There are no jobs. We are the lucky ones, on the farms. We still have food."

"We are not lucky," Loreda said.

"In the spring, when it rains—"

"We need to leave."

"Loreda, honey, I'd do anything for you—"

"But not this." Loreda stood up abruptly. "Not leave. You're saying no to me, just like you said no to Daddy."

Elsa released a heavy sigh and stood. "I'll say to you what I should have had the courage to say to your father: I love this land. I love this family. This is *home*. I want you to grow up here, knowing that this is your place, your future."

"But it's dying, Mom. And it will kill us where we stand."

"How do you know it's better in California? And don't give me that land-of-milk-and-honey nonsense. You saw the newsreel the other day. Half the country is out of work. Soup kitchens can't keep up with the demand. At least here we have some food and water and a roof over our heads. I can hardly get a railroad job as a single mother. And your grandparents . . ."

"They'll never leave," Loreda said.

Elsa unwrapped Rafe's shirt from around her throat. "I'd like you to have this. It's rather old and tattered, but it was made with love."

Loreda took Rafe's shirt carefully, as if it were made of spun dreams, and wrapped it around her neck. "I can still smell his hair pomade."

"Yes."

Tears brightened Loreda's eyes.

"I'm sorry, Loreda," Elsa said.

Loreda sighed heavily, touching the chambray at her neck as if it held magical powers. "We are going to be even sorrier. You watch."

꩜

AT LAST, THE LONG winter ended.

In the first week of March, the sun became a bright and shining friend that lifted their spirits and renewed their hope. One blue-sky day followed the other.

Today, as Elsa stood at the kitchen table, making a batch of creamy ricotta cheese, she thought, *Just a little rain,* and once again she could believe in it. Salvation. She could imagine a different view from here: Wheat growing tall. A field of gold that stretched to the horizon beneath an endless blue sky.

Rose drifted into the kitchen, pinning her kerchief in place. "Ricotta? What a treat."

"It's not every day a girl turns thirteen. I thought I'd splurge. I can feel the rain coming, can't you?"

Rose nodded, re-coiling her hair at the back of her neck.

Elsa brought a pot of coffee into the sitting room, along with an apronful of cups. One by one, she poured the rich, steaming brew into the speckled tin cups.

"Aw, Els, you're a godsend," Tony said, taking a sip.

Elsa smiled. "It's just coffee."

Tony reached for his fiddle and began to play.

Ant jumped up and said, "Dance with me, Lolo."

Loreda rolled her eyes—so put out—and then leapt to her feet and started doing a crazy version of the Charleston that was completely out of step with the music.

Everyone laughed.

Elsa couldn't remember the last time this house had filled with her children's laughter. It was a gift from God, just like the good weather.

Things would be better now; she could feel it. A new year. A new spring.

They would have sun—but not too much—and rain—but not too little—and those tender green plants would grow tall. Golden wheat stalks would rise and stretch toward the sun.

"Dance with me," Rose said, appearing in front of Elsa, who laughed.

"I haven't danced in . . . forever."

"None of us has." Rose placed her left hand on the small of Elsa's back and grasped her right hand, pulled her close.

"It was a long winter," Rose said.

"Not as long as the summer."

Rose smiled. "*Sì,* You're right about that."

Beside them, Ant and Loreda spun and danced and laughed.

Elsa was surprised by how comfortable she felt dancing with her mother-in-law. Almost light on her feet. She'd always felt so clumsy in Rafe's arms. Now she moved easily, let her hips sway in time to the music.

"You are thinking about my son. I see your sadness."

"Yes."

"If he comes back, I will hit him with a shovel," Rose said. "He is too stupid to be my son. And too cruel."

"Do yah hear that?" Ant said.

Tony stopped playing.

Elsa heard the *plunk-plunk-plunk* of rain hitting the roof.

Ant ran for the front door and swung it open.

They all ran out to the porch. A charcoal-gray cloud hovered overhead, another muscled its way across the sky.

Raindrops fell lightly, pattering the house, leaving starburst blotches on the dry ground.

Rain.

Big, fat droplets splattered the steps, gritty with dirt. More drops fell. The patter became a roar. A downpour.

They ran into the yard, all of them together, and turned their faces to the cool, sweet rain.

It doused them, drenched them, turned the ground to mud at their feet.

"We're saved, Rosalba," Tony said.

Elsa pulled her children into her arms and held them tightly, water running down their faces, sliding down their backs in cool, cold streaks. "We're saved."

⁂

THAT NIGHT, THEY SPLURGED on the evening meal, ate homemade fettuccine with bits of browned pancetta in a rich and creamy sauce. Afterward, while Tony played his fiddle in the sitting room amid the percussive beat of the rain, Elsa carried the ricotta cassata out to the family. The cake's golden top, covered with shiny preserved peaches, held a single burning candle.

Rose reached into the velvet pouch at her neck and pulled out the American penny that she'd worn for more than three decades. Elsa knew every word of the story of this penny, the family lore. Tony had found it in the street in Sicily and picked it up and showed it to Rose. *A sign,* they'd agreed. The hope for their future. It was the family talisman.

This penny had made the rounds every New Year's morning as each member of the family held it for a moment and said aloud what their hope for the new year was. They passed it around when they planted crops and on birthdays. On the back of it, curled on either side were beautiful, embossed shafts of wheat. It was little wonder Tony believed it had shown the Martinellis their destiny.

Rose handed the penny to Loreda, who stared solemnly down at it. "Make a wish, *cara.*"

"I don't believe in it anymore," Loreda said, handing the coin back to her grandmother. "It didn't keep our family together."

Rose looked stricken; it was a moment before she recovered and managed a smile.

Tony's music stopped.

Loreda stared at Elsa, teary-eyed. "He promised to teach me to drive when I turned thirteen."

"Ah . . ." Elsa said, feeling her daughter's pain. "I will teach you."

"It's not the same," Loreda said.

There was a short, sharp beat of awkward silence. Then Rose said, "You will believe again. And even if you do not, the coin has its power."

"I'll take her wish," Ant said. "Give me the penny."

Even Loreda laughed and dashed the tears from her eyes.

Tony played "Happy Birthday" on his fiddle and everyone sang.

IN THE DAYS AFTER the beautiful rainstorm, Elsa woke early each morning, fueled by hope, and went outside. She inhaled deeply, smelled the fecund scent of wet land, and knelt in the garden to tend her vegetables. She encouraged them to grow as she did her children: with a careful hand and a quiet voice. The ground looked alive again, not parched and dry; here and there, fragile green tips poked up from the dirt, seeking sunshine.

This morning, she saw Tony standing at the edge of the winter-wheat field. Not bothering with a sun hat—it was warm and kind, this sun, like an old friend—she walked past the chicken coop, heard them clucking. Their old rooster strutted along the wire fence, trying to hurry her past his brood. The windmill thunked in the breeze, bringing up water.

Elsa came to the edge of the field and stopped.

"Look at it," Tony said in a rough voice.

Green.

Rows of new growth, stretching to the horizon in straight rows.

Here was the essence of hope on a farm. The color of the future. Green now, and delicate, but with sunshine and rain, the wheat would become as sturdy as the family, as strong as the land itself, and turn into a sea of waving gold that would sustain them all.

At the very least, there would be grain for the animals. After four years of drought, that alone would be a blessing.

Elsa left Tony standing at the altar of his land, and headed toward the house. She knelt at her special patch of ground, beneath the kitchen window. Her aster was green. "Hey, you," she said. "I knew you'd come back."

FOURTEEN

On the day it happened, Elsa told herself it was nothing. They all did.

She woke early, feeling restless. She'd slept badly and didn't know why. She got out of bed and splashed water on her face and realized suddenly what was wrong: she was hot.

She braided her hair and covered it with a kerchief and went out into the kitchen, where she found Rose standing at the window.

Elsa knew they were both thinking the same thing: It was already hot. And it wasn't even seven o'clock in the morning.

"What's one hot day?" Elsa said, coming to stand by her mother-in-law.

"I used to love hot days," Rose said.

Elsa nodded.

They stared out at the blinding yellow sun.

EIGHT STRAIGHT DAYS OF hundred-degree heat. In mid-March.

They renewed their efforts to conserve: energy, water, food,

kerosene. They darkened the windows and carried water by the bucketful, poured it sparingly on the garden and on the grapes and in the
animal troughs, but it wasn't enough; the new growth began to wilt
in the inexorable heat. By the fourth day, the wheat was dead. Not a
hint of green for hundreds of acres. Elsa watched her father-in-law's
steady decline in spirit. He still woke early and drank a cup of bitter,
black coffee and read the newspaper. It wasn't until he opened the
door that his shoulders slumped. Each day, he was destroyed anew
at the sight of his land. Some days he spent hours at the edges of his
dead wheat field, just staring out. He would come home, smelling of
sweat and despair, and sit in the sitting room, saying nothing. Rose
tried everything she could to revive his spirit, but none of them had
much optimism left.

Still, even as the crops died and the fields dried up and their skin
burned, life went on.

Today, Elsa and Rose had to do laundry. In this blinding, headache-
inducing heat.

Elsa wanted to simply let her children wear dirty clothes, and say,
Who cares? Everyone was dirty these days, but what would that say
about the kind of mother she was or the lessons she was teaching them?
What if one of the few remaining neighbors stopped by and saw her
children in unwashed clothes?

So she washed out the tubs and filled them with water, and spent
more sweaty, exhausting hours washing towels and bedding and clothes.
First, of course, every item had to be carried outside and shaken. The
cistern had gone dry in this unseasonable heat, so all the water she
needed had to be hauled up from the well and carried into the house in
buckets. Thankfully, Loreda was good at hauling water and lately she
was too tired and dispirited to complain.

By the time Elsa finished the laundry, it was well past noon and over
105 degrees. The sheets were pinned onto the lines and flapping in the

breeze; she could barely lift her head, and every joint in her body ached. And all of it was a waste because dust would rise or fall or puff up from nowhere and leave a film on everything she'd just washed.

She returned to the dark, stuffy kitchen and started bread by mixing together last night's leftover potato water, a boiled potato, sugar, yeast, and flour. At two o'clock, Loreda walked into the kitchen.

"Good," Elsa said, covering the bread mixture with a dish towel. "You're just in time to help me bring in the laundry."

"Joy," Loreda said, following Elsa outside.

ON THE FIRST DAY OF spring—yet another sweltering day—Mom decided it was time to make soap. *Soap.* Loreda was too tired to complain—and it wouldn't do any good anyway. Mom and Grandma were warrior women. Nothing stopped them when they'd made up their minds.

Loreda followed her mother out to the barn.

Working together, they rolled a big black cauldron across the hard dirt yard and set it up. Mom knelt beside the three-legged pot and built a fire.

As flames took hold and licked upward, Mom said, "Start hauling water."

Loreda said nothing, just grabbed a pair of buckets and headed off. When she got back, Grandma was with Mom, watching the fire.

"We should have laid pipe," Grandma said. "Back when times were good."

"You know what they say about hindsight," was Mom's reply.

"Instead, we bought more land, a new truck, and a thresher. No wonder God is smiting us. Fools," Grandma said.

"Keep jawing," Loreda said. "I can handle all the water myself."

Grandma smacked her lightly in the back of the head. "*Basta.* Go."

By the time the cauldron had enough water in it, Loreda's neck ached, her knees hurt, and the dang heat was giving her a headache. She tugged the bandanna at her throat free and used it to blot her cheeks.

When the water began to boil, Grandma scraped lard into the pot and then carefully poured in the lye. The hot, humid air instantly turned toxic. Mom coughed and covered her mouth and nose.

The heat headache intensified behind Loreda's eyes. The blue of the horizon became hard to look at without blinking. She stared instead at the field of dead potatoes; the empty windmill platform made her miss her daddy, an emotion she clamped down quickly. She was done missing her dad. *Good riddance,* she thought (or tried to).

Mom stood at the pot, stirring the mixture of lye, grease, and water with a long, pointed stick until it was the right consistency.

Making soap to sell. As if *soap* would save them, as if it would make them enough money to feed them all this winter.

Mom ladled the soap into wooden molds while Grandma kicked sand on the fire to extinguish it.

"Loreda, help me carry these trays to the root cellar," Mom said.

Grandma wiped her hands on her apron and headed back to the house.

Loreda knew that as soon as the cauldron was cool they'd have to roll it back to the barn, and the thought of it made her want to scream in frustration. Instead, she grabbed a tray full of unset soap and followed her mother down into the dark, relative cool of the root cellar.

Empty shelves.

After years without a wheat harvest or much of a garden, they'd been living on the bounty of better years, but those supplies were going fast.

She and Mom exchanged a look, but neither of them spoke. There was no comfort in pointing out their lack of food supplies.

Loreda followed Mom back out into the heat. She was about to ask for a glass of water when she heard a strange sound. She stopped, listened. "Do you hear that?"

It was coming from the barn.

Mom headed toward the barn, opening the barn door in a giant sweep of creaking wood.

Loreda followed her inside.

Milo lay on his side, his sunken belly wheezing up and down as he tried to breathe. Dirty mucus slid from his nostrils, pooling on the ground.

Grandpa knelt beside the horse, stroking his damp neck.

"What's wrong with him?" Loreda asked.

"He collapsed," Grandpa said. "I was leading him out of his stall to water."

"Go to the house, Loreda," Mom said. She walked over to Grandpa, dragged a milking stool toward him, and sat down. She placed a hand on his shoulder.

"I got to shoot him, Elsa. He's suffering. The poor boy gave us his all."

Loreda stared at Milo, thinking, *No.* So many of her good memories included Milo. . . .

She remembered when Daddy taught her to ride on this old gelding. *He'll take care of you, Lolo, trust him. Don't be afraid.*

Loreda remembered Daddy swinging her up into the saddle, and Mom saying, *Isn't she too little yet?* And Daddy smiling. *Not my Lolo. She can do anything.*

Up on Milo's back, Loreda had conquered fear for the first time. *I did it, Daddy!*

It had been one of the best days of Loreda's life. She'd gone from a walk to a trot in one day, and Daddy had been so proud.

For years afterward, Milo had been her best friend on this vast farm. He followed her around like a puppy, nibbling at her shoulder, bumping her for carrots.

And now he'd fallen.

"Don't just sit there, do something," Loreda said, her eyes burning with tears. "He's suffering."

"I failed at all of it," Grandpa said.

"You didn't fail," Mom answered. "The land failed you."

"The government man said we did it to ourselves with greed and bad farming. If I'm a bad farmer, I got nothing, Elsa."

Milo shuddered, wheezed, made a low, desperate moan of pain, and kicked out his front legs.

Loreda walked dully to the workbench and picked up her grandfather's Colt revolver. She checked the chamber, closed it with a snap, and returned to Milo, who wheezed and snorted at her touch.

She saw the pain in his eyes, the muddy mucus in his nostrils as she stroked his damp neck. "I love you, boy," she said. Tears blinded her, blurred his beloved face. "You gave us everything you had. I should have spent more time with you. I'm sorry."

"Loreda, no," Grandpa said. "That ain't—"

Loreda put the muzzle of the pistol to the gelding's head and pulled the trigger. The gunshot cracked loudly.

Blood splattered Loreda's face.

After that, silence.

Tears streaked down Loreda's cheeks. She wiped them away impatiently. Useless tears. "The government will pay us sixteen dollars for him. Dead or alive," she said.

"Sixteen dollars," Grandpa said. "For our Milo."

Loreda knew what the grown-ups were thinking. They'd have sixteen dollars, but no means of transportation. And no crops. No food.

"How long before we all start falling to our knees and can't get up? How long?"

She threw down the gun and ran out of the barn. She might have headed for the driveway and kept running, all the way to California, but before she even reached the house, she felt the wind pick up. She looked out and saw it: dust storm, barreling down from the north.

Coming fast.

THAT WEEK, THE WIND became a clawing, screaming monster that shook the house and rattled the windows and pounded at the doors. Wind blew at over forty miles an hour, day after day, no reprieve, just an endless, terrifying assault. Dust rained down from the ceiling constantly. All of them breathed it in and spit it out and coughed it up. Birds were disoriented by the dust and slammed into walls and telephone poles. Trains stopped on the tracks; drifts of sand moved like waves across the flat land.

They woke to find outlines of their bodies in dust on the sheets. They put Vaseline in their noses and covered their faces with bandannas. The adults went out into the maw when they had to, following the rope that they'd strung from the house to the barn, going hand over hand, blinded by dust. The chickens were wild with panic and breathing in dirt day after day, and the children stayed in the house, wearing gas masks. Ant hated to keep his mask on—said it gave him a headache—even though the dust bothered him more than it did the rest of them.

Elsa worried about him, slept with him, sat in bed with him, reading as best she could in her scratchy voice. Stories were the one thing that calmed him down.

Now, on this fifth day of the storm, he was in her bed with the covers drawn up, wearing his gas mask, while Elsa swept the floor. Dirt slipped through cracks in the rafters and fell on everything.

She heard a *thump,* nearly lost in the maw of the storm.

Ant had dropped his picture book onto the floor.

Elsa set the broom aside and went to his bedside. "Ant, baby—"

"Momm—" He coughed violently; he'd never coughed this hard before; she thought it might crack his ribs.

Elsa pulled down her bandanna and eased the gas mask off of his face. Mud collected in the corners of his eyes, crusted his nostrils.

He blinked. "Mom? Is that you?"

"It's me, baby." She pulled him up, poured water into a glass, and made him drink it. She could see how much it hurt him to swallow. His breathing, even without the mask, was a terrible drawn-out wheezing.

Wind clattered at the windows, squealed through the cracks in the wood.

"My stomach hurts."

"I know, baby."

Grit. It was in all of them, in their tears, their nostrils, on their tongues, serrating their throats, collecting in their stomachs until they were all nauseated. Each of them lived with a gnawing stomachache.

But Ant felt the worst. His cough was brutal and he couldn't eat. Lately, he said the light hurt his eyes.

"Drink some more. I'll put some turpentine and hot towels on your chest."

Ant sipped at the water like a baby bird. When he finished, he slumped back, wheezing.

Elsa climbed into bed beside her son, taking him into her arms, murmuring prayers.

He lay frighteningly still.

She took some Vaseline out of a tin and smoothed it in Ant's raw, dirt-clogged nostrils, then refit the gas mask over his face. He blinked up at her, crying; mud formed in the corners of his red eyes.

"Don't cry, baby. This storm will stop soon and we'll take you to the doctor. He'll make you all better."

He wheezed through the gas mask. "O . . . kay," he said.

Elsa held him close, hoping he didn't see her tears.

⟩ₓ

NINE DAYS, AND STILL no respite from the storm. Wind rattled the walls and scratched at the door.

When Elsa woke to yet another day of wind, she checked on Ant, who slept beside her. He hadn't been strong enough to get out of bed in the last four days. He didn't even play with his soldiers anymore and didn't want to be read to. He just lay there wearing his gas mask, wheezing.

That terrible, drawn-out breathing was the first thing she listened for each morning when she woke and each night when she drew him close.

She heard his breathing and said a quick prayer to the Virgin Mary and got out of bed. Pulling the crusty bandanna down to her throat, she stepped down on the fine layer of silt that had collected on the floorboards overnight. Leaving footprints across the room, she went to the nightstand to wash her face.

The mirror stopped her, as it so often did these days.

"Lord," she croaked. Her face looked like a mile of desert in the summer—brown, cracked, furrowed. Her lips and teeth were brown with grit. Dust had gathered in the corners of her eyes and on her lashes. She washed and dried her face and brushed her teeth.

In the sitting room, she stepped into her boots by the door and paused, staring down at the rattling knob. The walls shook at the force of the wind. She slipped her bandanna back up over her nose and mouth, then put on her gloves and used all her strength to open the door.

Wind pushed her back. She leaned into it and squinted into the driving dust.

Finding the rope they'd strung between the house and the barn, she pulled herself across the yard, hand over hand, making her way slowly. At last she came to the barn. Once inside, she snapped a lead rope onto Bella's halter and led the poor, stumbling cow out of her stall and into the barn's wide center aisle. The walls clattered and shook; dust rained down from overhead.

Setting the pail in place, Elsa sat down on the milking stool and took off her gloves, tucking them into her apron pocket. Lowering her bandanna, she reached for the cow's dry, scabby teat. The barn rattled around them; wind whistled through the cracks, broke through boards.

Elsa's hands were so chapped and raw that it hurt her as much to milk as it did the cow. She took hold. The cow bellowed in pain.

"Sorry, girl," Elsa said. "I know it hurts, but my boy needs milk. He's . . . sick."

Thick brown milk came out in oozing muddy globs, splattered into the bucket.

"Come on, girl," Elsa urged, trying again.

And again. And again.

Nothing but milky mud.

Elsa closed her gritty eyes and rested her forehead on Bella's great, sunken side. The cow's tail swished at her, stung her cheek.

She didn't know how long she sat there, grieving for the lost milk, wondering how she would feed her children without milk or butter or cheese, grieving for this good animal who was breathing in dirt all day long and wouldn't live long. The other cow had stopped producing milk months ago and was even worse off than Bella.

With an exhausted sigh, Elsa put her gloves on and pulled her bandanna up and led Bella back into her stall.

By the time Elsa made it back to the house, her forehead was scraped raw and she could barely see. This wind grated skin away.

"Elsa? You okay?"

It was Tony. He came up beside her, put a steadying arm around her.

She pulled her bandanna down to talk. "No more milk."

Tony's quiet was heartbreaking. "So, we'll sell the cows to the government. Sixteen bucks apiece, wasn't it?"

Elsa tried to wipe the grit from her eyes. "We've still got soap to sell and a few eggs."

"Thank God for small miracles."

"Yeah," Elsa said, thinking of the root cellar's empty shelves.

FIFTEEN

*Q*uiet.

    No wind rattling the windows. No dirt raining down from the ceiling.

Elsa opened her eyes in the cautious way they'd all perfected. She pulled down the mud-encrusted bandanna that covered her nose and mouth, and brushed the dirt from her eyes. It took her a moment to focus. When she sat up, dirt pattered to the floor.

She checked on Ant first thing, wakened him by easing the gas mask off his small, bony face. "Hey, baby boy," she said. "Storm's over."

Ant opened his eyes. Elsa could see the effort it took. There was no white in his eyes at all, just a deep, angry red. "I can't . . . breathe." His dirty, blue-veined eyelids fluttered shut.

He's getting worse.

"Ant? Baby? Don't go to sleep, okay?"

He tried to wet his lips, kept trying to clear his throat. "I feel . . . bad . . . Mommy."

Elsa brushed the damp hair back from her son's forehead, felt how hot he was.

Fever.

That was new.

Elsa had a deep fear of fevers, a remnant from her youth, a reminder of her own illness.

Elsa uncovered the pitcher beside the bed and poured water into the crockery basin. Then she dipped a washrag into the lukewarm water and wrung out the excess and laid the cool, damp cloth across his forehead. Water dripped down the sides of his face.

Elsa poured a small bit of water into a glass, helped him to take two aspirin. "Pretend it's your grandma's lemonade. Sweet and tart." She gave him a teaspoon of sugar laced with turpentine. It was the only remedy they knew to combat the dust he breathed in, even with the mask on.

Ant drank a tiny amount and gulped down the sugar, then closed his eyes and sank deeper into the pillow.

Elsa had just released a breath when he suddenly arched up, his body seizing, his fingers curling into claws, his red eyes rolling back in his head.

Elsa had never felt so helpless in her life. There was nothing she could do; she sat there, watching the seizure wrack her little boy. The seconds seemed to last forever.

When it ended, she took him in her arms, held him tightly, too shaky and frightened to soothe him.

"Help me, Mommy," he said in a cracked voice. "I'm hot."

He needed help. *Now.*

She didn't care if there was no money. She'd beg if she had to.

"I'll help you, baby."

She scooped him into her arms, blanket and all, and carried him through the house. As if from a distance, she heard the family yell at her. She couldn't stop, didn't care about anything but Ant.

She made it out to the porch before she realized they had no horse.

Nothing to pull the wagon. The driveway stretched out in front of her, desolate and bare.

The ground was hard and flat in places, scoured to hardpan by the wind, which had also torn through barbed wire as if it were strands of hair, ripped it away, sent it flying. There were bits of it on every building; tumbleweeds stuck to it and then were covered in drifts of sand.

She saw a wheelbarrow standing upright, half buried in sand.

Could she do it? Push him two miles to town in a wheelbarrow?

Of course. She could take him as far as she needed to.

She walked unsteadily toward it and lay him down in the rusted scoop, his spindly legs hanging over the edge. She positioned his head carefully on the blanket.

"Mo-mmy?" he wheezed. "The light . . . hurts."

"Close your eyes, baby," she said. "Go to sleep. We're going to see Doc Rheinhart."

Elsa picked up the rough wooden handles and headed for the driveway.

"Elsa!" She heard Rose yelling for her, but didn't stop, didn't listen. She was in a panic to *go*, to get him help. She knew it was crazy, knew she was a little unhinged, but what else could she do?

"Elsa, let us help!"

Elsa plunged forward. The wheelbarrow seemed to fight back. She felt every bump in the driveway, every furrow like a blow to her spine. She made it to the main road.

Desolation. Sand in heaps. Sheds covered by it; fences fallen.

She turned onto the road and kept going, breathing hard.

Heat beat down on her. Sweat blurred her vision, ran between her breasts in itchy streams.

She stubbed her toe on something buried in the sand and stumbled. The wheelbarrow was wrenched out of her hands, clattered forward. Ant hit his head on the ground.

"I'm sorry, baby," Elsa said. Even she couldn't hear her words, her throat was so dry. She looked down at her left palm, skin torn away, bloody. Her blood darkened the handles.

She resettled Ant in the wheelbarrow and fought to move forward; before she'd taken a full step, she felt a hand on her shoulders.

Tony stood there, with Rose and Loreda on either side of him. "Are you ready to let us help you now?"

"You don't have to do it all yourself," Rose said.

"Yeah, Mom," Loreda said. "We've been yelling for you. Are you deaf?"

Elsa almost burst into tears. Very slowly, she set the wheelbarrow down.

Tony took hold of the handles, lifted the wheelbarrow up, and started off. Loreda moved in beside him, took over one side.

"You made it nearly a mile," Rose said, tenderly smoothing the damp hair from Elsa's dirty forehead.

"I'm just—"

"A mother." Rose reached down for Elsa's hands, lifted them, looked at the torn, bloody palms.

Elsa steeled herself. Her own mother would have scolded her for her stupidity in not wearing gloves.

Rose slowly lifted one of Elsa's hands, kissed the bloody skin. "That used to make it all better for my foolish son."

"It helps," Elsa said. It was the first time in her life someone had kissed an injury of hers to make it better.

"Come. My husband is not as young as he thinks. It will be my turn soon."

꒰

LONESOME TREE WAS A ghost town.

Tony pushed the wheelbarrow down Main Street, past the boarded-up storefronts. The once-thriving feed store had been taken over by the Red Cross and converted into a hospital.

The plains cottonwood was gone. Someone must have cut it up for firewood after it died of thirst.

At the makeshift hospital, Tony picked up Ant, who groaned and coughed.

Inside, the narrow building was shadowy and dark. The windows had been boarded up to keep out the dust and wind. Red Cross nurses wore uniforms that had once been starched white and were now a wrinkled gray. A doctor hurried from bed to bed, stopping just long enough at each to make an assessment and bark orders to the nurses following along behind him.

Tony carried Ant into the room. "I have a child here who needs help."

A nurse approached them. She looked as haggard and drawn as everyone else. "How bad is he?"

"Bad."

The nurse sighed heavily. "A bed came open this morning."

They all knew that meant someone had died from the dust.

The nurse gave Elsa a sad look. "It's been bad. Come."

Elsa followed Tony into the room full of wheezing and coughing patients.

They settled Ant on a cot in back, beneath a ten-foot window covered by wooden boards. Even so, the sill was stuffed with rags. To the left, a cot held an old man who fought for every breath. A mask covered his eyes.

Elsa knelt beside her son.

Heat radiated off of him. She touched his hot forehead. "I'm here, Ant. We all are."

Loreda sat at the end of the cot. "We're gonna play checkers. I'll let you win."

Ant coughed harder.

Moments later, Rose came back with the doctor. She was holding on to his sleeve in a death grip. No doubt Rose had grabbed the poor man and dragged him over here. Somehow, Rose still had a fire in her. Elsa couldn't imagine how she kept it lit in all this falling dirt. The doctor leaned down to take Ant's temperature.

The doctor read the thermometer, then examined Ant and sighed. "Your son is seriously ill, which I'm sure you know. He has a high fever and is suffering from severe silicosis. Dust pneumonia. Prairie dust is full of silica. It builds up in the lungs and tears away the air sacs."

"Which means?"

"He's breathing in dirt and swallowing it. Filling up with it. There's no other way to put it, but you've done the right thing to bring him here. This is the best place in town to be in a dust storm. We will take good care of him, I promise." The doctor glanced down at beds full of wheezing, coughing, sweating, dying patients. "Try not to worry."

"Is he dying?" Elsa asked quietly.

"Not yet." The doctor touched her shoulder, gave her a gentle squeeze. "You need to go home now, let me help him."

Elsa knelt beside Ant's cot. She buried her face in the hot crook of his neck, nuzzled him. "I'm here, baby boy." Her voice broke. "I love you."

Rose gently pulled Elsa to her feet. It took all of Elsa's self-discipline not to wail or scream or fall apart. She had no idea how she found the strength to turn around and meet her mother-in-law's sad gaze.

"We have some butter," Rose said in a tight voice. "We could make him a cookie or two, bring them back tomorrow, along with some toys and his clothes."

"I can't leave him."

The doctor stepped closer. "Everyone here is either an infant, a child, or an old person. Each one has someone who wants to sit with them. There's no room for visitors. Go home. Sleep. Let us take care of him. For a week at least. Maybe two."

"We can visit, can't we?" Loreda said.

"Of course," the doctor said. "Anytime you want. And there's other kids here for him to play with when he's feeling better."

Elsa said, "What if—"

The doctor stopped her. "You're going to ask what they all ask. Here's what I can say: If you want to save him, get him out of Texas. Take him somewhere he can breathe."

Rose put an arm around Elsa; it was the only thing that kept her upright. "Come, Elsa. Let's go make our boy some treats. We'll bring 'em by tomorrow."

ELSA STOOD AT THE edge of the dead wheat field. Dry brown dirt lay in dunes as far as she could see. It was nearly four o'clock now and still the sun beat down. Hot and dry. The windmill turned slowly, creaking, doing its best.

She wanted to believe that rain would come back and the seeds would sprout and this land would thrive again, but hope was something she could no longer afford, not when Ant was lying on a cot, coughing up the dirt in his lungs, burning with fever.

Dust pneumonia.

That was what they called it, but it was really loss and poverty and man's mistakes.

She heard footsteps behind her; they came with that new shuffling-sand sound, a kind of whisper, as if man were afraid now of disturbing the earth that had turned on him.

Tony came to a stop beside her. Rose stepped into place on her other side.

"He's dying here," Elsa said.

Dying.

It wasn't just Ant. It was the land, the animals, the plants. Every-thing. The sun had burned everything to dust and the wind had blown it all away. Millions of tons of topsoil gone.

"We need to leave Texas," Elsa said.

"Yes," Rose said.

"We can sell the cows to the government. That'll help some." Tony said. "They'll give us thirty-two bucks for the two cows."

Elsa drew in a deep, painful breath and stared out at the dead, brown land. She didn't want to go into the unknown with no job and almost no money. None of them wanted to leave. This was *home*.

Above their heads, the windmill creaked and the blades turned slowly.

Together, they walked back to the farmhouse, dust rising from their feet.

SIXTEEN

"I was thinking I could take Loreda hunting tomorrow," Grandpa said at dinner that night.

"That's a good idea," Grandma said, dipping her bread in a small bit of their precious olive oil. "The compass is in my dresser. Top drawer."

"We should clean out the barn," Mom said. "Rafe's old hunting tent is in there somewhere. And the wood-burning stove from the dugout."

Loreda couldn't take it another second. The grown-ups were jawing about nothing. They seemed to forget that Ant was in that dingy hospital without any of them. Or they thought she was too young to hear the truth. This stupid conversation was making her sick. The last thing they needed to do was to clean out the darn barn.

She got to her feet so suddenly the chair legs screeched. She kicked the chair out of her way, watched it crash to the floor. "He's dying, isn't he?"

Mom looked up at her. "No, Loreda. He's not dying."

"You're lying to me. And I'm not doing dishes." She stormed out of the house and slammed the door shut behind her.

Outside, there were no horses in the corral, no hogs in their pen. All they had left were a few bony chickens too hot and tired and hungry to cluck at her passing and two cows who were barely still standing. Soon, the cows would be sold to the government men and be taken away. Then all the pens would be empty.

She climbed up to the windmill platform and sat beneath the endless, star-splattered Great Plains night sky. Up here it felt—or it once had—as if she were a part of the heavens. She'd been so many things sitting here—a ballerina, an opera singer, a motion-picture star.

Dreams her father had encouraged before he left to follow his own.

Loreda bent her legs and wrapped her arms around her ankles. She could handle the dying farm and adults who lied to her. She could even handle her father abandoning them—her—but this . . .

Ant. Her baby brother, who curled up like a potato bug and sucked his thumb, who ran like a marionette, all arms and legs akimbo, who looked up at her at night and said, "Tell me a story," and hung on every word.

"Ant," she whispered, realizing it was a prayer. The first one she'd even begun in years.

The windmill shook. She looked down and saw her mother ascending, rattling the boards as she climbed up.

Mom sat down beside her, let her legs dangle over the edge.

"I'm not a baby, Mom. You can tell me the truth."

Mom took a deep breath and exhaled it. "We were talking about your dad's tent because . . . we're leaving Texas as soon as Ant is better. Going to California."

Loreda turned. "What?"

"I talked it over with Grandma and Grandpa. We have a bit of money and the truck runs. So, we will drive west. Tony is still strong. He'll find work, maybe on the railroad. I could do laundry for people, I hope. I hear Pamela Shreyer got work in a jewelry store. Imagine that. Her husband, Gary, is tending grapes."

"And Ant is coming with us?"

"Of course he is. As soon as he's better, we'll go."

"It's a thousand miles to California. Gas is nineteen cents a gallon. Do we have enough for that?"

"How do you know all of that?"

"After Dad left, when I was supposed to be studying Texas history, I studied maps of California. I thought about—"

"Running away to find him?"

"Yeah. Turns out I'm stupid, but not that stupid. California is a big state. And I don't even know for sure that he went west. Or that he stayed west."

"No. We don't know any of that."

Loreda leaned against her mother, who put an arm around her.

Leaving. Loreda thought about it for the first time, really thought about it. Leaving home.

"I wanted you to grow up on this land," Mom said. "I wanted to grow old here and be buried here and watch over your children's children. I wanted to see the wheat grow again."

"I know," Loreda said, with a sting of realization: there was a part of her that wanted that, too.

"We don't have a choice," Mom said. "Not anymore."

A WEEK LATER, MOST of the chicken coop was still buried in dirt, as was one whole side of the barn. The cows had been sold and taken away and the farm had been transformed by the eleven-day dust storm into a sea of brown waves. It was too much work to dig out from all that dirt, especially now that they were leaving. The big, wooden-slat-sided truck bed had been loaded with a few of the things they thought they'd need in their new life—the small wood-burning stove, barrels of goods and food, boxes of bedding, pots and pans, a gallon of kerosene, lanterns.

Elsa walked like a Bedouin up and down the dunes, past the windmill. At last she found some yucca, growing wild, its fibrous roots exposed by the wind and erosion.

She hacked up the roots, ripped them out of the ground, and dropped them into a metal bucket.

Back at the house, she saw Loreda seated at the kitchen table with Tony, maps laid out around them.

"What's that?" Rose said, coming out of the kitchen. She'd canned two chickens for the trip. That, along with the last of the canned vegetables, a sugar-cured ham, and some preserved Russian thistles, should get them to California.

"Yucca. We can boil it and eat it."

Loreda made a face. "A new low, Mom."

Outside, a car came into view. They looked at each other.

When was the last time they'd had visitors?

Elsa wiped her hands on a cement-sack dish towel and followed Tony out of the house.

The automobile rolled up the road, dodging this way and that to avoid cracks in the earth and sand dunes and coils of barbed wire. Yellow-brown dust billowed up from the thin rubber tires.

Tony crossed the porch and headed toward the automobile coming their way.

Elsa tented a hand to shield her eyes from the glare of the sun.

"Who is it?" Rose asked, coming up beside her, wiping her damp hands on her apron.

The automobile rumbled up into the yard and stopped in front of Tony. The cloud of dust dissipated slowly, revealing a 1933 Ford Model Y.

The door opened slowly. A man stepped out of the car, straightened. He wore a black suit, the buttoned-up coat strained over a well-fed gut, and a brand-new fedora. A thicket of gray sideburns bracketed his florid face.

Mr. Gerald, the only banker left in town.

Rose and Elsa walked down into the brown yard and stood with Tony.

"Morton," Tony said, frowning. "Are you here about the meeting tomorrow? I hear that government man is coming back to town."

"Yes, he is. But that's not why I'm here." Morton Gerald shut the car door gently, as if the automobile were a lover in need of care, and doffed his hat. "Ladies." He paused, looked uncomfortably at Tony. "Perhaps the ladies would like to give us some time to speak privately," he said.

Rose said firmly, "We'll stay."

"How can I help you, Morton?" Tony asked.

"Your note for the back hundred and sixty acres came due," Mr. Gerald said. To his credit, he looked unhappy with the news. "I'd roll it over if I could, but . . . well, as tough as times are for you farmers, there are men in the big cities speculating on land. You owe us nearly four hundred dollars."

"Take the thresher," Tony said. "Hell, take the tractor."

"No one needs farm equipment these days, Tony. But the rich men back East, the men who own the bank, they figure there's still money in land. If you can't pay, they're going to foreclose."

There was no answer, just the sighing of the wind, as if it, too, were disgusted.

"Can you pay something, Tony? Anything, so I can hold 'em off?"

Tony looked whipped, ashamed. "I have more land than I need, Morton. Go ahead, take those acres back," he said.

Mr. Gerald pulled a pink slip of paper out of his shirt pocket. "This is a formal foreclosure on your back one hundred sixty acres. Unless you repay your debt in full in the time stated, we will auction off that section of land on April sixteenth to the highest bidder."

꙳

ELSA'S SHOES SANK INTO the deep sand every now and then, upsetting her balance as she and Tony walked to town. On either side of the road, abandoned farmhouses and automobiles were buried in drifts of dirt; sometimes all she could see of a shed was the roof's peak, sticking up from a dune. Telephone poles had fallen down. Not a bird called out.

In town, an otherworldly quiet reigned. No automobiles rumbled up the street, no horses clopped in a steady rhythm. The school bell had been ripped away in the eleven-day storm and still hadn't been found. No doubt it was buried and would be revealed when the wind returned and shifted the landscape yet again.

At the makeshift hospital, Elsa came to a stop. "I'll meet you in thirty minutes?"

Tony nodded. He pulled the patched gray hat down over his eyes and headed toward the schoolhouse for the town meeting, his shoulders already slumped in defeat. No one expected much from the government man's return.

When Elsa entered the shadowy hospital, it took her eyes a moment to adjust to the hazy gloom. People hacked and coughed; babies cried. Tired nurses moved from bed to bed.

Elsa smiled at masked patients as she passed them. Most were either very young or very old.

Ant sat up in his narrow cot, pretending swordplay with a fork and a spoon. "Take that, matey," he said, clanging the fork into the spoon. His voice was still rough and the gas mask sat in readiness on the small table beside him. "You're no match for the Shadow!"

"Hey there," Elsa said, sitting down on the edge of his bed. He looked so much better today. For the past ten days, Ant had been lethargic and had remained listless even when someone came to visit. Here though, finally, was her boy. *He's back.* Elsa's relief was so sudden and staggering she felt tears sting her eyes.

"Mommy!" He launched himself at her, hugged her so fiercely she almost fell off the bed. She had difficulty letting him go.

"I'm playing pirates," he said, grinning at her.

"You lost a tooth."

"I did! And I really lost it. Nurse Sally thinks I swallowed it."

Elsa lifted the basket she'd brought with her. Inside was a bottle of *orzata,* the sweet syrupy drink they made each year from almonds purchased at the general store. This was the last precious bottle they had, made years ago and hoarded for special occasions. Elsa added a splash of it to a bottle she'd filled with canned milk and shook it to make bubbles, then handed it to Ant.

"Jeepers," he said, savoring his first sip. She knew he would try to drink it slowly and make it last, but he wouldn't be able to.

"And this," Elsa said, producing a single sugar cookie glazed with sweet icing.

Ant nibbled the cookie like a mouse, starting around the edges, working his way in to the chewy center.

"It looks like one lucky little boy has a mom who loves him," said the doctor, stopping by the bed.

Elsa stood. "He looks better today, Doctor."

"He must be improving; the nurses tell me he's becoming a handful," Dr. Rheinhart said, ruffling Ant's hair. "His fever finally broke last night and his breathing is much improved. He is absolutely on the mend. I want to keep an eye on him for a few days, but that's just to be safe."

Elsa offered the doctor a cookie. "It's not much, I know."

The doctor took the cookie and smiled, taking a bite. "So, Ant, would you like to go home soon?"

"Boy, would I, Doc. My toy soldiers miss me."

"How about Tuesday?"

"Yippee!" Ant said. A little cough accompanied his enthusiastic cry. Elsa's heart clutched at the sound. Would she feel a rush of fear at every cough from now on? "Thank you, Doctor," she said.

He gave her a tired smile. "See you Tuesday."

Elsa sat back down beside her son. His favorite book lay waiting for them. *The Tale of Little Pig Robinson* by Beatrix Potter. He could listen over and over to the story of Little Pig's escape on a rowboat to the land where the Bong-Tree grows, loving it anew each time. Or maybe it was the familiarity he loved, the idea that every time it ended in the same way.

He snuggled into the crook of her arm, eating the cookie while she read to him. Finally, she closed the book.

"Yah gotta go?" he said, looking forlorn.

"The doc wants to keep you here for a few days, just to make sure you're well, but in no time at all, we will be off on our adventure."

"To California," he said.

"To California." Elsa pulled him into her arms and held him tightly, then kissed his forehead and whispered, " 'Bye, baby boy.'"

Leaving him was always hard, but finally, there was hope. Ant would be coming home soon.

Outside, she glanced down the street and saw people coming out of the school. A glum, quiet gathering. She saw Tony exchange a few words with Mr. Carrio, then shake his hand.

Elsa waited for Tony on the boardwalk. He moved slowly toward her, looking beaten.

"How's our boy?" Tony asked.

"Doc says he can leave on Tuesday. Any news from the government man?" Elsa asked

Tony gave her a look so steeped in despair it took her breath away. "No good news," he said.

Elsa nodded.

They started the long, solemn walk home.

⟡

IN TWO DAYS, THEY were leaving this godforsaken land. And Elsa didn't say that lightly.

God forsaken.

How else could one describe it? God had turned His back on the Great Plains.

She'd spent the last few days packing for the trip. On this Palm Sunday, instead of going to church, Elsa had canned the jackrabbits Tony and Loreda shot yesterday; when that laborious chore was done, she'd moved on to the laundry.

Now at the end of the blue-skied day, Elsa knelt in front of her little aster plant, pouring a few precious cupfuls of water into the thirsty ground.

This flower, which she'd covered and protected and watered and talked to for so long, stood alone, defiantly green against all this brown.

She would have to leave it behind to die.

She dug up the small, tender plant. Carrying it in a bowl made from her gloved hands, she crossed the yard.

At the family's cemetery, the white picket fence lay in pieces; the headstones were half covered in dirt. Four gray, store-bought headstones with Rose's and Elsa's babies' names inscribed on them. Three girls and a boy.

How long would these markers last in the wind? And when the Martinellis were gone, who would tend to their children, buried all alone in the middle of nowhere?

Elsa knelt in the sand. "Maria, Angelina, Juliana, Lorenzo. This is all I can leave with you. I will pray it rains this spring so it flowers." She planted the flower in the powdery dirt in front of Lorenzo's half-buried headstone.

The aster sagged immediately, slumped to one side.

Elsa would not cry over this one little flower.

She closed her eyes in prayer. Too soon, she wiped her eyes and got slowly to her feet. As she straightened, she saw a black shadow rising in the distance; the blackest thing she'd ever seen, it lifted into the dark-blue early-evening sky, spread enormous black wings outward. Static electricity tingled the back of her neck, lifted her hair.

A black storm?

Whatever it was, it was moving this way. *Fast.*

She ran for the house, met Rose in the yard.

"*Madonna mia,*" Rose said. They stared at the blackness billowing toward them; it had to be a mile high. Birds flew overhead, hundreds of them, flying at their greatest speed.

Tony ran out of the barn and stood with them, watching.

It was eerily silent. Calm. There was no wind.

A burning smell filled Elsa's nostrils. The air felt sticky.

Static electricity arced in little bursts of blue fire through the air, dancing on bits of barbed wire and the windmill's metal blades. Birds fell from the sky.

All at once: complete darkness. Dust clogged their eyes and noses.

Elsa clamped a hand over her mouth and held on to her mother-in-law. The three of them made it to the house, stumbled up the stairs. Tony opened the door and shoved the women inside.

"Mom!" Loreda screamed. "What's happening?"

Elsa couldn't see her daughter; that was how dark it was. She couldn't see her own hands.

Tony slammed the door shut behind them. "Rose, help me with the windows."

"Loreda," Elsa yelled. "Put on your gas mask. Get to the kitchen. Sit under the table."

"But—"

"*Go,*" Elsa said to the daughter she couldn't see.

Elsa and Rose felt their way from room to room, closing the windows and covering them and pressing newspapers and oilcloth in every crack and crevice.

They kept their supplies—Vaseline, sponges, bandannas—in a basket in the kitchen. Elsa carried it through the inky dark and found a flashlight, clicked it on.

Nothing. Just a click.

"Is it on?" Rose asked, coughing.

"Who knows?" Elsa said.

"We need to get under the table, drape it with wet sheets," Rose said.

Something hit the house hard, a terrible *thwack*. Window glass shattered in a series of loud cracks and clattered to the floor.

The front door was ripped open. The swirling, biting black monster of a storm whooshed inside, hitting so hard Rose stumbled sideways. Tony raced over to shut the door again, and threw the bolt shut.

They found the buckets they kept filled with water in the kitchen and soaked some sheets to drape over the table and then dampened sponges and pressed them to their faces, breathing hard through them.

Elsa heard Loreda breathing heavily through the gas mask. She crawled forward, found the kitchen table. Pushing chairs aside, she crawled underneath it.

"I'm here, Loreda," she said, reaching out.

Elsa felt Loreda take her hand. They were sitting together, side by side, but couldn't see each other. Thank God Ant wasn't here.

Rose and Tony squeezed in under the table, past the draping of wet sheets.

Elsa held her daughter close as boards were ripped away and windows broke.

The walls shook so hard it seemed the house would shatter.

Suddenly it was freezing.

⠶

ELSA WOKE TO SILENCE; in it, she heard the wheezing cant of Loreda's labored breathing through the gas mask. Then, a scuttling sound—a mouse, probably—coming out of hiding, scurrying over the floor.

She pulled down her crusty, dirt-filled bandanna and peeled away the muddy sponge she'd been breathing through. Her first unprotected breath hurt all the way down her throat and into the pit of her gnawing, empty stomach.

She opened her eyes. Grit scraped her eyeballs.

Dirt blurred her vision, but she could see the dirty sheets draped around them, and her family, tucked in close to one another. Whatever it was, it was over.

She coughed and spat out a blob of blackish-gray dirt that was as thick and as long as a pencil nub. "Loreda? Rose? Tony? Is everyone okay?"

Loreda opened her eyes. "Yeah." The gas mask turned her voice raspy and monstrous.

Tony slowly lowered his bandanna.

Rose crawled out from under the table and staggered to her feet. She took Elsa by the hand, led her into the sitting room. Bright morning sunlight shone through the broken window. Impossibly, they'd slept through the night and outlasted the storm.

There was black dirt everywhere, a deep layer of it on the floor, gathered in dunes at every chair leg, falling down the walls like a mass of centipedes.

The front door wouldn't open; they'd been buried in.

Tony climbed out the broken window and dropped onto the porch. Elsa heard the scuffing *thwack* of the metal shovel on the porch boards as he dug sand away.

Finally, the door opened.

Elsa stepped outside.

"Oh, my God," she whispered.

The world had been reshaped and blanketed by the storm. Black dirt and dust, as fine as talcum powder, covered everything. There was nothing to see for miles except swelling dunes of inky sand. The chicken coop was completely buried; only the very peak of it poked up. The water pump rose up like a relic from a lost civilization. They could have walked right up to the top of the barn on one side.

Dead birds lay in heaps on the sand dunes, their wings still outstretched as if they'd died midflight.

"*Madonna mia,*" Rose said.

"That's it," Elsa said. "We are not waiting until tomorrow. We are going to get Ant and leave right now. This instant. Before this goddamned land kills my children."

She turned and strode back into the house. Every indrawn breath felt like swallowing fire. Her eyes burned. Grit lodged in her eyes, her throat, her nose, in the creases in her skin. It kept falling out of her hair.

Loreda stood by a broken window, her face blackened by dirt, looking dazed.

"We are leaving for California. Now. Go get the suitcases. I'm going to fill a tub with water for bathing in the yard."

"Outside?" Loreda said.

"No one will see you," Elsa said grimly.

For the next few hours, no one spoke. Elsa would have watered her aster, but the cemetery was gone, markers and picket fence and all, gone.

Tony shoveled the driveway so they could leave. They had strapped what they could to the truck—a few pots and pans, two lanterns, a broom and a washboard and a copper bathing tub. Inside the truck bed was their rolled-up camp mattress, a barrel full of food and towels and bedding, bundles of kindling and wood, and the black stove, strapped against the back of the cab. They packed as much as they could for their new life, but most of what they owned was still in the house and barn. The kitchen cabinets were nearly full, as were most of the closets. There was no way they could take it all. The furniture they would leave behind, like the pioneers who'd unloaded their covered wagons when the going got tough, leaving pianos and rocking chairs alongside their buried dead on the plains.

When they were completely packed, Elsa walked back to the house, over the dunes and troughs of sand.

Elsa looked around the house. They were leaving it full of furniture, with pictures still on the walls. Everything was covered in fine black dirt.

The front door opened. Tony walked in, holding hands with Rose. "Loreda is in the truck. She's impatient to go," Tony said.

"I'll make one last pass through the house," Elsa said. She walked through the powdery black dirt in the sitting room, over hills and across scrape marks. The kitchen window was gone; through it, the beautiful blue sky looked like an oil painting hung on a black wall.

Elsa walked into her bedroom and stood there, one last time. Books lined the dresser and the nightstands, each one draped in black dirt. Just like when she'd left her parents' home, she could only take a few of her treasured novels with her. Once again, she was starting over.

She quietly closed the bedroom door on this life and walked out of the house for the last time.

Rose and Tony stood on the porch, holding hands.

"I'm ready," she said, stepping onto the first riser of the porch steps.

"Elsinore?" Tony said.

It was the first time he'd ever used her given name and it surprised her. Elsa turned.

"We aren't going with you," Rose said.

Elsa frowned. "I know we planned to leave later, but—"

"No," Tony said. "That's not what we mean. We aren't going to California."

"I don't . . . understand. I said we needed to leave and you agreed."

"And you do need to go," Tony said. "The government has offered to pay us not to grow anything. They have forgiven mortgage payments for a while. So we don't have to worry about losing any more of the land. For now, at least."

"You said there was no good news after the meeting," Elsa said, feeling a rush of panic. "You lied to me?"

"This is not good news," he said softly. "Not when I know you must go for Ant's sake."

"They want us to plow differently," Rose said. "Who understands it? But they need the farmers to work together. How can we not try to save our land?"

"Ant . . . can't stay," Elsa said.

"We know that. And we can't go," Tony said. "Go. Save my grandchildren." His voice broke on that.

Tony curled his hand around the back of her neck, pulled her gently toward him, touched his forehead to hers; this was a man of the old world, a man who shut up and moved on and never stopped working. He poured all of his passion and love into the land. For his family. This touch was how he said, *I love you.*

And goodbye.

"Rosalba," Tony said. "The penny."

Rose took off the thin, black-ribboned necklace that held a velvet pouch.

Solemnly, she handed the pouch to Tony. He opened it, withdrew the American penny.

"You are our hope now," he said to Elsa, and then put the penny back in the pouch and pressed the necklace into the palm of her hand, forced her fingers to curl around it. He turned and walked back into the house, scuffling through the ankle-deep sand.

Elsa felt as if she were breaking apart. "You know I can't do this alone, Rose. Please . . ."

Rose laid a callused hand on Elsa's cheek. "You are everything those children need, Elsa Martinelli. You always have been."

"I'm not brave enough to do this."

"Yes, you are."

"But you'll need money. We took all the food—"

"We kept some for ourselves. And our land will provide."

Elsa couldn't speak. The last thing in the world she wanted was to drive across the country—over mountains and across vast deserts—with too little money and hungry children and no one to help her.

No.

The thing she couldn't bear would be to watch her son struggle to breathe again.

And there it was: the truth Rose had already come to.

"Tony put money in the glove box," Rose said "The tank is full of gas. Write to us."

Elsa slipped the necklace over her head, then reached for Rose's hand, afraid for a moment that once she touched this woman she loved, she wouldn't be able to let go, that she'd be too weak to leave.

"I can prove the penny's luck. It brought you to us," Rose said. Elsa wet her dry, dry lips.

"You are the daughter I always wanted," Rose said. "*Ti amo.*"

"And you are my mother," Elsa said. "You saved me, you know."

"Mothers and daughters. We save each other, *sì?*"

Elsa stared at Rose for as long as she could, memorizing everything about her, but at last, she had no choice. It was time to leave this place, this woman, this *home*.

She left Rose standing on the porch and walked across the hillocks of black sand to the loaded-up truck, where Loreda sat in the front.

Elsa got into the driver's seat and slammed the door shut and started the engine. It shuddered, coughed, started up.

Elsa drove slowly down the driveway and turned toward town.

The landscape was black and piled with sand. To the left, she saw an automobile half buried; a hundred feet farther on, a man lay dead, his hand outstretched, his open mouth full of sand. "Don't look," she said to Loreda.

"Too late."

Lonesome Tree was shrouded in black dirt.

Elsa pulled up in front of the makeshift hospital. It wasn't until she got out and went inside that she realized that she'd left the truck running and had said nothing to Loreda.

She saw the doctor and flagged him down. "I'm here for Ant."

Elsa saw that the hospital was full from end to end. People hacked and coughed; babies cried in a hacking way that broke her heart.

"Is he healthy?" Elsa asked. "You said he was ready to leave. That hasn't changed?"

"He's healthy, Elsa," the doctor said, patting her hand. "It may take as long as a year to really heal. But he's recovered. Might be he suffers with asthma later. You'll just have to keep an eye on him."

"I'm taking him to California," she said, unable to smile about it.

"Good."

"Can we ever come back?"

"I imagine so. Someday. Hardship ends. Kids are resilient."

"Mom!" Ant shuffled toward her, looking both scared and relieved. "Did you see that storm?"

"Thank you, Doctor." Elsa shook his hand. All she had to offer this man who'd saved Ant's life was her gratitude.

"Good luck to you, Elsa."

Outside, Ant looked at the deserted, sand-covered town, with its broken windows and tumbleweeds. "Jeepers," he said.

"Anthony," Elsa said. "Where are your shoes?"

"They broke."

"You have no shoes?"

Ant shook his head.

Elsa closed her eyes so he wouldn't see her emotion. *Going west with no shoes.*

"What's wrong, Mommy? Don't worry. I have tough feet."

Elsa managed a smile. She opened the truck door and helped him up into the bench seat. He sidled close to Loreda, who hugged him so tightly he had to claw his way free.

Elsa got into the truck and closed the door.

This was it.

They were leaving.

It was up to Elsa now, her alone, to keep them alive.

With no shoes.

She drove out of town and turned south. There wasn't another car on the road. Every house she passed looked deserted.

"Wait," Ant said, giving a short, sharp cough. "You forgot Grandpa and Grandma. Mom?"

Elsa looked at her son, thinner now, missing front teeth. He would know now, forever, as Elsa had known after her rheumatic fever, that he was fragile, that life was uncertain.

His gaze widened; she saw when he understood. He looked back—toward home—and then back at her, his eyes bright with tears. In that one look, she saw a bit of his childhood slip away.

1935

We draw our strength from the very despair in which we have been forced to live. We shall endure.

—CÉSAR CHÁVEZ

SEVENTEEN

⟩ℎ

Elsa kept her foot on the accelerator and her hands curled tightly around the steering wheel. They drove past a family of six walking on the side of the road, pushing a cart full of their belongings. People like them who had lost everything and were going west.

What was she thinking?

She didn't have the courage to set out on a cross-country journey into the unknown. She wasn't strong enough to survive on her own, let alone strong enough to care for her children. How would she make money? She had never lived on her own, never paid rent, never had a job. She hadn't graduated from high school, for gosh sakes.

Who was going to rescue them when she failed?

She pulled off to the side of the road and stopped, staring through the dirty windshield at the road ahead, at the devastation left by the black storm; buildings broken, cars in ditches, fences torn away.

The rosary that hung from the rearview mirror swung from side to side.

More than a thousand miles to California, and what would they find there? No friends, no family. *I could work in a laundry . . . or a library.*

But who would hire a woman when millions of men were out of work? And if she *did* get a job, who would watch the children? *Oh, God.*

"Mommy?"

Ant tugged at her sleeve. "Are you okay?"

Elsa shoved the truck door open. She stumbled away and stopped, breathing hard, fighting the tidal wave of panic.

Loreda came up beside her. "You thought Grandpa and Grandma would come?"

Elsa turned. "Didn't you?"

"They're like a plant that can only grow in one place."

Great. A thirteen-year-old saw what Elsa hadn't.

"I checked the glove box. They gave us most of the government money. And we have a full tank of gas."

Elsa stared down the long, empty road. Not far away, a crow sat on a shed that was buried almost to the peak in black dirt.

She almost said, *I'm scared,* but what kind of mother said those words to a child who counted on her?

"I've never been on my own," Elsa said.

"You're not on your own, Mom."

Ant popped his head out of the window of the cab of the truck. "I'm here, too!" he chirped. "Don't forget me!"

Elsa felt a rush of love for these children of hers, a soul-deep sense that was akin to longing; she drew in a deep breath, exhaled, and smelled the dry Panhandle Texas air that was as much a part of her life as God and her children. She'd been born in this county and always thought she'd die here. "This is home," she said. "I thought you'd grow up here and be the first Martinelli to go to college here. Austin, I thought. Or Dallas, a place big enough to hold your dreams."

"This will always be home, Mom. Just because we're leaving doesn't change that. Look at Dorothy. After all her adventures, she clicked her heels together and went home. And really, what choice do we have?"

"You're right."

She closed her eyes for a moment, remembered another time when she'd been scared and felt alone, back when she'd been sick. That was the first time her grandfather had leaned down and whispered, *Be brave,* into her ear. And then, *Or pretend to be. It's all the same.*

The memory calmed her. She could pretend to be brave. For her children. She wiped her eyes, surprised by her tears, and said, "Let's go."

She returned to the truck, took her seat, and banged the door shut beside her.

Loreda settled in beside her brother and opened up a map. "It's ninety-four miles from Dalhart to Tucumcari, New Mexico. That should be our first stop. I don't think we should drive at night. At least, that's what Grandpa told me when we were studying the map."

"You and Grandpa picked out a route?"

"Yeah. He's been teaching me stuff. I guess he knew all along he and Grandma weren't coming. He taught me all kinds of stuff—how to hunt for rabbits and birds, how to drive, and how to put water in the radiator. In Tucumcari, we pick up Route 66 west." She reached into her pocket, pulled out a battered bronze compass. "He gave me this. He and Grandma brought it with them from Italy."

Elsa stared down at the compass. She had no idea how to read it. "Okay."

"We can be a club," Ant said. "Like the Boy Scouts, only we're explorers. The Martinelli Explorers Club."

"The Martinelli Explorers Club," Elsa said. "I like it. Off we go, explorers."

꙳

As they neared Dalhart, Elsa found herself slowing down without thinking about it.

She hadn't been back here in years, not since the day her mother had taken one look at Loreda and commented on her skin color. Elsa might have taken her parents' criticism of herself to heart, but she would never let her children face it.

Dalhart had been as broken by the Depression and the drought as Lonesome Tree had; that much was obvious. Most of the storefronts were boarded up. A line of people stood at the church, metal bowls in hand, waiting for free food.

The truck bumped over the railroad tracks. Elsa turned onto Main Street.

"We're not supposed to turn here," Loreda said. "We go past Dalhart, not through it."

Elsa saw Wolcott Tractor Supply: closed, the windows covered by wooden boards.

She pulled up in front of the house she'd grown up in. The front door was off its hinges, and most of the windows were boarded up. A foreclosure notice had been pounded into the front door.

The front yard was ruined. Black sand, dirt, dunes everywhere. She saw her mother's garden, dead roses that had received more of Minerva Wolcott's love than Elsa ever had. For the thousandth time, Elsa wondered why her parents hadn't loved her, or why their version of love had been so cold and conditional. How did such a thing happen? Elsa had learned to love deeply on the day of Loreda's birth.

"Mom?" Loreda said. "Did you know the people who lived here? The house looks abandoned."

Elsa felt a shifting of time, an unpleasant sense of worlds colliding. She saw her children peering at her through worried eyes.

She'd thought it would hurt to see this place, but the opposite was true. This wasn't her home and the people who'd lived here weren't her family. "No," she said at last. "I didn't know the people who lived here . . . and they didn't know me."

☙

THE ROAD OUT OF Texas was miles of sand-duned nothingness broken up by a series of small towns. In New Mexico, they saw more people traveling west, in old jalopies weighed down with possessions and children, in cars pulling trailers, in mule- and horse-drawn wagons. There were people walking single file, pushing baby strollers and wheelbarrows.

When night began to fall, they passed a man dressed in rags, walking on bare feet, hat drawn low on his head, a fringe of long black hair against his ragged collar.

Loreda pressed her nose against the window, watching the man. "Slow down," she said.

"It's not him," Elsa said.

"It could be."

Elsa slowed down. "It's not him."

"Who cares?" Ant said. "He left."

"Shush," Elsa said. It was too late in the day for this. They were all exhausted after hours of driving. The gas gauge showed that they were nearly out of fuel.

Elsa saw a gas station and pulled into it, sidled up to the pump.

Nineteen cents per gallon. One dollar and ninety cents to fill the tank.

Elsa did the math in her head, recalculated the amount of money they would have when they drove away.

An attendant came out to pump their gas.

Across the street was a small auto court, with jalopies and trucks parked out front. There were people seated on chairs in front of their rooms, with their loaded-down vehicles parked in attached carports. A pink neon sign—turned off—read: VACANCY and $3.00/NIGHT.

Three dollars.

"Stay here," Elsa said to the kids.

She walked across the gravel parking lot to pay for the gas. There were a few people milling about in the falling night: a raggedy man standing over by the water pump, with a scrawny dog sitting on its haunches nearby. A kid kicking a ball.

A bell rang overhead as she opened the door. Her stomach growled loudly, reminding her that she'd given her lunch to the kids. She walked up to the cash register, which was operated by a woman with orange hair.

Elsa pulled her wallet out of her handbag and counted out one dollar and ninety cents and put it on the counter. "Ten gallons of gas."

"First day on the road?" the lady asked, taking the money as she rang up the sale.

"Yes. Just left home. How can you tell?"

"You don't got a man with you?"

"How—"

"Men don't let their women pay for gas." The woman leaned closer. "Keep your money somewhere besides your handbag, doll. There's a bad element out here. 'Specially in the last few days. Keep an eye out."

Elsa nodded and put her money back in her wallet. As she did so, she stared down at her left hand, at the thin wedding band she still wore.

"It ain't worth nuthin'," the clerk said, looking sad. "You'd best keep wearing it, too. A single woman can be prey out on the road. And don't stay at the auto court across the street. It's full of the shiftless kind. About four miles farther on, just past the water tower, there's a dirt road going south. Take it. If you go about a mile in, you'll find a nice copse of trees. If you don't feel like camping, keep going another six miles west on the main road. There's a clean motel called Land of Enchantment. Can't miss it."

"Thank you."

"Good luck."

Elsa hurried back to the truck. She had left the kids alone, with all their belongings and a full tank of gas and the keys in the ignition with shiftless men nearby.

Lesson one.

Elsa climbed into the truck. The children looked as hot and tired as she felt. "So, explorers. First order of business. We need a plan. There's a nice motel down the road that has beds and maybe hot water. It's at least three dollars a night. If we decide to stay in places like that, we'll use up about fifteen dollars. Or we can save that money and camp out."

"Camping!" Ant said. "Then it's a *real* adventure."

Elsa met Loreda's gaze over Ant's head.

"Camping," Loreda said. "Big fun."

Elsa drove on. Now and again, the headlights shone on more people walking alongside the road, headed west, carrying what they could, dragging wagons. A boy on a bicycle had a shaggy gray dog in the basket between the handlebars.

Four miles later, she turned onto a dirt road, past several jalopies that were parked for the night, campfires already going. She found a copse of trees growing well back from the road. She turned into it and parked.

"I'll see if I can find us a rabbit," Loreda said, taking the shotgun out of the rack.

"Not tonight," Elsa said. "Let's stay close together."

Elsa got out of the truck and reached into the bed for the supplies they'd brought with them. In a nice, flat spot not far away from the truck, she knelt down and started a campfire, using a little of the wood and kindling they'd packed.

"Do we get to sleep in the tent tonight?" Ant asked. "We ain't had a vacation before."

"Haven't," Elsa corrected automatically as she went back to the truck for food. She brought out two of their most precious supplies—a log-like roll of bologna and a half a loaf of store-bought light bread.

"Bologna sandwiches!" Ant said.

Elsa settled a cast-iron frying pan on the fire and put a scoop of lard in to sizzle, then peeled the yellow plastic casing away and cut thin slices of bologna from the roll. After snipping the edges so the meat wouldn't curl up, she dropped two slices into the bubbling fat.

Ant squatted on his haunches beside her, his hair as dirty as his face.

In the black pan, the bologna popped bits of hot lard.

Ant poked at the fire with a stick. "Take that, fire!"

Elsa opened the packaged bread and took out two white slices, rimmed in pale brown crust. This bread was practically weightless. Mr. Pavlov had begged them to accept this store-bought bread for their trip. His treat, he'd said. She smeared on some precious olive oil and sliced an onion. Placing the rings carefully onto a golden layer of oil, she then laid a crispy, browned slice of bologna on top.

"Loreda!" she called out. "Come on back. Food's ready."

Elsa pushed slowly to her feet and went back to the truck for more plates and their jug of water. As she came around the back of the bed, she heard something. A banging.

A man stood beside their truck, holding her gas cap in one hand and a hose in the other. Even in the fading light, she saw that he was ragged, pencil-thin. His shirt was tattered.

Fear immobilized her for a split second, but it was enough time for him to pounce. He grabbed her by the throat, his fingers tightening hard, and banged her up against the truck.

"Where's your money?"

"Please . . ." Elsa couldn't draw a good breath. "I . . . have . . . children."

"We all do," he said, showing off a mouth of decaying teeth. He banged her head against the truck. "Where is it?"

"N-no."

He tightened his grip on her throat. She clawed at his hands, tried to push him away.

There was a click.

A gun being cocked.

Loreda stepped out from behind the truck, holding their shotgun aimed at the man's head.

He gave a scratchy laugh. "You ent gonna shoot me."

"I can drop a dove in midflight. And I don't even want to hurt them. You, I kinda want to shoot."

He studied Loreda, appraised her intent. Elsa saw when he believed the threat.

He let go of Elsa's throat, stepped back, lifted his splayed hands in the air. Slowly, he backed away, step by step. When he reached the end of the trees and was out in the open, he turned and walked away.

Elsa let out a ragged breath. She wasn't sure which made her feel more unsteady, the attack or the grimness of her daughter's expression.

They would be changed by this, all three of them. How was it she hadn't thought of that before now? In Lonesome Tree they'd fought against nature for survival. They'd known the dangers of the physical world.

Out here, there were new dangers. Her children would learn that man could be dangerous, too. There was a darkness in the world of which they'd been innocent; already Loreda was losing that innocence. It would never return. "We'd best sleep in the back of the truck. I hadn't figured on anyone trying to steal our gas," Elsa said.

"I reckon there's a lot we ain't figured on," Loreda said.

Elsa was too tired to correct her daughter's grammar, and really, language seemed pretty small out here, in this vast expanse of nothing. She touched Loreda's shoulder, let her hand lie there. "Thank you," Elsa said softly. It felt, strangely, as if the world had just tilted somehow, slid sideways, taking them and everything they knew with it.

❧

DAY AFTER DAY, THEY drove west. Nine hundred miles over thin, potholed roads, making slow progress, stopping only when they had to eat or get gas, and to sleep at night. Elsa had grown used to the thump and rattle of the truck and the clanging of the stove and boxes in the back. Even when she got out of the car, her body remembered the jarring up-and-down and left her feeling dizzy.

The long, hot days driving had ground them all down. There had been conversation in the first, exciting hours of travel, talk of exploring and adventures, but heat and hunger and a bumpy road had finally silenced them all, even Ant.

Now, they were camped on a wild stretch of land, close to the road, where coyotes howled and bindle stiffs walked alone, many of them desperate enough to steal the pillow from beneath your head or the gas from your tank. That scared Elsa most of all: the gas in their tank. Gas was life now.

She lay on the camp mattress with her sleeping children tucked in close. Although she had needed sleep desperately last night, it hadn't come. She'd been plagued by nightmares of what lay ahead.

She heard a sound. A branch breaking.

She sat up fast and looked around.

Nothing moved.

Careful not to waken the children, she crawled out of bed and put her shoes on, then stepped onto the hard-packed dirt. Tiny pebbles and twigs poked at the thinning soles of her last pair of shoes. She was careful not to step on anything sharp.

Well away from the truck, she lifted her dress and squatted down to relieve herself.

As she returned to the truck, the sky turned a bright peony pink, broken here or there by the strange silhouette of a cactus. Some of them looked from a distance like thorny old men, raising their fists to an uncaring god. Elsa was stunned by the unexpected beauty of the morning. It reminded her of daybreak on the farm. She tilted her face skyward, felt the honest warmth of sunshine on her skin. "Watch over us, Lord."

Back at camp, she made a fire and started breakfast. The smell of coffee and honey-drizzled polenta cakes baking in the Dutch oven over an open flame roused the children.

Ant put on his cowboy hat and stumbled close to the fire and started to unbutton his pants.

"Not so close to camp," Elsa said, swatting his backside.

Ant giggled and walked out a ways to pee. Elsa saw him making patterns in the dry dirt with his urine stream.

"I know it takes nothing to entertain him," Loreda said. "But his own pee is a new low."

Elsa had too much on her mind to smile.

"Mom?" Loreda said. "What's wrong?"

Elsa looked up. There was no point lying. "The worst section of desert is ahead. If we cross it at night, hopefully our engine won't burn up. But if something goes wrong . . ."

Elsa shuddered at the thought of their truck rolling to a steaming, smoking halt in the middle of a desert that boasted triple-digit heat and no water. They'd heard horror stories about the Mojave Desert. Cars abandoned, people dying, birds picking at sun-bleached bones.

"We'll go as far as we can today and then sleep until dark," Elsa said.

"We'll make it, Mom."

Elsa stared out at the dry, unforgiving desert that stretched west, studded here and there with cactus. Along this thin ribbon of road that stretched east to west, there was civilization, but only now and then. In between towns there were great stretches of nothing. "We have to," she said. God help her, it was as encouraging as she could be.

EIGHTEEN

They rolled into town in a cloud of dust, belongings rattling in the back. At some point Ant's baseball bat had come loose and was rolling and thumping around in the bed of the truck, banging into things.

A brown windshield veiled the world and they couldn't waste water for cleaning it. At every gas stop, the attendant wiped the road dust and dead bugs away with a rag.

When they pulled into the gas station, they saw a grocery store not far away. A crowd had gathered in front of it: more people than they'd seen in one place since Albuquerque.

These weren't town folks, for the most part. You could tell by their ragged clothes and rucksacks. These were bindle stiffs—homeless men, the kind who jumped on and off trains in the middle of the night. Some were going somewhere; most were going nowhere. Elsa couldn't help looking at each one, searching for her husband's face. She knew Loreda did the same.

Elsa pulled up to the gas pump.

"Why are there so many people over there?" Loreda asked.

"It looks like a parade or sumpin'," Ant said.

"They look angry," Elsa said. She waited for an attendant to come out and pump her gas, but no one came.

"There may not be gas again for a long time," Loreda said.

Elsa understood. She and her daughter now shared an awareness of a different kind of danger on the road. If they didn't get gas here, they wouldn't make it across the desert.

Elsa honked her horn.

A uniformed attendant hurried toward the truck. "Don't get out, lady. Lock your doors."

"What's going on?" Elsa said, rolling down her window.

"Folks have had enough," he said, pumping gas into the tank. "That's the mayor's grocery store."

Elsa heard someone in the crowd yell, "We're hungry. Give us food."

"Help us!"

The crowd surged toward the store's entrance.

"Open the door," a man shouted.

Someone threw a rock. A window shattered.

"We want bread!"

The mob broke down the door and surged into the store, shouting and yelling. They swarmed the interior, breaking things. Glass shattered.

Hunger riots. In America.

The attendant finished filling the tank, then untied the jug from the front of the truck hood and filled it with water and retied it. All the while, he was watching the riot going on in the store.

Elsa rolled down her window just enough to pay for her gas. "Be safe," she said to the attendant, who said, "What's that these days?"

Elsa drove away. In the rearview mirror, she saw more people surge into the store, bats and fists raised.

AT FOUR O'CLOCK, ELSA pulled off to the side of the road, parked in the only shade she could find, and took a nap in the back of the truck. Her sleep was restless, uncomfortable, plagued by nightmares of parched earth and impossible heat. When she woke, hours later, still feeling groggy, her limbs aching, she sat up and pushed the damp hair out of her face. She saw her children, sitting in the dirt nearby, around a campfire. Loreda was reading to Ant.

Elsa got out of the truck and walked toward her children.

An overburdened jalopy rumbled past, headlights bright enough in the falling darkness to reveal a stoop-shouldered family of four walking along the shoulder of the road, going west, the mother pushing a carriage; beside her was a white sign posted for travelers: FROM HERE ON, CARRY WATER WITH YOU.

A year ago, Elsa would have thought it insane that any woman would think to walk from Oklahoma or Texas or Alabama to California, especially pushing a baby carriage. Now she knew better. When your children were dying, you did anything to save them, even walk over mountains and across deserts.

Loreda came up beside her. They watched the woman with the baby carriage. "We'll make it," Loreda said into the quiet.

Elsa didn't know how to repond. "We made it through the Dust Bowl," Loreda said, using the recently coined term to describe the land they'd left behind. They'd read a newspaper a few days ago, learned that April 14 had been dubbed Black Sunday. Apparently three hundred thousand tons of Great Plains topsoil had flown into the air that day. More soil than had been dug up to build the Panama Canal. The dirt had fallen to the ground as far away as Washington, D.C., which was probably why it made the news at all. "What's a few miles of desert to explorers like us?"

"Not a speck," Elsa said. "Let's go."

They walked back to the truck. Elsa paused, placed her hand on the warm, dusty metal of the hood. An amorphous fear—of so many bad outcomes—coalesced into a single word. *Please*. She trusted God to watch out for them.

After a late supper of beans and hot dogs and almost no conversation, Elsa herded her children into the back of the truck to sleep on the unfurled camp mattress they'd brought from home.

"You sure you're okay driving alone at night?" Loreda asked for at least the fifth time.

"It's cooler now. That will help. I'll drive as far as I can tonight and then pull over to sleep. Don't worry." She reached past her sagging collar for the small velvet pouch she wore around her throat. She removed the copper coin, looked down at Abraham Lincoln's craggy profile.

"The penny," Loreda said.

"It's ours now."

Ant touched the coin for luck. Loreda just stared at it.

Elsa put the penny back in its hiding place, kissed them good night, and then returned to the driver's seat. She started the engine and turned on her headlights; twin golden spears cut into the darkness as she put the truck in gear and drove away.

On the road, night erased everything except the path the headlights revealed. No cars were traveling east.

The road was as flat and black and rough as a cast-iron frying pan.

As the miles accumulated, so did her fear. It spoke to her in her father's voice: *You'll never make it. You shouldn't have tried. You and your children will die out here.*

Every now and then, she passed an abandoned vehicle, ghostly evidence of families who'd failed.

Suddenly the engine coughed; the truck did a little jerk. The rosary looped around the rearview mirror swung side to side, beads clattering together. A cloud of steam erupted from beneath the hood.

No no no no.

She pulled to the side of the road. After a quick check on the sleeping kids—they were fine—she went to the front of the truck.

The hood was so hot it took her several tries to unlatch it, open it. Steam or smoke tumbled out in the dark. She couldn't tell which it was.

Hopefully steam.

She couldn't add water until the engine cooled down. Tony had drilled that fact into her head as they'd prepared for the trip. She untied the jug of water from the hood, held it close.

All she could do was wait. And worry.

She looked up and down the road; no headlights for as far as she could see.

What would happen when the sun rose? Triple-digit heat.

How close was she to the end of the desert? They had maybe three gallons of water left in their canteens.

Don't panic. They need you not to panic.

Elsa bowed her head in prayer. She felt small out here, beneath this immense, starlit sky. She imagined the desertscape around her was alive with animals who survived in the dark. Snakes. Bugs. Coyotes. Owls.

She prayed to the Virgin Mary. Begged, really.

Finally, protecting her face with her bandanna, she opened the radiator and poured in the water. Then she retied the empty jug onto the truck and went back to her seat.

"Please, God . . ." she said, and turned the key in the ignition.

A click, then nothing.

Elsa tried it again and again, pumping the gas, her panic bumping up with each failed attempt.

"Steady, Elsa." She took a deep breath and tried again.

The engine coughed and sputtered to life.

"Thank you," she whispered.

Elsa drove back onto the road and kept going.

Sometime around four, the road began to rise, becoming a giant unfurling snake of a thing, turning and twisting.

The air coming in through the open window cooled. Elsa's sweat dried in itchy patches.

She drove up the steep, winding road, following the beam of her headlights, trying not to look at the cliff that crumbled away beside her.

Finally, when she could barely keep her eyes open, she pulled off the road into a wide patch of dirt ringed by tall trees.

She climbed into bed with her sleeping children, exhausted, and closed her eyes.

"Mom."

"*Mom.*"

Elsa opened her eyes.

Sunlight blinded her.

Loreda was standing by the truck. "Come here."

"Can I sleep for just—"

"No. Come. Now."

Elsa groaned. How long had she been asleep? Ten minutes? A glance at her watch told her that it was nine o'clock.

Numb with exhaustion, she climbed out of the truck. She and Loreda walked uphill, toward a break in the trees, where Ant was waiting impatiently, bobbing up and down on bare feet.

"I need coffee," Elsa said.

"Look."

Elsa glanced behind her, looking for a good spot to make a campfire.

"*Look,* Mom," Loreda said, shaking her.

Elsa turned.

They were standing at the top of a mountain, on a wide patch of flat land. Far below lay a vast swath of farmland, fields of green. Great rectangles of brown, newly tilled earth.

"California," Ant said.

Elsa had never seen land so beautiful. So fertile. So *green.*

California.

The Golden State.

Elsa swept her children into her arms and twirled them around, laughing so deeply it seemed to be the voice of her soul. Light returning to the dark. Relief.

Hope.

LOREDA SCREAMED.

Mom downshifted. The truck bucked and lurched and slowed, taking the hairpin turn at a crawl.

The cars behind them honked. They were a caravan of jalopies now, a bumper-to-bumper snake of cars going down a mountain.

Loreda clung to the metal door handle until her fingers ached and the sunburned ridge of her knuckles turned white.

The mountain road twisted again and again, some turns so sharp and unexpected that she was flung sideways.

Mom took a turn too fast, yelped in fear, and crammed the gearshift down.

Loreda screamed again. They barely missed hitting the wreckage of a jalopy in the ditch, lying on its side.

"Quit bouncing, Ant."

"I can't. My pee's startin' to come out."

Loreda slid to the side again. The door handle pinched her skin hard enough that she cried out.

And then, at last, a huge valley stretched out in front of them, an explosion of color unlike anything Loreda had ever seen.

Bright green grass, flowering bits of color, maybe weeds or wildflowers. Orange and lemon trees. Olive trees grew in swaths of silvery gray-green.

Cultivated green fields lay on either side of the wide black roadway. Tractors tilled large swatches of land, turned up the soil for planting.

Loreda thought of the facts she'd collected as they readied for this trip. This was the San Joaquin Valley, nestled between the Coast Mountains to the west and the Tehachapi Mountains to the east. Sixty miles north of Los Angeles.

Another mountain range dominated the northern horizon, rising up like something out of a fairy tale. These were the peaks John Muir thought should be named the Range of Light.

As Loreda stared out across the San Joaquin Valley, she felt a hunger open up inside her, one she'd never imagined. Seeing all of this unexpected beauty, such colors, such majesty, she wanted suddenly to see *more*. America the Beautiful—the wild blue Pacific, the snarling Atlantic, the Rockies. All the places she and Daddy had dreamed of seeing. She wondered what San Francisco looked like, the city built on hills, or Los Angeles, with its white-sand beaches and groves of orange trees.

Mom pulled over to the side of the road and sat there clutching the wheel.

"Mom?"

Mom didn't seem to hear her. She got out of the truck and walked into a field strewn with bright wildflowers. On either side, acres and acres of freshly tilled brown soil, ready for planting. The air smelled of rich earth and new growth.

Mom drew in a deep breath, exhaled. When she turned back to the truck, Loreda saw how shiny her mom's blue eyes were.

But why cry now? They'd made it.

Mom stood there, staring out. Loreda saw a trembling in her hands and realized for the first time that Mom had been afraid. "Okay," Mom said at last. "First Explorers Club meeting in California. Which way do we go?"

Loreda had been waiting for the question. "We're in the San Joaquin Valley, I think. South is Hollywood and Los Angeles. North is the Central Valley and San Francisco. I reckon the biggest town in these parts is Bakersfield."

Mom went to the back of the truck and made sandwiches while Loreda rattled off every relevant fact she'd memorized. The three of them walked out into a field full of wildflowers and tall grass and sat down to eat.

Mom chewed her sandwich, swallowed a bite. "The only thing I know is farming. I don't want to go to a city. No jobs. So no to Los Angeles. No to San Francisco."

"The ocean is west of us."

"I surely would love to see that," Mom said, "but not yet. What good will the sea do for us? We need work and a place to live."

"Let's stay here," Ant said.

"What did you call it, Loreda? The San Joaquin Valley? It sure is pretty," Mom said. "Looks like plenty of work here. They're getting ready to plant something."

Loreda looked out over the field of wildflowers and the distant mountains. "Y'all are right. There's no need to waste gas. We just need to find a place to stay."

After lunch, they climbed back into the truck and drove deeper into the valley on a road as straight as an arrow, toward the distant purple mountains. Green fields lay on either side of the road; in some of them, Loreda saw lines of stooped men and women working the land.

They passed fields of fattening cattle and a slaughterhouse that smelled to high heaven.

As they drove past a billboard for Wonder Bread, Loreda saw a bunch of dark heaps on the ground beneath the sign.

One of the heaps sat up; it was a painfully thin boy, dressed in rags, wearing a hat with no brim on one side.

"Mom—"

Mom slowed the truck. "I see them."

There were probably twenty of them: kids, young men, most of them dressed in rags. Worn, tattered overalls, dirty hats, shirts with torn collars. The land around them was flat and brown, unirrigated, as dry as lost hope.

"Some folks don't want to work," Mom said quietly.

"You think Daddy's over there?" Ant said.

"No," Mom said, wondering how long they all would be looking for Rafe. All their lives?

Probably.

They came to a four-way stop, where a grocery store and filling station faced each other across a strip of paved road. All around were cultivated fields. A sign read, BAKERSFIELD: TWENTY-ONE MILES.

Mom said, "We need gas, and since it's our first day in California, I say licorice whips for all!"

"Yay!" Ant yelled.

Mom pulled off the road and onto the gravel lot, easing to a stop at the pumps. A uniformed station attendant came running out to help.

"Fill it up, please," Mom said, reaching for her purse.

"You pay over yonder, ma'am. Same man owns the grocery store and the gas station."

"Thank you," Mom said to the attendant.

The three of them got out of the truck and stared across a cultivated field. Men and women were stooped over above the tufts of green. People working the fields meant *jobs*.

"You ever seen anything so pretty, Loreda?"

"Never."

"Can we go look at the candy, Mom?" Ant said.

"You bet."

Loreda and Ant ran across the street, toward the store, laughing and pushing each other excitedly. Ant clung to Loreda's hand. Mom hurried to keep up with them.

An old man sat on a bench out front, smoking a cigarette, wearing a battered cowboy hat drawn low.

Inside, the general store was murky and full of shadows. A fan turned lazily overhead, casting shadows and moving the air around, not creating any real coolness. The store smelled of wooden floors and sawdust and fresh strawberries. Of prosperity.

Loreda's mouth watered at all of the foodstuffs for sale in here. Bologna, bottles of Coca-Cola, packages of hot dogs, boxes full of oranges, wrapped loaves of Wonder Bread. Ant ran straight to the array of penny candy on the counter. Big glass jars full of licorice whips and hard candies and peppermint sticks.

The cash register was situated on a wooden counter. The clerk was a broad-shouldered man wearing a white shirt and brown pants held in place by blue suspenders. A brown felt hat covered his cropped hair. He stood as stiff as a fence post, watching them.

Loreda realized suddenly what they looked like after more than a week on the road (and years on the dying farm). Wan, thin, with pinched faces. Dresses hung together with dirt and hope. Shoes full of holes, or, in Ant's case, no shoes at all. Dirty faces, dirty hair.

Loreda self-consciously smoothed the hair back from her face, tucked a few flyaway strands back under her faded red kerchief.

"You'd best control those kids of yours," the man behind the counter said to Mom. "They can't touch things with their dirty hands."

"I'm sorry for our appearance," Mom said, stepping up to the counter as she unclasped her purse. "We've been traveling and—"

"Yeah. I know. Your kind pours into California every day."

"I got gas," Mom said, plucking one dollar and ninety cents in coins from her wallet.

"I hope it's enough to get you out of town," the man said.

There was a quiet after that, a drawing in of air.

"What did you say?" Mom asked.

The man reached under the counter, pulled up a gun, clanked it on the counter between them. "You best go."

"Children," Mom said. "Go back to the truck. We're leaving now."

She dropped the coins onto the floor and herded the kids out of the store.

The door banged shut behind them.

"Who does he think he is? Just 'cause he hasn't hit hard times, the crumb thinks he has the right to look down on us?" Loreda said, infuriated and embarrassed. He had made her feel *poor* for the first time in her life.

Mom opened the truck door. "Get in," she said in a voice so quiet it was almost frightening.

NINETEEN

꙳

E lsa was glad to put that place in her rearview mirror. She didn't know what she was looking for, what she was driving toward, but she figured she'd know it when she saw it. A diner, maybe. No reason she couldn't wait tables. She drove to Bakersfield and felt a little disoriented by the size of the city. So many automobiles and stores and people out walking around, so she turned onto a smaller road and kept driving. South, she thought, or maybe east.

She refused to let one man's prejudice hurt them after all they'd been through to get here. She was angry that Loreda and Ant had experienced such baseless prejudice, but life was full of such injustice. Just look at how her father had talked about the Italians, the Irish, the Negroes, and the Mexicans. Oh, he took their money and smiled to their faces, but his words were ugly the minute the door closed. Look at what her mother had seen when she'd looked at her newborn granddaughter: the wrong skin color.

Sadly, that ugliness was a part of life and not something Elsa could shield her children from entirely. Not even in California, in their new beginning. She simply had to teach them better.

They passed a sign for DiGiorgio Farms, saw people working in the fields.

A few miles later, outside a nice-looking town, Elsa saw a row of cottages set back from the road, all neatly cared for, with trees for shade. The middle one had a FOR RENT sign in the window.

Elsa eased her foot off the gas, let the truck coast to a stop.

"What's wrong?" Loreda asked.

"Look at those pretty houses," Elsa said.

"Could we afford that?" Loreda asked.

"We won't know if we don't ask," Elsa said "Maybe, right?"

Loreda did not look convinced.

"We could get a puppy if we lived here," Ant said. "I surely do want a puppy. I'd name him Rover."

"Every dog is named Rover," Loreda said.

"Is not. Henry's dog was named Spot. And—"

"Stay here," Elsa said. She got out of the truck and closed the door behind her. In the first few steps, she felt a dream open up and welcome her in. *A dog for Ant, friends for Loreda, a school bus that stops out front to pick them up. Flowers blooming. A garden . . .*

As she neared the house, the front door opened. A woman came out, wearing a pretty floral-print dress beneath a frilly red apron, and holding a broom. Her bobbed hair was carefully curled and a pair of wireless glasses magnified her eyes.

Elsa smiled. "Hello," she said. "The house is lovely. How much is the rent?"

"Eleven dollars a month."

"My. That's steep. But I can manage it, I'm sure. I could pay six dollars now and the rest—"

"When you get a job."

Elsa was relieved by the woman's understanding. "Yes."

"You'd best get in your car and head on down the road. My husband will be home soon."

"Perhaps eight dollars—"

"We don't rent to Okies."

Elsa frowned. "We're from Texas."

"Texas. Oklahoma. Arkansas. It's all the same. *You're* all the same. This is a good Christian town." She pointed down the road. "That's the direction you want to go. About fourteen miles. That's where your kind lives." She went back into her house and shut the door.

A few moments later, she took the FOR RENT sign out of the window and replaced it with a placard that read: NO OKIES.

What was wrong with these people? Elsa knew she wasn't as clean as she could be and was obviously down on her luck, but still. Most of America was. And she'd offered eight dollars a month. She wasn't asking for charity or a handout.

Elsa walked back to the truck.

"What's wrong?" Loreda asked.

"The house didn't look so nice up close. No room for a dog. That woman said we could find a place up the road about fourteen miles. Must be a campground or auto court for people coming west."

"What's an Okie?" Loreda asked.

"Someone they won't rent to."

"But—"

"No more questions," Elsa said. "I need to think."

Elsa drove past more cultivated fields. There were few farmhouses out here; mostly the landscape was a quilt of new green growth and brown, recently tilled fields. The first sign of civilization was a school, a pretty one, with an American flag flying out front. Not far beyond that was a well-tended-looking county hospital with a single gray ambulance parked by the entrance.

"This is about fourteen miles," Elsa said, slowing down.

There was nothing here. No stop sign, no farm, no motor court.

"Is that a campground, Mommy?" Ant asked.

Elsa pulled off to the side of the road. Through the passenger window she saw a collection of tents and jalopies and shacks set back from the road in a weedy field. There had to be a hundred of them, clustered here and there in community-like pods, but without any real plan or design. They looked like a flotilla of gray sailboats and abandoned automobiles on a brown sea. There was no road to the campground, just ruts in the field, and no sign welcoming campers.

"This must be the place she was talking about," Elsa said.

"Yay! A campground," Ant said. "Maybe there'll be other kids."

Elsa turned onto the muddy ruts and followed them. An irrigation ditch full of brown water ran the length of the field to her left.

The first tent they came to had a peaked roof and sloping sides; a stovepipe stuck out from the front like a bent elbow. The area in front of the open flaps was cluttered with belongings: dented metal wash buckets, whiskey barrels, gas cans, a chopping block with an ax stuck in it, an old hubcap. Not far away sat a truck with no tires. Someone had built up slatted sides and draped plastic over it all to create a dry place to live.

"Ewwww," Loreda said.

There seemed to be no rhyme or reason to the placement of the tents and shacks and parked jalopies.

Rail-thin children dressed in rags ran through the tent town, followed by mangy, barking dogs. Women sat hunched on the banks of a ditch, washing clothes in brown water.

One pile of junk turned out to be a dwelling; inside, three children and two adults huddled around a makeshift stove. A family.

A man sat on a rock, wearing only his torn trousers, his feet bare and black soled, his drying shirt and socks spread out in the dirt in front of him. Somewhere, a baby cried.

Okies.

Your kind.

"I don't like this place," Ant whined. "It stinks."

"Turn around, Mom," Loreda said. "Get us out of here."

Elsa couldn't believe people lived this way in California. In America. These folks weren't bindle stiffs or vagabonds or hobos. These tents and shacks and jalopies housed *families*. Children. Women. Babies. People who had come here to start over, people looking for work.

"We can't drive around wasting gas," Elsa said, feeling sick to her stomach. "We'll stay here one night, find out what's going on. Tomorrow I'll find work and we'll be on our way. At least there's a river."

"River? *River?*" Loreda said. "That is not a river and this is . . . I don't know what this is, but we do not belong here."

"No one belongs in a place like this, Loreda, but we only have twenty-seven dollars left. How long do you think that will last?"

"Mom, please."

"We need a plan," Elsa said. "Getting to California. That was all we thought about. Clearly it wasn't enough. We need information. Someone here will be able to help us."

"They don't look like they can help themselves," Loreda said.

"One night," Elsa said. She forced a thin smile. "Come on, explorers. We can handle anything for one night."

Ant whined again. "But it stinks."

"One night," Loreda said, staring at Elsa. "You promise?"

"I promise. One night."

Elsa looked out at the sea of tents and saw a break in them, an empty space between a ragged tent and a shack made of scrap wood. She drove into the empty area and parked on a wide patch of dirt tufted with weeds and grass.

The nearest tent was about fifteen feet away. In front of it was a collection of junk—buckets and boxes, a spindly wooden chair, and a rusted wood-burning stove with a bent pipe.

Elsa parked the truck. They got to work, set up their large tent, staked it in place, and laid the camp mattress in one corner, right down on the dirt floor, and covered it with sheets and quilts.

They unloaded only the supplies they would need for the night.

Their suitcases, the food (all of it would need to be guarded constantly in this place), and buckets both for carrying water and for sitting on. Elsa built a small campfire in front of the tent and placed overturned buckets nearby as chairs.

She couldn't help thinking that they now looked no different from everyone else here. She dropped a blob of lard into the Dutch oven, and when it started to pop, she added a precious chunk of ham along with a few canned tomatoes, a clove of garlic, and a potato cut into cubes.

Ignoring the buckets, Loreda and Ant sat cross-legged in the grassy dirt, playing cards.

When Elsa looked at her daughter, she felt an abiding sadness creep in. It was strange how you could stop seeing people who were right beside you, how images stuck in your head. Loreda was painfully thin, arms like matchsticks, knobby elbows and knees. One sunburn after another had left her cheeks full of freckles and peeling skin.

Loreda was thirteen; she should be filling out, not wasting away. A new worry. Or an old one, grown more vivid in the past hour.

As night fell, the camp livened up. Elsa heard distant conversations, dishes being filled and emptied, and fires crackling. Orange dots—open fires—sprouted here and there. Smoke drifted from tent to tent, carrying food aromas with it. A steady stream of people walked up from the road toward the tents.

Elsa heard footsteps and looked up. A family approached their campsite—a man, a woman, and four children—two teenaged boys and two young girls. The man, tall and whippet lean, wore stained overalls and a ripped shirt. Beside him stood a woman with shaggy, shoulder-length brown hair that was going gray in streaks. She wore a baggy cotton dress with an apron over it. There seemed to be nothing over her bones but a thin layer of skin; no muscle, no fat. The two skinny little girls wore burlap sacks that had cutouts for their arms and necks; their feet were dirty and bare.

"Howdy, neighbor," the man said. "Thought we'd come by to

welcome y'all." He held out a single red potato. "We brung yah this. Ain't much, I know. But we ain't too heeled, as y'all can tell."

Elsa was touched by the generosity of the gesture. "Thank you." She reached for one of their buckets, turned it over, and placed her sweater on it. "Sit, please," she said to the woman, who smiled tiredly and sat on the bucket, adjusting her housedress to cover her bare, dirty knees.

"I'm Elsa. These are my children, Loreda and Anthony." She reached sideways, withdrew two precious slices of bread from their loaf. "Please, take these."

The man took the bread in his callused hands. "I'm Jeb Dewey. This here's my missus, Jean, and our youngsters, Mary and Buster, Elroy and Lucy."

The kids moved over to a patch of weedy grass and sat down. Loreda started a new shuffling of the cards.

"How long have you been here?" Elsa asked the adults when the kids were out of earshot. She sat down on an overturned bucket near Jean.

"Almost nine months," Jean answered. "We picked cotton last fall, but winter here is hard. You got to make enough in cotton to tide you through four months of no pickin'. And don't let anyone tell you that California is warm in the winter."

Elsa glanced over at the Deweys' tent, which was about fifteen feet away. It was at least ten by ten; just like the Martinelli's. But . . . how could six people live in such tight quarters for nine months?

Jean saw Elsa's look. "It can be a mite hard to manage. Sweeping seems like a full-time job." She smiled, and Elsa saw how pretty she must have been before hunger had whittled her down. "It ain't like Alabama, I can tell you. We were better off there."

"I was a farmer," Jeb said. "Not a big place, but enough for us. It's the bank's farm now."

"Are most of the people here farmers?" Elsa asked.

"Some. Old Milt—he lives in the blue jalopy with the broke axle over yonder—he was a darn lawyer. Hank was a postman. Sanderson made fancy hats. You can't tell nothin' by lookin' at a fella these days."

"Watch out for Mr. Eldridge. He might come atcha when he drinks. He ain't been right since his wife and boy died o' dysentery," Jean said.

"There must be some work," Elsa said, leaning forward on the bucket.

Jeb shrugged. "We go out every mornin' to look. They're pickin' in Salinas right now if ya wanna go north. We pick fruit up north in the early summer. You gotta figgur on gas prices before you start movin'. But it's cotton that gets us along."

"I don't know anything about cotton," Elsa said.

Jean smiled. "It hurts like the dickens to pick, but it'll save you. The kids'll do good, too."

"The kids? What about school?"

"Oh." Jean sighed. "There's a school. Down the road a mile or so. But . . . last fall it took all of us, even the little ones, to pick enough to keep from starvin'. Not that the girls picked much, but I couldn't leave 'em behind all day, neither."

Elsa looked at the two little girls. What were they, four and five—in the cotton fields all day? She rushed to change the subject. "Can we get mail anywhere?"

"General delivery in Welty. They hold mail for us."

"Well." Jean stood, smoothing her dress. In the gesture, Elsa got a hint of who she had been before California—the quiet, respected wife of a small-town farmer. She'd probably cared about things like Fourth of July parades and wedding quilts and box socials. "Well. I should get supper on the stove. Best be takin' our leave."

"It ain't so bad as it looks," Jeb said. "You'll see. Just go to the relief office in Welty as soon as you can. It's up the road about two miles. You've got to register with the state for relief. Tell 'em you're here. We didn't register for a couple o' months and it cost us. Not that it'll help much now, since—"

"I don't want money from the government," Elsa said. She didn't want them to think she'd come all this way for government handouts. "I want a job."

"Yeah," Jeb said. "None of us want to live on the dole. FDR and his New Deals programs done good things to help the workin' man, but us small farmers and farmworkers sorta got forgot. The big growers got all the power in this state."

Jean said, "Don't worry. Y'all can learn to live with anything if you're together."

Elsa hoped she managed a smile, but she wasn't sure. She got to her feet, shook their hands, and watched the entire family walk over to that small, dirty tent.

"Mom?" Loreda said, coming up beside her.

Don't cry.

Don't you dare cry in front of your daughter.

"It's terrible," Loreda said.

"Yes."

And that awful smell pervaded everything. *Died o' dysentery.* No wonder, if people drank the water that ran in that irrigation ditch and lived . . . this way.

"I'll find work tomorrow," Elsa said.

"I know you will," Loreda said.

Elsa had to believe it. "This is not our life," she said. "I won't let it be."

⌇

ELSA WOKE TO THE sounds of a new day: fires igniting, tent flaps being unzipped, cast-iron pans hitting cookstoves, children whining, babies crying, mothers chiding.

Life.

As if this were a normal community instead of the last stop for desperate people.

Careful not to disturb her children, she exited the tent and started a campfire and made coffee with the last of the water from their canteens.

Dozens of men, women, and children ambled across the field, toward the road. In the rising sun, they looked like stick people. At the same time, women walked toward the ditch and bent down for water, squatted on wooden planks that lay along the muddy shore.

"Elsa!"

Jean sat in front of her own tent, in a chair by a cookstove. She waved Elsa over.

Elsa poured two cups of coffee and carried them next door, offering Jean one.

"Thank you," Jean said, wrapping her fingers around the cup. "I was just thinkin' I should get up and pour myself a cup, but once I set down, I just stuck."

"Did you sleep poorly?"

"Since 1931. You?"

Elsa smiled. "The same."

People walked past them in a steady stream.

"They all heading out to look for work?" Elsa asked, checking her watch. It was a little past six.

"Yep. Newcomers. Jeb and the boys left at four and ain't likely they'll find anything. It'll be better when they start weedin' and thinnin' the cotton. They're plantin' it now."

"Oh."

Jean pushed an apple crate toward Elsa. "Set a spell."

"Where are they looking for work? I didn't see many farmhouses . . ."

"It ain't like back home. Around here the farms are big business, thousands and thousands of acres. The owners hardly step onto their land, let alone work it. They got the coppers and the government on their side, too. The state cares more about linin' the growers' pockets than takin' care of the farmworkers." She paused. "Where's your husband?"

"He left us in Texas."

"That's happenin' all over."

"I can't believe people live this way," Elsa said, and immediately regretted her words when Jean looked away.

"Where can we go that's better? Okies, they call us. Don't matter where we're from. Nobody'll rent to us, but who can afford rent anyway? Maybe after cotton season you'll have enough money to head out. We didn't, though, not with four kids."

"Maybe in Los Angeles—"

"We say that all the time, but who knows if it's better there? At least here there's pickin' jobs." She looked up. "You got enough money to waste it on gas going somewheres else?"

No.

Elsa couldn't listen anymore. "I'd best go look for work. Will you keep an eye out on my children?"

"Course. And don't forget to register with the state. Tonight I'll introduce you around to the other women. Good luck to you, Elsa."

"Thank you."

After leaving Jean, Elsa carried two buckets full of fetid water from the ditch and boiled it in batches, then strained it through cloth.

She scrubbed her face and upper body as well as she could in the shadowy tent and washed her hair and put on a relatively clean cotton dress. She coiled her wet hair into a coronet and covered it with a kerchief.

This was the best she could do. Her cotton stockings were sagging but clean and the holes in her shoes couldn't be helped. She was grateful not to have a mirror. Oh, there was one somewhere, buried in one of the boxes in the back of the truck, but it wasn't worth rummaging around for.

She left a glass full of clean water inside the tent for the children and checked that they were still sleeping.

She left Loreda a note—*Looking for work/stay here/water in glass is safe to drink*—and headed out to the truck.

She drove out to the main road.

Every farm she came to had a line of people out front, waiting for work. More people walked single file along the road, looking. Tractors churned up the soil in brown fields; here and there, she saw a horse-drawn plow working the land.

After at least half an hour, she came to a HELP WANTED sign tacked to a four-rail fence.

She pulled off the road and onto a long dirt driveway lined with flowering white trees. Hundreds of acres of a low-growing green crop spread out on either side of the driveway. Potatoes, maybe.

She pulled up in front of a big farmhouse with a large screened-in porch and a pretty flower garden.

At her arrival, a man walked out of the house, let the screen door bang shut behind him. He was smoking a pipe and was well dressed, in flannel pants and a crisp white shirt and a fedora that must have cost a fortune. His hair was precisely trimmed, sideburns shorn, as was his pencil-thin mustache.

He came around to the driver's side of the truck. "A truck, huh? You must be new."

"Arrived yesterday, from Texas."

He gave Elsa an appraising look, then cocked his head. "Head that way. The missus needs help."

"Thank you!" Elsa hurried out of the truck before he could change his mind. *A job!*

She rushed toward the large house. Passing through an open picket gate and a rose garden that enveloped her in a scent that recalled her childhood, she climbed the few steps to the front door and knocked.

She heard the clip of high heels on hardwood floors.

The door opened to reveal a short, plump woman in a fashionable slit skirt dress with a flounced silken cravat at the high neckline. Carefully controlled platinum curls swept back from a center part and framed her face in a jaw-length bob.

The woman looked at Elsa and took a step back. She sniffed daintily, pressed a lace handkerchief to her nose. "Our farmhand deals with the vagrants."

"Your . . . the man in the fedora said you needed help with some household chores."

"Oh."

Elsa was acutely aware of how ragged she looked. All that effort to present herself for work meant nothing to this woman.

"Follow me."

Inside, the house was grand: oaken doors, crystal fixtures, mullioned windows that captured the green fields outside and turned them into a kaleidoscope of color. Thick oriental carpets, carved mahogany side tables.

A little girl came into the room, her Shirley Temple curls bouncing pertly. She wore a dress of pink polka dots and black patent leather shoes. "Mommy, what does the dirty lady want?"

"Don't get too close, dear. They carry disease."

The girl's eyes widened. She backed away.

Elsa couldn't believe what she'd heard. "Ma'am—"

"Don't speak to me unless I ask a direct question," the woman said. "You may scrub the floors. But mind you, I don't want to catch you shirking and I'll check your pockets before you leave. And don't touch anything but the water, bucket, and brush."

TWENTY

Loreda woke to the smell. It reminded her with every indrawn breath that they had spent the night in the last place on earth she wanted to be.

Loreda stayed in bed as long as she could, knowing that the clarity of day would reveal images she didn't want to see, but finally, the aroma of coffee urged her up. She eased away from Ant, who grumbled, and put a holey sweater on over her dress.

She stepped into her shoes and opened the tent flap, expecting to find her mother sitting on an overturned bucket by the campfire, drinking coffee. But neither Mom nor the truck were here. Instead, she found a glass of water and her mother's note.

Loreda looked out toward the road, across the flat, brown field rutted by foot and tire tracks and a cluster of tents and vehicles. The field—probably fifty acres altogether—held a hundred tents and dozens of trucks that had become homes. She saw hovels that had been cobbled together of scrap metal and wooden boards. Women moved through the camp herding ragged children, while mangy dogs ran through, barking for food or attention. Folks had lived here a long time, long enough to string laundry lines and create yards full of junk. No one would *want* to live this way, and yet here they were. The Great Depression.

For the first time, she understood. It wasn't just banksters running off with people's money or a movie theater closing its doors or people standing in line for free soup.

Hard times meant poverty. No jobs. Nowhere else to go.

Jean stepped out of her tent and waved at Loreda.

Loreda walked toward her, strangely glad for an adult nearby. "Hey, Miz Dewey," Loreda said.

"Your mama left about an hour ago, lookin' for work."

"My mom has never had a real job."

Jean smiled. "Spoken like a teenager. It don't matter, though. Experience, I mean. The jobs out here are field jobs, mostly. They won't hire us in diners and stores and such. They want them jobs for themselves."

"It's just wrong."

Jean shrugged, as if to say, *What difference does that make?* "When times is tough and jobs is scarce, folks blame the outsider. It's human nature. And raht now, that's us. In California it used to be the Mexicans, and the Chinese before that, I think."

Loreda stared out at the debris-strewn camp. "My mom never gives up," she said. "But maybe this time she should. We could go to Hollywood. Or San Francisco." Loreda hated how her voice broke on that. Suddenly she was thinking of her dad and Stella and her grandparents and the farm. More than anything right now, she wanted to be home, to have Grandma give her one of her no-nonsense hugs and slip her a bite of something.

"Come here, honey," Jean said, opening her arms.

Loreda walked into the woman's embrace, surprised by how much it helped, even from a stranger. "You'll have to grow up, I reckon," Jean said. "Your mom probably wants you to be young, but them days are gone."

Loreda held back tears. She didn't want to grow up, certainly not in a place like this.

She looked up at Jean's kind, sad face. "So, what should I do?"

"First, go to the ditch and carry lots o' water back. You got to boil and strain it before you drink it, mind. I'll give you some cheesecloth. Doin' laundry would help your mom out."

Loreda left Jean standing outside the tent and picked up a pair of buckets and walked to the ditch. A line of women was already squatted along the banks, or on wooden planks in the brown water, washing clothes. Children played at the edges of the dirty water.

Loreda filled both buckets with the ugly water and carried them back to the tent. She passed a family of six living in a shack made of tin and wood scraps.

By the time she got back to the tent, Ant was up and sitting in the dirt. He'd obviously been crying. "Everybody left me," he whined. "I thought—"

"I'm sorry," Loreda said, putting her buckets down.

Ant shot to his feet and tackled her. Loreda held him tightly.

"I was scared."

"Me, too, Antsy," Loreda said, as comforted by the feel of him as he was by her. When he drew back, his tears were gone and his smile was back. "Wanna play catch? I got my baseball somewhere."

"Nope. I got to boil this water and make breakfast. Then we're gonna wash clothes."

"Mom didn't tell us to do that," Ant whined.

"We've got to help."

Ant looked up suddenly. "She's comin' back, ain't she?"

"She's coming back. She's looking for work so we can move."

"Phew. You reckon she'll find it?"

"I hope so."

After a breakfast of tasteless wheat cereal, Loreda washed the dishes and put everything back into boxes, which were ready for packing up when the truck returned. That way they could leave this stinking place the second Mom got back.

>

By noon, Elsa's fingers ached and her hands were burned pink from bleach and lye. She had scrubbed the kitchen, dining, and sitting room floors, and then rubbed lemon-scented oil into the wood until the planks shone. She'd pulled dozens of leather-bound books out of bookshelves and dusted behind them, unable to stop herself from smelling the leather, the paper, even reading a sentence or two.

Her life as a reader felt far away.

When her cleaning was done, she scalded two plump chickens in boiling water and plucked them, her mouth watering at the idea of roasted chicken. An hour later, she hauled wet laundry outside and fed it through the metal wringer's presses, turning the crank until her shoulders screamed at the motion. All of this she did under the watchful eye of the woman of the house, who never offered Elsa a lunch break, a glass of water, or an introduction.

"That's it, then," the woman said at just past five o'clock, as Elsa was in the kitchen again, ironing a man's shirt. "You are done."

Elsa slowly released her hold on the iron and sighed in relief. She was parched and starving. "I noticed the pantry could use some organizing, ma'am, I—"

"Touching our food? Of course not. Crime around here is sky-high since your kind moved in. Our schools are full of your dirty children."

"Ma'am, certainly, as a Christian, you must—"

"How *dare* you question my faith? Out!" she said, flinging a pointed finger toward the door. "And don't you come back. The Mexicans are better workers than you dirty Okies. They don't sass and they don't stay in town after the crops are done. We never should have deported them."

Elsa was too tired and dispirited to argue. At least she'd found work.

Today's money was a start. She had to think of it like that. She said, "Fine, ma'am," and waited to be paid.

"What?" the woman said, crossing her arms.

"My pay."

"Oh. Right." The woman dug into her pocket and pulled out some coins and dropped them in Elsa's outstretched palm.

Four dimes.

"Forty cents?" Elsa said. "For ten hours?"

"Shall I take it back? I could tell my husband how insubordinate you've been."

Forty cents.

Elsa walked away, pushed through the door, let it bang shut behind her. She got in the truck and drove down the driveway, trying not to panic.

Forty cents for a day's work.

Now she knew why the folks in the camp walked to find work. Gas was already a luxury she couldn't afford.

Tomorrow she'd join the people leaving the ditch-bank camp before dawn in the hopes of finding work in the fields. The pay had to be better than this.

But she'd be damned if her children would work in the fields. They would go to school and get an education.

Out on the main road, she saw a slim man walking along the roadside, his shoulders hunched in defeat, carrying a tattered knapsack. Black hair hung in dirty strands from a holey hat. One foot was bare.

Rafe.

It couldn't be, but still . . .

She slowed the truck to a stop and rolled down the window. It was not her husband, of course.

"You need a ride, friend?" she asked.

The man glanced sideways. The skin on his face was tightly drawn over sharp bones. His cheeks were hollow. "Naw. Thanks, tho. Ain't nowhere to go and I got me a rhythm."

Elsa stared at him for a long moment, thinking, *Yeah, none of us has anywhere to go,* then she sighed and put her foot to the gas.

☙

THAT DAY IN CAMP, Loreda learned the flexibility of time. Until today, it had always seemed fundamental, reliable. Even in the midst of heartbreak—losing her father and her best friend, and Ant's illness—time had soothed with its consistency. *Time heals all wounds,* people told her, underscoring its essential kindness. She knew in fact that some wounds deepened over time instead of lessened; still, she'd relied on time's constancy. The sun rose and the sun fell every day; in between there were chores and meals and markers, a schedule of daily life.

Here, hobbled by misery, time crawled forward.

There was nowhere to go and nothing to do. She couldn't leave Ant and go hunting for doves or jackrabbits. Instead, she and her brother sat on the lumpy camp mattress and Loreda read *The Wonderful Wizard of Oz* out loud. But the book, with its terrible tornado in Kansas, wasn't as fantastic as it used to be, not when you were staying in a place that looked like a disaster zone. In fact, Loreda thought it might give them both nightmares.

It was just past five-thirty P.M. when Loreda heard the familiar rumble of their truck. She pushed Ant away and jumped out of bed.

Outside, on the rutted road, a crowd of people were walking this way.

Mom pulled up next to the tent and parked. Loreda waited impatiently for her to shut off the engine and step out of the truck. When Mom finally did exit the truck, she just stood there, hunched over, looking tired. Defeated.

"Mom?"

Mom straightened quickly and smiled, but Loreda saw that it was a lie, that smile. The defeat in Mom's blue eyes was frightening.

"I did laundry and soaked beans," Loreda said, suddenly wanting *Mom* back, the woman who was a full-charge-ahead workhorse, who never cried or gave up, who was never afraid. "We can leave after dinner."

"I got a job today," Mom said. "I worked all day for forty cents."

"Forty cents? That's not even enough to—"

"I know."

"Forty *cents*?"

"Now we know what we're up against, Loreda. We can't spend money on rent or gas."

"Wait. You promised we'd only stay one day."

"I know," Mom said. "I was wrong. We can't go anywhere yet. We need to make money, not just keep spending it."

"You want us to stay here? *Here?*" Loreda felt horror rise up and turn into a tremulous, terrifying anger, directed at her mother. In some small speck of her she knew it wasn't fair, but there was nothing she could do to draw it back. "No. *No.*"

"I'm sorry. I don't know what else to do."

"You *lied.* Just like he did. Everyone lies—"

Mom pulled Loreda into her arms. She fought to break free, but her mother held fast, tightened her hold until Loreda gave up and slumped forward and wept.

"I talked to Jean. Cotton-picking season is supposed to be the time we can save money and pay our bills. If we are really careful and save every penny, maybe we will be able to leave in December."

Loreda drew back, feeling shaky and uncertain. Angry. "Can we go back to Texas? We have enough for gas."

"The doctor said Ant's lungs wouldn't heal for at least a year. You remember how sick he was."

"But he refused to wear his gas mask in the beginning. Maybe now—"

"No, Loreda. That's not an option." She pushed the hair out of

Loreda's face with a gentle touch. "I need your help with Ant. He won't understand."

"*I* don't understand. This is America. How can this be happening to us?"

"Hard times," Elsa said.

"That's a darn lie."

"Language, Loreda," Mom said tiredly. Then she walked over to the truck and climbed up into the bed and began unstrapping the narrow, black wood-burning stove that Rose and Tony had used in the dugout years ago, before they'd built the farmhouse.

Loreda hated the idea of unpacking that stove with every fiber of her being. A stove meant home; it meant you were staying someplace, settling in. They'd imagined this stove heating a new house. With a sigh, she climbed up alongside her mom and untied the straps. Together, both of them grunting, they muscled the heavy stove out of the truck and onto the weedy grass in front of the tent. The buckets and a metal washbasin were beside it.

"Great," Loreda said. Now they looked like all the rest of the poor, desperate people living in tents in this ugly field.

"Yeah," Mom said.

There was nothing else to say.

They went into the tent, where Ant was lying on the dirt floor beside the mattress, playing with his toy soldiers. "Mom! You came back."

Loreda saw the pain flash across her mother's face. "I will always come back. You two are my whole life. Okay? Don't ever be afraid of that."

※

THAT NIGHT, ELSA LAY awake long after the kids had said their prayers and fallen asleep on either side of her. Moonlight illuminated the canvas walls, setting the small interior aglow. Careful not to disturb the kids, she found a scrap of paper and a pencil and sat up to write.

Dear Tony and Rose,

Greetings from California!

After a grueling drive that was more fun than any of us expected, we came to the San Joaquin Valley. It's a beautiful place. Mountains. Crops that are green and growing, rich brown earth.

Our tent is near a river. We've made friends with folks from the South. The kids are excited to start school tomorrow. How are things with you?

You can write to us care of General Delivery at the Post Office in Welty, California.

Pray for us as we pray for you.

Love,

Elsa, Loreda, and Ant

THE NEXT MORNING, ELSA woke before the sun rose and began carrying water back to the campsite, putting it on to boil on the stove.

In the darkness, smoke drifted from tent to tent; she heard the clang of water buckets being filled, of grease popping in cast-iron pans. People began to walk toward the road. Men, women, children.

At seven o'clock, she wakened the children, got them dressed, and herded them out of the tent, where she fed them some hot mush (not enough, but she knew now she had to save every single penny), and used the newly boiled, strained, and cooled water to wash their hair and faces. She was so grateful the kids had done laundry yesterday.

Ant tried to wiggle free. "Why do I gotta be cleaner?"

"Because today is the first day of school," Elsa said.

"Yippee!" Ant said, jumping up and down.

Loreda took a step back. "Tell me you're kidding."

"Education is everything, Loreda. You know that. You will be the first Martinelli to go to college."

"But—"

"No *buts*. Hard times don't last. Education does and y'all are behind the grind these days. Hurry up. We have a walk ahead of us."

"How am I supposed to go to school with no shoes?" Ant said. "Didja think of that?"

Elsa stared down at her son in horror. How in God's name had she forgotten that salient fact? "I . . . we . . ."

"Elsa?"

She turned, saw Jean walking toward her, carrying a scuffed, holey pair of boy's shoes. "I saw you carrying water," Jean said. "I figured you was washing the kids for school."

"I forgot my son had no shoes. How could I—"

Jean touched her shoulder, gave her a reassuring squeeze. "We do the best we can, Elsa. Here, these shoes belonged to Buster. He's outgrown 'em. You give 'em back when Ant outgrows them."

Elsa couldn't find words to express her gratitude. This generosity was nothing short of stunning, coming as it did from one with so little.

"It's how we get by," Jean said, patting Elsa's arm.

"Th-thank you."

"The school's a mile south." Jean cocked her head to the south. "They ain't real welcomin' there."

"I'd say that's true of the whole state so far," Elsa said.

"Yep."

"After you get 'em set in school, you'd best go register with the state. The relief office is north of here about two miles in Welty. You want them to know you're here."

Relief.

Elsa's stomach tightened at the thought. She nodded. "So, south to school and then go back north two miles from here to town. Got it."

Elsa handed Ant the shoes and loved how happy they made him. "All right, Martinellis," she said as he laced them up. "Let's go."

They walked out to the main road and turned south, joining a group of children walking in the same direction. There were probably nine children aged six to ten. Loreda was the oldest child in the group. Elsa was the only adult.

A blunt-nosed school bus rumbled past, spitting rocks and blowing dust. It didn't stop for the migrant children.

They passed a county hospital with a gray ambulance parked out front, and finally came to the school. Green grass and trees gave it an inviting look. A crowd of laughing, talking kids swarmed the yard. They were clean and well dressed. The migrant children moved woodenly, silently, among them.

"Look at them, Mom," Loreda said. "New clothes."

Elsa tipped Loreda's chin up with one finger, saw the tears gathering in her daughter's eyes. "I know what you're feeling, but don't you *dare* cry," Elsa said. "Not about this, not with all you've been through to get here. You're a Martinelli, and you're as good as anyone in California."

Tucking her children's hands in hers, she took them across the grass, beneath the billowing American flag.

Inside, the hallways were full of children. Elsa noticed the looks thrown their way and saw how the better-dressed children avoided them. A bulletin board held flyers for field trips and school functions and advertised the upcoming PTA meeting.

Elsa headed into the first office she saw. She stood with her children in front of a long counter. A placard on it read: BARBARA MOUSER, ADMINISTRATION.

Elsa cleared her throat. "Excuse me?"

The woman seated at a desk behind the counter looked up from her paperwork.

"I am here to enroll my children in school."

The woman sighed heavily and got to her feet. She was dressed in a pretty blue dress with a fabric belt, silk stockings, and sensible brown shoes. Elsa noticed that her nails were well cared for and her cheeks were nice and plump.

The woman walked up to the counter, on the other side of which Elsa and the children stood. "Did you bring report cards? Transfer papers? School records?"

"We left in a bit of a rush. Times back home were—"

"Hard for you Okies. Yes."

"We're from Texas, ma'am," Elsa said.

"What are their names?"

"Loreda and Anthony Martinelli. We call him—"

"Address?"

Elsa didn't know how to answer the question. "We . . . uh."

The woman turned her head, yelled, "Miss Guyman, come here. Squatters. Okies."

"We're from Texas," Elsa said firmly.

The woman pushed a piece of paper at Elsa. "Can you read and write?"

"Oh, for gosh sakes," Elsa said. "Of course."

"Names and ages." She handed Elsa a pencil.

As Elsa wrote down the children's names, a younger woman appeared in the office, dressed in a crisp white nurse's uniform and cap. The nurse marched over to the children, went to Loreda and began pawing through her hair.

"No lice," the nurse said. "No fever . . . yet. How old is this girl?" the nurse asked. "Eleven?"

"Thirteen," Elsa answered.

"Can she read?"

"Of course. She's excellent in school."

The nurse checked Ant's hair. "Fine," she said at last. "Most of your kind work the fields at eleven. I'm surprised your daughter is in school."

"Our *kind* are hardworking Americans who have hit hard times," Elsa said.

"Follow me," Mrs. Mouser said. "Not too close."

Elsa and the children followed the woman, who stopped at the end of the hall. "Boy. In there. Go."

Ant grabbed Elsa's sleeve, stared up at her.

"You're okay," Elsa said.

He shook his head, eyes pleading for a way out of this.

"Go," Elsa said.

Ant sighed heavily. His shoulders slumped in defeat. With a lackluster wave, he opened the door and disappeared into the busy classroom.

"No dawdling," the administrator said, walking on ahead.

Elsa had to force herself to keep walking. Loreda stayed close beside her.

At the last doorway, marked with a seven on it, the administrator stopped. "You," she said to Loreda. "Go on in. See those three desks in the back corner? Sit at one of them. Don't touch anyone or anything on your way. And for God's sake, don't cough."

Loreda looked at Elsa.

"You're as good as anyone," Elsa said.

Loreda opened the classroom door.

Elsa saw the way the clean, well-dressed children snickered at her daughter. A few of the girls even leaned away from Loreda as she passed them. A boy with red hair held his nose and a bunch of them laughed.

It took all the strength Elsa possessed to turn away from the closed door.

❧

ELSA WALKED BACK OUT to the main road and turned north. At the turnoff to the ditch-bank camp, she kept going. At last, she came to a small, well-tended town with a big cotton-boll-shaped sign that welcomed her to Welty, California. Main Street ran for four blocks; she saw a boarded-up theater, a city hall with columns out front, and a row of shops. She walked from shop to shop, seeing no help wanted signs in any windows.

The state relief office was off Main Street, tucked in a square full of park benches and flowering trees. A long line of people waited to get in.

She stepped into line. People didn't look at each other, nor did they speak.

Elsa understood. She could tell by the hard, shuttered looks on the men's and women's faces around her that they'd waited until they had no choice but to ask for help. And they were ashamed to need anything from the government. From anyone, really. Like her, they'd always worked for what they needed, not relied on the government for a handout.

Elsa's mind went blessedly blank as she stood there.

She finally made her way to the front of the line. Beneath a temporary awning sat a young man in a brown suit with a thin black tie over a crisp white shirt. A brimmed brown hat sat at a jaunty angle on his head.

"You here for relief?" he said, looking up, tapping his pen.

"No. I'll find a job, but I was told I needed to register. Just in case."

"Good advice. I wish more people heeded it. Name?"

"Elsinore Martinelli."

He wrote something down on a red card. "Age?"

"Lord," she said, laughing nervously. "Thirty-nine next month."

"Husband?"

She paused. "No."

"Children?"

"Loreda Martinelli, thirteen. Anthony Martinelli, eight."

"Address?"

"Uh."

"Side of the road," he said with a sigh. "Around here?"

"About two miles south."

He nodded. "Squatter's camp on Sutter Road. When did you arrive in California?"

"Two days ago."

The young man wrote all that down on her red card, then looked up. "We keep records of everyone who comes into the state. Your date for residency starts when you sign up, not when you actually arrive. There's no state relief until you're a resident, defined as being in the state for a year. Come back on April twenty-sixth."

"A year?" Elsa frowned. "But . . . I hear there's no work in the winter. Don't folks need help then?"

The man gave her a pitying look. "The feds'll give you some help. Commodities. Every two weeks." He cocked his head. "That's their line over there."

Elsa turned, saw the even longer line down the street. "What's commodities?"

"Beans. Milk. Bread. Food."

"So, all those folks are standing in line for food?"

"Yes, ma'am."

Elsa felt deeply sorry for the women she saw standing over there, skinny as rails, their heads bowed in shame. "That's not me," she said quietly. "I can feed my children."

For now.

TWENTY-ONE

At the end of the school day, Elsa stood at the flagpole, waiting for her children. She fought a wave of dizziness and realized that she'd forgotten to pack herself a lunch when she left this morning. After signing up for relief, she'd spent more hours walking through town, looking for work. It hadn't taken long to realize that no store proprietor or diner owner would hire someone who looked as ragged and poor as she did.

The school bell rang; children poured out of the school. The school bus doors wheezed open in welcome for some of the children.

She saw Loreda and Ant coming her way.

Ant had a black eye and his collar was ripped.

"Anthony Martinelli, what happened?" Elsa said.

"Nuthin'."

"Anthony—"

"Nuthin', I said."

She hugged her young son.

"You're choking me," he said, trying to get free.

Elsa forced herself to let go, and Ant pulled away. He walked on ahead, his empty lunch bag balled up in his fist.

"What happened, Loreda?"

"Some fifth-grader called him an ignorant Okie. Ant told him to take it back and when he wouldn't, Ant punched him. The kid punched back."

"I'll talk to—"

"The teachers know, Mom. The principal came out and said the boy shouldn't have punched Ant cuz we carry disease. He said, 'You know better than to touch 'em, Johnson.'"

"He's eight years old," Elsa said softly.

Loreda had no answer.

"I'll talk to him about turning the other cheek," Elsa said. It was all she could think of. What did she know of schoolyard fights or what it took to become a man?

Up ahead, Ant walked alone along the side of the road, looking small. Vulnerable. The few cars that passed them stirred up dust and honked at him to get out of the way.

"How about teaching him to kick a bigger boy in the privates?"

"I am not going to teach my son to kick another boy in . . . that area."

"Great. Teach him how to make an ice pack, then. Let him become a punching bag. Teach him we will always live this way."

"Oh, Loreda," she said. "I know how bad it is . . ."

"Do you? They ate fried chicken and had fruit-pie slices for lunch, Mom. One of them had something called a Twinkie. It smelled so good I accidentally made a sound and some of the girls laughed at me. One said, *Look at her, eating a potato.* And someone else said, *She probably stole it.*"

"Girls like that, unkind girls who think it's funny to laugh at another's misfortune, are nothing. Specks on fleas on a dog's butt."

"It hurts."

"Yes," Elsa said, remembering when she'd been called Anyone Else at school. "I know."

When they turned at last toward the camp along the ditch bank, she called out for Anthony. He stopped, waited for her. "Would Papa whup me for fighting?"

"For defending yourself? No. But let's fight with words from now on. Okay?"

"Yeah. Okay. How about if I say *fuck you*?"

Elsa almost laughed. God help her.

"No, Ant. You will not say that."

Ant's shoulders slumped. "I'm gonna get punched again. I know it."

"He is," Loreda said with a sigh.

All Elsa could think was, *We all are.*

⌒

THAT NIGHT, AFTER A dinner of ham-and-potato hash, Elsa got Ant settled in bed. None of them had said much during dinner. Loreda left the tent immediately after the meal, saying she couldn't stand the stuffiness. Elsa tucked Ant in bed and sat with him.

"It'll get better, Mom, right?" he said when he'd finished his prayers.

"Of course it will." Elsa stroked his head, ran her fingers through his hair until he fell asleep.

She eased out of bed and looked down at him.

The bruise around his eye was more pronounced now. Someone had punched him in the face, made fun of him. . . . It made her want to hit something. Hard.

Had she made a mistake in bringing them here? They'd given up everything they'd known and loved to start over here, but what if there was no new beginning here? What if it was just the same hardship and hunger they'd left behind? Or worse?

She withdrew the battered metal box she'd brought with her from

Texas. Opening it carefully, she stared down at the money: less than twenty-eight dollars. How long would that last if she didn't find work soon?

She closed the box and hid it inside the box of pots and pans, and then went outside, where she found Loreda sitting on an overturned bucket.

The camp lay in darkness. Elsa heard fiddle music coming from somewhere.

Loreda looked up. "It makes me think of Grandpa."

Elsa could only nod. A wave of homesickness threatened to topple her.

Jean approached their tent. "Come with me."

Loreda got to her feet. She looked as battered and demoralized by this day as Elsa felt.

The three of them walked through the camp, past open tents and closed-up cars. Dogs ran around barking.

At a flat, empty place along the ditch, a crowd had gathered. There were probably fifteen people here, men and women, standing around talking. Two men sat on rocks at the bank, playing fiddles.

Jean led Elsa and Loreda to a pair of women who stood near a spindly tree. "Gals, this here's Elsa Martinelli and her daughter, Lor-ay-da."

The women turned, both smiled. Elsa couldn't quite figure their ages. Late forties, maybe. Both were worn-looking, with wan smiles and kind eyes.

"Welcome, Elsa. I'm Midge," said the thinner of the women. "From Kansas. What they're calling the Dust Bowl, and, doll, it surely was."

Elsa smiled and put an arm around Loreda. "We're from the Texas Panhandle. We know dust."

"I'm Nadine," said the other woman in a beautiful drawling voice. She wore a pair of rimless round eyeglasses and smiled quickly. "From South Carolina. Can you believe I left a place where you could fish the waters? All those flyers about California being the land of milk and honey. *Pfffst.* How long y'all been here?"

"Just a few days," Loreda said. "But it seems longer."

Nadine laughed, adjusted her glasses. "Yeah. Time is odd here."

"You signed up for relief?" Midge asked.

Elsa nodded. "I did, but . . . well, I don't need relief just yet."

Midge and Nadine and Jean exchanged a knowing look.

They didn't say, *You will,* but they might as well have. That terrible sinking feeling came back into Elsa's stomach.

"You stick with us, doll," Nadine said. "We get each other through the days."

*

AFTER NEARLY FOUR WEEKS in California, they had settled into a routine; while Loreda and Ant went to school, Elsa looked for work. Any work. For any pay. She left earlier each morning, and walked up the road, sometimes going north, sometimes south, always hoping against hope to find a job weeding in the fields or doing laundry. More often than not she came up empty. Every time she bought food, her meager savings were being depleted. When she ran out of beans, she had to buy more. Ant had to have canned milk. He was a growing boy.

Now, after a long day looking for work and finding none, Elsa sat at the ditch bank, on an apple crate she'd found by the side of the road. It was nearing nightfall and there were about thirty people here: women washing clothes, men smoking pipes and talking, children playing tag and laughing. The heat of the day remained, giving a hint of what was to come in the next few months.

Someone played a harmonica; a dog howled in accompaniment. Ant had made friends with Mary and Lucy Dewey and the three of them ran around playing hide-and-seek. Loreda talked to no one, sat by herself, reading. Elsa knew she was determined not to make a friend here.

Jean hauled a metal bucket to the ditch bank and sat beside Elsa.

"It's starting to get warm already," Jean said. "Lord, these tents are uncomfortable in the summer."

"Maybe we'll all be working by then and be able to move."

Jean said, "Maybe," in a way that conveyed no hope at all. "How are the kids doing in school?"

"Not great, honestly. But I won't let them quit."

"Stay strong," Jean said, looking out at the people gathered along the ditch.

Elsa looked at her friend. "Do you ever get tired of being strong?"

"Oh, honey, of course."

FIVE WEEKS AFTER THEY arrived in California, they got their first letter from Tony and Rose. It bolstered everyone's spirits.

> *Dearest ones,*
>
> *The dust storms haven't given up, I'm sorry to say. Even so, there was another meeting this week. The government is offering us farmers ten cents per acre if we agree to contour the land. The work is slow going, but Tony is back to spending long hours on the tractor, and you know he'd rather be on his tractor than anywhere else. The Works Progress Administration is paying out-of-work men to help us. Now we just hope for these awful dust storms to stop. And if it rains, all this hard work might mean something.*
>
> *Yesterday, a man came through town and promised to bring rain, called himself a rainmaker. It was something to see, I'll say that. He shot something up in the sky. We're all waiting now to see if it works. I reckon you can't prompt God that way, but who knows?*
>
> *We miss you all and hope you are well.*
>
> *Hopefully Elsa's birthday was a grand event. Happiest of days!*
>
> *With love,*
>
> *Rose and Tony*

❧

On the last day of May, Elsa herded her children off to school and remained behind. Just this once, she was not looking for work. She had something else to do.

Without a husband to help out, Elsa felt the heavy burden of both working and caring for the children. So many chores and too few hours in which to do them. It was no surprise there were few single women out here. Loreda did more than her share; heck, these days everyone in the camp did more than their share of everything. Even Ant pulled his weight without complaint. He was responsible for making sure there was always plenty of firewood, kindling, and paper. He spent a lot of time rummaging through the camp and along the main road for whatever he could find; he also brought newspapers home from school. Yesterday he'd found a broken apple crate—a treasure.

It took Elsa two hours to carry enough water back to wash all of their clothes. By the time she boiled and strained the water and poured it into the copper tub they'd brought with them from Texas, she was sweating and exhausted. Once the clothes were washed, she hung them from the interior metal tent frame. They would take longer to dry inside, but at least they wouldn't be stolen. Then she put some lentils on to soak.

When those chores were done, she dragged the copper tub into the tent and then started hauling water again. Bucketful after bucketful; she hauled it from the ditch, boiled it and strained it and poured it into the tub.

Finally, she tied the tent flaps shut and disrobed—a thing she hadn't done in weeks. In the past month, they had learned, all of them, how to survive in these terrible conditions, packed in like prisoners. Baths had become luxuries rather than necessities.

She stepped into the tub and crouched down. The water was lukewarm, but still it felt heavenly. Using their last scrap of soap, she washed her body and her hair, trying not to care that in places she felt only her scalp.

Shivering as the water chilled around her, she stepped out and dried off, saving the water in the tub for the kids to bathe in. Heat radiated down from the canvas and up through the dirt floor as she brushed her thinning blond hair. There was no mirror in which to check her appearance, but she didn't want one. She covered her head with her cleanest kerchief, wishing that, today of all days, she still owned a hat.

The women would all be wearing hats.

Don't think about them. Or yourself.

This was for her children.

She unpacked her best dress.

Best dress. Made last year from scraps of pillowcase lace and flour sacks. The last time she'd worn it had been to church in Lonesome Tree.

Don't think about that.

She dressed carefully, pulling up her sagging cotton stockings and stepping into worn-down shoes. Then she stepped out of the tent and into the blazing afternoon sun.

Jean stood outside her own tent, holding a broom.

Elsa waved and walked over.

"I think you're lookin' for trouble," Jean said, looking worried.

"If I am, it's about time."

"I'll be here waitin' when you get back," Jean said.

Nadine walked over to join them. "She's really going?" she said to Jean.

Jean nodded. "She's going."

"Well, doll," Nadine said, "I wish I had your pluck."

Elsa was grateful for the support.

She walked out of camp. On the main road, the few automobiles that passed her honked for her to get off to the side. By the time she reached the school, she was covered in fine red dust.

She brushed as much of the dirt off of her as she could. She would *not* be a coward. Chin up, she crossed the lawn and bypassed the office and walked toward the library.

There was a sign on the door for the after-school PTA meeting.

She opened the door just as the school bell rang and children ran out into the hallway.

In the library, books lined every wall; there was a checkout desk, and bright overhead lights. A dozen or so women stood clustered together, sipping coffee from china cups. Elsa noticed how well they were dressed—silk stockings, fashionable dresses, matching handbags. Hair cut and styled. At one side of the room, a long table, draped in white, held trays of cookies and sandwiches and a silver coffee urn.

The women turned to stare at Elsa. Their conversations stalled and then stopped altogether.

Elsa wondered how it was she'd thought a clean flour-sack dress or a bath would help. She didn't belong here. How could she have thought otherwise?

No. This is America. I'm a mother. I'm here for my kids.

She took a step forward.

Eyes on her. Frowns.

At the clothed table, she poured herself a cup of coffee and took a sandwich. Her hand was shaking as she lifted it to her lips.

An older woman, in a tailored tweed skirt suit and heels, with tightly curled hair that peeked out beneath a beribboned felt hat, peeled away from the cluster of women and walked resolutely toward Elsa. As she neared, she raised one eyebrow. "I'm Martha Watson, president of the PTA. You're lost, I presume."

"I'm here for the PTA meeting. My children are in school here and I'm interested in the curriculum."

"People like you don't influence our curriculum. What you do is bring disease and trouble to our schools."

"I have a right to be here," Elsa said.

"Oh, really? Do you have an address in the community?"

"Well . . ."

"Do you pay taxes to support this school?"

The woman sniffed, as if Elsa smelled, and walked away, clapping her hands. "Come along, mothers. We need to plan the end-of-the-year raffle. We want to raise money to get those dirty migrants a school of their own."

The women fell in behind Martha, waddling like chicks behind the mama duck.

Elsa did what she'd always done when faced with derision and contempt. She walked away, defeated, left the library, went out into the now-deserted schoolyard.

She was almost to the flagpole when she stopped.

No.

This was not the woman she wanted to be anymore. Not the mother she wanted to be. These women looked at her and judged her and thought they knew her. They thought she was trash.

But she wasn't trash. And her children certainly weren't trash.

You can do it.

Could she?

They're bullies, Elsa. That was what Rose would say. *The only way to fight a bully is to stand your ground.*

Be brave, Grandpa Walt would say. *Pretend if you have to.*

Clutching her handbag strap, she walked back into the school. At the library door, she paused, but not for long, and then opened the door.

The women—a gaggle of geese, Elsa thought—turned to her. Mouths dropped open.

Martha took control. "I thought we told you—"

"I heard you," Elsa said. She was literally quaking inside. Her voice wavered. "Now you will hear me. My children go to this school. I will be a part of this. Period." She sidled into the back row and sat down, clamping her knees together, holding her purse on her lap.

Martha stared at her, lips pinched tightly together.

Elsa sat still.

"Fine. You can't impose manners or breeding. Ladies. Sit down."

The women took their seats, careful not to be near Elsa.

For the entire meeting—more than two hours—no one looked back at her. In fact, they were studiously avoiding her as they talked among themselves, saying things in strident voices: *dirty migrants . . . live like hogs . . . lice . . . don't know any better . . . shouldn't be allowed to think they belong.*

Elsa heard the message but didn't care, and not caring felt good.

Almost exhilarating, in fact. For once, she had not let someone else tell her where she belonged.

"The meeting is adjourned," Martha said.

No one moved. The women sat rigidly upright, facing Martha.

Elsa got it.

They wouldn't walk past her.

They carry disease, you know.

Elsa faked a sneeze. Everyone jumped.

Elsa got to her feet and walked casually toward the door, taking her time. As she passed the food table, she saw all that was there: little peanut-butter-and-pickle sandwiches on store-bought bread with the crusts cut off, deviled eggs, a Jell-O salad, and a plate of cookies.

Why not?

They thought she was a dirty Okie anyway. What beaten dog didn't jump at scraps?

Elsa picked up the plate of cookies and dumped all of them into her handbag. Next, she removed her headscarf and filled it with sandwiches. Then she snapped her handbag shut.

"Don't worry, ladies," she said, reaching for the door handle. "I'll bring a treat next time. I'm sure y'all *love* squirrel stew."

She walked out of the library and let the door bang shut behind her.

A HALF HOUR LATER, Elsa got her first whiff of the camp—the stench of too many people living without sanitation on a hot May day.

At their tent, she found Loreda and Ant sitting on boxes out front playing cards. Loreda had started making the lentil stew. Smoke puffed up through the stove's short metal pipe and drifted sideways.

At Elsa's arrival, Ant jumped up to greet her, but Loreda remained seated. Her daughter looked up and said, "Hey," in that new clenched voice of hers.

Ant produced a local newspaper that was stained and torn. Across the top in bold black type was the headline: "Criminal Element Rampant in Migrants Flooding into State. One Thousand Enter California Per Day." "I found this in the trash at school. I stole it. For the fire," he said.

"It ain't stealing if it's in the trash," Loreda said.

"I have a surprise," Elsa said.

"A *good* surprise?" Loreda said without looking up. "Or another bad thing happening?"

Elsa touched Loreda with the toe of her shoe. "It's good. Come on."

She herded her children toward the Deweys' tent. As they approached, Elsa smelled cornbread cooking.

Elsa called out a greeting at the closed flaps.

The tent flaps opened. Five-year-old Lucy stood there in her burlap-sack dress, skinny as a stalk of alfalfa, with four-year-old Mary standing so close the two girls looked conjoined.

Lucy smiled, showing off two missing teeth. "Miz Martinelli," she said. "What're y'all doing here?"

"I brought you something," Elsa said.

Inside the murky darkness that smelled of sweat, Elsa saw Jean sitting on a box, sewing by candlelight.

"Elsa," Jean said, getting to her feet.

"Come out," Elsa said. "I have a treat."

They gathered outside, around the small stove, where cornbread baked in a black cast-iron skillet. Jean sat down in the chair by the stove.

The four children plopped down in the weed-infested dirt, all cross-legged, and waited quietly.

Elsa opened her purse and took out a handful of cookies.

Ant's eyes lit up. "Wowza!" He cupped his hands together and reached out.

Elsa put a sugar-dusted cookie in each pair of hands, and then handed a small peanut-butter-and-pickle sandwich to Jean, who shook her head. "The kids need it more."

Elsa gave Jean a look. "You need to eat, too."

Jean sighed. She took the sandwich, took a bite, and moaned quietly.

Elsa tasted a cookie. Sugar. Butter. Flour. The single bite hurled her back in time to Rose's kitchen.

"How did it go?" Jean asked quietly.

"They made me president. Asked where I bought my dress."

"That good, huh?"

"I took all their treats. That was the highlight."

"I'm proud of you, Elsa."

Elsa couldn't remember anyone ever saying that to her. Not even Rose. It was surprising how much those few words could lift one's spirit. "Thank you, Jean."

The children ran off, laughing together. It was remarkable—and inspiring—to see how one sugary treat could revive them. Later, they'd have the sandwiches.

When they were alone, Jean said quietly, "I'm in trouble, Elsa."

"What's wrong?"

Jean put a hand on her flat stomach and looked sadly at Elsa.

"A baby?" Elsa whispered, lowering herself to sit on a crate beside Jean.

Born here?

Good Lord.

"How'm I gonna feed this one? I don't reckon I'll ever get milk in my breasts."

Once, Elsa would have said, *God will provide,* and she would have believed it, but her faith had hit the same hard times that had struck the country. Now, the only help women had was each other. "I'll be here for you," Elsa said, then added, "Maybe that's how God provides. He put me in your path and you in mine."

Jean reached over for Elsa's hand and held it. Elsa hadn't known until right then how much difference a friend could make. How one person could lift your spirit just enough to keep you upright.

TWENTY-TWO

Dearest Tony and Rose,

    June in California is beautiful. Hard red flowers have burst out in the cotton fields. Imagine the look of it across thousands of acres, with the mountains in the distance.

    The friends we have made promise plenty of work for all when the cotton is ready to pick.

    I must admit, it's hard to imagine myself working in someone else's fields. I'm sure it will make me think of you and the many wonderful hours we spent tending to our grapes and our fruit and our vegetables.

    We miss you and think of you often and hope you are well.

Love,

Elsa, Ant, and Loreda

IN JUNE, ELSA FOUND that if she woke at four A.M. and joined Jeb and the boys in line, there was usually work in the cotton fields, weeding and thinning the crop. Not every day, but most days she worked twelve hours for fifty cents. The pay wasn't good but she spent carefully and they survived. When Loreda's shoes wore out, instead of buying a new pair, Elsa cut out pieces of cardboard and fit them carefully inside the shoes.

Today, after a long, tiring day, she walked home with the others from the ditch-bank camp who'd found work at Welty Farms, which had nearly twenty thousand acres of cotton in California; the nearest field was about three miles north of the ditch-bank camp, past the town of Welty.

Jeb was beside her, walking back from work with his boys. "There's talk that Welty might cut wages," he said.

"How can they possibly pay us less?" Elsa said.

Another man said, "So many desperate folks floodin' into the state. More'n a thousand a day, I heard."

"Most of 'em'll take any pay at all if it means they can put food on the table," Jeb said.

"The durn farm owners can pay less and less," said another man. "I'm Ike," he said to Elsa, extending a thin-fingered hand in greeting. "I live at the Welty camp."

She shook his hand. "Elsa."

Fifty cents. That was what she'd earned today, and it wouldn't go far, and there was never any way of knowing how long this money had to last or when she'd get work again or what she'd be paid. What if they offered her forty cents tomorrow? What choice would she have but to agree?

"Once we're pickin' cotton, we'll be better," Jeb said.

The man named Ike made a sound. "I don't know, Jeb. I got a bad feeling. The price of cotton is down, and the damned Ag Adjustment Act is putting the squeeze on the growers again. The government wants less cotton planted to raise prices. You know what that means. Sooner or later, if the growers get squeezed, we get pounded."

"What about the summer months?" Elsa asked. "Once the cotton is thinned, it will be months before it's ready to pick. What work is there then?"

"Most of us move north pretty soon to pick fruit. We come back in the fall for cotton."

"Is it worth the gas money?" Elsa asked.

Jeb shrugged. "It's work, Elsa. We take it where we can, when we can."

Up ahead, Elsa saw women cooking in front of whatever dwellings they had. She heard the strains of a fiddle rising up and it made her smile.

Outside their tent, Loreda and Ant sat on the buckets on the ground. Beside them, a pot of beans simmered on the stove.

"Mom?" Loreda said. "I need to talk to you."

That couldn't be good. Lately, Loreda's anger had grown exponentially. She didn't complain much, or roll her eyes and storm off, but somehow that made it worse. Elsa knew her daughter was eating a steady diet of outrage and sooner or later she would explode. "Sure."

"Stay here, Ant," Loreda said, rising to her feet.

Elsa followed Loreda toward the ditch they pathetically called a river.

Beneath a spindly tree in full bloom, Loreda stopped and turned to face Elsa. "School ended two days ago."

"I'm aware of that, Loreda."

"Are you also aware that I'm the only thirteen-year-old in camp during the day?"

Elsa knew where this was going. She'd been expecting it. Dreading it. "Yes."

"Seven-year-olds are working in the fields, Mom."

"I know, Loreda, but . . ."

Loreda moved closer. "I'm not deaf, Mom. I hear what people say. Winter in California is bad. There's no work. We can't get state relief until next April. So the only money we have is what we make working in the fields. It will have to get us through four months with no work and no relief money."

"I know."

"Tomorrow I'm going to work with you."

Elsa wanted to say—to scream—*NO*.

But Loreda was right. They needed to save money for the winter.

"Just for the summer. Then you go back to school," Elsa said. "Jean can watch Ant."

"You know he'll want to work, too, Mom," Loreda said. "Ant's strong."

Elsa walked away, pretending she hadn't heard.

⟡

BY JULY, THE WORK in the cotton fields had ended again; there would be no more until it was time to pick the crop. Still, each day, new migrants walked or rode into the San Joaquin Valley. More workers, less work. The newspapers were full of outrage and despair on the part of the citizens, who worried that their tax dollars were being spent to help nonresidents. The schools and hospitals were overrun, they said, unable to survive the demands of so many outsiders. They worried about bankruptcy and losing their way of life and being made unsafe by the wave of crime and disease they blamed on migrants.

Elsa called an Explorers Club meeting and asked her children if they wanted to stay in the ditch-bank camp or follow the Deweys—and many of the camp's inhabitants—north to the Central Valley to find work picking fruit. As always, it was a difficult choice in which each of them was aware how precarious their survival was. Spend money or save it.

In the end, they made the choice that most of the migrants made: they packed their belongings in boxes and tore down the tent and re-packed the truck for travel. They headed north behind the Deweys;

in Yolo County, they moved into another field full of tents and set up camp. There, they learned to pick peaches. Elsa hated to bring Ant into the fields with her, but there was no choice. She was a single mother and her son was too young to stay alone all day, every day. With all of them picking, they made just enough to feed themselves and stay clothed. Certainly there were no savings.

When peach season ended, they picked up stakes again. For the rest of the summer, they joined the horde of migrants who moved from field to field, crop to crop, and learned to pick whatever was in season and be unseen by the good folks who needed their crops picked but didn't want to see the people who did the picking and expected them to move on when the season ended. They didn't go to town or see movies or even go into the libraries. They stayed in their camps, surviving together. Jean taught Elsa how to make hush puppies from ground corn and Elsa showed Jean how the cornmeal could be made into polenta cakes, which were delicious beneath a ladleful of soup or stew. They ate casseroles made of canned tomato soup and macaroni and chopped-up hot dogs. Through all of that long, hot summer, they waited for two words.

༯

COTTON'S READY.

The news swept the Central Valley in September. Elsa and the kids packed up in the middle of the night and drove back to the San Joaquin Valley and the ditch-bank camp that had been their first stop in California.

They turned onto the deep, dry ruts in the weedy field after a long, hot day of driving. Jeb's jalopy was in front of them, churning up dust.

"Jeepers," Ant said, peering through the dirty, bug-splattered windshield. "Look at that."

In the time they'd been gone, the population of the ditch-bank camp had increased dramatically. There had to be two hundred tents in the field now, filled with more desperate Americans looking for nonexistent jobs. The place looked like the aftermath from a tornado, all broken-down cars and junk spread out.

Jeb drove off to the right, away from the clot of tents and cardboard shacks. He found a nice spot, fairly level, with room for their tents to be side by side, but also each have a little privacy.

Elsa pulled up alongside him and parked.

"Long walk to the river," Loreda said, and then shook her head, muttering, "I can't believe I just called it a river."

Elsa pretended not to hear. "Let's go, explorers. Time to set up camp."

They got to work. They set up the tent and hauled out the stove and beat the lumpy, dirty camp mattress to redistribute the feathers. They stacked the buckets inside the copper tub and set them in front of the tent, alongside their washboard and broom.

"Great," Loreda said, returning with two buckets of water. "We're back where we started. Home, sweet home."

Elsa balled up a newspaper, saw the headline: "Relief Crippling the State Financially," and started a fire in the stove.

Loreda stood beside her. "You know school already started, right?"

"Yes."

"You know I'm not going back, right?" Loreda said.

Elsa sighed. All she wanted—all she'd ever wanted, really—was to be a good mother. How could she accomplish that if Loreda wasn't educated? And yet. They'd been in California for less than five months and they'd worked as hard as was possible, and Elsa still had less than twenty dollars to her name. With the gas it took to follow the crops north and the paltry wages and the cost of goods, there was no way to get ahead. And winter was coming. Their survival depended on cotton money and Loreda could pick as much as Elsa could. Double the wages.

"Yes," Elsa said. "I know you have to pick cotton, but Ant goes to school. Period." She looked at her daughter. "And the minute the cotton is done, you are back in school."

⟫

THE NEXT MORNING, LOREDA wakened before sunrise and listened for footsteps. At four A.M., she heard what she'd been waiting for: Jeb's voice at the tent flaps. "It's time."

Loreda and Elsa lurched out of bed already dressed, gathered up the rolled, twelve-foot-long canvas sacks they'd each paid fifty cents for, and went out of the tent.

Jeb and the boys, Elroy and Buster, were there.

The five of them walked out to the main road and turned right and kept walking until they came to the first Welty field.

There were already forty people or so in line, some of whom had probably slept on the roadside to ensure their place. Men, women, children as young as six. Mexicans, Negroes, Okies. Mostly Okies. Small particles of fluffy white cotton floated in the air, landed on Loreda's face, caught in her hair.

A row of trucks stood ready to be filled with cotton, their trailers lined with chicken wire.

At sunrise, a bell rang out. The crowd of pickers grew anxious. Not all of them would be chosen to pick. By now, there were hundreds of them in line.

The gates to the cotton field opened and a tall, ruddy-faced man wearing a ten-gallon hat walked out, surveying the crowd, moving along it, picking workers. "You," he said, pointing to Jeb.

Jeb rushed toward the gate.

"You," he said to Elsa, and then to Loreda, "And you . . ."

Loreda rushed into the fields, went to the row to which she was assigned.

She yanked her long canvas sack around, slung the leather strap over her shoulder.

The bell rang again and Loreda reached into the nearest cotton plant and yelped in pain. When she drew her hand back it was covered in blood. That was when she saw the spikes on the plant. They looked like darning needles. Wincing, she tried again, more slowly this time; still, she felt her flesh tear. She gritted her teeth and kept picking.

For hours the sun beat down, until heat and dust and human sweat were all Loreda could smell. Her throat was so dry it hurt to breathe. She had drunk all the water in her canteen—almost hot enough to scald—and now there was no more. Her bag grew heavier by the minute and her hands hurt.

Nearing noon, she dragged the heavy sack behind her and moved into the line formed at the giant scales. She unhooked the strap and dropped the load and learned instantly why the other pickers hadn't removed the strap in line: It was a bad idea. Now she had to haul the bag with her bloody, aching hands toward the scales.

She sagged in relief when it was finally her turn. A foreman slung a chain underneath her sack and hung it on the scales.

"Sixty pounds." The foreman stamped a ticket and handed it to her. "You can cash this in town. Pick faster if you want to keep a job."

Loreda retrieved her empty bag, backed away, and went back to work.

꒰

SEPTEMBER WAS ONE LONG, hot, backbreaking day after another in the cotton fields. Elsa's hands bled, her back ached, her knees hurt. Hour after scorching hour. Dawn to dusk, hunched over, picking bolls of cotton from between the razor-sharp spikes. There were no bathrooms in the fields, so it wasn't easy for a woman at certain times of the month, and Loreda had just begun menstruating.

Still, there was *work*. Steady work.

By mid-October, Elsa and Loreda had learned how to pick nearly two hundred pounds of cotton each per day. That meant four dollars a day in combined earnings. It felt like a fortune, even with the ten percent Welty charged to cash their wage chits. They'd been slow to get to the two-hundred-pound mark, but everyone knew there was a learning curve for picking.

$$\gamma$$

IN NOVEMBER, WHEN THE weather turned blessedly cool, and the last of the cotton had been picked, Elsa's metal cash box was stuffed with dollar bills. She had stocked up on food, bought bags of flour and rice and beans and sugar, as well as cans of milk and some smoked bacon. There was no refrigeration at the camp, no ice, so she learned to cook in a new way—everything came from bags or cans. No fresh pasta or sun-dried tomatoes, no homemade baked bread or nutty-flavored olive oil. The kids learned to love pork and beans doctored with corn syrup, and chipped beef on toast, and hot dogs cooked over an open fire, and saltine crackers fried in oil and dusted with sugar. American food, Loreda called it.

Elsa tried to hold back as much as she could for the winter, but after so many months of deprivation, she found her children's joy at suppertime and their full bellies to be her undoing.

Many of the camp's inhabitants, including Jeb and the boys, had moved on, looking for an extra few days' work in fields farther away, but Elsa had decided to stay put, as had Jean and her daughters.

It was time for Loreda to be back in school.

On this Saturday morning, Elsa got out of bed and swept the tent's dirt floor. She didn't know how it was possible, but dirt grew overnight, in the dark, like mushrooms. She swept the debris outside and opened the tent flaps to let in fresh air.

Outside, a layer of cool gray fog lay over the camp, blurring the sea of tents. She pulled an old newspaper from the salvaged fruit box where they stored every scrap of paper they could find, and read the local news as the coffee brewed.

The aroma brought Loreda stumbling out of the tent, her dark hair a snarl of tangles, her bangs a fringe well past her jawline. "You let me sleep," she growled.

"No work today," Elsa said. "You start school on Monday."

Loreda poured herself a cup of coffee. She pulled the bucket closer to the stove and sat down. "I'd rather pick cotton."

Elsa wished she had Rafe's gift for words, his eloquent way of shaping a dream. Loreda needed that now, she needed some spark to relight the fire she'd had before her father's abandonment and hardship had snuffed it out.

Unfortunately, Elsa didn't know much about dreaming, but she knew about school and the hardships that came from not fitting in. "I have an idea," she said.

Loreda gave her a skeptical look

"We are going to have breakfast and go somewhere."

"My joy is uncontainable."

Elsa couldn't help smiling, even as her daughter's hopelessness wounded her.

Elsa made a quick breakfast of oatmeal cooked in canned milk and topped with sugar for the kids, and then hurried them to get dressed. By nine o'clock, they were headed out from the camp, walking through a brown field draped in diaphanous gray fog.

"Where we goin', Mommy?" Ant asked, holding her hand.

She loved that he still held her hand in public.

"To town."

"Oooh," Loreda said. "What fun we'll have standing in line for the few dollars we earned this week."

Elsa elbowed her daughter. "No member of the Explorers Club is allowed to be unhappy on a Saturday adventure. New rule."

"Who made you President?" Loreda said.

"I did." Ant giggled. "Mo-mmy for President, Mo-mmy for President," he chanted, marching on the soft, wet grass.

Elsa pressed a hand to her heart. "It is such an honor. Why . . . I never expected such a thing. A woman President."

Loreda finally laughed and the mood lifted.

They turned onto the main road and walked all the way to Welty. By the time they reached the quaint little town, with its cotton-boll welcome sign, the fog had been burned away by a surprisingly warm sun. The mountains in the distance showed a new layer of snow. The trees along Main Street displayed their autumn finery.

"Wait here," Elsa said outside the Welty Farms office. Inside, she got into line and waited her turn to cash her chit.

"Here yah go," the man at the desk said, taking her chit worth twenty dollars and giving her eighteen dollars in exchange. Elsa rolled the money as tightly as she could, mentally calculating the total of their savings. It seemed like a lot now, but she knew it wouldn't be much by February.

But she wasn't going to think of that today. She returned to the street, where the children stood beneath a lamppost, waiting.

It was one of those sharp-as-a-tack moments when she *saw* them: Loreda, thin as a chicken bone in a threadbare dress and shoes that didn't fit and long, raggedly growing-out hair; Ant, scrawny and with dirty hair no matter how hard Elsa tried to keep him clean, still— thankfully—fitting into Buster's old shoes.

Elsa forced a smile as she walked out to meet them. Taking Ant's hand, she headed down Main Street, where the shops were opening for the day. She smelled coffee and freshly baked pastries as she passed the diner, and the familiar smell of baled hay and bags of grain as they passed the feed store.

There it was: the destination she'd had in mind when they left the camp this morning.

Betty Ane's Beauty Shop.

Elsa had seen the pretty little salon every time she came to town, seen well-dressed women coming out with stylish hair.

Elsa walked toward the salon. It was housed in an old-fashioned bungalow with a fenced yard out front.

Loreda stopped, shook her head. "No, Mom. You know how they'll treat us."

Elsa knew better than to make another hollow promise; she also knew that no matter how often you were knocked down, you had to keep getting up. She tightened her hold on Ant's hand and opened the gate.

Loreda wasn't following. Elsa knew it and kept going. *Come on, Loreda, be brave.*

Elsa and Ant walked up to the front door and Elsa opened it.

A bell jangled overhead.

Inside, the salon filled what had once been the bungalow's parlor. There were two pink chairs stationed in front of mirrors. Cords lay snaked on the floor, gathered up at a machine in the corner. Framed photographs of movie stars lined the pink walls.

A middle-aged woman in a white frock coat stood in the center of the salon holding a broom. She looked thoroughly, almost stubbornly modern, with waved, chin-length platinum-dyed hair and pencil-thin eyebrows. Her Clara Bow lips were painted a bright French red. "Oh," she said at the sight of them huddled together.

Loreda slipped in beside Elsa, took hold of her hand, and tugged it. "Let's go, Mom."

Elsa took a deep breath. "This is my daughter, Loreda. She's thirteen and about to start school on Monday, after a season of picking cotton. She expects to be teased, because . . . well . . ."

Loreda groaned beside her.

"Let me speak to my husband," the beautician said, and left the room.

"She's probably calling the police," Loreda said. "She'll say we're vagrants. Or worse."

A few moments later, the woman returned to the beauty parlor and faced them, pulling a comb out of her pocket. "I'm Betty Ane," she said, moving toward them, her high heels clicking on the hardwood floor. She came to a stop in front of Loreda. Close but not too close.

Please, Elsa thought, tightening her hold on Loreda's hand, *be kind to my girl.*

At the same moment, a large man in a brown suit came into the parlor from another room, carrying a big cardboard box.

"This is my husband, Ned," Betty Ane said.

"I understand," Elsa said. "You and Ned want us to leave. Go back to our kind."

Ned pulled the hat off of his head. "No, ma'am. We came here in '30. It was tough to make a living, but nothing like it is now." He offered her the box. "Here's some coats and sweaters and such. Winter can be cold here. There's a shower in our bathroom. Hot water. Why don't y'all help yourselves? A hot shower and new clothes can be a mighty bit of help in hard times."

Betty Ane smiled kindly at Loreda. "And I see a girl who needs a new hairstyle for her first day of school. Lord knows thirteen is hard enough without all of this." Betty Ane gave Loreda an appraising look. "You're a real beauty, doll. Let me work my magic."

TWENTY-THREE

Loreda sat in the tufted velvet chair and stared at her reflection in the mirror. Betty Ane had cut Loreda's black hair in a precise line along her chin and then coaxed it into waves that cascaded down from a deep side part. Her face, scrubbed clean with scented soap, was deeply tanned from work in the cotton fields. A new purple dress accentuated the startling blue of Loreda's eyes, and Betty Ane had talked Elsa into letting Loreda put a little pale-pink color on her lips.

"I forgot what I looked like," Loreda said, touching the silky tips of her hair.

Betty Ane stood behind her. "You may be the prettiest girl I've ever seen." She turned. "Elsa. Your turn."

Loreda hated to get out of the chair. It felt magical, a portal to a what-if world where ditch-dwellers turned into princesses.

Her legs were a little shaky, to be honest. In the mirror, she'd seen more than her face. She'd seen the girl she'd been before all of this. A dreamer, a believer. Someone who would *go places*. How had she forgotten all of that?

It gave her a newfound, or refound, hope, but it fed the anger in her, too. She thanked Betty Ane and moved away from the mirror. Mom touched her shoulder as they changed places.

"Say, is this your natural hair color?" Betty Ane said as Elsa sat down. "It's beautiful."

Loreda backed away. Without a glance at Ant, who was on the floor playing with a toy car, she went outside.

Even the air out here smelled different now.

She straightened to her full height, realizing all at once how life in the fields had hunched and diminished her. She'd spent months trying to be a cog in a wheel, unseen.

No more.

She strode confidently forward in the new-to-her dress with its Peter Pan collar. Her scuffed brown shoes hardly bothered her when coupled with lacy white socks.

She found the library on Pepper Street, set back from the town, on a pretty grass lot, with an American flag flapping from a white pole out front.

A library.

Magic.

She opened the door and walked right in, standing tall, the girl she'd been raised to be. A girl who believed in education and dreamed of being a reporter. Or a novelist. Something interesting, anyway.

The first thing she noticed was the smell of books. She inhaled deeply and felt transported for a moment to Lonesome Tree. *In her bedroom, light on, reading . . .*

Home.

"May I help you?"

"Yes. Please. I would love to find a book to read."

The librarian came out from around the desk. She was a sturdy woman with gray pin curls and black-rimmed glasses. "Do you have a library card?"

"No." Loreda was ashamed to admit it. She'd always had a library card in Texas. "We are . . . new to the state."

"Well." The librarian smiled kindly. "Thirteen?"

"Yes, ma'am."

"In school?"

"Yes, ma'am."

The librarian nodded. "Come with me."

She led Loreda through the library stacks to a large wooden student's table that was strewn with newspapers. "You can sit here. Let me find you something."

Loreda sat down at the oak desk, which had a lamp on it. She couldn't help flicking the light on and off and on again, marveling at the magic of electricity on demand.

The librarian returned with a book. "What's your name?"

"Loreda Martinelli."

"I'm Mrs. Quisdorf. You come back for your card, but I'll trust you with this for now." She set down a worn copy of *The Secret of the Old Clock*.

Loreda touched the book, lifted it to her face, and inhaled the remembered scent that made her think of reading at night . . . with Stella after school; listening to Daddy telling her bedtime stories. Like a flower that had been sucked dry in a drought and felt the first drop of spring rain, Loreda felt herself revive. "Do you have one I could take to my brother? He's eight. And maybe one for my mom? I'll bring them back, I promise."

Mrs. Quisdorf eyed her assessingly and finally smiled. "Miss Martinelli, I believe you are my kind of girl."

⁊

THAT NIGHT, AFTER THE children were asleep, Elsa swept the tent floor—again—and rearranged the collection of found fruit cartons that had become their pantry. They had sugar, flour, bacon, beans, canned milk, rice, and butter. A veritable feast. But even as the Depression had worsened, food prices had gone up. Five gallons of kerosene cost a dollar. Two pounds of butter cost fifty cents. Six pounds of rice cost nearly half a dollar. It was terrifying how fast it added up.

And today she'd spent seventy-five cents on haircuts for the three of them. She hoped she didn't regret it come winter.

Hefting the box of clothes she'd gotten today, she ducked out of the tent and walked over to see Jean, who sat in a chair by the woodstove, darning socks by lantern light. Jeb and the boys had taken the truck, hoping to find autumn work in the grape fields. No one expected them to find it this late in the year, though.

"Hey, Jean," Elsa said, coming out of the dark and into the lantern's pale light. She and the children had chosen what fit them from the box of clothes and saved the rest for the Deweys.

"Elsa. You look so pretty!"

Elsa felt her cheeks heat up as she set down the box of clothes. "Betty Ane tried."

Jean touched the wooden bucket nearest her with her toe. "Sit down."

Elsa settled herself on the bucket, ignoring the way it pinched into her bony buttocks. Lord, those beauty salon seats had felt heavenly.

"Why do you say things like that?"

Elsa looked through the box of clothes until she found what she was looking for. Her fingers felt soft, soft wool. "Like what?"

"Has no one ever said you were pretty?"

Elsa stopped rooting through the clothes and looked up. "I love a friend who lies."

"I'm not lying."

"I'm . . . not good with compliments, I guess." Elsa said, smoothing the silky, chin-length hair back from her face. She pulled out a soft lavender-blue baby blanket and held it out to Jean. "Look at this."

Jean took the blanket, stared down at it. "He was dancing up a storm yesterday," Jean said, putting a hand on her rounded belly.

Elsa knew Jean prayed every day to feel movement in her womb, and that with every movement she felt both joy and fear. "I had a dream last night. I had a job in a diner. I was serving apple pie to women who still wore hats that matched their dresses."

Jean nodded. "I reckon we all have that dream."

WINTER HIT THE SAN Joaquin Valley hard, a frightening combination of bad weather and no work. Day after day, rain fell from steel-wool-colored skies, fat drops clattering on the automobiles and tin-can shacks and tents clustered along the ditch bank. Puddles of mud formed and wandered, became trenches. Brown splatter marks discolored everything.

Elsa mourned every dollar spent, counting and re-counting her money on a daily basis. She was frugal, but even so, her savings diminished. She hated that she and the children had had no choice but to buy galoshes this month. There had been nothing in their sizes at the Salvation Army or the giveaway box at the Presbyterian church.

By late December, her savings had dwindled enough that she lived in a constant state of fear. Cotton hadn't earned them enough to last through the winter; she understood that now. She needed help to feed her children; it was as simple, as heartbreaking, as that. She couldn't get money from the state until April, but she could get food from the feds. It was better than standing in a line at a soup kitchen, bowl and spoon in hand, but she knew that could be her future if she wasn't careful. Honestly, she'd be doing it now if she hadn't heard that the supply at the soup kitchens was stretched to the limit; she didn't want to take free food out of the mouths of people who had no other choice, not while she still had some money.

"It ain't nothin' to be ashamed of," Jean said when Elsa told her.

They were standing in Elsa's tent, having a cup of coffee together in the relative quiet of mid-morning. Loreda and Ant had left for school hours ago. Rain thumped on the canvas, rattled the poles. "Really?" Elsa said, looking at her friend.

They both knew better. It *was* something to be ashamed of. Americans weren't supposed to take handouts from the government. They were supposed to work hard and succeed on their own.

"None of us got a choice," Jean said. "You don't get much—beans and rice—but every morsel matters."

That was the truth of it.

Elsa nodded. "Well, I won't get help standing here wishing life were different."

"Ain't it the truth?" Jean said.

The women exchanged a smile.

Jean left the tent, closed the flaps behind her. Elsa buttoned up her hooded coat and stepped into her oversized galoshes and began the walk into Welty. In this weather, it was slow going.

Nearly an hour later, splattered with mud, bedraggled by rain, Elsa stepped into the long line of people in front of the federal relief office. She stood in line for two more hours. By the time she reached the interior of the office, she was shivering violently.

"Els-s-s-inore Martinelli," she said to the young man seated at a desk in the small office. He ran through a tin box full of red cards, pulled one out.

"Martinelli. Registered arrival in the state on April 26, 1935. Two children. One woman. No husband."

Elsa nodded. "We've been here almost eight months."

"Two pounds of beans, four cans of milk, a loaf of bread. Next." He stamped the card. "Come back in two weeks."

"That's supposed to last us two weeks?" she said.

The young man looked up. "You see how many people need help?"

he said. "We're overwhelmed. There just isn't enough money. The Salvation Army has a soup kitchen on Seventh."

Elsa picked up her box of commodities and settled it uncomfortably in her arms. With a tired sigh, she stepped back out into the rain.

"Join us, raise your voices. Workers of the valley unite!"

Elsa looked over at the man standing at the corner, shouting; he wore a long, dark-colored duster and a hood. Rain slashed at him.

He raised a fist for emphasis. "Unite! Don't let them make you afraid. Come to the Workers Alliance meeting."

Elsa saw how people moved away from him, drew back. None of them could afford being seen with a Communist.

A police car rolled up, lights flashing. Two officers got out and grabbed the man and started beating him.

"You see this?" the Communist shouted. "This is in America. The coppers are hauling me away for my ideas."

The cops shoved him into the squad car and drove away.

Elsa resettled the box of commodities in her arms and began the long walk back to the camp. It was late afternoon when she reached the field.

There were almost a thousand people living here now, more than four times the number that had been here when they had arrived.

Elsa splashed through ankle-deep mud toward her tent.

A few people were out and about, scavenging for anything that they could use.

She stopped at the Deweys' tent. "Anyone home?"

The flaps were opened by Lucy. Elsa saw the whole family—all six of them—gathered inside. Jeb and the boys had been as unable to find work as everyone else.

Jean smiled tiredly, her hand resting on her big belly. The buttons of her dress gaped; one was missing. "Hey, Elsa. How did it go?"

Elsa reached into the box and withdrew two cans of milk, as well as a few slices of bread from the loaf she'd been given. It wasn't much, and yet it was. The two families shared whatever good fortune came their way. "Here you go," she said, offering the food.

"Thank you," Jean said, giving her an understanding look.

Elsa returned to her own tent and ducked inside. The floor was mud now. No wonder people were getting sick. Ant sat on the mattress they all shared, doing his homework.

Loreda sat on an apple crate sewing a black button onto the purple dress she'd gotten at the beauty salon. At Elsa's arrival, she looked up. "How was it?"

"Fine." Elsa's hands were so cold, she almost dropped the box.

Loreda got up and wrapped a blanket around Elsa, who sat down gingerly on the edge of the mattress.

"You should have seen how many people there were in line, Loreda," Elsa said. "The soup kitchen line was twice as long."

"Hard times," Loreda said woodenly. It was what they always said.

"What would Tony and Rose say if they knew we were living on the dole?"

"They'd say Ant needed the milk," Loreda said.

Elsa knew now how Tony had felt when his land died. There was a deep and abiding shame that came with asking for handouts.

Poverty was a soul-crushing thing. A cave that tightened around you, its pinprick of light closing a little more at the end of each desperate, unchanged day.

꒰

CHRISTMAS MORNING DAWNED BRIGHT and clear, the first dry day in nearly a week. Elsa woke to blissful quiet. She had slept in. They all had. These days there was no reason to rise before dawn. There was no work to be found and school was closed for the holiday.

She got out of bed slowly, moving like an old woman. Indeed, she felt like one. The combination of cold, hunger, and fear had aged her. All she wanted to do was climb back in bed with her kids and cuddle under the covers and sleep. It was her only escape. But she knew how dangerous escape could be. Survival took grit and courage and effort. It was too easy to give in. No matter how afraid she was, she had to teach her children every day how to survive.

She grabbed the water jug and went outside to make coffee.

The camp wakened with her. People came out of their tents, blinking mole-like at the unexpected sunlight. Folks smiled and waved. Someone was playing a fiddle. A banjo joined in. Someone somewhere began to sing.

Elsa wrapped a blanket around her shoulders and followed the music to a group gathered by the ditch, now swollen with fast-moving brown water. She found Jean and Midge standing together beside a tree. There were men sitting on rocks or fallen trees along the bank, playing the instruments they'd brought across the country. Women stood with buckets they'd filled and set down.

Jean and Midge began to sing. "*Will the circle be unbroken . . .*"

Others joined in.

"*. . . by and by Lord, by and by.*"

Elsa felt the music rise up in her. In it, she heard the best of her past, church services with Rose and the family, Tony playing his fiddle, box suppers, even the one time Rafe had danced with her at Pioneer Days.

She went back to the tent and wakened the children and hustled them out to the bank. The three of them stood alongside Jean and Midge.

Within moments, Jeb and the Dewey kids showed up. A crowd formed around them.

Elsa held her children's hands. They stood on the muddy bank and looked up to the bright heavens and sang hymns and Christmas songs, and by the end, none of them cared that the local churches denied them entry or that their clothes were ragged and dirty or that Christmas dinner would be small. They found strength in each other. Elsa and Jean looked at each other as they sang the words *be unbroken.*

When the men finally stopped playing, people looked each other in the eye for the first time in weeks, wished each other a merry Christmas.

Elsa held on to her children's hands as they walked back to the tent.

Loreda stoked the fire, then poured two cups of coffee and handed one to Elsa.

Ant dragged a stool and two fruit crates outside. They sat in front of the tent, close to the stove's warmth. They'd made a tree out of nailed-together tin cans and kindling and decorated it with whatever they could find—utensils, hair ribbons, strips of cloth.

Elsa pulled a small, muddied, crumpled envelope out of her pocket and opened the letter that had arrived last week, general mail at the post office.

"A letter from Grandma and Grandpa!" Ant said.

Elsa unfolded it and read aloud.

My dearest daughter and grandchildren,

Another dust storm hit this week, and after that, a cold snap.

It has been a tiresomely cold winter, I must tell you. We are envious of your California warmth. Mr. Pavlov tells us you must have seen a palm tree by now. And perhaps the ocean. What grand sights.

Your grandfather thinks the soil conservation program shows promise. Much of what we planted was hit hard by the continuing drought, but after a light rain this month, we see a little sprouting.

Still, thanks to the Virgin, the well is working. We have enough water for the household and the chickens, so we carry on, hoping again for a crop. The ten cents per acre we get from the government has kept us afloat.

Your last letter spoke of cotton picking. I must say, it is hard to imagine you in the fields, Elsa, but more power to you all for thriving in these difficult times.

Hard times don't last. Love does. We are sending along small
gifts for our beloved grandchildren so that they remember us well.

With love,
Rose and Anthony

Elsa pulled two pennies out of the envelope and handed one to each of them.

Ant's eyes lit up. "Candy money!" he cried.

"And there are more gifts in my suitcase," Elsa said, warming her hands around her cup of coffee. "Because I know a young man who likes to snoop."

Ant wheeled around and went into the tent and came out with two packages, one wrapped in newspaper, the other in cloth.

Ant ripped his open. Elsa had made him a handsome vest from the seat fabric of an automobile that had been abandoned in the camp, and she'd bought him a Hershey's chocolate bar.

Ant's eyes rounded. He knew the candy bar cost five cents. A fortune. "Chocolate!" He peeled back the wrapper slowly, revealing a sharp brown corner, which he bit off in a mouselike nibble. Savoring.

Loreda opened her gift. Elsa had repaired Loreda's shoes, used tire rubber to fashion a new set of soles, which would last longer and be more comfortable than cardboard. Beneath the shoes lay Loreda's brand-new library card and *The Hidden Staircase*.

Loreda looked up. "You went back? In the rain?"

"Mrs. Quisdorf picked that book out for you. That card, though, that's the real gift. It can take you anywhere, Loreda."

Loreda's fingers traced the card reverently. Elsa knew that a library card—a thing they'd taken for granted all of their lives—meant there was still a future. A world beyond this struggle.

Ant bounced up and down on the stool in excitement. "Can we give Mommy her present now?"

Loreda walked over to the truck and pulled out a small package wrapped in newsprint.

"Open it!" Ant said, bouncing to his feet.

Elsa carefully unwrapped the gift, not wanting to rip the newspaper or lose the strips of cloth that bound it all. Everything mattered these days.

Inside lay a slim leather-bound journal full of blank paper. The first few pages of the book had been ripped away and the cover was water damaged. Several pencils—sharpened down to stubs—rolled out and plopped onto the ground.

Loreda looked at her. "I know you have stuff you need to say, but we're kids so you stay quiet. I thought maybe writing it down would make you feel better."

"I thought that, too," Ant said. "I got the pencils from school! All by myself."

The journal reminded Elsa of who she'd once been: the girl with the bad heart who had read books and dreamed of going away to college to study literature. She'd dreamed of one day writing.

Do you have some hidden talent of which we are all unaware?

Elsa hated that she heard her father's voice now, of all moments, at this time when her love for her children almost bowled her over and she thought, even in the midst of all this hardship and failure, *I have raised good children.* Kind, caring, loving people.

"I'll write something," Elsa said.

"Will you let us read it, Mommy?" Ant asked.

"Maybe someday."

1936

One thing was left, as clear and perfect as a drop of rain—the desperate need to stand together . . . They would rise and fall and, in their falling, rise again.

—SANORA BABB,
WHOSE NAMES ARE UNKNOWN

TWENTY-FOUR

O n the last day of January, a cold front moved into the valley and
stayed for seven days. The ground turned hard; fog lay for hours
every morning. There was still no work.

Their savings decreased, but Elsa knew they were the lucky ones;
they'd saved cotton money and there were only three of them. The
Deweys had six mouths to feed and soon it would be seven. The migrants who had just arrived in the state, most of them with nothing,
were trying to survive on federal relief—paltry amounts of food handed
out every two weeks. They lived on flour-and-water pancakes and fried
dough. Elsa could see the ravages of malnutrition on their faces.

Now it was past suppertime, which had been a cup of watery beans
and a slice of skillet bread for each of them. Elsa sat on an overturned
bucket by the wood-burning stove, with the metal box open on her lap.
Ant sat beside her, taking his daily nibble off his Christmas Hershey's
chocolate bar. Loreda was in the tent, rereading *The Hidden Staircase*.

Elsa counted their money again.

"Elsa! It's time!"

She heard Jean shout her name. Elsa stood up so fast she nearly upended the box of money.

The baby.

Ant looked up. "What's wrong?"

Elsa ran into the tent and hid the box of money. "Loreda," she said. "Come with me."

"Where—"

"Jean's having her baby."

Elsa ran to the Deweys' tent. She found Lucy outside, crying. "Loreda, take the girls to our tent. Tell them to stay with Ant and not to come back until you come to get them. Then come back to help me."

Elsa entered the Deweys' dark, dank tent.

A single lantern glowed, barely banishing the shadows. She saw gray lines in the dark: a pile of food stores, a makeshift washbasin.

Jean lay on her side on a mattress on the floor, as still as a held breath.

Elsa knelt beside the mattress. "Hey," she said, touching Jean's damp forehead. "Where's Jeb?"

"Nipomo. Hopin' to pick peas." Jean panted. "Somethin ain't raht, Elsa."

Not right. Elsa knew what that meant; every woman who'd lost a child did. A mother's instinct was strong at a time like this.

Loreda came into the tent.

"Help me get her to her feet," Elsa said to Loreda.

Together they got Jean upright. Jean leaned heavily on Elsa. "I'm taking you to the hospital," Elsa said.

"No . . . sense."

"It's not nonsense. This isn't a child with a cough or a fever, Jean. This is an emergency."

"They . . . won't . . ." Jean's face tightened as another contraction hit.

Elsa and Loreda got Jean settled in the passenger seat of the truck. "Watch the kids, Loreda."

Elsa started the engine and hit the lights and they were off, rattling down the muddy road, driving too fast.

"Can't . . ." Jean said, clutching the armrest. "Take . . . back . . ."

Another contraction.

Elsa turned into the hospital parking lot; the building glowed with expensive electrical lighting.

Elsa slammed on the brakes. "Wait here. I'll get help."

She ran into the hospital, rushed down the hallway, and stopped at the desk. "My friend is having a baby."

The woman looked up, frowned, and then wrinkled her nose.

"Yeah, yeah. I smell," Elsa said. "I'm a dirty migrant. I get it. But my friend—"

"This hospital is for *Californians*. You know, the folks who pay taxes. For citizens, not vagrants who want to be taken care of."

"Come on. Be human. Please—"

"You? Telling me to be human? Please. Look at yourself. You women pop out babies like champagne corks. Find one of yours to help you." The woman finally rose. Elsa saw how well-fed she was, how plump her calves were. She reached inside a drawer, pulled out a pair of rubber gloves. "I'm sorry, but rules are rules. I am allowed to give you these." She held out the gloves.

"Please. I'll scrub floors. Clean bedpans. Anything. Just help her."

"If it's as dire as you say, why waste time begging with me?"

Elsa snatched the gloves and ran back to the truck.

"They won't help us," she said through gritted teeth as she climbed in. "The good, God-fearing folk of California don't care about a baby's life, I guess."

Elsa drove as fast as she could back to camp, rage trapped inside of her, tightening her breathing.

"Hurry, Elsa."

At the Deweys' tent, Elsa helped Jean into the dank interior.

"Loreda!" Elsa shouted.

Loreda ran into the tent, banged into Elsa. "Why are you back?"

"They turned us away."

"You mean—"

"Go get water. Boil a lot of it." When Loreda didn't move, Elsa snapped, "*Now!*" and Loreda ran out.

Elsa lit a kerosene lamp and helped Jean to the mattress on the floor.

Jean convulsed in pain, gritted her teeth to keep from crying out.

Elsa knelt beside her, stroking her hair. "Go ahead and scream."

"It's coming," Jean said between pants. "Keep . . . the kids . . . away. Scissors in that . . . box. And there's some string."

Another contraction.

Elsa stared at Jean's writhing belly and knew she only had a few moments. Elsa ran back to her tent, ignoring the children, who looked at her with frightened eyes. There wasn't time to comfort them now.

She grabbed a stack of saved newspapers and ran back to Jean's tent, where she laid the newspapers down on the dirt floor, grateful that they were relatively clean.

Headlines flashed out at her: "Typhoid Outbreak in Migrant Camps."

Elsa helped Jean roll onto the newspapers. Elsa then put on the gloves.

Jean screamed.

"Go ahead," Elsa said, kneeling beside her. She stroked Jean's wet hair.

"It's . . . *now*," Jean cried out.

Elsa moved quickly, positioned herself between Jean's open legs. The top of the baby's head appeared, slimed and blue. "I see the head," Elsa said. "Push, Jean."

"I'm too . . ."

"I know you're tired. Push."

Jean shook her head.

"Push," Elsa said. She looked up, saw the fear in her friend's eyes. "I know," Elsa said, understanding Jean's deep fear of this moment. Babies died in the best of circumstances, and these were the worst. They also lived in spite of all odds. "Push," she said, meeting Jean's fear with a quiet hopefulness.

The baby whooshed out in a stream of blood into Elsa's gloved hands. Too tiny, spindly almost. Smaller than a man's shoe.

Blue.

Elsa felt a roar of anger move through her. *No.* She wiped the blood from the tiny face, cleaned out her mouth, begged the infant, "Breathe, baby girl."

Jean pushed up to her elbows. She looked too tired to breathe herself. "She ain't breathin'," she said softly.

Elsa tried to help the baby breathe. Mouth-to-mouth.

Nothing.

She smacked the tiny blue bum, said, "*Breathe.*"

Nothing.

Nothing.

Jean pointed to a straw basket. In it was the soft lavender blanket.

Elsa tied off the umbilical cord and cut it, then got slowly to her feet. Weak. Shaky. She wrapped up the tiny, still baby.

As she offered the baby to Jean, tears blurred her vision. "A girl," she said to Jean, who took her with a gentleness that broke Elsa's heart.

Jean kissed the blue forehead. "I'm namin' her Clea, after my mom," Jean said.

A name.

The very essence of hope. The beginning of an identity, handed down in love. Elsa backed away from the heartbreak of watching Jean whisper into the baby's blue ear.

Outside, Elsa found Loreda pacing.

Elsa looked at her daughter, saw the question, and shook her head.

"Oh, no," Loreda said, slumping her shoulders.

Before Elsa could offer comfort, Loreda turned and disappeared into their tent.

Elsa stood there, unmoving. That terrible, terrible image of a baby coming into the world on a crumpled newspaper over a dirt floor wouldn't go away.

I'll name her Clea.

How had Jean even been able to speak?

Elsa felt tears rise up, overtake her. She cried as she hadn't cried since Rafe left her, cried until there was no moisture left inside of her, until she was as dry as the land they'd left behind.

⤶

AT A LITTLE PAST ten o'clock that night, Loreda finished digging the small hole and dropped her shovel.

They were far from camp, in an area surrounded by trees; a place as dark as the mood of the two women and one girl standing beneath them.

Anger suffused Loreda, overwhelmed her; she felt it poisoning her from the inside out. She'd never felt its like before, not even when Daddy left them. She had to hold it inside her one breath at a time; if she let it go, she'd scream.

And look at her mother. Standing there, holding a dead baby in a clean lavender blanket, looking sad.

Sad.

The sight of it doubled Loreda's rage. This was no time to be sad.

She fisted her hands at her side, but who was there to hit? Mrs. Dewey looked dazed and unsteady. Ghostly.

Mom knelt down and carefully placed the dead baby in the small grave and began to pray. "Our Father—"

"Who the hell are you praying to?" Loreda snapped.

She heard her mother sigh and slowly get to her feet. "God has—"

"If you tell me He has a plan for us, I'll scream. I swear I will."

Loreda's voice broke. She felt herself start to cry, but she wasn't sad; she was furious. "He lets us live like this. Worse than stray dogs."

Mom touched Loreda's face. "Babies die, Loreda. I lost your brother. Grandma Rose lost—"

"THIS ISN'T LIKE THAT!" Loreda screamed. "You're a coward, staying here, making us stay here. Why?"

"Oh, Loreda . . ."

Loreda knew she'd gone too far, had said too cruel a thing, but there was no stopping this rage, no slowing it. "If Daddy were here—"

"What?" Mom said. "What would he do?"

"He wouldn't let us live like this. Burying dead babies in the dark, working our fingers to the bone, standing in line for two hours to get a can of milk from the government, watching people get sick around us."

"He left us."

"He left *you*. I should do the same, get out of here before we're all dead."

"Go, then," Mom said. "Run away. Be like him."

"I might," Loreda said.

"Good. Go." Mom bent down, picked up the shovel, began filling the grave with dirt.

Scrape, thunk.

In minutes there would be nothing to show that a baby had been buried here.

Loreda marched back through the squalid camp, past tents over-filled with people, past mangy dogs begging for scraps from folks who lived on scraps. She heard babies crying and people coughing.

The Dewey tent was closed up, but Loreda knew the little girls were in there, waiting for their mother to comfort and reassure them.

Words. Lies. Nothing would get better.

She was done living like this.

At her tent, she flung the flaps open, found Ant curled up on the mattress, his body as small as he could make it. They'd all learned how to sleep together on the too-small bed.

Her heart gave a hard ping at the sight of him.

Loreda knelt beside the bed, ruffled his hair. He mumbled in his sleep. "I love you," she whispered, kissing the hard bone of his cheek. "But I can't stay another second."

Ant nodded in his sleep, murmured something.

Loreda went to the small suitcase that held all of her ragged clothes and her beloved library card. From the food crate, she took three potatoes and two slices of bread, and then opened the metal box that held their money. All they had in the world. Loreda felt a twinge of guilt.

No.

She'd wouldn't take much. Just two dollars. It was her money as much as Mom's. God knew Loreda had worked for it. She carefully counted out the money and then scrounged for a piece of paper. She found a bit of crumpled newsprint. Smoothing it as best she could, she used one of Ant's pencil stubs to write a note to her mother and Ant, leaving it beneath the coffeepot.

She carried her suitcase to the tent flaps, looked back one last time, and walked away.

She passed the truck, full of things they should have left behind. Ant's baseball bat lay cocked against a mantel clock, neither of which they needed, but neither Loreda nor her mother had the heart to tell Ant his baseball days were over before they'd begun. God knew if they'd ever need a mantel clock again. They would have packed differently if they'd known. Or maybe if they'd known what waited for them in California, they'd have stayed in Texas.

They shouldn't have left.

Or maybe they should have gone farther.

It was Mom's fault. She'd chosen to stop here, said, *We have to.* Everything had gone wrong from then.

From that first fatal lie: one night.

Well, it had been a lot of nights, and Loreda was getting the hell out.

᚜

ELSA AND JEAN STOOD together in the darkness, staring down, holding hands. Time fell away, passed in long swaths of silence between women who knew there were no words at a time like this.

There was no marker here to commemorate the baby, nor markers to commemorate the others buried in this section of the camp.

"We'd best get back," Elsa said at last, buttoning up her ill-fitting wool coat. "You're shivering."

"I'll be along," Jean said.

Elsa squeezed her friend's hand. With a sigh that felt drawn from deep in her tired bones, she carried the shovel back to camp and threw it in the back of the truck, where it landed with a clang.

Thoughts of Loreda pushed their way in. Elsa should have comforted Loreda at the grave site. What kind of mother snapped at a grieving thirteen-year-old? Loreda had seen too much loss. Elsa knew that. There must be words Elsa could find that would help.

Elsa just had nothing left right now. She felt emptied by the baby's death. The last thing she could do was face her daughter's fury.

Better to let a little time smooth over the edges. A night, at least. Tomorrow the sun would shine and Elsa would take Loreda aside and offer what comfort she could.

Coward.

"No," Elsa said out loud to reinforce the decision. She would not look away from this. She would hit it head-on, try to comfort Loreda as best as she could.

She lifted the tent flap and went inside.

The quilts were tangled, but it was clear that Ant was in bed alone.

Loreda wasn't in the tent.

Elsa went to the truck, banged on the side of the bed. "Loreda? Are you in there?"

She examined the bed, saw the boxes of goods they'd brought with them, things they'd thought they'd need: candlesticks, porcelain dishes, Ant's baseball bat and mitt, a mantel clock. "Loreda?" she said again, her voice spiking in worry when she saw that the cab was empty, too.

Elsa stepped back.

He left you. I should do the same . . . get out of here before we're all dead.

Go, then. Go. Be like your father. Run away.

Maybe I will.

Good. Go.

A chill moved through Elsa. She ran back into the tent.

Loreda's suitcase was gone. So was her sweater and the blue wool coat she'd gotten at the salon.

Elsa saw a note peeking out from beneath the coffeepot. Her hand shook as she reached for it.

> *Mom,*
> *I can't take it anymore.*
> *I'm sorry.*
> *I love you both.*

Elsa ran out of the tent and didn't stop running until there was a stitch in her side and her breathing was ragged.

The main road stretched north and south. Which way would Loreda go? How could Elsa even guess?

Elsa had told her thirteen-year-old daughter to *go*, to run away and be like a man who didn't want to be found. To *go* out into a world full of bindle stiffs walking the roads and riding the trains, gangs of desperate, angry men with nothing to lose, who lurked like packs of wolves in the shadows.

She screamed her daughter's name.

The word rang out through the night and faded away.

><

LOREDA WALKED SOUTH UNTIL her shoe broke and her back ached, and still the empty road stretched in front of her, bathed in moonlight. How much farther to Los Angeles?

She had always dreamed of finding her father, just bumping into him, but now, standing here alone on the side of the road, she understood what her mother had said to her once.

He doesn't want to be found.

How many roads were there in California, going how many directions, to how many destinations? So what if her father dreamed of Hollywood? That didn't mean he'd gotten there, or that he'd stayed there.

And how far had she walked? Three miles? Four?

She kept walking, determined not to turn around. She was not going to go back and admit she'd made a mistake by leaving. She couldn't stand this life anymore. Period.

But Ant would wake up and miss her. He'd think he was easy to leave, that there was something wrong with him. Loreda knew that because it was how she'd felt when Daddy had left.

She didn't want to hurt her brother.

She saw headlights in front of her, coming up the road. A truck rolled up to her and stopped. It was an old-fashioned truck, with a square wooden and glass cab that appeared to have been stuck on the truck's black chassis. The hinged windshield was open.

The driver reached over and rolled down the passenger window. He was as old as Mom, with a face that was like most men's these days—sharp and bony. He needed to shave, but Loreda wouldn't call him bearded. Just scruffy. "What're you doing out here all by yourself? It's midnight."

"Nothing."

His gaze flicked down to her suitcase. "You look like a girl who is running away."

"What do you care?"

"Where are your parents? It's dangerous out here."

"None of your business. Besides, I'm sixteen. I can go where I want."

"Yeah, kid. And I'm Errol Flynn. Where are you headed?"

"Anywhere but here."

He looked up the road. It was at least a minute before he looked at her again. "There's a bus station in Bakersfield. I'm headed north. I can give you a lift. I just have to make a stop along the way."

"Thanks, mister!" Loreda tossed her suitcase in the back of the truck and climbed in.

TWENTY-FIVE

I'm Jack Valen," the man said.

"Loreda Martinelli."

He put the truck in gear and they drove north. The suspension on the truck was shot. The leather seat burped up and down at every bump.

Loreda stared out the window. In the brief flash of their headlights or in the glare of billboards lit up by streetlights, she saw people camped on the side of the road, and hobos walking with packs slung over their backs.

They passed the school and the hospital and the squatter's camp, which lay shrouded in darkness.

And then they were past the places Loreda knew, past the town of Welty. Out here, there was nothing but road.

"Hey, what do you have to do this late at night?" she said. It occurred to her suddenly that she could have put herself in danger.

The man lit a cigarette, exhaled a stream of blue-gray smoke through his open window. "Same as you, I imagine."

"What do you mean?"

He turned. For the first time she saw his entire face, the tanned roughness of it, the sharp nose and black eyes. "You're running away from something. Or someone."

"And you are, too?"

"Kid, if you aren't running away these days, you aren't paying attention. But no, I'm not running." He smiled in a way that made him almost handsome. "I don't want to get caught out here, either."

"My dad did that."

"Did what?"

"Ran out in the middle of the night. Never came back."

"Well . . . that's a hell of a thing," he said at last. "What about your mom?"

"What about her?"

He turned onto a long dirt road.

Darkness.

Loreda didn't see lights anywhere, just blackness. No houses, no streetlights, no other cars on the road.

"W-where are we going?"

"I told you I had a stop to make before I dropped you at the bus station."

"Out here? In the middle of nowhere?"

He let the truck roll to a stop. "I need your word, kid. You won't talk about this place. Or me. Or anything you see here."

They were in a huge grassy field. A barn stood alongside a dilapidated ranch house, both bathed in moonlight. A dozen or so cars and trucks were parked in the grass, their headlights off. Thin yellow lines in between the boards of the barn indicated that there was something going on inside. "No one listens to people like me," Loreda said. She couldn't bring herself to say the word she meant: *Okies*.

"If you don't give me your word, I'll turn around right now and drop you off on the main road."

Loreda looked at him. He was impatient with her, she could tell. A tic pulled at the corner of his eyes, but otherwise he appeared calm. He was waiting for her to decide, but he wouldn't wait long.

She should tell him to turn around right now, take her back to the road. Whatever was going on in that barn this late at night couldn't be good. And grown-ups didn't demand this kind of promise from kids.

"Is it bad, what's going on in there?"

"No," he said. "It's good. But these are dangerous times."

Loreda looked into the man's dark eyes. He was . . . intense. A little frightening, perhaps, but alive in a way she hadn't seen before. Here was a man who wouldn't live in a dirty tent and eat scraps and be grateful for it. He wasn't broken like the rest of them. His vitality called out to her, reminded her of better times, of the man she'd thought her father to be. "I promise."

He drove forward, threading his way through the parked cars. Near the doors, he parked the truck and turned off the engine.

"You stay in the truck," he said, opening his door.

"How long will you be?"

"As long as I need to be."

Loreda watched him walk toward the barn and open the door. She saw a flash of light, and what looked like shadow people gathered within. Then he closed the door behind him.

Loreda stared at the dark barn, the streaks of light bleeding through the cracks. What were they doing in there?

An automobile chugged up alongside the truck, parked. Its headlights snapped off.

Loreda saw a couple get out of the car. They were well dressed, all in black, both smoking cigarettes. Definitely not migrants or farmers.

Loreda made a snap decision: she got out of the truck and followed the couple to the barn.

The barn door opened.

Loreda slipped in behind the couple and immediately pressed herself back against the rough boards of the barn.

She couldn't have said what she was expecting to see—grown-ups drinking hooch and dancing the Lindy Hop maybe—but whatever she'd expected, it wasn't this. Men dressed in suits mingled with women, some of whom were wearing pants. *Pants.* They seemed to be all talking at once, gesturing with their hands as if arguing. The place felt alive, hive-like with activity. Cigarette smoke created a haze that blurred everyone and stung Loreda's eyes.

There were about ten tables set up in the barn's dusty, shadowed interior, with lanterns set on each one, creating pockets of light shot through with dust and smoke. Typewriters and mimeograph machines were positioned on the tables. Women sat in chairs and smoked and typed. There was a strange aroma in the air, mixed in with the smell of smoke. Stacks of papers lined the tabletops. Every once in a while Loreda heard the *briiiiing* of a carriage return.

When Jack strode forward, people stopped what they were doing and turned toward him. He pulled a newspaper off a table in front of him and climbed up several loft steps, then faced the crowd. He lifted the newspaper up. The headline read: "Los Angeles Declares War on Migrants."

"Police Chief James 'Two Guns' Davis, with the support of the big growers, the railroads, the state relief agencies, and the rest of the state fat cats, just closed the California border to migrants." Jack threw the paper to the straw-covered floor. "Think of it. Desperate people, good people, *Americans,* are being stopped at the border at gunpoint and turned away. To go where? Many of them are starving back home or dying of dust pneumonia. If they won't turn back, the coppers are jailing them for vagrancy and judges are sentencing them to hard labor."

Loreda was hardly surprised. She knew what it was like to come here looking for better and be treated as worse.

"Bastards," someone yelled.

"All across the state of California, the big growers are taking advantage of the people who work for them. The migrants coming into the state are so desperate to feed their families, they'll take any wage. There are more than seventy thousand homeless people between here and Bakersfield. Children are dying in the squatters' camps at a rate of two a day, from malnutrition or disease. It's not right. Not in America. I don't care if there is a Depression. Enough is enough. It's up to us to help them. We have to get them to join the Workers Alliance and stand up for their rights."

There was a roar of approval from the crowd.

Loreda nodded. His words struck a nerve with her, made her think for the first time, *We don't have to take this.*

"Now is the time, comrades. The government won't help these people. It is up to us. We have to convince the workers to stand up. Rise up. Use any means at our disposal to stop big business from crushing the workers and taking advantage of them. We must stand together and fight this capitalist injustice. We will fight for the migrant workers here and in the Central Valley, help them organize into unions and battle for better wages. The time . . . is now!"

"Yes!" Loreda shouted. "Yes!"

Jack jumped down from the riser on the loft ladder, but just before he did, Loreda saw him look directly at her.

He strode toward her, making his way easily through the crowd.

Loreda felt the intensity of his gaze; she felt like a mouse paralyzed by the gaze of a hunting hawk.

"I thought I told you to stay in the truck."

"I want to join your group. I could help."

"Oh, really?" He towered over her, was even taller than her mom. She drew in a tight, ragged breath. "Go home, kid. You're too young for this."

"I am a migrant worker."

He lit a cigarette, studied her.

"We live in the ditch-bank camp off Sutter Road. I picked cotton this fall when I should have been in school. If I hadn't, we would have starved. We live in a tent. We wanted the jobs in the fields so badly that sometimes we slept in ditches at the side of the road to be first in line. The boss—that fat pig, Welty—he doesn't care if we make enough to eat."

"Welty, huh? We've been trying to unionize the migrant camps. We've met with resistance. The Okies are stubborn and proud."

"Don't call us that," she said. "We're people who just want jobs. My grandparents and my mom . . . they don't believe in government hand-outs. They want to make it on their own, but . . ."

"But what?"

"It's not going to work, is it? Us coming here for a better life and actually getting it?"

"Not without a fight."

"I want to fight," Loreda said, realizing as she said it that she'd been itching for this fight for a long time. *This* was what she'd run away to find, not her lily-livered father. *This* was the passion she'd lost. She felt the heat of it.

"How old are you, really?"

"Thirteen."

"And your old man ran out on the family when he lost his job in . . . St. Louis."

"Texas," Loreda said.

"Kid, men like that aren't worth shit. And you're too young to be walking around on your own. How'd you get to California?"

"My mom brought us."

"All by herself? She must be tough."

"I called her a coward tonight."

He gave her a knowing look. "Is she going to be worried?"

Loreda nodded. "Unless they went looking for me. What if they're gone?" At that, homesickness gripped her; not the kind for a place, but for people. Her people. Mom and Ant. Grandma and Grandpa. The people who loved her.

"Kid, the people who love you stay. You've already learned that. Go find your mom and tell her you've been as dumb as a box of marbles. And let her hold you tight."

Loreda felt the sting of tears.

A police siren wailed outside.

"Shit," Jack said, taking her by the arm, dragging her across the barn, through the panicking crowd.

He shoved her up the ladder in front of him and pushed her into the loft. "There's fire in you, kid. Don't let the bastards put it out. Stay here till morning or you might end up in the hoosegow."

He dropped down the loft ladder to the barn floor.

The door cracked open. Cops appeared in the opening, holding guns and billy clubs. Behind them, red lights flashed. Cops streamed into the barn, scooped up the papers and the typewriters and the mimeograph machines.

Loreda saw a cop hit Jack in the head with his club. Jack staggered but didn't fall. Weaving a little, he grinned at the copper. "That's all you got?"

The cop's face tightened. "You're a dead man, Valen. Sooner or later." He hit Jack again, harder.

"Round 'em up, fellas," the policeman said, as blood splattered his uniform. "We don't want Reds in our town."

Reds.

Communists.

⊱

ELSA WALKED BENEATH AN anemic moon into the town of Welty. At this hour, the streets were deserted.

There it was: the police station, tucked on a side street, not far from the library.

She didn't believe that anyone in authority would actually help her, or even listen to her, but her daughter was missing. This was all she could think of to do.

The parking lot was empty but for a few cruisers and an old-fashioned truck. In the light cast downward from a streetlamp, she saw a bindle stiff standing beside the truck smoking a cigarette. She didn't make eye contact but felt him watching her.

Elsa straightened to her full height, unaware that she'd become hunched on her walk here.

She moved past the vagrant and entered the station. Inside, the lobby was austere; one row of chairs against a wall, each one empty. Light shone down from the ceiling onto a man in uniform, smoking a hand-rolled cigarette, at a desk with a black phone.

She tried to look confident. Clutching her fraying handbag strap, she crossed the tile floor, made her way to the officer at the desk.

He was tall and thin, with slicked-back hair and a thin mustache. He wrinkled his nose at her disheveled appearance.

She cleared her throat. "Uh. Sir. I'm here to report a missing girl." She tensed, waited for it: *We don't care about your kind.*

"Uh-huh?"

"My daughter. She's thirteen. Do you have children?"

He was silent so long she almost turned away.

"I do. A twelve-year-old, in fact. She's the reason I'm losing my hair."

Elsa would have smiled any other time. "We had a fight. I said . . . Anyway, she ran away."

"Do you have any idea where she'd go? What direction?"

Elsa shook her head. "Her . . . father left us a while ago. She misses him, blames me, but we have no idea where he is."

"Folks are doing that these days. Last week we had a fella kill his whole family before he killed himself. Hard times."

Elsa waited for more.

The man stared at her.

"You won't find her," Elsa said dully. "How could you?"

"I'll keep my eye out. Mostly, they come back."

Elsa tried to compose herself, but his kindness unraveled her more than cruelty could. "She has black hair and blue eyes. Well, almost violet, really, but she says only I see that. Her name is Loreda Martinelli."

"Beautiful name." He wrote it down.

Elsa nodded, stood there a moment longer.

"My recommendation is to go home, ma'am. Wait. I bet she'll come back. It's obvious you love her. Sometimes our kids don't see what's right in front of them."

Elsa backed away, unable to even thank him for his kindness.

Outside, she stared across the empty parking lot and thought: *Where is she?*

Elsa's legs started to give out on her. She stumbled, nearly fell.

Someone steadied her. "You okay?"

She wrenched sideways, pulled away.

He backed off, lifted his hands in the air. "Hey, I'm not going to hurt you."

"I—I'm fine," she said.

"I'd say you're further from fine than anyone I've ever met."

It was the bindle stiff she'd seen by the truck on her way into the station. An ugly bruise discolored one of his cheekbones. Dried blood flecked his collar. His black hair was too long, raggedly cut, threaded with gray at the temples.

"I'm fine."

"You look exhausted. Let me drive you home."

"You must think I'm stupid."

"I'm not dangerous."

"Says the bloodied-up man at the police station at one in the morning."

He smiled. "A good beating makes them feel better."

"What did you do?"

"Do? You think you need to commit a crime to get beaten up by the coppers? I'm just unpopular these days. Radical ideas," he said, still smiling. "Let me drive you home. You will be safe with me." He put a hand to his chest. "Jailbird's honor."

"No, thanks."

Elsa didn't like the way he was staring at her. He reminded her of the hungry men who lurked in shadows to steal what they wanted. Deep-set black eyes peered out from his craggy face; he had a jutting nose and pushed-out chin. And he needed a shave. "What are you looking at?"

"You remind me of someone, that's all. A warrior."

"Yeah. I'm a warrior, all right."

Elsa walked away. Out on the main road, she turned left, toward the camp. It was the only thing she could think of to do. *Go home.* Ant was there.

Wait and hope.

TWENTY-SIX

After a long, sleepless night in the barn, Loreda climbed down from the loft as dawn turned the sky lavender and then pink and then golden.

She walked down the road, carrying her suitcase.

At Sutter Road, she looked out at the spray of tents and broken-down automobiles and cobbled-together shacks clustered in the winter-dead field.

Please still be here.

Loreda stayed away from the muddy ruts and kept to the grassy high ground as she headed for their tent. She passed a hovel built of metal scraps; inside, a man and woman huddled around a nub of a candle. The woman held a very still baby in her arms.

Up ahead, Loreda saw their truck parked by the tent. Her knees almost buckled in relief. *Thank God.* They were still here.

Loreda rounded the truck and saw the Deweys' tent. Mrs. Dewey sat in a chair out front, hunched over, hands curled around a cup of coffee. Mom sat on an overturned apple crate beside her, writing in her journal.

Loreda slowed her step, moved quietly forward. In the silence that should have held a baby breathing, Loreda saw how broken both women looked.

Jean looked up first, smiled at Loreda, and touched Elsa's arm. "It's your girl. I told you she'd come back."

Mom looked up.

Loreda felt a breathtaking rush of love for her mother. "I'm so sorry," she said.

Mom closed her journal and stood up. She tried to smile, and in the failure, Loreda glimpsed the pain she'd caused by running away. Mom stood still, didn't move toward Loreda.

Loreda knew this distance between them was hers to cross. "I've been as dumb as a box of marbles, Mom," Loreda said, moving toward her.

A little laugh erupted from her mother; it sounded like joy.

"Really. I've been a real crumb to you, Mom. And . . ."

"Loreda—"

"I know you love me, and . . . I'm sorry, Mom. I love you. So much."

Mom pulled Loreda into her arms, held her tightly.

Loreda clung fiercely to her mother, afraid to let her go. "I was afraid you'd leave when I was gone . . ."

When Mom drew back, her eyes were bright and she was smiling. "You are *of* me, Loreda, in a way that can never be broken. Not by words or anger or actions or time. I love you. I will always love you." She tightened her hold on Loreda's shoulders. "You taught me love. You, first in the whole world, and my love for you will outlive me. If you had not come back . . ."

"I'm here, Mom," Loreda said. "But I learned something last night. And I think it's important."

＞

ELSA GRASPED LOREDA'S HAND, unable to let go, and let her daughter lead her back to the tent and pull her inside.

"I can't wait to tell you where I was," Loreda said as she unbuttoned her coat.

The reunion was over, apparently. Loreda was on to new business. Elsa couldn't help smiling at the quick change in her daughter's demeanor.

Elsa sat down on the mattress beside Ant, who was still sleeping. "Where did you go?"

"To a Communist meeting. In a barn."

"Oh. That is hardly what I would have guessed."

"I met a man."

Elsa frowned. She started to get up. "A man? A grown man? Did he—"

"A Communist!" Loreda sat down beside Elsa. "A whole group of them, really. They were meeting in a barn north of here. They want to help us, Mom."

"A Communist," Elsa said slowly, trying to process this new and dangerous information.

"They want to help us fight the growers."

"Fight the growers? You mean the people who employ us? The people who pay us to pick their crops?"

"You call that pay?"

"It is pay, Loreda. It buys us the food we eat."

"I want you to come to a meeting with me."

"A meeting?"

"Yes. Just listen to them. You'll like what—"

"No, Loreda," Elsa said. "Absolutely not. I am not going and I forbid you to go. The people you met are dangerous."

"But—"

"Believe me, Loreda, whatever the question is, communism is not the answer. We're Americans. And we can't get on the wrong side of the growers. We're close enough to starvation as it is. So, no."

"But it's the right thing."

"Look at this tent, Loreda. Do you think we have the luxury of fighting our employers? Do you think we have the luxury of waging a philosophical war? No. Just no. And I don't want to hear about it again. Now, come, let's get a little sleep. I'm exhausted."

>

RAIN FELL FOR DAYS. The land along the ditch bank became a pond. People started getting sick: typhoid, diphtheria, dysentery.

The burying ground doubled in size. Because the county hospital refused to treat most of the migrants, they had to help themselves as best they could.

Everyone was hungry and lethargic. Elsa spent as little as she possibly could on food, and still she watched their savings dwindle.

On this stormy winter night, Loreda and Ant were in bed, trying to sleep, burrowed beneath a pile of quilts.

Rain hammered the canvas, rippled the grayed fabric, and sluiced down the sides.

Elsa sat on an apple crate, writing in her journal by the meager light of a single candle.

For most of my life, weather was a thing remarked upon by the old men in their dusty hats who stopped to jaw with each other outside Wolcott Tractor Supply. A topic of conversation. Farmers studied the sky the way a priest read the word of God, looking for clues and signs and warnings. But all of it from a friendly distance, all of it with a faith in the essential kindness of our planet. But in this terrible decade, the weather has proven itself to be cruel. An adversary that we underestimated at our peril. Wind, dust, drought, and now this demoralizing rain, I fear—

Thunder exploded in a deafening *craaaaack.*

"That was a bad one," Loreda said. Ant looked scared.

Elsa closed her journal and got up. She was halfway to the flaps when the tent collapsed around them. Water rushed in, sucked at Elsa's legs. She shoved her journal in the bodice of her dress and reached out blindly for her children. "Kids! Come to me."

She heard them clawing at the wet canvas, trying to find their way. "I'm here," Elsa said.

Loreda reached her, held her hand, kept one arm around her brother.

"We have to get out," Elsa said, fighting to find the tent flaps.

Ant was crying beside her, clinging to her.

"Hang on to me," Elsa shouted to him. She found the split in the fabric, wrenched the flaps open, stumbled out with the children. The tent whooshed past them, taking their belongings with it.

The money.

A gush of water hit Elsa so hard she almost fell.

Lightning flashed; in the light, she saw utter destruction. Garbage and leaves and wooden crates floated past, riding the torrent, there and gone in a second.

Holding tightly to her children's hands, she slogged against the rising tide of water and made her way to the Deweys' tent. "Jean! Jeb!"

The tent collapsed just as the Deweys crawled out.

The sound of people screaming rose above the howl of the storm.

Elsa saw headlights out on the road, turning. Coming their way.

She spat rain, pushed the wet hair out of her eyes, and yelled, "We need to go that way, toward the road."

The two families stayed close together, all holding hands. Elsa's boots filled with muddy water. She knew her children were barefoot in this cold, wet water.

Together they fought their way toward the headlights. There was a row of cars parked on the main road, headlights pointed at the camp. Halfway there, Elsa saw a line of people with flashlights. A tall man stepped forward, wearing a brown canvas duster and a hat that sagged in the rain. "This way, ma'am," he yelled. "We're here to help you."

The Deweys made it to the row of volunteers. Elsa saw someone hand Jean a raincoat.

Elsa looked back. Their tent was gone now, washed away, but the truck was still there. If she didn't get it now, she would lose it.

She pushed her children forward. "Go," she said. "I have to get the truck."

"No, Mom, you can't," Loreda shouted.

Rushing water tried to push Elsa over. She pulled Ant's wet hand out of hers and shoved him at Loreda. "Get yourselves to safety."

"No, Mom—"

Elsa saw the tall volunteer heading their way again. She pushed her children toward the man, said, "Save them," and turned back.

"Ma'am, you can't—"

Elsa fought her way to the truck, which was running-board deep in water. A plastic doll in a muddy pink dress floated by, blue marble eyes staring upward. Mud and water had swept their campsite away; everything was gone. The stove had been knocked over; water swirled over it. She thought about the box that held their money and knew she'd never find it.

She climbed into the truck, grateful for once that she kept the keys in the glove box. Auto theft was low on anyone's mind when gas was unaffordable.

Please start.

Elsa turned the key in the ignition.

It took five tries and five prayers before the truck grumbled and groaned and came to life.

She turned on the headlights and put the truck in gear.

The truck jostled from side to side, fighting its way out of the mud. Elsa kept her hands tight on the wheel; her feet worked the pedals. The vehicle rolled and bucked and sometimes the engine whined, but finally the tires found purchase.

Elsa drove slowly out to the road, where a string of volunteers helped people into cars. She saw Loreda step out of an old-fashioned, wooden-cabbed truck into the pouring rain and wave her hands in the air. "Follow us, Mom!"

$$\gamma$$

ELSA FOLLOWED THE OLD truck into Welty. On a small, deserted street by the railroad tracks, it pulled up in front of a boarded-up hotel. On either side of the hotel were businesses that had been shut down. A Mexican restaurant and a laundry and a bakery. The street-lights were off. A shuttered gas station boasted a hand-lettered sign that read: THIS IS YOUR COUNTRY. DON'T LET THE BIG MEN TAKE IT AWAY FROM YOU!

Elsa had never seen this street. It was several blocks from the main section of Welty. The few houses she could see looked dilapidated and deserted. She pulled up alongside the other truck and parked.

She stepped out into the driving rain. Her children immediately ran to her; she drew them in close, holding them tightly, shivering.

"Where are the Deweys?" Elsa yelled to be heard over the storm.

"They left with other volunteers."

The driver of the truck stepped out. At first all she noticed was his height and the familiarity of the dark brown duster he wore. It was an old-fashioned coat, something a cowboy would wear. She'd seen it before, somewhere. He walked toward Elsa, through the headlights' rain-beaded glare.

It came to her: she'd seen him spouting Communist rhetoric in town once, and again outside the jail, where he'd been beaten on the night Loreda ran away.

"The jailbird," she said.

"The warrior," he answered. "I'm Jack Valen. Come. Let's get you warm."

"He's the Communist I met, Mom," Loreda said.

"Yes," Elsa said. "I've seen him in town."

He led them to the padlocked hotel door and put a key in the lock. The big black lock clattered to the side. He pushed the door open.

"Wait. The hotel looks boarded up," Elsa said.

"Looks can be deceiving. In fact, we count on that," Jack said. "A friend owns this place. It only looks abandoned. We keep it boarded up, for— Well, never mind. You can have one or two nights here. I wish it could be more."

"We are grateful for anything," Elsa said, shivering.

"Your friends the Deweys were taken to the abandoned grange hall. We are doing what we can. It came on so suddenly. There will be more help in place in the morning."

"From Communists?"

"I don't see anyone else here, do you?"

He led them inside the small hotel, which smelled of decay and cigarette smoke and must.

It took Elsa's eyes a moment to adjust. She saw a burgundy desk with a wall of brass keys behind it.

She followed Jack up to the second floor. There he opened a door to reveal a small, dusty room with a large canopy bed, a pair of night-stands, and a closed door.

He walked past them into the room and opened the closed door.

"A bathroom," Elsa whispered.

"There's hot water," he said. "Warm, at least."

Ant and Loreda shrieked and ran for the shower. Elsa heard them turn it on.

"Come on, Mom!"

Jack looked at Elsa. "Do you have a name besides 'Mom'?"

"Elsa."

"It is nice to meet you, Elsa. Now I must go back out to help."

"I'm coming with you."

"There's no need. Get warm. Stay with your children."

"Those are my people, Jack. I'm going to help them."

He didn't argue. "I will meet you downstairs."

Elsa went into the bathroom, saw her children in the shower to-gether, fully dressed, laughing. She said, "I'm going to help Jack and his friends, Loreda. You guys get some sleep."

Loreda said, "I'll come!"

"No. I need you to watch Ant and get warm. Please. No fighting with me."

Elsa hurried back outside. Now there were several automobiles in the parking lot with their lights on.

Volunteers gathered in a semicircle around Jack, who was clearly their leader. "Back to the ditch-bank camp off of Sutter Road. We need to save as many of them as we can. The grange hall has room, and so do the depot and the barns at the fairground."

Elsa climbed into Jack's truck. They joined a steady stream of blurred yellow headlights in the falling rain. Jack leaned sideways, grabbed a ratty brown sack from behind Elsa's seat. "Here, put these on." He dropped the bag in her lap.

Fingers shaking with cold, she opened it, found a pair of men's pants and a flannel shirt, both huge.

"I have something to tie the pants tight," he said.

He pulled off to the side of the road at the destroyed encampment. Drenched, dislocated people walked toward the road, clutching what-ever they'd been able to save.

In the darkness beside the truck, Elsa stripped out of her wet dress and into the oversized flannel shirt, and then put on the pants. Her journal fell out of her bodice, surprising her. She'd forgotten she'd saved it. She set it on the truck's seat, then stepped back into her wet galoshes and out into the rushing water.

Jack yanked off his tie and fit it through the belt loops on her bor-rowed pants, cinching the waistband tightly. Then he took off his coat and put it around her shoulders.

Elsa was too cold to be polite. She put on the coat, buttoned it up. "Thank you."

He took her by the hand. "The water is still rising. Be careful."

Elsa held on to his hand as they slogged through the cold, muddy, rising water. Ruined belongings floated past them. She saw a broken-down truck with a pile of junk tarped in the back. And a face. "There," she yelled to Jack, pointed.

"We're here to help," Jack shouted.

The black, shiny tarp slowly lifted. Huddled beneath it, Elsa saw, was a bony woman in a wet dress, holding a toddler. Both her face and the toddler's were blue with cold.

"Let us help you," Jack said, reaching out.

The woman pushed the tarp aside and crawled forward, holding her child close. Elsa immediately put an arm around the woman, felt how thin she was.

At the side of the road, volunteers—more now—were waiting with umbrellas and raincoats and blankets and hot coffee.

"Thank you," the woman said.

Elsa nodded and turned back to Jack. Together, they trudged back to the camp.

Water and wind beat at them; mud filled Elsa's boots with cold.

They worked through the long, wet night. Along with the rest of the volunteers, they helped people get away from the flooded encampment; they took as many as they could to warmth, got them settled in whatever buildings they could find.

By six in the morning, the rain and the flooding had stopped and dawn revealed the devastation caused by the flash flood. The ditch-bank camp had been washed away. Belongings floated in the water. Tents lay in tangled masses, ruined. Sheets of cardboard and metal lay scattered, as did boxes and buckets and quilts. Jalopies were up to their fenders in water and mud, trapped in place.

Elsa stood by the side of the road, staring at the flooded land.

People like her who had almost nothing had lost everything.

Jack came up beside Elsa and wrapped a blanket around her shoulders. "You are dead on your feet."

She pushed the wet hair out of her eyes. Her hand trembled at the effort. "I'm fine."

Jack said something.

She heard his voice but the vowels and consonants were stretched out of shape. She started to say, *I'm fine,* again, but the lie got lost somewhere between her brain and her tongue.

"Elsa!"

She stared at him, uncomprehending.

Oh, wait. I'm falling.

⤛

ELSA WAKENED IN JACK'S truck as it rattled to a stop in front of the boarded-up hotel. Elsa sat up, feeling dizzy. She saw her journal on the seat beside her and picked it up.

The parking area was crowded with people now. It had become a disaster staging area. Volunteers offered food and hot coffee and clothes to the flood victims, who walked around with a dazed look.

Elsa got out of the truck, staggered sideways.

Jack was there to catch her.

She tried to pull away. "I should go to see my children—"

"They're probably still sleeping. I'll make sure they're fine and tell them where you are. For now, though, you are getting some sleep. I saved a room for you."

Sleep. She had to admit it sounded good.

He helped her up the stairs and into the room next to her children's. Once inside, he led her straight into the bathroom, where he turned on the shower water and waited impatiently for it to get warm; when it did, he wrenched back the curtain. Elsa couldn't hold back a sigh. Warm water. She tossed her journal onto a shelf above the toilet.

Before she fully understood what he was doing, Jack had removed her galoshes and peeled the heavy canvas duster off of her and pushed her into the spray of water, fully dressed.

Elsa tilted her head back, let the hot water run through her hair.

Jack pulled the shower curtain shut and left her.

The water at Elsa's feet turned black with the mud. She stripped out of Jack's clothes—probably ruined now—and reached for the soap in the dish and rubbed it in her hands. *Lavender.*

She washed her hair and scrubbed her skin until it tingled. When the water began to cool, she stepped out, dried off, and wrapped herself in the towel. Steam hung in the room. She washed Jack's clothes in the sink, then draped the shirt and pants and her undergarments and socks over the towel rack and returned to the bedroom.

Clean sheets.

What a luxury.

Maybe Jack was right. A short nap might help.

Elsa thought of all the laundry she'd done in her life, the joy she'd always taken in hanging sheets to dry, but never until now had she fully, deeply appreciated the sheer physical pleasure of clean sheets on naked skin. The fresh smell of lavender soap in her hair.

She rolled onto her side and closed her eyes. Within moments, she was asleep.

TWENTY-SEVEN

W hen Loreda woke up, she didn't know where she was.

She sat up slowly, feeling a cloud-soft mattress beneath her. Hair lay across her face in tangles; it smelled of lavender. *Mom's soap.* But it wasn't quite the right aroma, and they hadn't had lavender soap in years.

The flood. The ditch-bank camp.

It came back to her in a flash, the muddy water rushing past them, the tent collapsing, people screaming.

Loreda eased out from underneath the covers and found Ant curled up beside her, wearing only his saggy underwear and an undershirt.

Their slightly damp clothes hung from hooks on a wooden dresser. Loreda got up and took her clothes with her into the bathroom. After she used the toilet, she couldn't help herself: she took another shower but didn't wash her hair. Then she put on her dress and sweater. Her coat was gone. As was all of their money and food.

"Oh, no, yah don't," Ant said, flinging the covers aside when she walked back into the room barefoot.

"What do you mean?"

"You ain't leavin' me here alone. I'm not a baby anymore. I'm starting to think things happen that I don't know nuthin' about."

Loreda couldn't help smiling. "Get dressed, Antsy."

He dressed in last night's still-damp clothes—all they had left now—and together they left the room, walked on bare feet down the narrow stairway to the lobby below. Halfway down, they heard voices.

The small lobby was filled with people; the air smelled of sweat, wet clothes, and drying mud. Loreda and Ant pushed their way through.

Outside, a bright sun shone on the wet street, which had been cordoned off to traffic. Several organizations had set up tents in the street—the Red Cross and the Salvation Army, some state relief organizations. A couple of church groups. Each held a table and chairs, along with donuts and sandwiches and hot coffee, as well as boxes of goods and clothes for giveaway.

"It's like a carnival," Ant said, shivering in his damp clothes. "But I don't see no rides."

"Any rides," Loreda said, crossing her arms for warmth.

The displaced migrant families were obvious; they gathered in bedraggled groups, wearing blankets and looking dazed, sipping hot coffee.

Loreda saw a tent set back from the others. A banner hung from one tent pole to the other, WORKERS ALLIANCE: FDR'S NEW DEAL SHOULD WORK FOR YOU.

Communists.

"Come on." Loreda dragged Ant to the tent, where a woman in a black coat stood all by herself smoking a cigarette. She wore black wool pants and a creamy white sweater and a beret. Bright red lipstick accentuated the pallor of her skin.

Loreda approached the tent. "Hello?"

The woman pulled the cigarette from her bright red lips and turned. Her dark eyes narrowed into an assessing gaze that swept Loreda from head to foot. "Would you like some coffee?"

Loreda had never seen a woman like this. So . . . elegant, or maybe it was just boldness. She was probably Mom's age, but her style and beauty were somehow ageless. "I'm Loreda."

The woman extended a hand. Bright red lacquer polish brightened her short fingernails. "I'm Natalia. You're freezing."

"W-wet clothes. But that doesn't matter. I want to join your group."

The woman took a drag of her cigarette, exhaled slowly. "Really?"

"I know Mr. Valen. I have . . . been to a barn meeting."

"Really?"

"I'd like to join the fight."

Natalia paused. "Well, I imagine you have more reason than most. Today, though, we are not fighting. Today we are helping."

"Helping people gets their attention."

"Smart girl."

"I want to be a part of . . ." She lowered her voice. "You know. Rise up. Stand up."

Natalia nodded. "Good for you. A girl who thinks for herself. You can start by getting some dry clothes and shoes for you and the boy. Put them on. Stop shivering. Then you may help me pour coffee."

༞

VOLUNTEERS ARRIVED IN A steady stream. By noon there were hundreds of people in the valley, handing out hot coffee and warm clothes and sandwiches. The Red Cross had set up a temporary shelter in an abandoned automobile dealership and given folks a place to stay overnight. The Salvation Army had taken over the local grange hall. According to Jack, half the Communists and socialists in Hollywood had come to help or sent donations. There was even word that some movie stars were here, although Loreda hadn't seen any. Or maybe Natalia was an actress; she certainly had the glamour.

Loreda and Ant had spent the last few hours helping flood victims in any way they could. Loreda had found dry, warm clothes and shoes for the three of them. The clothing—their only real belongings now—sat in a box in the Communists' tent. She'd found a dress and sweater for Mom and had taken them up to her room. Seeing Mom asleep, Loreda had left the clothes for her. Now Loreda sat in the Communists' tent beside Natalia. In front of them, the table held a big metal coffeepot and a nearly empty tray of sandwiches. And a stack of flyers, very few of which had been taken, if any.

Natalia lit up a cigarette, offered Loreda one.

"No, thanks. I'd rather eat than smoke."

Natalia leaned forward and took the last bologna sandwich, handing it to Loreda.

Taking a bite, Loreda stared out at the diminished crowd. There were fewer people out here now. Most had been relocated or helped in some way.

Out in the cordoned-off street, Jack threw a softball back and forth with Ant. Loreda found herself mesmerized by Ant's joy in such a simple thing. It made her think about Daddy and who they'd all been before he left. His leaving was still the worst thing that had happened to their family. The drought and the Depression would end. Daddy leaving them in the middle of it would hurt forever.

She looked at Jack. Even with all they'd been through, the long, terrible night, there was a strength in him that comforted her. You could count on a man like that, she thought. A man who didn't just spout ideas, but fought for them, took beatings for them, and stayed in place. If only her father had been more like Jack.

A rebel instead of a dreamer. Daddy had given Loreda words; it was actions that mattered. She knew that now. Leaving. Staying. Fighting. Or walking away.

Loreda wanted to be like Jack, not like her faithless father. She wanted to stand for something and tell the world she was better than this, that America should be better than letting her live this way.

But look at the stack of flyers left on the table. Very few had been taken. People had taken coffee and sandwiches, but apparently they didn't want words. Especially not fighting words. And the only name on the Workers Alliance sign-up sheet was Loreda's.

"How do you know Jack?" Loreda said, looking at him.

"I met him years ago at a John Reed Club. We were both young and full of ourselves." Natalia dropped her cigarette and stubbed it out with her fashionable shoe. "He was the first person I know to start talking about workers' rights in the fields. He got us to fight the deportation of Mexicans a few years ago. It was an ugly time, but . . ." She shrugged. "People get scared when they lose their jobs and they tend to blame outsiders. The first step is to call them criminals. The rest is easy. You know about that," she said, eyeing Loreda.

"I do."

"Several years ago, the Mexicans organized and joined the union and struck for better wages, but it came with violence. Men died. Jack spent a year in San Quentin. When he came out, he was even more determined."

Loreda hadn't considered *prison*. "How is it illegal to ask for better wages?"

Natalia lit up another cigarette. "It isn't, technically. But this is a capitalist country, run by big-money interests. After the state's anti-immigration campaign, when they rounded up all the illegals and deported them back to Mexico, the growers would have had a real problem, but then . . ."

"We started coming."

Natalia nodded. "They sent flyers across America, telling workers to come. And they came, too many of them. Now there are ten workers for every job. We're having trouble getting your people to organize. They're—"

"Independent."

"I was going to say stubborn."

"Yeah. Well, a lot of us are farmers, and you have to be stubborn to survive sometimes."

"Are you stubborn?"

"Yeah," Loreda said slowly. "I reckon so. But more than anything, I'm mad."

ELSA WOKE TO SUNSHINE coming through glass windows and it made her miss the farmhouse in Lonesome Tree. She would write about that in her journal later, about the simple joy of seeing sunshine through clean glass, golden, pure as the gaze of God, and how it could lift one's spirit.

It was better than writing about the new and terrifying truth of life: their money was gone.

Their belongings, their tent, their stove, their food. Gone.

Still, someone had left a pale blue dress and a red sweater hanging over the dresser. *Small blessings.*

Moving slowly—everything hurt after last night—she slipped into the new clothes and still-muddy galoshes and went to the room next door to find her children. When no one answered her knock on the door, she went downstairs.

The street in front of the hotel was cordoned off to traffic. The Red Cross had set up a tent, as had the Salvation Army and a local Presbyterian church. She saw Ant and Loreda handing out food on trays. The sight of them helping others when they themselves had lost everything made her proud. After all they'd suffered—the hardship, the loss, the disappointment—there they were, smiling and handing out food. Helping people. It gave her hope for the future.

Jack stood in a nearby tent, talking to a woman in a beret. Elsa headed toward him.

He gave her a smile. "Coffee?"

"I'd love some."

He pulled out a chair for her. She saw stacks of flyers on the table around him. *Unionize Now! Communism Is the New Americanism.* Some of the flyers were in Spanish. A sign-up sheet asked for people to join the Workers Alliance. There was one name on it: Loreda's.

"Offering a little radical ideology with the coffee?" she said, crumpling the sign-up sheet into a ball. "My daughter is not signing this."

He sat down near her, scooted closer. "Loreda has been following me around like a bird dog on the scent."

"She's thirteen." Elsa glanced at the people gathered in the street. "She could get in trouble just talking to you, let alone joining the Communist Party. The growers don't want unions."

"A sad comment on the times. This is America, after all."

"Not the America I know." She turned to him. "Why communism?"

"Why not? I've done my time in the fields. I know how hard life is for migrant workers. Big growers helped elect FDR. He's beholden to them. Ever wonder why his policies help almost all workers except farmworkers? I want to make it better."

He looked at her. "I have a feeling you know struggle. Maybe you can tell me why most of the folks coming into the state don't want to unionize?"

"We're proud," she said. "We believe in hard work and a fair chance. Not one for all and all for one."

"Don't you think a little all-for-one might help your folks?"

"I think what you want will cause trouble." Elsa finished her coffee and handed him her empty cup. As he took it from her, she noticed his ratty wristwatch, which didn't tell the right time. It surprised her, that small insight. She'd never known a man who didn't care about time. "I appreciate your help, Jack. Truly. Your people were the first to help us, but . . ."

"But what?"

"I don't have time for communism. I need to find a place for us to live."

"You think I don't understand, Mrs. Martinelli, but I do. Better than you can imagine."

The way he said her surname surprised her somehow; he made it sound exotic almost, tinged with an accent she didn't recognize. "Call me Elsa, please."

"Will you let me do one thing for you?"

"What?"

"Will you trust me?"

"Why?"

"There's no *why* to trust. It either is or isn't. Will you trust me?"

Elsa stared at him, looked deeply into his dark eyes. There was in him an intensity that unnerved her; maybe she would have found him frightening in her life before all of this. She remembered the day she'd seen him proselytizing in the town square and getting punched by the police, and the bruises she'd seen on his face when she saw him outside the police station. He and his ideas came with violence, there was no doubt about that.

But he'd saved her children and given them a place to stay. And, strangely, beneath the fierceness she saw in him, she sensed pain. Not loneliness, exactly, but an aloneness she recognized.

Elsa stood. "Okay," she said, her gaze steady.

He led her to the Red Cross tent, where Loreda and Ant were handing out sandwiches.

"Mommy!" Ant cried out at the sight of her.

Elsa couldn't help smiling. What in the world was more restorative than a child's love?

"You should see how good I've been at food, Mommy," Ant said, grinning. "And I didn't eat *every* donut."

Elsa ruffled his clean hair. "I'm proud of you. And now Mr. Valen promises to show us something interesting. Explorers Club outing?"

"Yay!"

Loreda said, "Let me get our new stuff." She ran back to the

Communist tent and returned with a box full of clothes and bedding and food.

Jack touched Elsa's arm gently. When she looked up at him, she saw a surprising understanding in his eyes, as if he knew how it felt to lose everything, or maybe just to have nothing to lose.

"Follow me. I'm in that truck."

Elsa walked with her children to their own muddy truck and climbed in. The truck bed held the few goods and belongings they'd never unpacked; things they didn't need in this broken-down version of their life.

As they headed north following Jack, storm damage was evident everywhere; splintered, fallen trees, rocks and rubble in the street, slumps of land that covered roadways. Water in gullies, in puddles, in falls by the street.

People walked in a steady stream along the side of the road, carrying whatever they had left.

They passed another ditch-bank camp that was destroyed. A sea of mud and belongings, but already people were slogging back onto the wet land, digging through the mud and standing water for their belongings.

At a sign that read WELTY FARMS, Jack pulled over to the side of the road and parked. Elsa did the same. He walked over to her side of the truck. She rolled down the window.

"This is Welty's camp. He houses some pickers here. I heard that a family left yesterday."

"Why would a family leave?"

"Someone died," he said. "Tell the man at the guardhouse that Grant sent you."

"Who is Grant?"

"A boss. He drinks too much to remember who uses his name."

"Will you come with us?"

"I've got a bad reputation around here. They don't like my ideas." He flashed her a smile and walked back to his own truck.

He was gone before Elsa could thank him. She drove slowly onto Welty land, noticing that it was soggy from rain but hadn't been flooded. The camp was situated between two cotton fields and set well back from the road. A guardhouse stood at the fenced entrance to the camp.

Elsa came to it and stopped.

A man stood there holding a shotgun. He was whippet-thin, with a pencil neck and an elbow-sharp chin. A hat covered close-cut gray hair.

"Hello, sir," she said.

The man stepped up to the truck, peered inside. "You flooded out?"

"Yes, sir."

"We only take families here," he said. "No riffraff. No Negroes. No Mexicans." He eyed the three of them. "No single women."

"My husband is coming home tomorrow," Elsa said. "He's picking peas." She paused. "Grant sent us."

"Yep. He knows I've got an open cabin."

"A *cabin*," Loreda whispered.

"It's four bucks a month for electricity, and a buck apiece for two mattresses."

"Six dollars," Elsa said. "Can I get the cabin without electricity or mattresses?"

"No, ma'am. But there's work here at Welty and if you live in our cabins, you're the first to get our jobs. The big man owns twenty-two thousand acres of cotton. Most of our folks live on relief until the cotton season. We have our own school, too. And a post office."

"School? On the property?"

"It's better for the kids. They don't get hassled so much. You want it or not?"

"She *definitely* wants it," Ant said.

"Yes," Elsa said.

"Cabin Ten. We take payment right out of your pay. There's a store where you can buy goods and even get a little cash if you need it. On credit, of course. Go on."

"Don't you need my name?"

"Nah. Go on."

Elsa continued on the muddy road toward a collection of cabins and tents, set up almost like a town. She followed the signs to Cabin 10 and parked beside it.

The cabin was a concrete and wooden structure that was about ten feet by twelve feet. The sides began as a layer of concrete block and then became metal panels with wood supports. There were no windows, but two of the upper walls had long metal vents that could be pushed up and locked in place on hot days.

They got out of the truck and went inside. It was gloomy, cast in shadows. A bare light bulb hung from a cord on the ceiling. "Electricity," Elsa said, marveling.

A small hot plate on a wooden shelf and two rusted metal bed frames with mattresses took up half of the space in the cabin, but there was room for chairs, maybe even a table. There was a cement floor. A *floor.*

"Wowza," Ant said.

"This is *great,*" Loreda said.

Electricity. Mattresses. A floor beneath their feet. A roof over their heads.

But . . . six dollars. How in the world could she pay for this? They'd lost every cent they had.

"Are you okay, Mom?" Loreda asked.

"Can we go exploring?" Ant asked. "Maybe there's other kids here."

Elsa nodded distractedly, stood there. "Go on. Don't be gone long."

Elsa left the cabin after them. She could see several cabins and at least fifty tents spread out across five or six acres. People milled about, gathering firewood, chasing children. It looked more like a town than a ditch-bank camp, with signs that pointed the way to toilets and laundry and school.

The good fortune of being here was tempered by her fear of losing it. How long could she live on credit?

She went back to her truck and picked up the box of supplies Loreda had gathered from the Salvation Army. Clothes, shoes and coats for the children, sheets, a single frying pan. And some food—enough for two days if they were careful.

What then?

She carried it into their cabin and closed the door.

"Hey," Jack said, seated on one of the beds.

Elsa almost dropped the box in surprise.

"I'm sorry," he said. "I didn't mean to scare you. It seems I couldn't stay away."

"I thought you weren't supposed to be here."

"I have a fondness for breaking rules."

Elsa set the box on the floor and sat down beside him. "I don't know how I'll pay for this. I'm grateful. Truly. It's just . . ."

"It costs money you don't have."

"Yes." It felt good to say it out loud. "We lost everything in the flood."

"I wish I had money to give you, but a job like mine doesn't pay much."

"I'm surprised it pays at all." She looked at him. "What is your job, exactly?"

"I work for the Workers Alliance. The Popular Front. Whatever you want to call it."

"The Communist Party."

"Yes. There are about forty of us on the payroll across the state. Support in Hollywood is high right now, with what's going on in Europe. I write for the *Daily Worker*, sign up new members, lead study groups, and organize strikes. Basically, I do whatever I can do to help people who are being taken advantage of by the capitalist system. And I spread the word that there's a better way." He met her gaze and returned it with a steady one of his own. "How did you end up living in that camp? As a single woman . . ."

She tucked her hair behind one ear. "You've heard my story before, believe me. We left bad times in Texas and found it worse in California."

"Your husband?"

"Gone."

"So, he's a fool."

Elsa smiled. She'd never quite thought of it that way, but she liked it. "That's my position, yes. And you? Are you married?"

"Nope. Never been. Women tend to be scared of the trouble I bring. The big, bad Communist."

"Everything is frightening these days. How much more trouble can there be?"

"I've been in prison," he said quietly. "Does that scare you?"

"It would have. Once." Elsa was unused to the way he stared at her. "I'm not going to get any prettier, you know."

"You think that's what I'm thinking when I look at you?"

"Why do you take the risk? Of communism, I mean. You must know it won't work in America. And I see what it costs you."

"For my mother," he said. "She came here at sixteen because she was starving and had been disowned by her family because of me. I still don't know who my father is. She worked like a dog to support us, doing whatever she had to do, but each night, at bedtime, she kissed me good night and told me I could be anything in America. It was the dream that had brought her here and she passed it on to me. But, it was a lie. For people like us, anyway. Folks who are from the wrong place, or have the wrong color skin, or speak the wrong language, or pray to the wrong God. She died in a factory fire. All of the doors were locked to keep the workers from taking cigarette breaks. This country used her up and spit her out and all she ever wanted was for me to have opportunities. A better life than she'd had." He leaned toward her. "You understand. I know you do. Your people are starving, dying. Thousands are homeless. They can't make enough money picking to survive. Help me convince them to strike for better wages. They'll listen to you."

Elsa laughed. "No one has ever listened to me."

"They will. We need someone like you."

Elsa's smile faded. He was serious. "What good is a strike if you lose your job? I have children to feed."

"Loreda is a firebrand. She would love—"

"She needs to be in school. Education is what will give her a better life, not joining the Communists." Elsa got slowly to her feet. "I'm sorry, Jack. I'm not brave enough to help you. And please, please, keep your people away from my daughter."

Jack rose. She could see the disappointment in his eyes. "I under-stand."

"Do you?"

"Of course. Fear is smart until . . ." He headed for the door, paused as he reached for the knob.

"Until what?"

He looked back at her. "Until you realize you're afraid of the wrong thing."

⅂

THAT NIGHT, WHILE THE children slept, Elsa got her journal out of the box that had been in the truck. She turned through the pages. The children had been right that writing helped. Words jumped out at her: *rain, baby in a lavender blanket, no work, waiting for cotton, the demoralizing rain.* Tonight, later, she would write about her constant fear, how it strangled her all the time and the constant effort it took not to show it to her children. Writing about it would remind her that they had survived. As bad as the flood had been, they were still here.

Although this journal meant the world to her, now it was the only paper they had. She ripped a sheet out and wrote a letter to Tony and Rose.

Dear Tony and Rose:

We have an address!

We are—at last—out of our tent and into a home with real walls and a floor. The children are enrolled in a school that is a stone's throw away from our own front door. We feel so blessed. That's the good news. The not so good news is that a flood destroyed our tent and most of our belongings. Imagine that, a flood. I know you'd love a little of that water to come your way.

Lord, I miss home so much sometimes I can hardly breathe.

How is the farm? The town? You both?

Please write to us soon.

Love,

Elsa, Loreda, and Ant

TWENTY-EIGHT

꙳

L ast night, they'd eaten a meal that almost filled their bellies and which had been cooked on an electric hot plate inside a cabin with four walls and a roof overhead and a floor to stand upon. After supper, they'd climbed into real beds on real mattresses that weren't on the floor. Loreda had slept deeply, with her little brother tucked in close, and awakened the next morning refreshed.

After breakfast, they each dressed in the new garments and shoes they'd gotten from the Salvation Army and stepped outside into a bright sunlit day.

The Welty camp was situated on a few acres tucked in between cotton fields. Although the camp hadn't flooded, evidence of too much rain was everywhere. The grass had been stomped into mud, but Loreda could see it would be a green pasture under better conditions. Now many of the trees, scattered randomly throughout the camp, were broken-limbed by the storm. Ditches full of muddy water ran here and there. Ten cabins and about fifty tents created a makeshift town in the center of the camp. Between the cabins and the first of the tents, Loreda saw a long building that was the laundry, and four restrooms—two for women and two for men—each of which had long lines of people waiting their turn. Most important, there were two faucets at each entrance. Clean water. No more hauling water from the ditch, boiling and straining it before each use.

At the company store, more people waited in line, mostly women, standing with their arms crossed, children close by. A hand-painted sign pointed the way to the school.

"What if I said we'd start tomorrow?" Loreda said glumly.

"I'd say you were just bumping gums," Mom said. "I'm going to do laundry and get some food and you're going to school. End of story. Start walking."

Ant giggled. "Mom wins."

Mom led the way toward a pair of tents positioned at the far end of the camp in a grove of spindly trees. She paused beside the largest of the tents, which had a wooden sign posted out front: LITTLE KIDS SCHOOL.

The tent next door read: BIG KIDS SCHOOL.

"I reckon I'm big," Ant said.

Mom said, "I don't think so," and eased Ant toward the Little Kids tent.

Loreda moved fast.

The last thing she wanted was to be walked into her classroom by her mother. She went to the Big Kids tent and peered inside.

There were about five desks. Two were empty. A woman wearing a drab gray cotton dress and rubber boots stood at the front of the room. Beside her was an easel that held a chalkboard. On it, she'd written: *American history.*

Loreda ducked inside and sat at the empty desk in the back.

The teacher looked up. "I'm Mrs. Sharpe. And who is our newest pupil?"

The other kids turned to look at Loreda.

"Loreda Martinelli."

The boy in the next desk scooted so close his desk edge banged into hers. He was tall, she could tell. Lanky. With a dirty cap pulled down so low she couldn't see his eyes. His blond hair was too long. He wore faded overalls over a denim shirt; one bib strap was untied and the corner flapped over like a dog's ear. A winter coat hung on him, too big and missing most of the buttons. He pulled off his cap. "Lor-ay-da. I ain't heard that name before. It's pretty."

"Hi," she said. "Thanks. And you are?"

"Bobby Rand. You moved into Cabin Ten? The Pennipakers left just before the flood. The old man died. Dysentery." He smiled. "Glad to have someone my age here. My pa makes me go to school if there's no pickin'."

"Yeah. My mom wants me to go to college."

He laughed, showing off a missing tooth. "That's rich."

Loreda glared at him. "Girls can go to college, I'll have you know."

"Oh. I thought you were jokin'."

"Well, I'm not. Where are you from, the Stone Age?"

"New Mexico. We had a grocery store that went bust."

"Students," the teacher said, rapping a ruler on the top of the easel. "You are not here to jaw. Open your American history books to page one-twelve."

Bobby opened a book. "We can share. Not that we're gonna learn anything that matters."

Loreda leaned toward him, looked at the open book. The chapter heading was "The Founding Fathers and the First Continental Congress."

Loreda raised her hand.

"Yes . . . Loretta, is it?"

Loreda didn't correct the pronunciation of her name. Mrs. Sharpe didn't look like much of a listener. "I'm interested in more recent history, ma'am. The farmworkers here in California. The anti-immigration policies that deported the Mexicans. And what about workers' unions? I'd like to understand—"

The teacher rapped her ruler down so hard it cracked. "We do *not* talk about unionism here. That's un-American. We are lucky to have jobs that put food on our tables."

"But we don't really have jobs, do we? I mean—"

"Out! Now. Don't come back until you're ready to be grateful. And quiet, as young women should always be."

"What is wrong with everyone in this state?" Loreda said, slamming the book shut on Bobby's finger. He yelped in pain.

"We don't need to learn about what old rich men did more than one hundred years ago. The world is falling apart *now*." She strode out of the tent.

What now?

Loreda marched through the grassy mud toward . . . what?

Where was she going? If she went back to the cabin, Mom would put her to work doing laundry.

The library. It was the only thing she could think of.

She walked out of camp and turned onto the paved road and walked to town.

In Welty, which was less than a mile away, she turned onto Main Street, where a series of awninged shops had obviously once offered everything a person could need if you had money. Tailors, druggists, grocers, butchers, dress shops. Now most of them were closed. A movie theater stood in the center of town, its marquee unlit, its windows boarded up.

She passed a boarded-up hat shop; a man sat on the stoop, one leg stretched out, the other bent. He draped an arm over the bent knee, a brown hand-rolled cigarette dangled between his fingers.

He peered up at her from beneath the brim of his tired-looking fedora.

A look of understanding passed between them.

Loreda paused for a moment outside the library. She hadn't been here since the day of her haircut. It already felt like a lifetime ago.

Today she looked bedraggled, unkempt, skinny. At least she was wearing the relatively new hand-me-down dress, but the mud splattered lace-up shoes and socks were not a good look on anyone.

Loreda forced herself to open the door. Once inside, she stepped out of her muddy shoes, left them by the door.

The librarian looked Loreda up and down, from her dirty stockinged feet to the ratty lace of her hand-me-down collar.

Remember me, please. Don't call me an Okie.

"Miss Martinelli," she said. "I hoped you'd return. Your mother was so pleased to pick up your library card."

"It was my Christmas present."

"A fine gift."

"I . . . lost the Nancy Drew books in the flood. I'm so sorry."

Mrs. Quisdorf gave her a sad smile. "Nothing to fret about. I'm just glad to see you looking well. What can I find on the shelves for you?"

"I'm interested in . . . workers' rights."

"Ah. Politics." She walked away. "Give me a moment."

Loreda glanced at the newspapers spread out on the table beside her. One from the *Los Angeles Herald-Express* had the headline: "Stay Away from California: Warning to Transient Hordes."

Nothing new there.

"Relief for Migrants to Bankrupt State."

Loreda flipped through the pages, saw article after article that claimed the migrants were bankrupting the state by demanding aid. Called them shiftless and lazy and criminal, reported that they lived like dogs "because they don't know any better."

She heard footsteps again. Mrs. Quisdorf came up beside her and laid a slim book on the table beside the newspapers. *Ten Days That Shook the World,* by John Reed.

"John Reed," Loreda said. The name struck a chord, but she couldn't remember where she'd heard it. "Thank you."

"A warning, though," Mrs. Quisdorf said quietly. "Words and ideas can be deadly. You be careful what you say and to whom, especially in this town."

·⟩⟨·

THE CAMP'S LAUNDRY WAS housed in a long wooden building and had six large metal tubs and three hand-cranked wringers. And—miracle of miracles—clean, running water at the turn of a handle. Elsa spent her first morning in camp washing the sheets they had gotten from the Salvation Army and the clothes they'd worn in the flood, putting it all through a wringer instead of twisting the water out of each item by hand. When everything was clean, she carried the damp bundle back to her cabin and set up a makeshift laundry line and hung it all to dry.

Then she retrieved the letter she'd written last night and dropped it off at the post office. Just that—the fact that she could walk fifty feet and mail a letter—was a staggering bit of good fortune.

And now, shopping. Right here. In camp. What a convenience.

The company store was in a narrow green clapboard building, with a peaked roof and slim windows positioned on either side of a white door. She had to walk through mud to get there—mud everywhere, of course, since the flood and the rain—and climb two mud-streaked steps.

As Elsa opened the door, a bell tinkled overhead, sounding surprisingly gay.

Inside, she saw rows and rows of food. Cans of beans and peas and tomato soup. Bags of rice and flour and sugar. Smoked meats. Locally made cheeses. Fresh vegetables. Eggs. Milk.

One whole wall was clothing. Bolts of fabric, everything from cotton to wool. There were boxes of buttons and ribbons and spools of thread. Shoes in every size. Galoshes and raincoats and hats. There were cotton- and potato-picking sacks and canteens and gloves.

Everything was priced high, she noticed. Some things—like eggs—were more than twice the price they were in town. The cotton-picking sacks that hung from hooks on the wall were priced three times what Elsa had paid in town.

She picked up an empty basket.

In the back of the store, a long counter ran nearly from end to end; behind it stood a man with muttonchop sideburns and bushy eyebrows. He wore a dark brown hat, a black sweater, and pants with suspenders. "Hullo there," he said, pushing the wire-rimmed spectacles higher on his nose. "You must be the new resident of Cabin Ten."

"I am," Elsa said. "We are, actually, my children and me. And my husband," she remembered to add.

"Welcome. You look like a fine new member of our little community."

"We were . . . flooded out of our . . . home."

"As so many were."

"Our money was lost. All of it."

He nodded. "Indeed. Again, a common tale."

"I have children to feed."

"And rent to pay now."

Elsa swallowed hard. "Yes. Your prices . . . they're very high . . ."

Behind her, the bell tinkled again. She turned and saw a big man walk in. A toothy smile dominated his florid, fleshy face. He hooked his thumbs into the suspenders that held up his brown woolen pants and ambled casually forward, eyeing the goods on either side of him as he walked.

"Mr. Welty," the store clerk said. "A good morning to you."

Welty. The owner.

"It'll be better when the damn ground dries, Harald. And who have we here?" He came to a stop beside Elsa. Up close, she saw the quality of his clothing, the cut of his coat. It was how her father had dressed for work—a man choosing clothes to make a statement.

"Elsa Martinelli," she said. "We are new here."

"The poor family lost everything in the flood," Harald said.

"Ah," Mr. Welty said. "Then you're in the right place. Stock up on food to feed your family. Get whatever suits your fancy. Come cotton season, you will make plenty. Do you have children?"

"Two, sir."

"Fine, fine. We love our children pickers." He slapped a hand down on the counter hard enough to rattle the jar of candy by the register. "Give her some candy for her children, by God."

Elsa thanked him, although she was pretty sure he didn't hear, or wasn't listening. Already he was turning away, walking out of the store.

The bell jangled.

"So," Harald said, opening a book. "Cabin Ten. I will put you down for six dollars this month on credit. That's for rent. Now, what else do you need?"

Elsa looked longingly at the smoked meat.

"Just take what you need," Harald said gently.

Elsa couldn't do that. If she did, she'd take it all, and run like a thief. She couldn't let herself be seduced by the idea of credit. Nothing in this life was free, for migrants most of all.

Still.

She walked the aisles slowly, adding up every price in her head. She placed items in her basket with great care, as if they might detonate on impact: cans of milk, smoked ham, a bag of potatoes, a bag of flour, a bag of rice, two tins of chipped beef, a small amount of sugar. A bag of beans. Coffee. Some laundry and hand soap. Toothpaste and toothbrushes. A blanket. Two envelopes.

She carried the basket to the counter and withdrew the items one by one.

As she did so, a terrible sinking feeling filled her, a sense of impending doom. She had never bought anything she couldn't pay for. Sure, the Wolcott family had bought things in town on credit, but that had been a convenience. Her father paid his tab promptly, from savings in the bank. The idea of asking for credit when there were no savings to draw upon felt to Elsa like begging.

"Eleven dollars and twenty cents," Harald said, writing the total down in the book below the heading of Cabin 10.

At this rate, Elsa would accrue a lot of debt between now and April 26, when—hopefully—state relief would give her some help.

"You know," she said quietly, "I only need one can of chipped beef."

ELSA HAD NO SHELVING in the cabin, so she stacked the food carefully in the one box they had and tucked it under the bed. She'd withheld two cans of milk, a pound of coffee, and a bar of soap. Those items she put back in the bag she'd gotten at the store and carried it out of the cabin.

She got into her truck and drove south, past the town of Welty, to the ditch-bank camp, and parked on the side of the road. The field was a sea of standing water and mud, studded with debris. Goods, tree limbs, sheets of metal lay scattered and floating. With nowhere else to go, people had begun to move back onto the land and set up camp.

Elsa saw the Deweys' big farm truck off to the right, half buried in mud. A group of people stood around it.

She carried the groceries across the field, her boots pressing down into the squishy mud, standing water lapping across her ankles now and then.

Jeb and the boys were busy hammering nails into salvaged sheets of plywood. The two girls sat in the back of the truck, playing with ruined dolls in muddy dresses. A broken chair leaned against the mud-clogged stove they had hauled all the way from Alabama, thinking it would go into a house.

They were living in the truck, all six of them.

Elsa saw Jeb and waved. He gave her an ashamed look. "Jean's at the ditch."

Elsa's throat was too tight to allow for words, so she nodded and set the groceries down on the broken chair. Saying nothing, she picked her way through the muddy, debris-strewn field to the ditch.

Jean was at the bank, trying to draw water into a bucket. Elsa came up quietly behind her, feeling guilty that she'd gotten out of this place and ashamed at how grateful she was for it. "Jean," she said.

Jean turned. In the split second before she smiled, Elsa saw the depth of her friend's despair. "Elsa," Jean said. "As you can see, the neighborhood has gone to hell without you."

Elsa didn't feel much like joking. "Nadine? Midge?"

"Nadine and them moved on. Jest started walkin'. Ain't seen Midge since the flood."

Jean got slowly to her feet, set the bucket of dirty water down beside her.

Elsa approached cautiously, afraid that she might cry. She understood at last what her grandfather had meant when he said, *Pretend to be brave if you have to.* She did that now, managed a smile even as she felt the sting of tears. "I hate you being here."

"I hate it, too." Jean coughed into a dirty handkerchief. "But Jeb is going to rig some kind of structure on the back of the truck. Maybe even make us a covered porch. It won't be so bad soon. The land'll dry." She smiled. "Maybe you'll come back for tea."

"Tea? I think we should start drinking gin."

"You'll visit, though?"

Elsa glimpsed Jean's fear, and it matched her own. "Of course. And you'll let me know if you need me. Whenever. Day or night. We're in Cabin Ten at Welty's growers' camp. Just up the road. I . . . brought you food." *Not enough.*

"Aw, Elsa . . . how can I thank you?"

"You don't need to thank me. You know that."

Jean picked up her bucket. The two women walked back to the broken-down truck. How would the Deweys follow the crops in the coming months?

Elsa didn't know how to leave them here, but there was nothing she could do. She knew that others were even worse off, without even a car to live in.

"It will get better," Jean said.

"Of course it will."

A look passed between them, a knowledge of their shared lie.

"We'll drink gin and dance the Charleston, like them society girls," Jean said. "I always wanted dance lessons. Did I tell you that? As a girl in Montgomery. I begged my mama for lessons. I've still got two left feet. You shoulda seen me at my weddin'. Jeb and me dancing was a terrible thing to see."

Elsa smiled. "It couldn't be worse than Rafe and me. Someday soon we will teach each other to dance, Jean. You and me, with music. And we won't care who is watching or what they think," she said. She pulled Jean into a tight hug and found it difficult to let go.

"Go on," Jean said. "We're fine here."

With a crisp little nod and a wave to the rest of the family, she headed back across the soggy field. She saw her own stove, half buried in mud, lying on its side, the pipe gone. With each breath, she almost cried; each moment she held it back was a triumph. She found a bucket sticking up from the mud and picked it up and kept walking. Then she found a coffee cup and she picked that up, too.

In Welty, she walked to the gas station and washed out the bucket at the faucet by the pumps. She held her muddy boots under the water, cleaning them, too, and then she put them back on. All the while she was thinking about her friend, living in a truck in the middle of a sea of mud in the winter.

"Elsa?"

She shut off the water and turned.

Jack stood there, holding a sheaf of papers. Flyers, no doubt, urging people to rise up in anger about the way they were treated.

She shouldn't move toward him, not right out here in public, but she couldn't help herself. She felt fragile and alone.

So alone.

"Are you okay?" he asked, meeting her more than halfway.

"I've been out . . . to the ditch-bank camp. Jean . . . and the children . . . are living . . ." On that, her voice broke.

Jack opened his arms and she walked into his embrace. He held her close, said nothing while she cried. Even so, his arms comforted her, his shirt soaked up her tears.

Finally, she drew back, looked at him. He let her go and wiped the tears from her face with the pad of his thumb.

"That's no way to live," she said, clearing her throat. Already the moment of intimacy between them was dissolving. She felt embarrassed for letting him hold her. No doubt he thought her needy and pathetic.

"No, it isn't. Let me drive you home?"

"Back to Texas?"

"Is that what you want?"

"Jack, what I want doesn't matter one whit. Not even to me." She wiped her eyes, ashamed by the weakness she'd revealed.

"It's not weak, you know. To feel things deeply, to want things. To need."

Elsa was startled by his perceptiveness. "I need to go," she said. "The kids will be out of school soon."

"Goodbye, Elsa."

She was surprised by how sad he looked when he said it. Or maybe disappointed in her. It was probably that. "Goodbye, Jack," she said, and walked away, left him standing there. Somehow, she knew he was staring after her, but she didn't look back.

꒰ꗃ꒱

BY THE END OF March, the ground had dried, the ditch-bank camp had filled again, Loreda had turned fourteen, and the Martinelli family was deeply in debt. Elsa did the math obsessively in her head. So far, she and Loreda would have to pick three thousand pounds of cotton just to pay their debt. But she still had to pay rent and buy food. It was a violent, vicious cycle that would start all over again when winter came. There was no way to get ahead, no way to get out.

Still, she went out each day, looking for work while the kids were in school. On good days, she made forty cents weeding or doing someone's laundry or cleaning someone's house. She and the kids made weekly visits to the Salvation Army to pick through the give-away clothing bins.

In April, she counted down the days until she officially became a resident of the state and could qualify for relief. It no longer even crossed her mind to refuse aid from the government.

On the appointed day, she woke early and made flour-and-water pancakes for the kids and poured them each a half glass of the watered-down apple juice they sold by the quart in the company store.

Still sleepy eyed, the kids dressed and put on their shoes and filed out of the small cabin and headed for the bathrooms, where there would be a long line.

When they returned, Elsa served them two pancakes each—doctored with a precious dollop of jam. They sat on their bed, side by side.

"You need to eat something, Mom," Loreda said.

For a moment Elsa saw her fourteen-year-old daughter in heart-breaking relief: bony face, prominent cheekbones. A gingham dress hung on her thin body; her clavicle stuck up from the hollowed-out skin on either side.

She was supposed to be going to square dances and having her first crush on a boy at this age . . .

"Mom?" Loreda said.

"Oh. Sorry."

"Are you dizzy?"

"No. Not at all. Just thinking."

Ant laughed. "That's no good, Ma. You know better."

Ant stood up. He was all knobs and sticks, this boy who had just turned nine; with elbows and knees and feet that were all too big for his skinny limbs. In the past few months, he'd found friends and begun to act like a boy again; he refused to have his hair cut, hated any sort of games, and called her Ma.

"Guess what today is," Elsa said.

"What?" Loreda said, not bothering to look up.

"We get state relief," Elsa said. "Real cash money. I can start paying down our debt."

"Sure," Loreda said, plunging her empty plate into the bucket of soapy water.

"We registered with the state a year ago," Elsa said. "We can get aid as residents now."

Loreda looked at her. "They'll find a way to take it back."

"Come on, Miss Sunshine," Elsa said, offering Ant his coat.

Elsa didn't bother with her own coat. She put on her galoshes and wrapped a blanket around her shoulders.

They stepped out into the busy camp. Now that the threat of frost had passed, men were busy in the fields. Tractors worked ceaselessly, readying the soil, churning it up, planting seeds.

"It makes me think of Grandpa," Loreda said.

They all stopped, listened to the sound of the tractors' motors. The smell of freshly turned soil hung in the air.

"It does," Elsa said, feeling a wave of homesickness.

They kept walking, three abreast, until they reached the school tents.

"'Bye, Ma. Good luck with relief," Ant said, running off.

Loreda ducked into her tent.

Elsa stood there a moment, listening to the sounds of children talking and laughing, of teachers telling them to take their seats. If she closed her eyes—which she did, just for a moment—she could imagine a whole different world.

Finally, she turned away. Paths between the tents and cabins had been worn into ruts by hundreds of feet. At the bathrooms, she got in line and waited her turn.

It wasn't a bad wait at this time of day—less than twenty minutes for the toilets. She wanted to take a shower, but with only two showers, the wait was always an hour or more.

She went into her cabin and washed the breakfast dishes and put them in the salvaged apple crate that was their cupboard. In the past months since the flood, they had become good at scavenging.

She made her bed and put on her coat and left the cabin.

In town, a long line of sad-looking men and women snaked in front of the state relief office. Most didn't look up from their own clasped hands. They were Midwesterners or Texans or Southerners, most of them. Proud people who weren't used to being on the dole.

Elsa took her place at the back. People moved in behind her quickly, seemed to come from the four corners of town to get in line.

"Are you okay, ma'am?"

She gave herself a little shake, forced a smile. "Forgot to eat, I guess. I'm fine. Thank you."

The scrawny young man in front of her wore dungarees that must have been bought when he weighed fifty pounds more. He needed a shave but his eyes were kind. "We all forgot that," he said with a smile. "I ain't eaten since Thursday. What day is it?"

"Monday."

He shrugged. "Kids, you know."

"I know."

"You got relief before?"

She shook her head. "I didn't qualify until today."

"Qualify?"

"You have to be in the state a year to get relief."

"A year? We could be dead by then." He sighed and stepped out of the line and walked away.

"Wait!" Elsa called out. "You need to register now!"

The young man didn't turn around and Elsa couldn't step out of line to follow him. Losing her place would cost her hours.

She eventually made her way to the front. Once there, she looked down at the bright-faced young woman seated at the desk, with a portable typewriter in front of her. Beside it was a long index-card box. "Name?"

"Elsa Martinelli. I have two children. Anthony and Loreda. I registered last year on this date."

The woman rifled through the red cards, pulled one out. "Here you are. Address?"

"Welty growers' camp."

The woman put the card in the typewriter and added the information. "All right, Mrs. Martinelli. Three people in the family. You'll get thirteen dollars and fifty cents per month." She pulled the card out of the typewriter.

"Thank you." Elsa rolled the bills into as small a cylinder as she could and tightened her fist around them.

As she left the state relief office, she noticed a commotion down the street at the federal relief office. A crowd of people were shouting.

Elsa walked cautiously toward the melee, keenly aware of the money in her hand.

She stopped beside a man at the edge of the crowd. "What's going on?"

"The feds cut relief. No more commodities."

Someone in the crowd yelled, "That ain't right!"

A rock sailed through the relief office window, breaking the glass. The mob surged toward the office, shouting.

Within minutes a siren could be heard. A police car rolled up, lights flashing. Two uniformed men jumped out holding billy clubs. "Who wants to go to jail for vagrancy?"

One of the policemen grabbed a raggedly dressed man, hauled him over to the police car, and shoved him in. "Anyone else want to go to jail?"

Elsa turned to the man beside her. "How can they just end the commodities relief? Don't they care about us?"

The man gave her a disbelieving look. "You tryin' to be funny?"

⤳

AFTER LEAVING THE RELIEF office, Elsa walked to the ditch-bank
camp on Sutter Road.

In the months since the flood, more people had moved onto this
land. Old-timers pitched their tents and parked their cars and built
their shacks on higher ground, if they could find it. Newcomers set
up near the ditch. The ground was studded with spring grass and old
belongings, some of which poked up here and there in the dirt. A pipe
edge, a book, a ruined lantern. Most things of value had been dug up
already or were buried too deeply to be found.

She came to the Deweys' truck. They'd built a shack around it with
scavenged wood and tar paper and scrap metal.

She found Jean sitting in a chair beside the truck's front fender.
Mary and Lucy sat in the grass beside her cross-legged, poking sticks
into the ground.

"Elsa!" Jean said, starting to rise.

"Don't get up," Elsa said, seeing how pale her friend was, how gaunt.
Elsa sat down on the overturned bucket beside Jean.

"I don't have any coffee to offer you," Jean said. "I'm drinking hot
water."

"I could use a cup," Elsa said.

Jean poured Elsa a cup of boiling water and handed it to her.

"The feds cut relief," Elsa said. "People are rioting in town."

Jean coughed. "I heard. Don't know how we're gonna make it till
cotton."

"We'll make it." Elsa opened her hand slowly, looked down at the
thirteen dollars and fifty cents she had to feed her family until next
month. She peeled off two one-dollar bills and handed them to Jean.

"I can't take that," Jean said. "Not money."

"Of course you can." They both knew that the twenty-seven dollars the Deweys got from the state wasn't nearly enough to feed six people. And Elsa could get things on credit from the store. The Deweys couldn't.

Jean reached for the bills, trying to smile. "Well. I am saving up for our bottle of gin."

"You bet. We will get rip-roaring drunk real soon. Bad-girl drunk," Elsa said, smiling at the thought. "I was only a bad girl once in my life, and you know what it got me?"

"What?"

"A bad husband and a beautiful new family. So, I say we be bad."

"That a promise?"

"You bet. Someday soon, Jean."

>

ELSA WALKED BACK TO Welty Farms and went to the company store. On the way home from the relief office, she had made calculations in her head. If she used half of her relief money to pay down her debt each month, it would be tight, but they'd have a chance.

In the store, she picked out a loaf of bread and one of bologna and a can of chipped beef, some hot dogs, and a bag of potatoes. A jar of peanut butter, a bar of soap, several cans of milk, and some lard. More than anything, she wanted to add a dozen eggs and a Hershey's candy bar. But that was how people were ruined by credit.

She placed her items on the counter.

Harald smiled at her as he rang up the items. "Relief day, eh, Mrs. Martinelli? I can tell by your smile."

"It's a relief for sure."

The cash register clattered and rang. "That'll be two dollars and thirty-nine cents."

"That sure is steep," Elsa said.

"Yep," he said, giving her a commiserating look.

She withdrew the cash from her pocket, began counting it out.

"Oh. We don't take cash, missus. Just credit."

"But I have money, finally. I wanted to pay on my bill, too."

"It doesn't work that way. Credit only. I can even give you a little spending money . . . on credit. With interest. For gas and such."

"But . . . how do I get out from my debt?"

"You pick."

The reality of the situation sank in. Why hadn't Elsa figured it out before? Welty *wanted* her in their debt, wanted her to spend her relief money lavishly and be broke again next winter. Of course they'd give you cash for credit—probably at a high interest rate—because poor folks worked for less, asked for less. All she could do was try to use her relief money to buy goods in town, at lower prices, to offset her accruing debt at the company store, but it wouldn't make much of a dent. They couldn't live on thirteen dollars a month. She reached into the basket and removed a can of chipped beef, which she set back on the counter. "I can't afford this."

He recalculated her credit total, wrote it down. "Sorry, ma'am."

"Are you? What about going north, to pick peaches? I suppose I'd have to pay for the cabin in advance while I'm gone."

"Oh, no, ma'am. You'd have to give up the cabin and the sure-thing job of picking cotton."

"We can't follow the crops?" Elsa stood there a moment staring at him, wondering how he could stand to be a part of this system. They couldn't follow the crops and keep the cabin, which meant they had to stay here, without work, waiting for cotton, living on relief and credit. "So, we're slaves."

"Workers. The lucky ones, I'd say."

"Would you?"

"Have you seen the way folks live out by the ditch bank?"

"Yes," Elsa said. "I've seen it."

Holding her bag of groceries, she walked out of the store.

Outside, people milled about: women hanging laundry, men scavenging for wood, young children looking for any bit of junk to call a toy. A dozen stoop-shouldered women in baggy dresses stood in line for the two women's toilets. There were more than three hundred people living here now; they'd pitched fifteen new tents on concrete pads.

She looked at the women, really *looked*. Gray. Slanted shoulders. Kerchiefs on untended hair. Drab dresses mended and re-mended. Fallen stockings. Worn shoes. Thin.

Still, they smiled at one another in line, talked, wrangled their runaway children, those young enough not to be in school. Elsa had stood in that line enough to know that the women talked about ordinary things—gossip, children, health.

Life went on, even in the hardest of times.

TWENTY-NINE

In May, the valley dried out beneath sunny days and everything grew and blossomed. In June, the cotton plants flowered and needed to be trimmed. True to Welty's word, those who lived at Welty Farms growers' camp were the first to get these precious jobs; Elsa spent hours working beneath the hot sun. Most of the valley's ditch-bank residents, including Jeb and the boys, had hitchhiked north for work. Jean stayed back with the girls and the stuck-in-the-ground truck that was all they had left.

Today, just before dawn, a big truck pulled into the Welty camp, chugging smoke. The people standing in line barely waited for it to stop before they climbed aboard. Men and women got into the back and crammed in tightly, hats drawn low, gloves on (gloves they'd had to purchase at the company store for an exorbitant price).

Loreda looked up at Mom, who was pressed close to the wooden slats directly behind the cab. She had been the second person in line when the truck pulled up this morning.

"Make sure Ant does his homework," Mom said.

"Are you sure I can't—"

"I'm sure, Loreda. You can pick cotton when it's ready; that's it. Now go to school and learn something so you don't end up like me. I'm forty and most days I feel a hundred. Besides, there's only a week of school left anyway."

A man closed the gate at the back of the truck. Within moments the truck was chugging out to the road, heading to the cotton fields. It wasn't hot yet, but it soon would be.

Loreda went back into the cabin. Already the small interior had begun to grow warm. Though she knew it was a harbinger of summer heat to come, Loreda still appreciated the warmth after the cold of winter. She opened the air vents and went to the hot plate and started the oatmeal she and Ant would have for breakfast.

As light came into the cabin, Ant stumbled out of bed and walked to the door. "I gotta pee."

He came back fifteen minutes later, scratching his privates. "Did Mom get work?"

"She did."

He sat on a wooden crate at the table they'd scavenged. After they finished eating, Loreda walked Ant to school. "I'll meet you at the cabin after school," she said. "Don't dawdle. Today's laundry."

"It'll be hot." Ant grimaced and went into his classroom.

Loreda headed to her own classroom. As she reached the tent flap, she heard Mrs. Sharpe say, "Today the girls are going to learn to mix cosmetics, and the boys will do a science project."

Loreda groaned. Making cosmetics.

"We all know how important beauty is in finding a man," Mrs. Sharpe said.

"No," Loreda said aloud. "Just . . . no."

She put her foot down on making cosmetics. Last week the girls had spent hours learning to sift dry ingredients and knead bread, while the boys had been taught how to "fly" in a replicated plywood airplane cockpit with painted-on instruments.

She didn't skip school often, because she knew how much her mother cared about education, but honestly, sometimes Loreda just couldn't stand it. And Lord knew Mrs. Sharpe would give Loreda the evil eye either way. Her questions in class were not appreciated. She ducked into their cabin, found her latest library book, and headed out of camp.

Out on the main road, she felt her spine straightening, her chin lifting. She swung her arms as she walked to town. What could be better than skipping school to visit the library? She'd read *The Communist Manifesto* this week and she was eager to find something equally enlightening. Mrs. Quisdorf had mentioned something by a man named Hobbes.

Main Street was busy today. Men in suits and women in spring dresses walked toward the movie theater; the marquee read: TOWN MEETING.

Loreda walked into the library and headed straight for the checkout desk.

She handed Mrs. Quisdorf the book.

"And what did we learn from this?" Mrs. Quisdorf asked in a lowered voice, although it didn't look like anyone else was here. The library was empty most days.

"It's all about class struggle, isn't it? Serfs against landlords throughout history. Marx and Engels are right. If there was only one class, where everyone worked for the good of all, it would be a better world. We wouldn't have people like the big growers making all the money and people like us doing all the work. We starve while the rich get richer."

"From each according to his ability, to each according to his needs," Mrs. Quisdorf said, nodding. "That's the general idea. Who's to say if it actually works, though."

"Hey, what's going on at the theater? I thought it was closed down."

Mrs. Quisdorf looked back through the windows. "Town meeting. It's politics, I guess you could say. Happening right under our noses."

"Would they let me in?"

"It's open to the public, but . . . well . . . sometimes it's better to study politics from a nice, safe historical perspective. The real thing can be pretty ugly."

"How can they stop me from going? I'm a resident of the state now."

"Yes, but . . . well, be careful."

"I'm reliably careful, Mrs. Q.," Loreda said.

Outside, a hot June sun shone down. She left the side street and emerged onto Main, passing a soup kitchen with a long line of people out front.

Loreda merged into the well-dressed crowd and entered the theater. Inside, red velvet curtains bracketed a raised stage. Gilt trim highlighted intricately carved woodwork. Within minutes, most of the seats were taken.

Loreda took a seat on the aisle beside a man in a black suit and hat who was smoking a cigar. The smell of the smoke made her feel slightly sick.

A man stepped up onto the stage, took his place behind the podium. The crowd quieted.

"Thank you all for coming. We all know why we're here. In 1933, the Federal Emergency Relief Administration was set up to be temporary help for folks coming into the state. We didn't know we'd be overrun with migrants. And who knew so many of them would be of weak moral character? Who knew they'd want to live on relief? Thanks to FDR's support for business, we've ended federal relief, but the state still pays people who have been here for a year. And frankly, the state just doesn't have the resources to handle the need."

Weak moral character?

A man in the crowd stood up. "We hear they aren't going to pick. Why should they? They're living the good life on the dole. From my taxes!"

"What if there aren't enough workers to pick our cotton crop?"

"And what about that durn tent camp the feds are building for migrants in Arvin? It'll be a hotbed for agitators. I hear they're talking about giving them gosh darn healthcare."

A man stood. Loreda recognized Mr. Welty. He liked to walk through camp, with his chest all puffed up, and look down on his workers.

"The damn relief workers are coddling the Okies," Welty said. "I say we stop *all* relief during the picking season. What if they get a hankering to unionize? We can't afford a strike."

Strike.

The man at the podium held out his hands to quiet the audience. "That's why we're here today. The CSA shares your concerns. We will not let the crop—or your bottom line—suffer. The state knows how important the crop is to our economy. Just as we know how important it is to manage the disease in the camps so our own children remain safe. We need to build a migrant school, a migrant hospital. Keep them to themselves."

"The damn Red agitators were at my farm this week stirring up trouble. We gotta stop a strike before it happens."

A man strode down the aisle as if he owned the place. He wore a brown suit coat that was dusty and out of date. Loreda saw him and sat up straighter.

Jack.

"They're *Americans,*" Jack said. "Do you have no shame at all? You don't mind breaking their backs when the cotton is ready, but as soon as it's done, you throw them away like they're garbage. Just as you've always done to the people who pick your crops. Money, money, money. It's all you care about."

A shouting match erupted throughout the audience. Men stood, shouted, pumped their fists in anger.

"A man can't feed his family on one cent for every pound of cotton he picks. You know it and you're scared. You should be scared. You kick a dog long enough, he's going to bite," Jack said.

Two policemen rushed in. One of them grabbed Jack and hauled him away.

Loreda ran outside, blinking for a moment in the brightness. Flyers stuck to the sidewalk, along the curb, drifted down the street. *Workers Unite for Change!*

Jack lay sprawled on the ground. His hat had fallen off and lay beside him.

"Jack!" Loreda yelled, running over to him, kneeling.

"Loreda." He grabbed his hat, crushed it to his head, and stood up, giving her a slow-building smile. "My little commie-in-training. How the hell are you?"

How could he smile with blood running down from a cut at his temple?

A police siren wailed.

"Come on," Jack said, taking her by the arm. "I've had enough jail time this week." He gathered up his flyers, and then pulled her across the street and into a diner.

Loreda climbed up onto the stool next to him. Taking a napkin, she dabbed at the blood at his temple.

"Does it give me a rakish look?"

"That's not funny," she said.

"No. It's not."

"What was all of that about?"

He ordered Loreda a chocolate milkshake.

"Cotton prices are down. That's bad for the industry and bad news for the workers. The growers are getting nervous."

Loreda slurped up the sweet, creamy milkshake so fast it gave her a headache. "That's why they had that meeting and called us names?"

"They call you names because they don't want to think of you as like them. They're worried about you forming unions, demanding more money. The so-called Bum Blockade—the closing of state borders—is over, so migrants are pouring into the state again."

"They don't want to pay us enough to live on."

"Exactly."

"How do we make them pay?"

"You'll have to fight for it." He paused, looked at her, trying to appear nonchalant. "Now, tell me, kid, how's your mom?"

$$\sim$$

AFTER TEN HOURS OF hard labor beneath a hot sun, Elsa climbed down from the truck. She had her work chit in one gloved hand. It wasn't worth much, but it was something. The company store charged the camp residents ten percent to convert the chit to credit, but they couldn't cash it anywhere else; if they wanted cash instead of credit, they had to pay interest. So, in point of fact, as little as they were paid, it was really even ten percent less. Exhausted, her hands and shoulders aching in pain, she walked over to the store and went inside. The bell that jangled at her entrance grated on her nerves. All she could think about in this place was her growing debt and the grinding truth that there was no way out of it.

A new man was at the counter, someone she didn't know.

"Cabin Ten," she said.

The new man opened the book, looked at the chit, and wrote down the amount she'd earned. Turning, she chose two cans of milk from the aisle beside her. She hated to pay what they charged for it, but Ant and Loreda needed milk to keep their bones strong. "Put this on my bill," she said without looking back.

She joined the women in line for the bathroom. Usually she struck up a conversation with the women around her, but after ten hours in the cotton field, she didn't have the energy.

When it was finally her turn, she went into the dark, smelly bathroom and used the toilet.

She washed her hands at a pump outside and then headed back to her cabin. A foreman followed her part of the way, stopped to listen to a pair of men talking along the fence line. It was happening more and more lately, the growers sending spies to listen to what the workers said when they weren't in the fields.

At her cabin door, she paused, collected herself, and managed a smile just as she opened the door. "Hello, explor—"

She stopped.

Jack sat on Elsa's bed, hunched forward, as if telling a story to Ant, who sat on the concrete floor in front of him cross-legged, looking rapt.

"Ma!" Ant said, springing up. "Jack is tellin' us about Hollywood. He's met a bunch of movie stars. Ain't that right, Jack?"

Elsa saw the stack of flyers on the chair beside her. *Workers Unite for Change!*

Jack stood. "I met Loreda in town today. She invited me here."

Elsa looked at Loreda, who had the grace to blush. "Loreda was in town. On a school day. How interesting. And she invited you—a Communist—back to our tent, with your flyers. How very thoughtful of her."

"I skipped school and went to the library," Loreda said as Elsa put the milk away. "Mrs. Sharpe was teaching the girls in class how to make cosmetics, Mom. I mean . . . we can't buy books and we're hungry, and making eyeliner is important?"

"Loreda tells me you've been working hard lately," Jack said, coming toward her. "It was sure hot today."

"It's still hot. And I'm lucky to have the work," she said. When he was close enough to hear her whisper, she said, "You endanger us with your presence."

"I promised the kids an adventure," he whispered back. "Ant tells me you have an Explorers Club. May I join?"

"Please, Mom," the kids said in unison.

"They have the hearing of jackals when they want to," Elsa said.

"Pleeeeeease."

"Okay, okay. But I should feed us—"

"No," Jack said. "You are in my care now. I'll meet you out at the road. My truck's there. It's best not to be seen with me."

"I'm pretty sure it's best not to *be* with you," Elsa said.

Loreda jumped up and led Jack to the door, closing it behind him. Slowly, she turned, making a face. "About school—"

Honestly, Elsa was too hot and tired to care about skipped school right now. She washed and dried her face and brushed her hair. "We'll talk about it tomorrow." She made Ant turn around, then stripped out of her work clothes and into the pretty cotton dress from the Salvation Army.

They left the cabin and walked out to the main road, where Jack's truck was parked.

All the way there, she worried that they were being watched, but she didn't see any foremen skulking about.

They crammed into Jack's old truck. Elsa held Ant on her lap.

"And we're off!" Ant said as Jack steered their way out to the road.

Soon they turned onto the road where the abandoned hotel was. "Wait here." He parked the truck and bounded out and went into a small Mexican restaurant that appeared to be standing-room-only busy inside. Moments later, he came out with a basket, which he put in the back of the truck.

Well out of town, they turned onto a road Elsa had never been on before. It twisted and turned as it rose into the foothills.

At last Jack pulled over and parked at the edge of a large, grassy area, alongside a dozen or so other parked cars. People walked among the newly planted trees; children and pets ran across the grass. Elsa could see three lakes; one was dotted with people in paddleboats. People swam along the shore, laughing and splashing. Off to the left, in a copse of trees, a band played a Jimmie Rodgers song. A string of concession booths had been set up along the shore. The air smelled of brown sugar and popcorn.

It was like going back in time. Elsa thought of Pioneer Days and how she and Rose had cooked all day to be ready, how Tony had played his fiddle, and everyone had danced.

"It's like home," Loreda said beside her.

Elsa reached out for her daughter's hand, held it for a moment, and then let her go.

The kids ran off toward the lake.

"It's beautiful," Elsa said.

Jack got the basket from the back of the truck. "The WPA built it with FDR's funds. It put men to work and paid them a good wage. This is opening day."

"I thought you commies hated everything in America."

"Not at all," he said solemnly. "We agree with the New Deal. We believe in justice and fair wages and equal opportunity for all, not just the rich. Communism is really just the new Americanism; I think it was John Ford, the director, who said that first. At one of the early meetings of the new Hollywood Anti-Nazi League."

"You take it very seriously," she said.

"It is serious, Elsa." He took her arm, began strolling through the park. "But not today."

Elsa felt people looking at her, judging her worn clothes and bare legs and shoes that didn't quite fit.

A tall woman in a blue crepe dress walked past, her gloved hands holding fast to her handbag. She sniffed ever so slightly as she turned her head away.

Elsa stopped, feeling ashamed.

"That old bag has no right to judge you. Stare her down," Jack said, and urged her to keep walking.

It was exactly the kind of thing her grandfather would have said to her. Elsa couldn't help smiling.

They went to the edge of the lake and sat down in the grass. Ant and Loreda were splashing in water up to their knees. Elsa and Jack took off their shoes; Jack set his hat aside.

"You remind me of my mother," he said.

"Your mother? Have I aged that much?"

"It is a compliment, Elsa. Believe me. She was a fierce woman."

Elsa smiled. "I'm hardly fierce, but I'll accept any compliment these days."

"I often wondered how my mother did it, survived in this country, a single woman who barely spoke the language, with a kid and no husband. I hated how other women treated her, how her boss treated her. I don't know why I'm telling you this."

"You probably think she was lonely, worry that you weren't enough. Believe me, I know lonely, and I'm sure you were the thing that saved her from it."

He was silent for a moment, studying her. "I haven't talked about her in a long time."

Elsa waited for him to go on.

"I remember the sound of her laughter. For years, I've wondered what she had to laugh about . . . now I see you, here, with your children . . . I see the way you love them and I think I understand her a little."

Elsa felt his gaze, steady and searching, on hers, as if he wanted to know her.

"Come in with us, Mommy!" Ant said, waving her over.

Grateful for the distraction, Elsa broke eye contact with him and waved at her children. "You know I can't swim."

Jack got up and pulled Elsa to her feet. They were so close she could feel his breath against her lips. "No, really," she said. "I can't swim."

"Trust me." He pulled her toward the water. She would have fought, but they were garnering enough looks as it was.

At the shore, he picked her up and carried her into the water.

Cool water slapped Elsa in the back, and then suddenly she was in the water, in his arms, staring up at the bright blue sky.

I'm floating.

She felt weightless, a perfect combination of sun and water, cold and hot, steady in his arms. For a magnificent moment, the world fell away and she was somewhere else, before now, or long from now, and she wasn't hungry or tired or scared or angry. She simply was. She closed her eyes and felt at peace for the first time in years. *Safe.*

When she opened her eyes, Jack was staring down at her. He leaned down, so close she thought he might kiss her, but he whispered, "Do you know how beautiful you are?"

She wanted to laugh at the obvious joke, but she couldn't make a sound, not with him staring at her. After a moment, her silence turned the moment awkward. Still, she had no idea what she should have said.

He carried her back to the grassy shore and set her down and left her there, shivering and confused, both by his words and her sudden feelings for him.

He returned with a serape, which he wrapped around her shoulders. Opening the basket, he called for the kids, who ran up, dripping water from their clothes.

Ant collapsed beside Elsa. She pulled him under the serape with her.

Jack opened the basket and pulled out bottles of Coca-Cola and tamales filled with beans and cheese and pork and a deliciously spiced sauce.

It was the best day any of them had had in years, since before the dust and the drought and the Depression.

"It reminds you, doesn't it?" Loreda said much later, when the park had emptied and the sky had darkened and the stars had come out to shine.

"Of what?"

"Home," Loreda said. "I swear I can hear the windmill."

But it was just the water, slapping rhythmically against the shore.

"I miss it," Ant said.

"I'm sure they miss us, too," Elsa said. "We will write them tomorrow and tell them all about this wonderful day." She looked at Jack. "Thank you."

"You're welcome."

The exchange felt oddly intimate, or maybe it was the way he looked at her, or the way his look made her feel. *You scare me,* she wanted to say, but it was ridiculous and what did it matter anyway? This was just one day, a vacation. "And now . . ."

She didn't have to finish the sentence. Jack stood. So did Ant and Loreda. He got them settled in the back of his truck and then opened the cab door for Elsa.

Back to the camp. Real life.

The road home was long and lonely and winding. In her head Elsa started a dozen conversations with him, found bits and pieces to say, but in reality she sat in silence, too confused to say much of anything. Today had felt . . . special, but what did she know of things like that? She didn't want to humiliate herself by imagining some feeling that wasn't there.

At the entrance to the Welty camp, Jack pulled off to the side of the road and parked. Elsa watched him walk through the headlights' yellow glow to open her door.

She stepped out; he took her hand.

"I'm going up to Salinas soon. To try to unionize the workers up there. Maybe head over to the canneries. I'll be gone awhile. So . . ."

"Why are you telling me that?"

"I didn't want you to think I just . . . ran off. I wouldn't do that to you."

"That's an odd thing to say to a woman you barely know."

"If you'll notice, I'm trying to change that, Elsa. I want to know you. If you'll just give me a chance."

"You scare me," she said.

"I know," he said, still holding her hand. "The growers are scared, the townspeople are angry, the state is bleeding money, and people are desperate. It's a volatile situation. Something's gotta give. The last time it exploded, three union organizers were dead. I don't want to put you in danger."

The funny thing was, Elsa hadn't meant that at all. She was afraid of him as a man, afraid of the things she felt when he looked at her, afraid of the feelings he had awakened in her.

"Aren't you a union organizer?" she said.

"I am."

It made her think for the first time about the danger he was putting himself in. "So, I am not the only one who needs to be careful, am I?"

THIRTY

All that long, hot summer, Elsa and Loreda did their best to find work. They didn't dare leave the growers' camp to look elsewhere, and didn't want to use relief money for gas, so they stayed in Welty and found what work they could. On days when there was no work, Elsa did her chores and then walked Loreda and Ant to the library, where Mrs. Quisdorf kept them busy with books and projects. With the kids safe at the library, Elsa often walked to the ditch-bank camp and sat with Jean by the muddy water or the buried-in-dirt truck and talked.

"Where is he?" Jean said on a particularly hot day in late August. The camp smelled to high heaven in this heat, but neither one cared. They were just happy to get a little time together.

"Who?" Elsa said, sipping the lukewarm tea Jean had made.

Jean gave Elsa that look, the one they'd perfected with each other. "You know who I mean."

"Jack," Elsa said. "I try not to think about him."

"You need to try harder," Jean said. "Or just admit he's on your mind."

"I don't have a good history with men."

"You know the thing about history, Elsa? It's over. Already dead and gone."

"They say people who don't heed history are doomed to repeat it."

"Who says that? I ain't never heard it. I say folks who hang on to the past miss their chance for a future."

Elsa looked at her friend. "Come on, Jean," she said. "Look at me. I wasn't pretty in the best of times—when I was young and well fed and clean and wore fine clothes. And now . . ."

"Ah, Elsa. You got a wrong picture of yourself."

"Even if that is true, what does a person do about it? The things your parents say and the things your husband doesn't say become a mirror, don't they? You see yourself as they see you, and no matter how far you come, you bring that mirror with you."

"Break it," Jean said.

"How?"

"With a gosh dang rock." Jean leaned forward. "I'm a mirror, too, Elsa. You remember that."

❧

COTTON'S READY.

Word spread through the Welty camp on a hot, dry day in September. Airy white tufts floated above the crop, lifted into the clear blue sky. Notices on each cabin and tent advised the folks to be ready to pick at six in the morning.

Elsa dressed in pants and a long-sleeved blouse and made breakfast, then woke the children, who now sat on the edge of their bed, eating hot, sweet polenta, chewing it silently.

It broke Elsa's heart that they would be picking with her today. Especially Ant. But they hadn't had a meeting about it, not this season. Last year they'd been naïve; Elsa had thought she could keep her children in school while she made enough money to feed and house and clothe them. Now she knew better. They'd been in the state long enough to understand: Cotton was their lifeblood. Even the children had to pick.

They'd had no choice but to fall into the cycle the growers wanted them in: living on credit, building up debt, and never making enough, even with relief, to break out. They had to pick enough to pay off this year's debt, so they could start living on credit again in the winter when the work vanished.

She rolled up their cotton sacks and filled their canteens and packed their lunches, and then hurried the kids out of the cabin to the row of waiting trucks.

"You," the boss said, pointing at Elsa. "Three of you?"

No, Elsa wanted to say.

"Yes," Loreda said.

"The kid's scrawny," the boss said, spitting tobacco.

"He's stronger than he looks," Loreda said.

The boss leaned over to the truck bed beside him and pulled out three twelve-foot-long canvas picking bags. "Go to the east field. A buck and a half apiece for the bags. We'll put 'em on your account."

"A dollar fifty! That's highway robbery," Elsa said. "We have our own bags."

"If you live on Welty land, you use Welty bags." He looked at her. "You want the job?"

"Yes," Elsa said. "Cabin Ten."

He threw them the three long sacks.

Elsa and the kids climbed into the truck with the other pickers and were driven five miles to another Welty field, where each was assigned their own row. Elsa unfurled her long, empty bag and strapped it to her shoulder and let it splay out behind her, then showed Ant how to do it.

He looked so small in the row. She and Loreda had spent time explaining the work to him, but he would have to learn as they had—by getting bloody hands.

"Quit starin' at me like that, Ma," he said. "I ain't a baby."

"You're my baby," she said.

He rolled his eyes.

A bell rang to start them off.

Elsa stooped over and got to work, reaching into the spiny cotton plant, wincing as the needle-sharp pins stuck deep into her flesh. She pulled off the bolls, separated them from leaves and twigs, and stuffed the white handfuls of cotton into her bag. *Don't think about Ant.*

Over and over and over she did the same thing: pick, separate, shove into bag.

As the sun rose higher in the sky, Elsa felt her skin burning, felt sweat scrape the sunburn and collect at her collar. Behind her, the bag became heavier and heavier; she dragged it forward with every step.

By lunchtime, it was well over one hundred degrees in the field.

The water truck rolled forward, positioning itself at the end of the rows, which meant they had to walk nearly a mile for a drink of water.

Elsa saw how many workers were lined up outside the field hoping for work, standing for hours in the hot, hot sun. Hundreds of them.

Desperate enough to take any wage to feed their families.

Elsa kept picking, hating with every moment, every breath, that her children were out here picking alongside her.

When her bag was full, she muscled it out of her row and over to the line at the scales.

Loreda came up beside her. They were both red-faced and sweating profusely and breathing hard.

"Would it kill them to put in a bathroom?" Loreda said, sopping her brow.

"Hush," Elsa said sharply. "Look at all the people waiting to take our jobs."

Loreda looked out over the line at the entrance. "Poor folks. Even worse off."

A truck rattled up the dirt road, dust clouding up around it. The sides were painted with a white cotton boll and read WELTY FARMS.

The truck came to a rattling stop. Mr. Welty climbed out. He was a big man, powerful-looking, with a shock of white hair that looked like cotton tufts beneath his felt fedora. Behind him, in the bed of the truck, were coils of barbed wire.

Everyone stopped working, turned.

The owner, was heard being passed in whispers among the workers. *It's him.*

He climbed up on to the platform that held the scales. He looked out over his fields and his workers, then glanced pointedly at the hundreds of people waiting for work. "Thanks to the feds, I had to plant less cotton this year. There is less cotton to pick and more people to pick it. So, I'm cutting what we pay by ten percent."

"Ten percent?" Loreda shouted. "We can't make a—"

Elsa clamped a hand over her daughter's mouth.

Welty looked directly at Elsa and Loreda. "Anyone want to quit? Take the cut in pay or walk away. I've got ten men wanting to work for each person here. Doesn't matter to me who picks my cotton." He paused. "Or who lives in my camp."

Silence.

"I thought not," he said. "Back to work."

A bell rang.

Elsa slowly lowered her hand from Loreda's mouth. "You want to be one of them?" she said, cocking her head toward the line of people waiting for work.

"We are them!" Loreda cried. "This is *wrong.* You heard Jack and his friends—"

"Hush," Elsa hissed. "That's dangerous talk, and you know it."

"I don't care. This is *wrong.*"

"Loreda—"

Loreda yanked free. "I won't be like you, Mom. I won't just take it and pretend it's okay as long as they don't *actually* kill us. Why aren't you furious?"

"Loreda—"

"Sure, Mom. Tell me to be a nice girl and be quiet and keep working while we go into debt every month at the company store."

Loreda dragged her bag up to the scale and said loudly. "Yes, sir. Pay me less. I'm happy for the job."

The man at the scales handed her a green chit for the cotton. Ninety cents for one hundred pounds, and the company store would charge her another ten percent.

>€

"You're awful quiet," Mom said as they walked back to their cabin.

"Consider it a blessing," Loreda said. "You wouldn't like what I have to say."

"Really, Ma," Ant said. "Don't ask her."

Loreda stopped, turned to her mother. "How is it you aren't as mad as I am?"

"What good does it do to be mad?"

"At least it's *something*."

"No, Loreda. It's nothing. You've seen the people pouring into the valley every day. Fewer crops, more workers. Even I understand basic economics."

Loreda threw her empty cotton bag down and ran, dodging this way and that among the cabins and tents. She wanted to keep running until California was only a memory.

She was at the farthest reaches of the camp, in a thicket of trees, when she heard a man say: "Help? When did this durn state ever do anything to help us?"

"They cut wages again today, across the valley."

"Now, Ike. Be careful. We got jobs. And a place here. That's something."

Loreda hid behind a tree to listen to the men gathered in the shadows.

"You remember the squatters' camp. We're living better now."

Ike stepped forward. He was a tall, skinny pike of a man with a pale ring of gray hair beneath a pointed bald spot. "You call this living? This is my second cotton season and I can tell you already that I'll work my ass off, as will my wife and children, and we will end up with about four cents left over after our debt is paid. *Four cents.* And you know I'm not being sarcastic. Everything we make goes to the store for our cabins and tents, our mattresses, our overpriced food."

"You *know* they're cheatin' us with their bookkeepin'."

"They charge ten cents per dollar for converting our chits into cash but we can't cash 'em anywhere else. Every penny we make picking cotton goes to pay our debt at the company store. Ain't no way to get ahead. They make sure we don't ever have money."

"I got seven mouths to feed, Ike," said a tall man in patched overalls and a straw hat. "Most of us have family depending on us."

"We can't do anything. I don't care what this Valen says. It's dangerous to listen to him."

Jack.

She should have known he'd somehow be a part of this. He was a *doer.*

Loreda stepped out from behind the tree. "Ike's right. Valen's right. We have to stand up for ourselves. These rich farmers have no right to treat us this way. What would they do if we stopped picking?"

The men looked nervously at each other. "Don't talk about a strike . . ."

"You're just a girl," one man said.

"A girl who picked two hundred pounds of cotton today," Loreda said. She held out her hands, which were red and torn. "I say *no more.* Mr. Valen's right. We need to rise up and—"

A hand clamped around Loreda's bicep, squeezed hard. "Sorry, boys," Elsa said. "My daughter had a rough day. Don't pay her any mind." She hauled Loreda back toward their cabin.

"Dang it, Mom," Loreda hollered, yanking free. "Why did you do that?"

"You get pegged as a union rabble-rouser and we're finished. Who can say there wasn't a grower spy in that group? They're everywhere."

Loreda didn't know how to live with this gnawing anger. "We shouldn't have to live like this."

Mom sighed. "It won't be forever. We'll find a way out."

When it rains.

When we get to California.

We'll find a way out.

New words for an old, never realized hope.

>

TENSION BEGAN TO TAKE up space in the valley. It could be felt in the fields, in the relief lines, around camp. The lowered wages had frightened and unsettled them all. Would it happen again? Nobody was saying the word out loud, but it hung in the air anyway.

Strike.

At night, in the growers' camps and the ditch-bank settlements, field foremen began to show up, clubs in hand. They walked from cabin to cabin and tent to tent and shack to shanty, listening to what was being said, their appearance designed to have a chilling effect on conversation. Everyone knew that there were spies living among them, people who had chosen to stay in the growers' good graces by passing along names of anyone who expressed discontent or stirred up trouble.

Now, after a long day spent picking cotton, Loreda was slumped on her bed, watching her mom heat up a can of pork and beans on the hot plate.

She heard footsteps outside.

A piece of paper slid under the cabin door.

No one moved until the footsteps went away.

Then Loreda launched herself off the bed and grabbed the paper before her mother could.

FARMWORKERS UNITE

A call to action.

We must fight for better wages.

Better living conditions.

A coincidence our wages are cut now?

We don't think so.

Poor, hungry, desperate folks are easier to control.

Join us.

Break free.

The Workers Alliance wants to help.

Join us Thursday at midnight

in the back room at the El Centro Hotel.

Mom grabbed the paper, read it, crumpled it.

"Don't—"

Mom lit a match and set fire to the paper; she dropped it to the concrete floor, where it burned to ash.

"Those people will get us fired and thrown out of this cabin," Mom said.

"They'll *save* us," Loreda argued.

"Don't you see, Loreda?" Mom said. "Those men are dangerous. The farmers are opposing unionization."

"Of course they are. They want to keep us hungry and at their mercy so we'll work for anything."

"We are at their mercy!" Mom cried.

"I'm going to that meeting."

"You are not. Why do you think they're meeting at midnight, Loreda? They're *scared*. Grown men are scared to be seen with the Communists and union organizers."

"You're always talking about my future. Your big dreams for me. College. How do you think I'm going to get there, Mom? By picking cotton in the fall and starving in the winter? By living on the dole?" Loreda moved forward. "Think about the women who fought for the vote. They had to be scared, too, but they marched for change, even if it meant going to jail. And now we can vote. Sometimes the end is worth any sacrifice."

"It's a bad idea."

"I can't take being kicked around and treated badly, barely surviving anymore. It's *wrong* what they're doing. They should be held accountable."

"And you, a fourteen-year-old girl, are the one to make them pay, are you?"

"No. Jack is."

Mom frowned, tucked her chin in. "What does Mr. Valen have to do with this?"

"I'm sure he'll be at the meeting. Nothing scares him."

"I've said all I'm going to on this subject. We are staying away from union Communists."

THIRTY-ONE

O n Thursday, after ten hours of picking cotton, Loreda's entire
body hurt, and tomorrow morning, she would have to get up
and do it all again.

For ten percent less in wages.

Ninety cents for a hundred pounds of picked cotton. Eighty cents if
you counted the cut taken by the crooks at the company store.

She thought about it endlessly, obsessively; the injustice of it gnawed
at her.

Just as she thought about the meeting.

And her mother's fear.

Loreda understood the fear more than her mother suspected. How
could Loreda *not* understand it? She'd lived through the winter in California, been flooded out, lost everything, survived on barely any food,
worn shoes that didn't fit. She knew how it felt to go to bed hungry and
wake up hungry, how you could try to trick your stomach with water
but it never lasted. She saw her mother measuring beans out for dinner
and splitting a single hot dog into three portions. She knew Mom regretted every penny she added to their debt at the store.

The difference between Loreda and her mother wasn't fear—they shared that. It was fire. Her mother's passion had gone out. Or maybe she'd never had any. The only time Loreda had seen genuine anger from her mother was the night they'd buried the Deweys' baby.

Loreda *wanted* to be angry. What had Jack said to her the first day they met? *You have fire in you, kid. Don't let the bastards snuff it out.* Something like that.

Loreda didn't want to be the kind of woman who suffered in silence. Refused to be.

Tonight was her chance to prove it.

At eleven o'clock, she lay in bed wide awake. Waiting. Counting every minute that passed.

Ant lay beside her, hogging the covers. Usually she wrenched them back and maybe even gave him a kick for good measure. Tonight she didn't bother.

She eased out of bed and stepped onto the warm concrete floor. For as long as she lived, she would be grateful for flooring. Always.

A quick sideways glance confirmed that her mother was asleep.

Loreda grabbed a blouse and her overalls from the coatrack and dressed quickly, buttoning the bib after she'd stepped into her shoes.

Outside, the world was still. The air smelled of ripe fruit and fecund earth. A hint of woodsmoke from extinguished fires. Nothing ever really left here; things lingered. Scents. Sounds. People.

She closed the door quietly behind her, listening for footsteps. Her heart was pounding; she felt afraid . . . and keenly alive.

She waited, counted to ten, but she didn't see any foremen out and about.

Moving quietly, she headed into the night.

In town, she walked past the theater and City Hall, and turned onto a back street, where the grass was overgrown and most of the houses and businesses were boarded up. Dodging the streetlights, she stuck to the shadows until she came to the hotel they'd stayed in during the flood.

It was so quiet out here, she hoped they hadn't canceled the meeting. All day, as she'd sweated and strained in the field, dragging her heavy sack behind her, pocketing the coupon that devalued her labor, she thought about tonight's meeting.

There were no lights on in the El Centro Hotel, but a few cars were parked out front, and she saw that the heavy chain that locked the doors together hung slack from one of the doorknobs.

Loreda cautiously opened the front door.

A man with a beak of a nose and small round spectacles stood behind the reception desk, staring at her.

"You need a room?" he said in a heavily accented voice.

Loreda paused. Could she be arrested for just showing up? Or was this man an employee of the big farmers, here to identify rabble-rousers? Or was he a friend of Jack's, here to make sure only the right people made it to the meeting?

"I'm here for the meeting," she said.

"Downstairs."

Loreda moved toward the stairs. Nervous, suddenly. Excited. Scared.

She touched the smooth wooden banister as she made her way down the narrow stairs, past a broom closet and laundry room.

She heard voices, followed the sound to a room in the back, its door open to reveal a crowd inside.

People stood shoulder to shoulder. Men, women, and a few kids. Bobby Rand waved at her.

Jack stood in the front of the room, commanded attention. Although he was dressed like many of the migrants around him, in faded, stained overalls and a frayed denim shirt beneath a dusty brown suit coat, there was vibrancy to him, an *aliveness* that was like no one she'd ever met before. Jack *believed* in things and fought to make the world a better place. He was the kind of man a girl could count on.

"... one hundred and fifty strikers were herded into cages," he was saying in a passionate voice. "Cages. In America. The big farmers and their corrupt coppers and citizens-turned-vigilantes put your fellow Americans in *cages* to break a strike of workers who just wanted an even shake. Two years ago, a bunch of Tulare farmers shot into a crowd of people just for *listening* to strike organizers. Two people were killed."

"Why are you tellin' us this?" someone yelled. Loreda recognized him from the squatters' camp they'd lived in. A man with six kids and a wife who had died of typhoid. "You trying to scare us off?"

"I'm not going to lie to you good people. Striking against the big farmers is dangerous. They'll oppose us with everything they've got. And, folks, as you know, they've got it all: money, power, the state government." He picked up a newspaper, held it out for everyone to see. The headline read: "Workers Alliance Un-American." "I'll tell you what's un-American, and that's big farmers getting richer while you get poorer," Jack said.

"Yeah!" Jeb said.

"What's un-American is cutting pickers' wages just because the growers are greedy."

"Yeah!" the crowd yelled back.

"They don't want you to organize, but if you don't, you'll starve, just like the pea pickers did in Nipomo last winter. I was there. Children died in the fields. Starved. In America. The big growers are planting less because cotton prices are down, so they pay less. God forbid their profit diminishes. They aren't even pretending to give you a living wage."

Ike yelled out: "They think we ain't human!"

Jack looked out at the crowd, made eye contact one by one with his audience. Loreda felt an electricity of hope move from him to the crowd. "They need you. That's your power. Cotton has to be picked while it's dry and before the first frost. What if no one picks it?"

"A strike!" someone called out. "That'll show 'em."

"It isn't easy," Jack said. "Cotton is spread out over thousands and thousands of acres and the growers stand together. They pick a price to pay and stick with it. So we need to stand together. Our only chance is to join forces, all of the workers. Everyone, everywhere. We need you all to spread the word. We have to shut down the means of production completely."

"Strike!" Loreda yelled.

The crowd joined in, chanting, "Strike, strike, strike."

Jack saw Loreda at the same time someone grabbed her arm. Loreda yelped in pain and wrenched free, turning.

Her mother stood there, looking angry enough to blow smoke. "I can't *believe* you'd do this."

"Did you hear what he said, Mom?"

"I heard." Mom glanced sideways, across the room, saw how many people were here.

Jack pushed through the crowd, coming their way.

"Your speech was great," Loreda said as he drew near.

"I noticed you showed up alone," he said. "It's late for a girl your age to be out by herself."

"Would you say that to Joan of Arc?" Loreda said.

"You're Joan of Arc now, are you?" Mom said.

"I want to go on strike, Jack—"

"Loreda," Mom said sharply. "It's Mr. Valen. Now go upstairs and let me speak to him. I'll deal with you later."

"You can't make me—"

"Go, Loreda," Jack said evenly. He and Mom stared at each other.

"Okay, but I'm striking," Loreda said.

"*Go,*" Mom said.

Loreda turned away and trudged up the stairs. She didn't care what her mother said. She didn't care how much trouble she got in or how dangerous it was.

Sometimes a person had to stand up and say enough was enough.

⋎

"How long have you been back in Welty?" Elsa asked Jack when they were alone.

"A week or so. I was going to send word to you."

"Oh, I'd say you sent word." She stared at him, wishing that things were different, that she was different, that she had her daughter's fire and courage. "She's a fourteen-year-old girl, Jack, who snuck out in the middle of the night and walked a mile to get here. You know what could have happened to her?"

"What does that tell you, Elsa? She *cares* about this."

"What does that prove? We all know it's wrong, but your solution won't make our lives better. You'll just get us fired, or worse. Our survival hangs by a thread, do you get that?"

"I get it," he said. "But if you don't stand up, they'll bury you, one cent at a time. Your daughter understands that."

"She's fourteen," Elsa said again.

Jack lowered his voice to match hers. "A fourteen-year-old who is picking cotton all day. I assume Ant is, too, because it's the only way for you to feed them."

"Are you judging me?"

"Of course not," he said. "But your daughter is old enough to decide for herself about this."

"Says the man with no children."

"Elsa—"

"I'm making the decision for her."

"You should teach her to stand up for herself, Elsa. Not to lie down."

"And now you are definitely judging me. If you thought I was a brave woman, you've misjudged me."

"I don't think so, Elsa. I think you believe it, though, which is tragic."

"Stay away from Loreda, Jack. I mean it. I won't let her be a casualty in this war you're playing at."

"No one is playing, Elsa."

She walked away.

He started to follow her.

"Don't," she snapped, and kept walking.

Outside, she grabbed Loreda's arm and half dragged her out to the street, where they began walking home in the dark. Automobiles rumbled past them, headlights bright.

"Mom, if you'd listen to him—"

"No," Elsa said. "And neither will you. It's my job to keep you safe. By God, I've failed at everything else. I will not fail at that. Do you hear me?"

Loreda stopped.

Elsa had no choice but to stop, too, and turn back. "What?"

"Do you really think you've failed me?"

"Look at us. *Walking* back to a cabin smaller than our old toolshed. Both of us skinny as matchsticks and hungry all of the time. Of course I've failed you."

"Mom," Loreda said, moving close. "I'm alive because of you. I go to school. I can think because you want to make sure I always do. You haven't failed me. You've saved me."

"Don't you try to turn this around and make it about thinking for yourself and growing up."

"But it is about that, Mom. Isn't it?"

"I can't lose you," Elsa said, and there it was: the truth.

"I know, Mom. And I love you. But I need this."

"No," Elsa said firmly. "No. Now start walking. We have an early wake-up."

"Mom—"

"No, Loreda. *No.*"

LOREDA WOKE AT FIVE-THIRTY and had to force herself out of bed. Her hands hurt like the dickens and she needed about ten hours of sleep and a good meal.

She put on her tattered pants and a shirt with long, ripped sleeves and trudged out to get in line at the bathroom.

The camp was strangely quiet. People were out and about, of course, but there wasn't much conversation. No one made eye contact for long. A field foreman stood at the chain-link fence, hat drawn low, watching people. She knew there were more spies about, listening for any talk of a strike.

She got in line for the bathroom. There were about ten women in front of her.

As she waited, she saw a flash of movement back in the trees. Ike, at the water pump, filling a bucket. Loreda wanted to walk right over to him, but she didn't dare.

She finally made it to the front of the line and used the bathroom.

She exited from the back door, closing it quietly behind her. She looked around, didn't see anyone loitering or watching. Trying to look casual, she strolled over to the water pump.

Ike was still there. He saw her coming and stepped aside. She bent over and washed her hands in the cold water.

"We're meeting tonight," Ike said quietly. "Midnight. The laundry."

Loreda nodded and dried her hands on her pants. It wasn't until she was halfway back to her cabin that she felt a prickling of awareness along the back of her neck. Someone was watching her or following her.

She stopped, turned suddenly.

Mr. Welty stood there in the trees, smoking a cigarette. Staring at Loreda. "Come here, missy," he said.

Loreda walked slowly toward him. The way he looked at her, through narrowed eyes, sent a shiver down her spine. "Yes, sir?"

"You pick cotton for me?"

"I do."

"Happy for the job?"

Loreda forced herself to meet his gaze. "Very."

"You hear any of the men talking about a strike?"

Men. They always thought everything was about them. But women could stand up for their rights, too; women could hold picket signs and stop the means of production as well as men.

"No, sir. But if I did, I'd remind them what it's like not to have work."

Welty smiled. "Good girl. I like a worker who knows her worth."

Loreda slowly walked back to the cabin, shutting the door firmly behind her. Locking it.

"What's the matter?" Mom said, looking up.

"Welty questioned me."

"Don't draw that man's attention, Loreda. What did he ask?"

"Nothing," Loreda said, grabbing a pancake from the hot plate. "The trucks just drove up."

Five minutes later, they were all out the door, walking toward the line of trucks parked along the chain-link fence.

Quietly, they joined their fellow workers and climbed up into the back of a truck.

When the sun rose on the cotton fields, Loreda saw the changes that had been made by the growers overnight: coils of spiked barbed wire topped the fencing. A half-finished structure stood in the center of the field, a tower of some kind. The clatter and bang of building it rang out. Men she'd never seen before paced the path between the chain-link fence and the road, carrying shotguns. The place looked like a prison yard. They were readying for a fight.

But with *guns*? It wasn't as if they could shoot people for striking. This was America.

Still, a ripple of unease moved through the workers. It was what Welty wanted: the workers to be afraid.

The trucks rumbled to a stop. The workers got out.

"They're afraid of us, Mom," Loreda said. "They know a strike—"

Mom elbowed Loreda hard enough to shut her up.

"Hurry up," Ant said. "They're assigning rows."

Loreda dragged her sack out behind her, took her place at the start of the row she'd been assigned.

When the bell rang, she bent over and went to work, plucking the soft white bolls from their spiked nests. But all she could think about was tonight.

Strike meeting. Midnight.

At noon the bell rang again.

Loreda straightened, tried to ease the cricks out of her neck and back, listening to the sound of men hammering.

Welty stood on the scales' raised platform, looking out at the men and women and children who worked themselves bloody to make him rich. "I know that some of you are talking to the union organizers," he said. His loud voice carried across the fields.

"Maybe you think you can find other jobs in other fields, or maybe you think I need you more than you need me. Let me tell you right now: that is not the case. For every one of you standing on my property, there are ten lined up outside the fence, waiting to take your job. And now, because of a few bad apples, I have had to put up fencing and hire men to guard my property. At considerable cost. So, I am lowering wages another ten percent. Anyone who stays agrees to that price. Anyone who leaves will never pick for me or any other grower in the valley again."

Loreda looked at her mother over the row of cotton that stood between them.

The structure in the middle of the field was nearly complete. It was easy now to see what they'd been building all morning: a gun tower. Soon one of the foremen would be up there, pacing, carrying a rifle, making sure the workers knew their place.

You see? Loreda mouthed.

❧

ELSA LAY AWAKE, DEEP into the night, worrying about the ten percent cut in wages.

Across the small, dark room, she heard the other rusted metal bed-frame squeak.

Elsa saw the shadow of her daughter in the moonlight through the open vent. Loreda quietly got out of bed.

Elsa sat up, watched her daughter move furtively; she dressed and went to the cabin door, reached for the knob.

"Where do you think you're going?" Elsa said.

Loreda paused, turned. "There's a strike meeting tonight. In camp."

"Loreda, no—"

"You'll have to tie me up and gag me, Mom. Otherwise, I'm going."

Elsa couldn't see her daughter's face clearly, but she heard the steel in her voice. As scared as Elsa was, she couldn't help feeling a flash of reluctant pride. Her daughter was so much stronger and braver than Elsa was. Grandpa Wolcott would have been proud of Loreda, too. "Then I'm going with you."

Elsa slipped into a day dress and covered her hair with a kerchief. Too lazy to lace up her shoes, she stepped into her galoshes and followed her daughter out of the cabin.

Outside, moonlight set the distant cotton fields aglow, turned the white cotton bolls silver.

The quiet of man was complete, unbroken, but they heard the scuttling of creatures moving in the dark. The howl of a coyote. She saw an owl, perched in a high branch, watching them.

Elsa imagined spies and foremen everywhere, hidden in every shadow, watching for those who would dare to raise their voices in protest. This was a stupid idea. Stupid and dangerous.

"Mom—"

"Hush," Elsa said. "Not a word."

They passed the newer section of tents and turned into the laundry—a long, wooden structure that held metal washbasins, long tables, and a few hand-cranked wringers. Men rarely stepped foot in the place, but now there were about forty of them inside, standing in a tight knot.

Elsa and Loreda slipped to the back of the crowd.

Ike stood at the front. "We all know why we're here," he said quietly.

There was no answer, not even a movement of feet.

"They cut wages again today, and they'll do it again. Because they can. We've all seen the desperate folks pouring into the valley. They'll work for anything. They have kids to feed."

"So do we, Ike," someone said.

"I know, Ralph. But we gotta stand up for ourselves or they'll destroy us."

"I ain't no Red," someone said.

"Call it whatever you want, Gary. We deserve fair wages," Ike said. "And we aren't going to get 'em without a fight."

Elsa heard the distant sound of truck engines.

She saw people turn around, look behind them.

Headlights.

"Run!" Ike yelled.

The crowd dispersed in a panic, people running away from the laundry in all directions.

Elsa grabbed Loreda's hand and yanked her back toward the stinking toilets. No one else was going this way. They lurched into the shadows behind the building and hid there.

Men jumped out of the trucks, holding baseball bats, sticks of wood; one had a shotgun. They formed a line and began walking through the camp, backlit by their headlights, their footsteps muffled by the chug of their engines. They beat their weapons into the palms of their hands, a steady thump, thump, thump.

Elsa pressed a finger to her mouth and pulled Loreda along the fence line. When they finally made it back to the cabins, they ran for their own, slipped inside, locked the door behind them.

Elsa heard footsteps coming their way.

Light flashed through the cracks in the cabin; men moved past, accompanied by the sound of baseball bats hitting empty palms.

The sound came close—*thump, thump, thump*—and then faded away. In the distance, someone screamed.

"You see, Loreda?" Elsa whispered. "They'll hurt the people who threaten their business."

It was a long time before Loreda spoke, and when she did, her words were no comfort at all. "Sometimes you have to fight back, Mom."

THIRTY-TWO

"Can we drive to relief this week, Ma?" Ant said at the end of another long, hot, demoralizing day picking cotton.

Elsa had to admit that the idea of walking to town and back after a day in the fields was hardly appealing.

But these were the kinds of decisions that came back to haunt a woman when winter came.

"Just this once. In fact, Ant, if you want to, you can stay in the camp and play with your friends if you'd like."

"Really? That'd be swell."

"I'll stay and watch him," Loreda said.

Elsa gave her daughter a pointed look. "You, I'm not letting out of my sight."

They left Ant at the cabin and got into the truck.

"Can I practice driving? Grandpa said I should keep practicing," Loreda said. "What if there's an emergency?"

"An emergency that requires you to drive?"

"It's possible."

"Fine."

Loreda got behind the wheel.

Elsa climbed into the passenger seat. Lord, but it was hot. Loreda started the engine.

"You remember how to work the pedals? Do it slowly, carefully. Find the—"

The truck lurched forward and died.

"Sorry," Loreda said.

"Try again. Take your time."

Loreda worked the pedals, put the truck in first gear. They moved slowly forward.

The engine revved.

"Second gear, Loreda," Elsa said.

Loreda tried again and finally got it into second.

They drove in fits and starts down the road to the state relief office, where there was already a crowd of people waiting. The line snaked out the door and through the parking lot and down the block.

Elsa and Loreda got in line.

As they stood there, the sun began to set slowly, gilding the valley for a few beautiful moments before the sky darkened.

They were almost to the head of the line when a pair of police cars drove into the parking lot. Four uniformed policemen exited the vehicles. Moments later a Welty truck drove up and Mr. Welty stepped out.

People in line turned to look, but no one said anything.

Two of the policemen and Mr. Welty cut to the head of the line and strode into the relief office. They didn't come back out.

Elsa clung to Loreda's hand. In normal times, the folks in line might have turned to one another, asked what was going on, but these weren't ordinary times. There were spies everywhere; people wanted to take a place at Welty, wanted a job.

Elsa finally stepped into the small, hot office, where a pretty young woman sat at the desk with the file box full of residents' names in front of her.

Welty stood beside the woman, appeared almost to be looming over the poor girl. Two policemen stood beside him, hands rested on their gun belts.

Elsa eased Loreda away and walked up to the desk alone. Her throat was so dry she had to clear it twice to speak. "Elsa Martinelli. April 1935."

Welty pointed at Elsa's red card. "Address Welty Farms. She's on the list."

The woman looked at Elsa with compassion. "I'm sorry, ma'am. No state relief for anyone who is capable of picking cotton."

"But . . ."

"If you can pick, you have to," she said. "It's the new policy. But don't worry, as soon as cotton season is over, you'll be put back on the relief rolls."

"Wait a minute. Now, the state is cutting my relief? But I'm a resident, and I am picking cotton."

"We want to make sure you keep picking it," Welty said.

"Mr. Welty," she said. "Please. We need—"

"Next," Welty said loudly.

Elsa couldn't believe this new cruelty. People needed this relief to feed their children, even if they did pick cotton. "Have you no shame?"

"Next," he said again. A policeman came up to physically move Elsa out of the line.

She stumbled away, felt Loreda steady her.

Elsa stepped out of the relief office (what a joke that title was) and stared at the long line of people, many of whom didn't yet know their relief had been cut. So, the state was helping the growers avoid a strike by cutting relief to people who were already barely surviving.

She heard a shout and turned.

Two policemen slammed a man against the building wall, said, "Where's tonight's meeting? Where is it?" They shoved the man into the wall again. "How are you going to feed your family from San Quentin?"

"Elsa!"

She saw Jeb Dewey rushing toward her. He looked frantic.

"Jeb. What's wrong?"

"It's Jean. She's sick. Can you help?"

"I'll drive," Elsa said, already running toward the truck.

Elsa drove out to the old squatters' camp and parked near the Deweys' truck. She and Jeb and Loreda got out. A wood and metal roof had been built over the bed. Another roof extended out to the side, created a covered cooking area where the children now sat. Jean lay on a mattress in the back of the truck.

"Tell us what to do," Jeb said.

Elsa climbed up into the truck bed and knelt beside Jean. "Hey, you."

"Elsa," Jean said, her voice almost too soft to be heard. Her eyes had a glassy, unfocused look. "I told Jeb you'd be at relief today."

Elsa placed a hand on Jean's forehead. "You're burning up." She yelled to Jeb: "Get me some water."

Moments later, Loreda handed Elsa a cup of warm water. "Here, Mom."

Elsa took the cup. Cradling Jean's neck, she helped her sip water. "Come on, Jean, take a drink."

Jean tried to push her away.

"Come on, Jean." Elsa forced the water down Jean's throat.

Jean looked up at her. "It's bad this time."

Elsa looked down at Jeb. "You got any aspirin?"

"Nope."

"Loreda," Elsa said. "Take the truck to the company store. Buy us some aspirin. And a thermometer. The keys are in the ignition."

Loreda ran off.

Elsa settled herself in closer to Jean, held her in her arms, and stroked her hot brow.

"It's the typhoid, I reckon," Jean said. "You should probably stay away."

"I'm not that easy to get rid of. Just ask my husband. He had to run off in the middle of the night."

Jean smiled weakly. "He was a fool."

"Jack said the same thing. So did Rafe's mom, come to think of it."

"I sure could use me some of that gin we been talkin' about."

Elsa ran her fingers through Jean's damp hair. Heat radiated from Jean's body to Elsa's. "I could sing . . ."

"Please don't."

The women smiled at each other, but Elsa saw Jean's fear. "It'll be okay. You're strong."

Jean closed her eyes and fell asleep in Elsa's arms.

Elsa held Jean, stroked her hot brow, and whispered quiet words of encouragement until she heard the rumbling sound of the truck returning. *Thank God.*

Loreda drove up and parked. She opened the truck's door and got out, banging the door shut behind her. "Mom!" she yelled. "The store wasn't open."

Elsa craned her neck to see Loreda. "Why not?"

"Probably because of the strike talk. They want to remind us how much we need them. Pigs."

Jean's body suddenly arched and stiffened. Her eyes rolled back in her head. Her body began to shake violently.

Elsa held her friend until she stilled.

"There's no aspirin, Jean," Elsa said.

Jean's eyes fluttered open. "Don't fret none, Elsa. Just let me—"

"*No,*" Elsa said sharply. "I'll be right back. Don't you dare go anywhere."

Jean's breathing slowed. "I might go dancin'."

Elsa eased Jean's head back and got out of the truck. "You stay here," she said to Loreda. "Try to get Jean to drink more water. Keep a wet rag on her forehead. Don't let her kick the covers away." She turned to Jeb. "I'll be right back."

"Where yah going?" Jeb asked.

"I'm getting her aspirin."

"Where? You got any money to buy some?"

"No," Elsa said tightly. "They make sure we never have money. Stay here."

She ran to the truck and started it up, drove out to the main road.

At the hospital, she walked across the parking lot and pushed through the doors, leaving dirty brown footprints across the clean floor as she walked to the front desk, where a woman sat alone, playing solitaire.

"I need help," Elsa said. "Please. I know you won't let us come to the hospital, but if you could just give me some asprin, it would be such a help. My friend has a fever. Really high. It could be typhoid. Help us. Please. *Please.*"

The woman straightened in her chair, craned her neck to look up and down the hall. "You know that's contagious, right? There's a nurse at the new government tent camp in Arvin. Ask her for help. She treats your kind."

Your kind.

Enough is goddamned enough.

Elsa walked out of the hospital, went back to the truck, and grabbed Ant's baseball bat from out of the bed. Carrying it, she walked across the parking lot, trying to stay calm.

This time she banged through the doors, took one look at the woman sneering up at her, and slammed the baseball bat down on the front desk hard enough to dent the wood.

The woman screamed.

"Ah, good. I have your attention. I need some aspirin," Elsa said calmly.

The woman spun around, yanked open a cabinet. With shaking hands, she started pawing through medicine. "Darn Okies," the woman muttered.

Elsa smashed a lamp. Then the phone.

The woman grasped a pair of bottles and thrust them at Elsa. "You people are animals."

"So are you, ma'am. So are you."

Elsa took the aspirin.

She was almost to the front door when a big man came lumbering down the hallway toward her.

"Stop her, Fred! She's a criminal!" the woman at the desk yelled.

He blocked the door.

Elsa stepped closer to the man in the brown security uniform, holding the bat down at her side. Her heart was thundering, but strangely, she felt calm. In control, even. She had the medicine and no one was going to stop her from getting it to Jean. "How badly do you want to stop me, Fred?"

The man's gaze softened. "The missus and I came here from Indiana about five years ago. It was a helluva lot easier then. I'm sorry for the way you're treated." He pulled out a five-dollar bill. "Will this help?"

Elsa almost cried at the small kindness. "Thank you."

"Now go. Alice is probably calling the coppers already."

Elsa sprinted out of the hospital, threw the baseball bat into the truck bed, then started the engine and stomped on the gas. The old truck fishtailed in the gravel and slowly straightened out on the dark road.

She turned onto the road to the squatters' camp and pulled up in front of the Deweys' truck.

She found Jeb in the bed of the truck with Jean, cradling his wife in his arms; the children stood with Loreda beneath the wooden overhang close to the side of the truck. The boys held the little girls' hands.

"She keeps askin' for gin," Jeb said, looking bereft and confused. "She don't drink."

Elsa climbed up into the bed of the truck, settled in on Jean's other side. "Hey, you, bad girl. I've got some aspirin."

Jean's eyes fluttered open.

"I hear you're making trouble, demanding gin," Elsa said.

"One martini before I die. Don't seem too much to ask."

Elsa helped Jean swallow two aspirin and drink a glass of water, and then stroked her friend's hot forehead. "Don't you give up, Jean . . ."

Jean stared up at Elsa, breathing heavily, sweating. "You dance, Elsa," she said, almost too quietly to be heard. "For both of us." Jean squeezed Elsa's hand. "I loved you, girlfriend."

Not past tense. Please.

She heard Jeb start to cry.

"I love you, too, Jean," Elsa whispered.

Jean slowly turned her head to look at her husband. "Now . . . where . . . are my babies, Jeb?"

Elsa had to force herself to move away, get out of the truck. The four Dewey children climbed up and gathered around Jean.

Elsa heard whispering. Elroy said, "I will, Ma," as the girls cried.

And then Jean's broken voice: "I had so much more to say to y'all . . ."

Loreda touched Elsa's shoulder. "Are you okay?"

Elsa's answer was a primal scream.

Once she started, she couldn't stop.

Loreda pulled Elsa into her arms and held her while she cried for all of it—the way they lived, the dreams they'd lost, the future they'd so blindly believed in. For the children who would grow up not knowing Jean. Her humor, her gentleness, her steel, her hopes for them.

Elsa cried until she felt emptied inside.

She pulled away from Loreda, who looked frightened. "I'm sorry," Elsa said, wiping her eyes.

"Sometimes it just . . . breaks you," Loreda said. "It helps to get mad."

"You're right," Elsa said. *Enough.* "If I wanted to find Mr. Valen and his Communist friends, would you know where to look?"

"I think so."

"Where?"

"There's a barn where they make flyers and stuff. Out at the end of Willow Road."

"Okay." Elsa drew in a deep breath and released it slowly. "Okay, then."

⁂

LATER, WHEN NIGHT FELL across the valley and stars came out to blanket the sky, Elsa quietly herded her children out of the cabin and toward the truck. None of them spoke as they climbed into the vehicle and drove away. Each understood the danger of what they'd decided to do tonight.

"Turn here," Loreda said.

Elsa turned onto a dirt road that cut through brown, uncultivated fields. At the end of the road, a gray-brown barn stood next to an old ranch house with broken windows and boarded-up doors. There were six or seven automobiles parked out front.

Elsa parked next to a dusty Packard. She and Loreda and Ant got out of the truck and walked toward the barn. Loreda pushed open the half-broken door.

The interior was lit by lanterns. There were several tables set up on the straw-covered dirt floor; chairs were placed randomly along the walls. At least a dozen people were at work: some at typewriters, others at mimeograph machines. Cigarette smoke thickened the air but couldn't obliterate the sweet smell of hay.

Elsa and the children walked among the Communists; no one seemed to notice them. Elsa saw a paper come out of a mimeograph machine. "WORKERS UNITE!" was the bold headline. She smelled an odd odor of ink and metal.

They passed a small dark-haired woman wearing spectacles who paced as she dictated to another woman, who was typing. "We cannot allow the rich to get richer while the poor get poorer. How can we call ourselves the land of the free when people are living on the streets and dying of hunger? Radical change requires radical methods ..."

Loreda elbowed Elsa, who looked up.

Jack was coming toward them.

"Hello, ladies," he said, staring intently at Elsa. "Loreda," he said, "Natalia is at the mimeograph machine. She could use some help."

"You, too, Ant," Elsa said. "Stay with your sister."

Jack led Elsa outside, to a firepit around which was arranged a collection of mismatched furniture. Several ashtrays overflowed with bent cigarette butts. "So, Communists sit around a fire and smoke like everyone else," Elsa said.

"We are almost human that way." He moved closer. "What happened?"

"Jean died. There was no way for us to save her. The company store was closed to teach us a lesson and the hospital wouldn't help. I even used a ... baseball bat to get their attention. All I got was some aspirin. Oh, and they culled our names from the relief rolls today. If you can pick cotton, you have to. No state relief."

"We heard. The growers bullied the state into it. They're calling it the No Work, No Eat policy. They're afraid that relief will allow you to feed your children while you strike for better wages."

Elsa crossed her arms. "All my life I've been told to make no noise, don't want too much, be grateful for any scrap that came my way. And I've done that. I thought if I just did what women are supposed to do and played by the rules, it would ... I don't know ... change. But the way we're treated ..."

"It's unfair," he said.

"It's wrong," she said. "This isn't who we are in America."

"No."

"A strike." She said the frightening word quietly. "Can it work?"

"Maybe."

She was grateful for his honesty. "They'll hurt us for trying."

"Yeah," he said. "But life is more than what happens to us, Elsa. We have choices to make."

"I'm not a brave woman."

"And yet here you are, standing at the edge of battle."

His words touched a chord in her. "My grandfather was a Texas Ranger. He used to tell me that courage was a lie. It was just fear that you ignored." She looked at him. "Well, I'm scared."

"We're all scared," he said.

"I have children to worry about, children I have to feed and clothe and keep safe. I can't risk their lives."

He said nothing, and she knew why. He was letting her say it.

"They're already at risk," she said. "They can't be taught that this is what we deserve, that this is America. I have to teach them to stand up for themselves."

Elsa felt both a stunning sense of relief, almost of coming home, finding herself . . . and a deep, abiding fear. *Courage is fear you ignore.* But how did one do that, really? In practical terms.

"The rifle tower they built in the field . . . that's to scare us, right? What we're doing—a strike—it's legal."

"It's legal. Hell, it's the very essence of America. We were built on the right to protest, but laws are enforced by the government. By the police. You've seen how they support big business."

Elsa nodded. "What do we do?"

"First we need to get out the word. We've set a strike meeting for Friday. But it's dangerous even to tell people, let alone to show up for the meeting."

"Everything is dangerous," she said. "So what?"

He laid a hand along her cheek.

She leaned into his touch, taking strength and comfort from it.

THIRTY-THREE

In the dark just before the dawn, Loreda opened the cabin door and stepped outside. Last night's gathering of the Workers Alliance had energized her, galvanized her. The Communists were working hard to bring about a strike, but they needed people like Loreda to spread the word through the camps. The Communists couldn't do it on their own.

It's dangerous, though, Natalia had said to Loreda last night. *Don't forget this. When I was a girl, I saw revolution up close. Blood runs in the streets. Don't forget for one moment that the state has all the power—money and weapons and manpower.*

We have heart and desperation, had been Loreda's answer.

"Yeah," Natalia had said, exhaling smoke. "*And brains. So, use yours.*"

Loreda closed the door behind her and walked out into the camp. She could hear people readying for the day, serving food, packing lunches. There was a long line at the toilets.

But the quiet was new and unnerving. No one laughed or even talked. Fear had moved into the camp. Everyone knew they were being watched by people whose loyalty was to the grower, not to the workers. Unfortunately, you never knew who the traitor was until you said the wrong thing to the wrong person and a knock at your door came in the middle of the night. They had heard the cries of families being hauled out of camp.

The first colors of sunrise cast light on the coiled barbed wire that topped the new fencing. She walked toward the line for the toilets and waited her turn. Afterward, she saw Ike filling his canteen at the waterspout outside the laundry. Loreda tried to look completely casual as she moved toward him, but she may have failed. She was filled with adrenaline, scared and exhilarated and excited.

She stepped in close to him, said, "Friday," without stopping. "The barn on Willow Road. Eight o'clock. Pass the word."

She kept going, didn't even look back to see if he heard. She walked back to the cabin, very slowly, expecting every minute to be stopped.

She closed the door behind her.

Mom and Ant looked at her.

"Well?" Mom said quietly.

Loreda nodded. "I told Ike."

"Good," Mom said. "Let's go pick cotton."

THAT NIGHT, AFTER ANOTHER long, hot day in the fields, there was a letter from Tony and Rose to cheer them all. After supper, the children climbed into bed with Elsa and she opened the envelope and withdrew that letter. It had been written on the back side of Elsa's last letter to them. No reason to waste paper.

> *Dearest ones,*
>
> *It has been a hot, dry summer. The good news is that the wind and dust have given us a respite. No dust storms for ten days. Not enough to call an end to them, but an answer to prayers anyway. August and the first half of September were entirely unpleasant. All we did, it seems, was sweep, but these last few days have so far*

been kinder. Also, the government has finally realized that the help
we most need is water and it is being delivered by the truckload. We
pray there will be a crop of winter wheat. At least enough to feed
our two new cows and the horse. But hope is hard to come by.

Sending you all much love. Miss you terribly.

Love, Rose and Tony

"Do you think we will ever see them again, Mom?" Loreda asked in the silence that followed Elsa's reading of the letter.

Elsa leaned back against the rusted metal bed frame. Ant resettled himself, laid his head on her lap. She stroked his hair.

Loreda sat opposite Elsa, against the narrow foot of the bed.

"Remember that house I stopped at in Dalhart, on the day we left for California?"

"The big one with the broken window?"

Elsa nodded. "It was big, all right. I grew up there . . . in a house that had no heart. My family . . . rejected me, is I guess the best way to put it. Looks mattered to my family, and my unattractiveness was a fatal flaw."

"You're—"

"I am not fishing for compliments, Loreda. And God knows I'm too old for lies. I'm answering your question. This one, and one you haven't asked in a while. About me and your grandparents and your father. Anyway, my point is that as a girl, I was lonely. I could never understand what I'd done to deserve my isolation. I tried so hard to be lovable." Elsa drew in a deep breath, released it. "I thought everything had changed when I met your father. And it did. For me. But not for him. He always wanted more than life on the farm. Always. As you know."

Loreda nodded.

"I loved your dad. I did. But it wasn't enough for him, and now I realize it wasn't enough for me, either. He deserved better and so did I." As she said the unexpected words, Elsa felt them reshape her some-how. "But you know how my life really changed? It wasn't marriage. It was the farm. Rose and Tony. I found a place to belong, people who loved me, and they became the home I'd dreamed about as a girl. And then you came along and taught me how big love could be."

"I treated you like you had the plague."

Elsa smiled. "For a few years. But before all of that, you . . . You couldn't stand to be apart. You cried for me at naptime, said you couldn't sleep without me."

"I'm sorry," Loreda said. "For—"

"No sorries. We fought, we struggled, we hurt each other, so what? That's what love is, I think. It's all of it. Tears, anger, joy, struggle. Mostly, it's durable. It lasts. Never once in all of it—the dust, the drought, the fights with you—never once did I stop loving you or Ant or the farm." Elsa laughed. "So, my long-winded answer to your question is this: Rose and Tony and the farm are home. We will see them all again. Someday."

"They were crazy," Loreda said. "Your other family, I mean. And they missed out."

"On what?"

"You. They never saw how special you are."

Elsa smiled. "That's maybe the nicest thing you've ever said to me, Loreda."

ON FRIDAY EVENING, AFTER another long day of picking cotton, Elsa and her children snuck out of camp and drove to the end of Willow Road for the strike meeting.

Inside the barn, typewriters clattered; people talked loudly and moved about. Communists, mostly. Not many of the workers were here.

Jack saw them in the doorway and came over. "The growers are getting nervous," he said. "I heard Welty is fit to be tied."

"The camp was full of men with guns last night. They didn't threaten us, but we got the message," Loreda said.

"We can hardly blame people for staying away," Jack said.

"The Brennans ain't comin'," Ant said. "They said we're crazy to come."

"We're not on grower land. There's no law saying we can't *talk*," Loreda said.

"Sometimes legal rights don't matter as much as they should," Jack said.

Natalia walked up to Jack. As usual she was impeccably dressed, in black pants and a fitted tan blazer with a white silk blouse buttoned to the throat. It was little wonder Loreda idolized the woman. In the midst of a dangerous meeting, she managed to look glamorous and calm. How did a woman become so steady?

"Come," she said, taking Jack by the arm. "All of you."

Natalia led them to the barn door.

In the field between the barn and the road, Elsa saw a steady line of vehicles driving toward the barn. One after another, cars parked out front; doors opened. People stepped out, gathered uncertainly; more arrived. More people came on foot across the bare grass pasture.

Elsa saw the way folks moved as they congregated—nervously, eyes darting back to the road and out across the empty fields.

By eight o'clock, Elsa estimated the crowd at over five hundred. More people walked up the road, merged into the audience gathered in front of the barn. They talked among themselves, but quietly. Everyone was afraid to be there, afraid of the consequences of just listening to talk of a strike.

"You should talk to them," Jack said to Elsa.

She laughed. "Me? Why would anyone listen to me?"

"You know these people. They'd listen to you."

"Go on," she said, giving him a shove. "Convince them the way you convinced me."

Jack hauled a table out from the barn and set it in front of the big double doors, then jumped up on it.

The crowd stilled. Elsa looked out at the familiar faces: folks who'd come from the Midwest or the South, Texas and the Great Plains; folks who'd worked hard all of their lives and still wanted that, who had fallen on such inexplicably hard times that they were confused, undone. All of them thought, or had thought, as Elsa had, that if they could just get an even break, a chance, they could right the ship of their lives.

"Eight years ago, Mexicans picked almost all of the crops in this great valley," Jack said. "They came across the border, moved into these fields, and picked the crops and moved on. February for peas in Nipomo. June for apricots in Santa Clara. Grapes in August in Fresno, and September here for cotton. They came, they picked, and they returned home for the winter. Invisible to the locals at every stage. Until the Crash of '29 broke the system and made Californians afraid for their jobs. They feared who Americans always fear: the outsider. So the state cracked down on illegal immigrants and called the Mexicans criminals and deported them. By '31, the majority of them were gone or in hiding. It would have been a catastrophe for the agriculture business, but then . . ."—Jack held out his arms—"the Dust Bowl. The drought. The Great Depression. Millions lost their jobs and their homes. You came west, needing jobs, just wanting to put food on your tables and feed your families. You took the Mexicans' places in the fields. Now, your people make up ninety percent of the pickers. But you don't want to be unseen, do you? You came to live here, to put down roots, to be *Californians.*"

"We're Americans!" someone yelled from the crowd.

"We got every right to be here!"

"Rights," Jack said, looking out at them. "They matter in America, don't they?"

"Yes!"

"Here you have the right to be paid for your labor, and fairly. You have the *right* to a living wage, but you have to fight for it. They won't just give it to you. They care more about their wallets than your survival. We have to join together. Men, women, and children who pick their crops. We have to band together and rise up and say *NO MORE*. We won't be treated as worthless. We are going to make a stand on the sixth of October. Pass the word. We will be peaceful. That's critical. This is a protest, not a brawl. You will go into the cotton fields and sit down. Simply that. If we can slow the means of production, even for a day, we will get their attention."

"Their attention is dangerous," someone yelled. "They'll want to hurt us."

"They hurt you every day. We have to remember what we're fighting for," Jack said. "On the sixth, my comrades are leading strikes at every field and farm we can throughout the valley. If we can strike everywhere at once, we can—"

Sirens cut him off.

Police. Barreling up the road in cruisers, lights flashing.

"Coppers!" someone yelled.

"Strike on the sixth," Jack said. "Spread the word. All of us on one day. Every field."

Behind the police cars were trucks filled with men standing in back holding bats and shovels and clubs.

A man on a loudspeaker, standing in the back of one of the trucks, said, "Please disperse. You are engaged in illegal activity."

The vehicles pulled up and parked. Men jumped down, carrying their weapons.

The crowd broke apart. People screamed and pushed one another aside.

"Loreda!" Elsa couldn't see her children in the pandemonium. "Ant!"

People ran in all directions. Those who had driven jumped in their cars and drove away. The others ran for their lives across the fields.

Elsa saw Loreda and Ant, clinging to each other, being carried forward by the tide of people.

She started to run for them, but something hit her in the head, hard, and she fell to the ground unconscious.

⟩⟨

ELSA CAME AWAKE IN stages. Her mouth was dry. She was thirsty.

The last thing she remembered was—

"Loreda! Ant!" She sat up so fast she felt dizzy.

Jack was beside her. "I'm here, Elsa," he said.

She was in bed. But not in a room she'd ever seen before. There was an empty chair beside the bed.

Jack handed her a glass of water and sat down in the chair.

"Where are my children?"

"Natalia got them to your cabin. She drove your truck back."

"How do you know this?"

"I told her to. Natalia never fails. She will be in the cabin, with the door locked. She will shoot anyone who tries to harm them."

"Will they know I'm safe?"

"Natalia knows you are with me, so yes. She trusts me as I trust her."

"Quite a relationship you two have."

"We've been through a lot together."

Elsa downed the water and slumped back. There was a ringing in her ears and a painful throbbing in the back of her head. She touched it gingerly. Her fingertips came back bloodied. "What happened?"

"One of their thugs hit you."

Elsa saw the bloody, scraped ridge of Jack's knuckles. "You punched him?"

"And then some." He put a washrag in a basin of water, wrung it out, and placed it on her forehead.

The coolness soothed. "How long ago?"

"An hour, maybe. They got what they wanted: people are scared to strike."

"They were scared before, Jack, but they showed up. Was anyone besides me hurt?"

"Several. A few were arrested. They burned down the barn. Took all our mimeograph machines and typewriters."

Elsa glanced around the small room, saw the spartan décor: an old dresser, a nightstand with a brass lamp on it, a rag rug. Stacks of papers and books and magazines and newspapers lined every wall, covered most surfaces. No mirror. No closet. Just a few men's clothes hanging from hooks on the wall. It all had a very temporary look. Or maybe this was how men lived without women in their lives. "Where are we?" she asked, but she knew.

"I sleep here when I'm in town." He paused.

"Interesting you don't say you live here."

"My life. It's . . . more of an idea. A cause. Or it has been."

"What do you mean?"

"For years, I've been fighting to make the rich pay their workers a living wage. I hate the inequity between the haves and the have-nots. I've been beaten and gone to prison for it. I've seen my comrades beaten, but tonight . . . when I saw you get hit . . ."

"What?"

"I thought . . . it's not worth that." He looked at her. "You've unbalanced me, Elsa."

Elsa felt a sense of connection but didn't know what to do with it, how to reach for him without humiliating herself. "I'm not myself around you, either," was all she could think of to say.

He reached for her hand, held it.

The silence became awkward. He seemed to be waiting for her to say something, but what?

"There's blood on your face and in your hair. Maybe you'd like to bathe before I take you back to your cabin. So the kids don't see you like this."

He helped her out of bed and steadied her as they walked into the small bathroom. Jack turned on the water in the porcelain bathtub, and then left her alone.

She undressed and stepped into the bath. With a sigh, she slid down into the hot water.

It relaxed her as nothing had in a long time. She washed her hair and body and felt rejuvenated.

But all the while, she was thinking of Jack.

Do you know how beautiful you are? She had never forgotten him saying those remarkable words, and now, he'd claimed to be unbalanced by her. Certainly, she was equally undone by him.

She stepped out of the tub and dried off, then wrapped the towel around her naked body and reached down for her ragged dress.

She stopped.

When she put that dress back on, she would be Elsa again.

She didn't want that. At least she didn't want to be the Elsa who stayed silent and accepted less and thought it her due. She'd rather reach for love and fail than never reach at all.

She turned the door handle slowly.

Even as she opened the door, she couldn't quite believe she was doing this: she, who had ached for her husband's touch for more than a dozen years but never once had the courage to reach for him, was going to walk out of this bathroom wearing only a towel.

It felt like the most courageous act of her life. She opened the door and walked into the bedroom.

Jack stood against the wall, arms crossed. When he saw her, he uncrossed his arms and walked toward her.

She dropped the towel, trying not to be ashamed of her scrawny body.

He stopped, then moved closer, said her name softly.

Elsa couldn't believe the look in his eyes, but it was there. Desire. For her.

"Are you sure?" he asked, touching a lock of her hair, lifting it from her bare shoulder.

"I'm sure," she said.

He took her hand and led her to the bed. She reached for the lamp, to turn it off. He stopped her, said, "Don't," in a rough voice. "I want to see you, Elsa."

He threw his shirt and undershirt aside, kicked off his pants, and took her into his arms.

"Tell me what you want," he murmured, his lips on hers.

He was asking for words she didn't know, answers she didn't have.

"Maybe you want me to kiss you here? Or here?"

"Oh, my God," she said, and he laughed, kissing her again. His touch was magic, created a need she could neither control nor deny, made her desperate for more.

His hands were all over her, touching her with an intimacy she'd never imagined. The world disappeared, spiraled down to nothing except her desire and her need. No one had ever known her like this; he showed her the power of her own body, the beauty of her need. She dared with him all the things she'd always dreamed of. Relief came in waves; she felt ethereal, bodiless, at one with the air in the room. Floating. When she finally came back to herself—and that was what it felt like, becoming corporeal again after being nothing but need—she opened her eyes.

Jack lay on his side, staring at her.

She leaned boldly forward, kissed his lips, his temple. Somewhere in all of it, she realized she was crying.

"Don't cry, my love," he whispered, drawing her into his arms, holding her close. "There's more where that came from. I promise you. This is just the beginning."

My love.

﹅

"You are going to wear a groove in the floor," Natalia said, exhaling smoke.

Loreda stopped pacing. "It's been two hours. Maybe she is dead."

Ant shot up. "You think she's dead?"

Loreda shook her head. *Stupid.* "No, Antsy. I don't."

"She'll be back," Natalia said. "Jack will see that she is returned."

Loreda heard footsteps outside.

"Ant," she said harshly, "come over here."

He darted to her side, pressed up against her hip. She put a hand on his shoulder protectively.

Natalia got to her feet, stood in front of them as the door opened.

Jack and Mom walked in.

"Mommy!" Ant hurled himself at their mother.

"Whoa," Mom said. "Slow down, buddy. I'm fine." She leaned down and kissed the top of his head.

Jack said, "She should sleep now." He helped Mom over to bed and got her settled in.

Ant immediately climbed up onto the foot of her bed and curled up like a puppy.

Loreda, Natalia, and Jack moved toward the door.

"Is she really okay?" Loreda asked.

"Yes," he answered. "A nasty blow to the back of the head, but it will take more than that to slow your mother down. She's a warrior."

"It's dangerous," Loreda said, realizing for the first time how true those words were. Everyone had told her, but she hadn't truly understood until tonight. They were risking everything to strike. Not just their jobs. It could go really badly.

"You see now," Jack said. "A fight like this isn't romantic. I was in San Francisco when the National Guard went after strikers with bayonets."

"People died that day," Natalia said. "Strikers. They called it Bloody Thursday."

"We have to fight them, though," Loreda said. "With whatever we have. Like when Mom took the baseball bat into the hospital to get aspirin for Jean."

"Yeah," Jack said, looking grim. "We do."

THIRTY-FOUR

O n the morning of the sixth, just before dawn, Elsa and the children climbed into one of the waiting Welty trucks.

The workers were quiet, subdued. People were reluctant to make
eye contact. Elsa didn't know if that meant they were with the strike
or against it, but they all knew about it. Strike talk was everywhere.
Careful words, spoken in dark corners. Everyone who worked in the
valley knew a strike was happening today. Which meant the growers
knew.

"I want you and Ant always in my sight," Elsa said as the truck
pulled up in front of the cotton field. Jack's truck was parked in the
middle of the road; he, Natalia, and several of their comrades waited for
the strikers, held picket signs. The gate to the field was open.

"Fair pay! Fair pay! Fair pay!" Jack chanted as the workers climbed
down from the truck.

Several cars and trucks appeared on the road behind Jack and Natalia, drove slowly forward. In minutes, Jack and his comrades would be
caught between the strikers in front of them and the growers behind
them, hemmed in on either side by fenced cotton fields.

The workers stopped en mass, stood clustered together, facing the Communists.

The first car stopped behind Jack's truck. Three men got out; each one held a rifle.

A truck stopped beside it. Two more men jumped onto the road.

A third truck rolled into place and Mr. Welty stepped out, holding a shotgun. He walked forward, stopped about three feet behind Jack, and faced the strikers. "Wages are lowering today to seventy-five cents for a hundred pounds of cotton," Welty said. "If you don't take the wage and pick, there are plenty who will."

Five armed men fanned out behind him, guns at the ready.

Jack turned to face Welty, walked boldly toward the owner, went toe to toe with him, became the tip of the arrow of the strikers.

"They won't pick for that," Jack said.

"You don't even work for me, you lyin' Red," Welty said.

"I'm trying to help these workers. That's all. Your greed is un-American. They aren't going to pick for seventy-five cents. That's not a living wage." Jack turned to the workers. "He *needs* you to pick but he doesn't want to pay you. What do we say?"

No one answered.

Welty's men smacked their gun barrels against their palms.

"They're smarter than you are, Red," Welty said.

Elsa knew what they were supposed to do now; they all did. Jack had told them at the barn. *Go into the fields peaceably. Sit down.*

If they didn't move, didn't act, this strike would be over before it began and they would lose and the bosses would be even stronger.

Elsa placed a hand on each of her children's shoulders. "Come on, kids. Into the field."

They walked forward, moved through the crowd and then emerged from it, three lone figures, out in front, moving toward the entrance to the field.

The spiked barbed wire that topped the chain-link fencing glittered in the sunlight; an armed man stood at the parapet of the gun tower, his rifle aimed at the workers.

"See?" Welty said to Jack. "This little lady knows who pays her. Seventy-five cents is better than nothing."

Elsa walked past Jack and Welty without looking at either man. She and her children walked into the cotton field.

Loreda looked back. "No one is following us, Mom."

Follow us, Elsa thought. *Please. Don't let us be alone. It will all be for nothing then.* Jack said they all needed to do it, together, to stop the means of production.

"Fair pay!" Jack shouted behind her. "Fair pay!"

The walk into the cotton field was the longest six minutes of Elsa's life. She took her place in a row and turned around.

For a moment the crowd of pickers stood there, motionless, staring at Elsa and her children, alone in the field.

Ike stepped forward first, pushed his way out of the crowd, and began walking toward the open gate.

"Look, Mom," Loreda said under her breath as one by one the workers followed Ike, walked into the fields, and filled the rows.

As one, the workers turned to face Welty.

"Get to work, men," Welty yelled.

As if there were only men here.

Elsa stared out at the people standing in the rows of cotton, *her* people. Her kind. Their courage humbled her. "You know what to do!" Elsa yelled.

The workers sat down.

>-

AS DUSK DREW NEAR, the strikers stood up and walked out of the fields, under the angry gazes of the boss and his men.

The strikers had filled the fields all day, sitting quietly.

Jack waited for them down the road. He had a bloody lip and a blackening eye; still, he gave the group a smile. "Good job, everyone. We got their attention. Tomorrow we need to get an even earlier start. They'll be ready this time, and they won't send trucks to pick you up. We'll meet at four A.M. Outside the El Centro Hotel."

They began the long walk home, all of them together.

Loreda was jubilant. "Not a single boll of cotton was picked today. That'll teach Mr. Fat Cat not to take advantage of us anymore," she said.

Elsa walked beside Jack. She wished she could feel as happy as her daughter did, but her worry outpaced her enthusiasm. She could tell most of the strikers felt as she did. Looking at Jack's bruised face, she said, "You certainly got their attention, I see."

He moved closer. His fingers brushed hers as they walked. "When a man resorts to violence, he's scared," Jack said. "That's a good sign."

"Did we make it worse for ourselves?"

"They'll be ready for us tomorrow," Jack said.

"How long will all this last?" she asked. "Without relief, we are going to be in trouble, Jack. They won't give us credit at the store if we don't pick, and none of us has any savings. We can't hang on for long . . ."

"I know," Jack said.

They came to the Welty growers' camp. The workers who lived there turned in, heading back to their tents and cabins. Loreda and Ant ran off ahead. Others kept walking down the road.

Jack and Elsa stopped, looked at each other. "You were amazing today," he said quietly.

"All I did was sit down."

"It was bold and you know it. I told you they'd listen to you."

She touched the swollen purple skin below his eye. "You need to be careful tomorrow."

"I'm always careful." He gave her a smile that should have been comforting but wasn't.

LATER THAT NIGHT, ELSA stood at the hot plate stirring a pot of beans.

Someone pounded on the door so hard the walls rattled.

"Kids, get behind me," she said, and then went to the door, opening it.

A man stood there, holding a hammer. "Well, well," he said. "If it isn't the woman at the front of the line. The Red's whore."

Elsa shielded the children with her body. "What do you want?"

He shoved a piece of paper at her. "Can you read?"

She yanked the notice out of his hand and read it.

To John Doe and Mary Doe, whose true names are unknown:

You will please take notice that you are required to vacate and surrender up to me the premises now occupied by you; said premises being known as California Lands Unit 10.

This is intended to be three days' notice to vacate said property on the grounds that you are in unlawful possession thereof, and unless you do vacate the same as the above stated, the proper action at law will be brought against you.

Thomas Welty, owner, Welty Farms

"You're evicting us? How am I here unlawfully?" Elsa said. "I pay six dollars a month for this cabin."

"These are pickers' cabins," the man said. "Did you pick today?"

"No, but—"

"Two more nights, lady," the man said. "Then we come back here and take all your shit and throw it in the dirt. You've been notified."

He left.

Elsa stood in the open doorway, stared out at the pandemonium in camp. A dozen men moved ominously forward, pounding notices on doors, kicking doors open, handing out eviction notices, and nailing them on posts near every tent.

"They can't do that!" Loreda screamed. "Pigs!"

Elsa yanked her children inside, slammed the door shut.

"They can't evict us for exercising our rights as Americans," Loreda said. "Can they?"

Elsa saw when it settled into place for Loreda, when she really understood the risk. As bad as ditch-bank living had been before, they'd had a tent, at least. Now, if they got kicked out of here, they had nothing.

The growers knew all of this, knew tomorrow it would be harder for the workers not to pick, and harder still the day after that.

How long could hungry, homeless, starving people stand up for an idea?

᚜

ELSA WOKE TO A hand clamped over her mouth.

"Elsa, it's me."

Jack. She sat up.

He took his hand away from her mouth.

"What's wrong?" she whispered.

"There's talk of trouble. I want you and the kids out of the camp tonight."

"Yes. They evicted all of us today. I think that's just the beginning." She threw back the covers and got out of bed. His hand slid down her side in a quick caress.

Elsa closed the window vent, then lit a kerosene lamp and went to wake the children.

Ant grumbled and kicked at her and rolled over.

"What?" Loreda said, yawning.

"Jack says there may be trouble tomorrow. He wants us to move out."

"Of the cabin?" Loreda said.

In the faint light, Elsa saw the fear in her daughter's eyes. "Yes," Elsa said.

"All right, then." Loreda elbowed her brother. "Get up, Ant. We're on the move."

They packed their few belongings quickly and stowed the boxes in the back of the truck, along with the crates and buckets they'd salvaged in the last few months.

At last, Elsa and Loreda stood at the door, both staring at the two rusted metal bed frames with mattresses and the small hot plate, thinking what luxuries they were.

"We can move back in when the strike is over," Loreda said.

Elsa didn't answer, but she knew they wouldn't live here again.

They left the cabin and walked out to their truck.

The children climbed into the back and Elsa got into the driver's seat. Jack took his place beside her.

"Ready?" he said.

"I guess."

She started the engine but didn't turn on the headlights. The truck grumbled down the road.

Elsa parked in front of the boarded-up El Centro Hotel, where they'd stayed during the flood.

Jack unlocked the heavy chain from the front door and led them inside.

The lobby stank of cigarette smoke and sweat. People had been here, and recently. In the dark, Jack led them up the stairs and stopped at the first closed door on the second floor. "There are two beds in here. Loreda and Ant?"

Loreda nodded tiredly, let her half-sleeping brother angle against her.

"Don't turn on the lights," Jack said. "We'll come get you in the morning for the strike. Elsa, your room is . . . next door."

"Thank you." She squeezed his hand and let him go, then got the kids settled in their separate beds.

In no time, Ant was asleep; she could hear his breathing. It struck her with painful clarity that this simple sound was the very essence of her responsibility. Their *lives* depended on her and she was letting them strike tomorrow.

"You're wearing your worried face," Loreda said when Elsa sat down on the bed beside her.

"It's my love face," Elsa said, stroking her daughter's hair. "I'm proud of you, Loreda."

"You're scared about tomorrow."

Elsa should have been ashamed that Loreda saw her fear so clearly, but she wasn't. Maybe she was tired of hiding from people, of thinking she wasn't good enough; she'd filled that well for years and now it was empty. The weight of it was gone. "Yes," she said. "I'm scared."

"But we'll do it anyway."

Elsa smiled, thinking again of her grandfather. It had taken decades, but she finally knew exactly what he'd meant by the things he'd told her. It wasn't the fear that mattered in life. It was the choices made when you were afraid. You were brave because of your fear, not in spite of it. "Yes."

She leaned down and kissed her daughter's forehead. "Sleep well, baby girl. Tomorrow will be a big day."

Elsa left her children and went into the room next door, where Jack sat on the bed, waiting for her. A single candle burned in a brass holder on the nightstand. The few boxes that held their belongings were stacked along one wall.

Jack stood.

She walked boldly up to him. In his eyes, she saw love. For *her*. It was young, new, not deep and settled and familiar like Rose and Tony's, but love just the same, or at least the beautiful, promising start of it. All of her life she'd waited for a moment like this, yearned for it, and she would not let it pass by unnoticed, unremarked upon. Time felt incredibly precious in these hours before the strike. "I promised a girlfriend something crazy."

"Oh, yeah?"

She brought her hands up, linked them behind his head. "I've never asked a man to dance. And I know there's no music."

"Elsa," he whispered, leaning in to kiss her, moving to a song that wasn't being played. "We are the music."

Elsa closed her eyes and let him lead.

For you, Jean.

THIRTY-FIVE

Elsa was awakened by a kiss. She opened her eyes slowly. Last night was the best night's sleep of her life, which seemed almost obscene, given the circumstances.

Jack leaned over her. "My comrades should be downstairs by now."

Elsa sat up, pushed the tangled hair from her eyes. "How many of you are there?"

"Across the state, thousands. But we are fighting on many fronts. We have organizers at every field we can from here to Fresno." He kissed her again. "See you downstairs."

Elsa got out of bed and walked—naked—over to one of the boxes that held their belongings. Burrowing through, she found her journal and the latest pencil nub Ant had found in the school's trash can.

Settling back in bed, she opened the journal to the first blank page and began to write.

Love is what remains when everything else is gone. This is what I should have told my children when we left Texas. What I will tell them tonight. Not that they will understand yet. How could they?

I am forty years old, and I only just learned this fundamental truth myself.

Love. In the best of times, it is a dream. In the worst of times, a salvation.

I am in love. There it is. I've written it down. Soon I will say it out loud. To him.

I am in love. As crazy and ridiculous and implausible as it sounds, I am in love. And I am loved in return.

And this—love—gives me the courage I need for today.

The four winds have blown us here, people from all across the country, to the very edge of this great land, and now, at last, we make our stand, fight for what we know to be right. We fight for our American dream, that it will be possible again.

Jack says that I am a warrior and, while I don't believe it, I know this: A warrior believes in an end she can't see and fights for it. A warrior never gives up. A warrior fights for those weaker than herself.

It sounds like motherhood to me.

Elsa closed the journal and dressed quickly, then went to the room next door.

Ant was bouncing on the bed, saying, "Lookit me, Loreda. I'm flying."

Loreda ignored her brother, paced, chewing on her thumbnail.

At Elsa's entrance, they both stilled.

"Is it time?" Loreda asked, bright-eyed. She looked excited, ready to go.

Elsa felt a clutch of worry. "Today will be—"

"Dangerous," Loreda said. "We know. Is everyone downstairs?"

"I thought we should—"

"Talk more?" Loreda said impatiently. "We've talked plenty."

Ant jumped off the bed, landed on bare feet beside his sister. "I'm the Shadow! No one can scare me."

"Okay," Elsa said. "Just stay close today. I want to see you two every second."

Loreda pushed Elsa toward the door while Ant tugged on his boots, yelled, "Wait for the Shadow!"

The lobby was empty when the three of them got downstairs, but within minutes there was a crowd. Members of the Workers Alliance gathered in pods; they stacked leaflets on the table and leaned picket signs against the walls. Workers from the ditch-bank camp and Welty Farms and the newly constructed Resettlement Administration camp in Arvin stood silently by, looking anxious.

Elsa saw Jeb and his children in the back corner and Ike with some of the Welty camp workers.

Loreda picked up a sign that read FAIR PAY and stood by Natalia, whose sign read WORKERS UNITE.

Jack stood at the front of the room. "Friends and comrades, it is time. Remember our plan: Peaceable strike. We go to the fields and sit down. That is all. We hope it happens all across the state on this morning, as we hope that more workers join us. Let's go."

They filed out of the hotel and gathered in the street. There were fewer than fifty of them altogether. Natalia got into the driver's seat of Jack's truck and started the engine. Jack stood in the wooden-slatted bed of the truck and faced the small gathering. "The world can be changed by a handful of courageous people. Today we fight on behalf of those who are afraid. We fight for a living wage." He yelled out, "Fair pay! Fair pay!"

Loreda held her sign in the air and chanted with him. "Fair pay! Fair pay!"

The truck rolled forward; the strikers followed. Jack reached down for a megaphone and amplified his chant. "Fair pay! Fair pay!"

Elsa and her children and the strikers walked behind the truck, listening to Jack.

They passed a Lucky Strike billboard. Several of the people living beneath it stood up, ambled across the brown field, and joined the strikers.

A quarter of a mile later, a group of clergymen joined them, holding up signs that read MINIMUM WAGE FOR WORKERS!

At every new road or camp, more people joined. Their voices rose up. *Fair pay! Fair wages!*

More people merged in.

Elsa turned at one point, saw the crowd. There had to be six hundred people here now, all coming together to fight for a decent wage.

She elbowed Loreda, cocked her head so Loreda would look back and see the people behind them.

Loreda grinned and chanted louder. "Fair pay! Fair pay!"

Jack and the Workers Alliance were right. The growers would have to treat the workers fairly if they wanted their cotton picked before the weather changed and frost ruined the crop. This wasn't about being a Communist or a rabble-rouser. This was about fighting for the rights of every American.

A mile later, they turned a corner, nearly a thousand of them now, marching and chanting, signs held high, and neared the entrance to Welty Farms. The road stretched out in front of them, a straight line, bordered on each side by fenced cotton fields. A single man waited for them, stood in the middle of the road.

Welty.

Natalia stopped the truck directly in front of him.

Still standing in the back of the truck, Jack spoke to the huge crowd through the megaphone. "This is your day, workers. Your moment. The owners will hear you. They can't ignore so many of you saying, *No more.*"

Loreda responded loudly, shouting, "No more! No more!"

The crowd joined in, waving their signs for emphasis.

"We will be peaceful, but we will stand our ground," Jack said through the megaphone. "No more being pushed around and starved. You deserve a fair day's wage for a day's work."

Elsa heard the rumble of engines. She knew the rest of them heard it, too. The chanting faded.

"Go into the field," Jack said. "Sit down. Break down the gate if you must."

Elsa turned, saw a hay truck full of workers pull up behind the strikers. The driver honked the horn to be let through.

"Strikebreakers. They're here to take your jobs," Jack said. "Don't let them in."

The crowd spread out, blocked the truck's path to the gates with their bodies.

"No work! Fair pay!" Jack shouted.

Welty walked around to the side of Jack's truck and faced the strikers. "I'm paying seventy-five cents today," he said. "Who wants to feed their family and move into one of my cabins? Who wants credit at the company store come winter and a mattress to sleep on?"

"Hell, no!" Jack yelled.

A roar of agreement rose up from the crowd.

A truck appeared on the road behind Welty, drove toward the strikers. A man exited the truck, carrying a rifle casually over one shoulder. He walked to the field and opened the gate.

"They aren't gonna shoot. We ain't done nothin' wrong," Ike called out. "Stay strong!"

The man with the rifle went to the top of the guard tower and aimed his gun at the strikers.

"He can't shoot us for nothin'," Ike yelled. "This is still America."

More trucks full of migrant workers willing to pick for seventy-five cents pulled up behind the strikers, honked to be let through.

"Don't let 'em through," Jack yelled.

Sirens.

Police cruisers and cars and trucks barreled down the distant road, creating a cloud of dust. One by one they turned onto this road, and parked in a straight line that created a blockade in front of Jack's truck.

The doors opened. Masked men stepped out of the vehicles, holding clubs and bats and guns.

Vigilantes. Ten of them.

Policemen stepped out of their cruisers, guns drawn.

The vigilantes walked slowly forward.

The crowd of strikers backed away; the chanting quieted.

"Men wear masks because they're ashamed of what they're doing," Jack said through the megaphone. "They know this is wrong."

Elsa stared at the masked men coming toward her and the children. She held her children close, began to back away.

"Mom, no!" Loreda cried.

"Hush," Elsa said, pulling Loreda closer.

"Stand your ground," Jack said. He looked directly at Elsa, said, "Don't be afraid."

Three vigilantes jumped up into the back of Jack's truck. One cracked Jack in the back with his bat. Jack dropped the megaphone and staggered forward. The vigilantes grabbed Jack by the hair and dragged him out of the truck; one of them cracked Jack in the head with the butt of his rifle. Jack dropped to his knees.

"Get to work," Welty yelled. "This strike is over."

The vigilantes circled Jack, began beating and kicking him.

The workers backed away; some edged toward the cotton field. The strikebreaker trucks honked to be let through.

"Elsa!" Jack yelled, and was kicked hard for it.

She knew what he wanted. *They'll listen to you.*

Elsa climbed up into the back of the truck and took up Jack's megaphone and faced the strikers. Her hands were shaking. "Stop!" she cried out.

The workers stopped backing away, looked up at her.

She was breathing hard. Now what?

Think.

She knew these people, *knew* them. They were her people. *Her kind,* the Californians said derisively, but it was a compliment.

They were like her. Today, they were part of a new group: people who stood up, used their voices to say *No more*. They'd woken in the middle of the night, hungry, to stand up for their rights, and now it was Elsa's time to show her children what her grandfather had taught her long ago. She wrapped her fingers around the soft velvet pouch at her throat. *Saint Jude, patron saint of desperate cases and lost causes, help me.*

"What?" someone yelled.

"Hope," Elsa said. The megaphone turned her whispered word into a roar that quieted the crowd. "Hope is a coin I carry. An American penny, given to me by a man I came to love. There were times . . . in my journey, when it felt as if that penny and the hope it represented were the only things that kept me going. I came west . . . in search of a better life . . . but my American dream has been turned inside out by hardship and poverty." She looked at Welty. "And greed. These years have been a time of things lost: Jobs. Homes. Food. The land we loved turned on us, broke us all, even the stubborn old men who used to talk about the weather and congratulate each other on the season's bumper wheat crop. 'A man's got to fight out here to make a living,' they'd say to each other."

Elsa looked out at the crowd, saw all the women and children who were here, looking up at her. She saw her life in their eyes, her pain in the slant of their shoulders.

"A man. It was always about the men. They seem to think it meant nothing to cook and clean and bear children and tend gardens. But we women of the Great Plains worked from sunup to sundown, too, toiled on wheat farms until we were as dry and baked as the land we loved. Sometimes, when I close my eyes, I swear I can still taste the dust."

Elsa paused, surprised by how loud and forceful her voice had become. She stared out at the workers, saw for the first time that their ragged clothes and hungry faces were badges of courage, of survival. They were good people who didn't give up. "We came to find a better life, to feed our children. We aren't lazy or shiftless. We don't want to live the way we do. It's time," she said. "Time to say, *No more*. No more company store cheating us and keeping us poor. No more lowering wages. No more using us up and spitting us out and pitting us against each other. We deserve better. *No more*."

"No more!" Ike yelled.

Loreda shouted, "No more!"

There was a moment's pause, and then the crowd rallied, blocked the strikebreakers, and chanted back at Elsa in unison.

"No more. No more. No more!"

The crowd raised their voices and their signs, ignoring the gunman in the tower and the policemen and masked vigilantes.

Their courage stunned and invigorated Elsa, who chanted with them.

"Fair wages!" the pickers chanted, lifting their picket signs into the air.

Elsa heard a high whistling sound, then a thunk of something metal landing at her feet. A second later, smoke erupted, blanketing everything, obscuring the world.

Elsa's eyes stung. She saw the strikers run blindly into each other, panicked. They backed away from the truck.

Someone shouted, "They're throwing tear-gas bombs!"

More whistling, metal tear-gas canisters landed among the crowd; smoke billowed up.

Elsa lifted the megaphone. "Run into the fields, not away," she cried out, coughing hard. She wiped her eyes but it didn't help. "Don't give up!"

The workers panicked, ran in every direction, bumped into each other. No one could see much through the stinging tear gas.

A shot rang out, loud even in the pandemonium.

Elsa felt something hit her so hard she staggered, clutched her side.

Warm, wet, sticky.

I'm bleeding.

She heard Loreda scream, "Mom!" and Elsa wanted to answer, to say, *I'm fine,* but the pain.

The pain.

She dropped the megaphone, heard it thunk to the back of the truck. Through the burning, stinging haze of smoke, she saw Loreda pushing through the crowd, screaming, and Ant stumbling along beside her.

All Elsa wanted was to let them get to her, stay awake, tell them how much she loved them, but pain was overtaking her, squeezing until she couldn't breathe . . . *My babies,* she thought, reaching out for them.

༘

IT SEEMED TO HAPPEN in slow motion: the sound of a gunshot, Mom staggering forward, blood turning her dress red. Jack throwing men off of him.

Loreda screamed and grabbed Ant's hand, fighting her way toward the truck, through the panicking crowd. She saw Jack hit one of the vigilantes with his own bat and fell another with a punch.

"They shot her!" someone yelled. The vigilantes backed away from the truck.

Jack jumped into the back of the truck, took Mom in his arms.

"Is she alive?" Loreda screamed.

Mom opened her red, teary eyes and looked at Jack. "We failed."

Jack lifted Mom into his arms and carried her out of the truck.

He stood in front of the strikers, holding Elsa. Her blood dripped through his fingers and onto the ground. Tear gas drifted past them.

"Strike . . . lead them," Mom whispered, and Loreda understood.

"Arrest them!" Welty shouted to his henchmen, but the policemen backed away from the woman covered in blood. The vigilantes froze. Some dropped their weapons. The strikebreakers fell silent.

Loreda saw a rifle on the ground at her feet. She picked it up, walked over to Welty, who blocked the entrance to the field, and aimed the gun at his chest.

Welty raised his hands into the air. "You wouldn't dare—"

"Wouldn't I? If you don't get out of our way, I'll kill you. As sure as I stand here."

"It won't do any good. I'll break your damn strike."

Loreda cocked the gun. "Not today."

Welty stepped aside, moving slowly.

Ike stepped forward, pushed his way through the crowd. He walked past Jack and headed into the field. Then Jeb and his children followed . . . and Bobby Rand and his father.

The workers filed silently, solemnly into the field, taking up space in the rows, making sure no one could pick this cotton today.

In Jack's arms, Mom lifted her head, looked out at the strikers gathered in front of her. She smiled and whispered, "No more."

As scared and shaken as Loreda was, she'd never been prouder of anyone in her life.

Ж

JACK HELD MOM IN his arms and kicked the hospital door open. "My wife needs help."

The woman at the front desk looked horrified as she raised up out of her cushy chair. "You can't—"

"I'm a goddamn California resident," Jack said. "Get a doctor."

"But—"

"*Now,*" Jack said in a voice so dangerous even Loreda felt a flash of fear.

The woman called for a doctor.

While they waited, blood dripped onto the clean floor. Ant saw it and started to cry. Loreda pulled him close.

A man in white bustled toward them, flanked by a nurse in a starched uniform.

"Gunshot in the abdomen," Jack said. His voice broke halfway through the sentence and Loreda saw his fear. It heightened her own.

The doctor called for help and within moments Mom was on a gurney, being rushed away from them.

Jack pulled Ant close, held him. Loreda moved in to be with them. Jack's arm circled her.

All Loreda could think about was how mean she'd been to her mom. For years. There was so much to say now, to undo. She wanted to tell her mother how much she loved and admired her, how she wanted to be just like her when she grew up. Why hadn't she said it all before?

Loreda wiped her tears, but more kept falling. She couldn't even be strong for Ant. She prayed for the first time in years. *Please, God, save her.*

I can't live without my mom.

⤳

WHITE.

Lights too bright.

Stinging.

Pain.

Elsa opened her eyes again, squinted at the intensity of the light overhead.

She was in bed.

She turned her head slowly. Every breath hurt.

Jack sat in a chair beside her, holding Ant on his lap. Her son's eyes were red, bloodshot. Tears streaked his freckled cheeks.

"Elsa," Jack said softly.

"She's awake," Ant said.

Loreda rushed in, almost pushed Jack and her brother aside. "Mommy," she said.

Mommy.

That one word brought everything back: Elsa rocking Loreda to sleep, reading her stories, teaching her to make fettuccine, whispering *Be brave,* into her ear.

"Where ..."

Jack touched her face. "You're in the hospital."

"And?"

She saw the answer in her loved ones' eyes. They were already grieving.

"They couldn't repair the damage," Jack said. "Too much internal bleeding, and your heart ... they say there's something wrong with it. Can't keep up or some damn thing. They've given you pain medication ... there's nothing else they can do."

"But they're wrong," Loreda said. "Everyone's always been wrong about you, Mom. Haven't they? Like me." Loreda started to cry. "You'll be fine. You're strong."

Elsa didn't need them to tell her she was dying. She could feel her body shutting down.

But not her heart. Her heart was so full it couldn't hold all of the love she felt when she looked at these three who had shown her the world. She'd thought she had a lifetime to show them her love.

Time.

Hers had gone too fast. She'd only just discovered who she was.

She had counted on a lifetime to teach her children what they needed to know, but she didn't have that gift of grace and time. Still, she had given them what mattered: they were loved and they knew it. Everything else was decoration.

Love remains.

"Ant," she said, opening her arms.

He climbed like a monkey from Jack's arms to hers. His weight pressed down on her, caused an agonizing pain. She kissed his wet cheek.

"Don't die, Mommy."

That hurt worse than her gunshot. "I'll . . . watch over you . . . all your life. Like . . . the Shadow. At night . . . while you sleep."

"How will I know?"

"You'll . . . remember me."

He cried. "I don't want you to leave."

"I know, baby." She wiped his tears, felt the start of her own.

Jack saw her pain and pulled Ant into his arms. It broke her heart to see him holding her son. Here was a flash . . . a glimpse of the future that was slowly being lost. The family they could have become.

She stared up at Jack. "God, what a life we could have had."

He leaned closer, still holding Ant, and kissed her on the lips, stayed there long enough that she tasted his tears.

She lifted a hand, pressed her palm to his cheek so he could feel her touch one last time. "Take them home for me," she whispered against his lips.

He nodded. "Elsa . . . God, I love you . . ."

Loreda slipped in beside Jack, who stepped aside, soothed Ant, stroked his back.

"Hey, Mom," Loreda said in a thready voice.

Elsa stared up at her brash, beautiful, impetuous daughter. "I wanted to watch you take on the world, baby girl."

"I can't do it without you."

"You can . . . and you will."

"It's not fair," Loreda said. "No one will ever love me like you do."

Elsa had trouble breathing. It felt as if she were drowning from the inside out. She reached up slowly, every movement hurting, and untied the necklace at her throat. She took the velvet pouch in shaking hands and placed it in her daughter's palm. "Keep . . . believing in . . . us." Elsa paused to catch her breath. Every second hurt more than the last.

Loreda took the pouch in her hand, held it as her tears fell. "What do I do without you?"

Elsa tried to smile but couldn't. She was too tired. Too weak. "You live, Loreda," she whispered. "And know . . . every single second . . . how much I loved you." *Find your voice and use it . . . take chances . . . never give up.*

Elsa couldn't keep her eyes open anymore. There was so much more to say, a lifetime's worth of love and advice to bestow on her children, but there was no more time . . .

Be brave, she might have said, or maybe she only thought it.

THIRTY-SIX

"S he wants us to go home," Loreda said. The unexpected word—
home—gave her a bit of steadiness; something to hold on to.
Grandma and Grandpa. She needed them now.

"That's what she said."

Jack held Ant, who had cried himself to sleep.

"Good. I won't bury her here," Loreda said. "And Ant and I can't
stay. Even if they are still having dust storms in Texas. We can't stay
here. I *won't* stay here."

"I'll drive you back, of course, but . . ."

"Money," Loreda said dully. Everything came down to that.

"I'll talk to the Workers Alliance. Maybe—"

"No," Loreda said sharply, surprised by the suddenness of her anger,
the burning heat of it.

Enough was enough.

Goddamned enough.

Desperate times called for desperate measures. She knew what
Mom had done for Jean at a moment like this.

"I know where we can get what we need," she said. "Can I take your truck?"

"It doesn't sound like a good idea . . ."

"It isn't. Can I have your keys?"

"They're in the truck. Don't make me regret this."

"I'll be back as soon as I can."

Loreda rushed out of the hospital and drove Jack's truck north. *Look, Mom, a driving emergency,* she thought, starting to cry again.

In town, she passed vigilantes driving up and down the streets with loudspeakers, telling people to get back to work or be arrested for vagrancy, promising hard labor.

She could do this.

She *could.*

And if she died or went to hell or went to jail, well, okay. She was, by God, going to get her mother home so she could be buried on the land she loved, and not here, in this place that had broken and betrayed them.

She pulled up in front of the El Centro Hotel and ran up to Mom's room. There, she grabbed the shotgun, stuffed some clothes in a laundry bag, and went back down to Jack's truck and drove north.

Not far from the Welty camp, she parked behind an Old Gold cigarettes billboard. She grabbed the shotgun and laundry bag and darted into the camp and past the empty guardhouse.

The camp was quiet; eviction notices fluttered on every cabin door. She snagged some boys' clothes from a laundry line—a pair of wool pants, a black sweater—and found a floppy black hat in a mud puddle. She pulled the boys' oversized clothes on over her faded dress and tucked her hair up under the hat, then smeared mud on her cheeks.

Hopefully she looked like a boy going rabbit hunting.

A heavy pall of defeat lay over the place. The vigilantes were gone, but the point had been made. Power reestablished. Loreda had no doubt that even though Mom had given her life for this strike, it would be broken. If not today, then tomorrow or the next day. Starving, desperate people could only fight for so long.

She passed a few women and children standing in lines—for the showers, for the bathrooms, for the laundry—and made eye contact with none. She didn't recognize many of them anyway; the camp was already filling with new folks, ready to pick for any wage to put food on the table.

The camp store sat off by itself, lights on inside, ready to trap more unwary newcomers into debt.

Loreda opened the door cautiously, peered in.

No customers.

She breathed a sigh of relief.

She let the door bang shut behind her and did her best to swagger forward in her boy's disguise. She kept her eyes cast downward.

There was a new man at the register, one she had never seen before.

A lucky break.

Loreda raised the shotgun and aimed it at him.

The man's eyes widened. "What're you doin', son?"

"I'm robbing you. Give me the money in the register."

"We're a credit business."

"Don't insult me. I know you give cash for credit." She cocked the gun. "You ready to die for Welty's money?"

The man wrenched open the cash register and pulled out all the bills, shoved them toward Loreda on the counter.

"Coins, too."

He jangled up the coins and stuffed all the money in a burlap sack. "There. That's everything we got. But Welty will find you and—"

She grabbed the bag. "Get down in the corner. If I see you run out after me, I'll shoot you dead. Believe me, I am mad enough to do it."

She backed out of the store, kept the gun aimed at his hunched back.

Once outside, she threw the gun in the bushes and ran for the trees at the back of the camp, pulling off the boy's sweater as she went. She used the sweater to scrub the dirt off her face; she took off the hat and stepped out of the pants, then tossed it all in a trash can and shoved the burlap bag full of money into her laundry sack.

Now she was just a skinny girl in a faded dress.

She was halfway to the guardhouse when she heard a whistle blow.

Men with guns ran into camp, stopped at the store.

Loreda went to the laundry and got in line.

Someone hollered, "Got his gun!"

"Fan out, look everywhere! Welty wants this boy found."

Sure. They didn't mind cheating people, these big growers, but they hated being robbed. They would love to put someone away for armed robbery.

Loreda inched forward in line, her heart pounding, her mouth dry, but none of the vigilantes even glanced at the women standing in line to do laundry.

Sometimes it was good to be a woman.

The men ran through the camp, looking for boys, questioning them, snatching anything from their hands, barking out questions.

Then it was over.

When they were finally gone, Loreda stepped out of line and walked along the fence line out of the camp, carrying her laundry bag full of money. No one looked at her twice.

On the main road, she saw red lights flashing. Police going from camp to camp questioning, yanking bystanders aside.

Loreda drove back to the hospital.

There, she parked and counted the money.

One hundred and twenty-two dollars. And ninety-one cents.

A fortune.

❧

THAT NIGHT THEY MADE an arrowed beeline over the mountains and across the worst part of the Mojave Desert in a darkness devoid of stars, with a pine coffin in the bed of the truck.

There were few other cars on the road. Loreda couldn't see much beyond what lay in the glow of the headlights. Ant lay sleeping up against her. He hadn't said a single word since Mom died.

At midnight, just past Barstow, Jack pulled off the road and parked.

Without a tent, they laid blankets and quilts on a flat patch of ground and stretched out, with Ant positioned between Jack and Loreda.

"You want to tell me now?" Jack said quietly, over the sound of Ant's snoring.

"Tell you what?"

"How you got the money?"

"I did a bad thing for a good reason."

"How bad?"

"Baseball-bat-in-a-hospital-to-get-aspirin bad."

"Did you hurt anyone?"

"No."

"And you won't do it again and you know it was wrong?"

"Yeah. The world's topsy-turvy, though."

"It is."

Loreda sighed. "I miss her so much I can't breathe. How will I make it like this for the rest of my life?"

She was grateful he didn't answer. There was truth in his silence. She already knew this was a grief she would never get over.

"I never said I was proud of her," Loreda said. "How could I—"

"Close your eyes," Jack said. "Tell her now. I've been talking to my mom that way for years."

"Do you think she hears?"

"Moms know everything, kid."

Loreda closed her eyes and thought of all the things she wished she'd said to her mother. *I love you. I'm proud of you. I've never seen anyone so brave. Why was I so mean for so long? You gave me wings, Mom. Did you know that? I feel you here. Will I always?*

When she opened her eyes, there were stars overhead.

EPILOGUE

1940

I AM STANDING BEHIND the farmhouse in a field of blue-green buffalo grass. To my left, a sea of golden wheat waves in the breeze. My grandparents' farm has been recontoured, as have all the big farms in the county. Newspapers credit the President's soil conservation plan for rescuing the Great Plains, but my grandmother says it was God who saved us; God and His rain.

I look like any other girl my age, but I am different from most. A survivor. There is no way to forget what we went through in the Great Depression or to unlearn the lessons of hardship. Even though I am only eighteen, I remember my childhood as a time of loss.

Her.

She is what I miss every day, what I cannot replace.

I walk toward the family cemetery behind the house. It has been restored in the past few years: New white fencing surrounds the square of lush grass. One of us waters it every day. Asters bloom along the fence. Every new bud brings a smile. Nothing is ever taken for granted.

I mean to take a seat on the bench my grandfather built, but for some reason I remain standing, staring down at her headstone. She should be here today, beside me. It would mean so much to her . . . and more to me. I hold tightly to her journal. The few words she wrote will have to last me a lifetime.

I hear the gate open behind me. I know it is my grandmother, following me. She can sense when the sadness rises in me; some days she gives me space with my grief, some days she takes my hand. I don't know how, but she always knows which I need.

The gate creaks shut.

My grandmother moves in to stand beside me. I can smell the lavender she puts in her soap and the vanilla she has used in today's baking. Her hair is white now; she calls the color her badge of courage. "This came for you in the mail today. From Jack."

She hands me a large yellow envelope, with a return address in Hollywood. Jack is on to another fight these days, against fascism, now that there is war in Europe.

I open the package. Inside is a slim book with a marked page. I open the book to that page.

It is a grainy black-and-white photograph of my mother, standing in the back of a truck, with a megaphone to her mouth. The caption reads: *Union organizer Elsa Martinelli leads strikers amid a spray of tear-gas bombs and bullets.*

I touch the picture, as if I'm blind and my fingers can somehow reveal a deeper image. I close my eyes and remember her standing there, shouting, "*No more, no more . . .*"

"The day she found her voice," I say.

My grandmother nods. It is a thing we have spoken about often in the past few years.

"You should have seen her," I say. "I was so proud of her."

"As she would be of you today," Grandma says.

I open my eyes and see the headstone in front of me.

Elsa Martinelli

1896–1936

Mother. Daughter.

Warrior.

"I wish I'd told her I was proud of her," I say quietly. Regret re-emerges at the oddest moments.

"Ah, *cara*, she knows."

"But did I say it? Everything was so terrible, and I . . . looked past her. I kept thinking my life was *out there*, somewhere else, when it was right beside me. She was right beside me."

"She knew," Grandma says gently. "And now it is time to go."

"How can I leave her?"

"You won't. As she will never leave you."

In the distance, I hear Ant's laughter. I turn and see him and our golden retriever running this way, bumping into each other. Grandpa is waiting by the windmill to drive me to the train station so that I can go to college in California, in a city near the sea.

California, Mom. I'm going back.

Unbroken.

"A train does not wait," my grandmother says. "Do not dawdle."

I hear her walk away and know that she is giving me a last moment here alone, as if the words I have been unable to find for years will suddenly come to me. "I'm going to college, Mom."

A breeze moves through the buffalo grass; in it, I swear I hear her voice and remember her long-forgotten words: *You are of me, Loreda, in a way that can never be broken. You taught me love. You, first in the whole world, and my love for you will outlive me.*

It is a single perfect memory. A goodbye that gives me peace and courage. Her courage. If I have even a sliver of it, I will be lucky.

Be brave.

It was the last thing she said to me in this world, and I wish I'd told her that her courage would always guide me. In my dreams, I say, *I love you*, I tell her every day how she shaped me, how she taught me to stand up and find my woman's voice, even in this man's world.

This is how my love for her goes on: in moments remembered and moments imagined. It's how I keep her alive. Hers is the voice in my head, my conscience. I see the world, at least in part, through her eyes. Her story—which is the story of a time and land and the indomitable will of a people—is my story; two lives woven together, and like any good story, ours will begin and end and begin again.

Love is what remains.

"Goodbye," I whisper, although I don't really give the word away, I hold it close. I look at her headstone, see that word, the one that will forever define her for me: *warrior.*

Smiling, I turn and look back over the farm that will always be home, where she will await my return.

But for now, I am an explorer again, made bold by hardship and strengthened by loss, going west in search of something that exists only in my imagination. A life different than one I've known before.

Hope is a coin I carry, given to me by a woman I will always love, and I hold it now as I journey west, part of a new generation of seekers.

The first Martinelli to go to college.

A girl.

AUTHOR'S NOTE

On September 6, 1936, in his fireside chat to the nation, President Franklin D. Roosevelt said,

> I shall never forget the fields of wheat so blasted by heat that they cannot be harvested. I shall never forget field after field of corn stunted, earless and stripped of leaves, for what the sun left the grasshoppers took. I saw brown pastures which would not keep a cow on fifty acres.
>
> Yet I would not have you think for a single minute that there is permanent disaster in these drought regions, or that the picture I saw meant depopulating these areas. No cracked earth, no blistering sun, no burning wind, no grasshoppers are a permanent match for the indomitable American farmers and stockmen and their wives and children who have carried on through desperate days, and inspire us with their self-reliance, their tenacity, and their courage. It was their fathers' task to make homes; it is their task to keep those homes; it is our task to help them with their fight.

Their tenacity and courage. Their self-reliance. Words that describe the Greatest Generation. Words that stay with me and have deep meaning. Especially now.

As I write this note, it is May 2020, and the world is battling the coronavirus pandemic. My husband's best friend, Tom, who was one of the earliest of our friends to encourage my writing and who was our son's godfather, caught the virus last week and has just passed away. We cannot be with his widow, Lori, and his family to mourn.

Three years ago, I began writing this novel about hard times in America: the worst environmental disaster in our history; the collapse of the economy; the effect of massive unemployment. Never in my wildest dreams did I imagine that the Great Depression would become so relevant in our modern lives, that I would see so many people out of work, in need, frightened for the future.

As we know, there are lessons to be learned from history. Hope to be derived from hardships faced by others.

We've gone through bad times before and survived, even thrived. History has shown us the strength and durability of the human spirit. In the end, it is our idealism and our courage and our commitment to one another—what we have in common—that will save us. Now, in these dark days, we can look to history, to the legacy of the Greatest Generation and the story of our own past, and take strength from it.

Although my novel focuses on fictional characters, Elsa Martinelli is representative of hundreds of thousands of men, women, and children who went west in the 1930s in search of a better life. Many of them, like the pioneers who went west one hundred years before them, brought nothing more than a will to survive and a hope for a better future. Their strength and courage were remarkable.

In writing this story, I tried to present the history as truthfully as possible. The strike that takes place in the novel is fictional, but it is based on strikes that took place in California in the thirties. The town of Welty is fictional as well. Primarily where I diverged from the historical record was in the timeline of events. There are instances in which

I chose to manipulate dates to better fit my fictional narrative. I apologize in advance to historians and scholars of the era.

For more information about the Dust Bowl years or the migrant experience in California, please go to my website KristinHannah.com for a suggested reading list.

ACKNOWLEDGMENTS

I'd like to thank Sharon Garrison, who took me on a lengthy, personal tour of the "Weedpatch" camp in Arvin, California, which was built in 1936 by the Works Progress Administration to house migrant workers. Thank you, Sharon, for sharing your memories with me. Thank you, also, to the many volunteers who keep the era alive in the yearly Dust Bowl Days celebration. I am grateful to have met with and spoken to so many people who lived at the camp.

Thank you to the University of Texas at Austin and the Harry Ransom Center. The original papers of Sanora Babb were invaluable. Her novel *Whose Names Are Unknown* is a must-read for anyone interested in the time period.

A big shout-out to my creative "village." I couldn't do this without you. In no particular order, thanks to Jill Marie Landis, Jennifer Enderlin, Andrea Cirillo, Jane Berkey, Ann Patty, Megan Chance, Jill Barnett, and Kimberly Fisk. Sometimes I lose my mind during either the editorial or writing process (sometimes both), and I am grateful for the smart women who keep me on track and make me laugh.

Thank you to the crack team at Jane Rotrosen Agency. This year marks twenty-five years of us working together. It's gone by in a flash, and I couldn't imagine better partners on the roller-coaster journey of publishing.

To Matthew Snyder, who is an absolute blast to work with and guides me through the inexplicable world of movies and TV with steadiness and good humor. And to Carol Fitzgerald, who does her best to keep me in the virtual world. Thanks to Felicia Forman and Arwen Woehler for help in researching the era, and Cindy Urrea for her invaluable advice.

To the people who really bring it all together at St. Martin's Press, I love working with all of you: Sally Richardson, Lisa Senz, Dori Weintraub, Tracey Guest, Brant Janeway, Andrew Martin, Anne Marie Tallberg, Jeff Dodes, Tom Thompson, Kim Ludlam, Erica Martirano, Elizabeth Catalano, Don Weisberg, Michael Storrings. And, of course, to the captain of the ship, John Sargent. I am more grateful than you can know to be a part of the team.

Thanks to my godmother, Barbara Kurek. I love you.

And this year, a special thanks to the people on the front lines of the pandemic—the first responders, the healthcare workers, the essential workers, and everyone keeping our communities safe. You are rock stars.

Thanks to Tucker, Sara, Kaylee, and Braden. And last but not least, to my husband, Ben. For love, for laughter, for keeping me steady. For everything.